More praise for Charles Baxter's *Shadow Play*

"*Shadow Play* is so wonderfully rich—funny and generous and serious and surprising—I read it through without a pause. Charles Baxter knows the magic thing about fiction: how it can capture the enchantedness of the real world."   —Josephine Humphreys

"*Shadow Play* is irresistible! Charles Baxter draws the reader in with the intrigue of our supposed 'everyday lives.' Wyatt is Baxter's pilgrim, trying to find his way, taking risks we all might have considered (but shied away from) and becoming, ultimately, the good father, husband, and son we should wish to be. Baxter succeeds in deepening the mystery in our lives without frightening us away— a wise and compelling novel."   —Robert Coles

"Big, moving, rich with life and story. . . . Baxter has . . . gone into the ordinary and secret places of people—their moral and emotional quandaries, their typically American circumstances, their burning intelligence, their negotiations with what is trapped, stunted, violent, sustaining, decent or miraculous in their lives." —Lorrie Moore, *New York Times Book Review*

"Remarkable . . . *Shadow Play* is pure Charles Baxter. Which is to say: this is a very important work of art." —*The Hungry Mind Review*

"[Baxter's] mainstream American characters gradually reveal fascinating quirks, unexpected depths of feeling . . . even some visionary madness—in other words, some of the qualities we recognize lying just beneath the surface of our everyday selves." —*Philadelphia Inquirer*

"Baxter tells his tale in language so carefully honed it sings; his metaphors . . . are striking and luminous. . . . This lyrical, witty, dramatic and moving story has the clarity of sunshine, the haunting suggestion of shadow play." —*Publishers Weekly*

SHADOW PLAY

A NOVEL

CHARLES BAXTER

W. W. NORTON & COMPANY
New York   London

The stanzas from "Didymus" by Louis MacNeice are reprinted from
The Collected Poems of Louis MacNeice, by permission of the publisher,
Faber and Faber Limited.

The text of this book is composed in Bembo, with the display set in Anna.
Composition by the Haddon Craftsmen, Inc.
Manufacturing by Quebecor Fairfield
Book design by Charlotte Staub

Library of Congress Cataloging-in-Publication Data
Baxter, Charles
Shadow play : a novel / Charles Baxter.
p. cm.
I. Title.
PS3552.A8543S5 1993
813'.54—dc20   92-10377

ISBN 0-393-03437-2
ISBN 0-393-32274-2-pbk.

W. W. Norton & Company, Inc.
500 Fifth Avenue, New York, N.Y. 10110
www.wwnorton.com

W. W. Norton & Company Ltd.
Castle House, 75/76 Wells Street, London W1T 3QT

1 2 3 4 5 6 7 8 9 0

For
Martha Hauser Baxter
and
Carol Houck Smith

Refusing to fall in love with God, he gave
Himself to the love of created things,
Accepting only what he could see, a river
Full of the shadows of swallows' wings

That dipped and skimmed the water; he would not
Ask where the water ran or why.
When he died a swallow seemed to plunge
Into the reflected, the wrong sky.

—Louis MacNeice

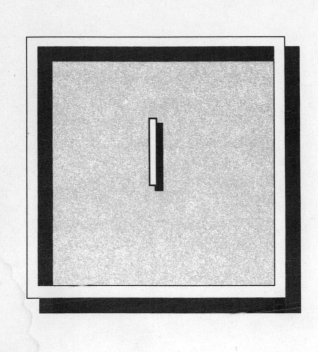

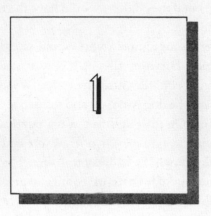

Behind the house a crow cawed irritably as the rains began

Inside, close enough to an open window to hear the crow, Wyatt was packing. He had had enough. It was time to leave, to move on. He had opened his suitcase so that its lid fell back over the edge of the bed, and he had carefully folded a few pairs of underwear, some socks and trousers, and laid them out neatly so that they wouldn't get jumbled together.

He put his favorite sport shirt, speckled green like an unripe banana, at the top, next to a pair of tennis shoes, his teddy bear, and a night-light. The night-light took a fifteen-watt bulb and had Scottie dogs painted on its sides. He didn't know if they had electrical outlets where he was going, wherever that was, but if they did, he would have the light. He was eight years old.

There were some animals who would wonder what had become of him. Dictator, the sheltie, was sleeping in the bathroom on the cool tiles near the toilet. Wyatt patted him on the head, and the dog woke up and slurped at Wyatt's face, his tail wagging. On the dog's face was a puzzled expression. Was there going to be fun? Or not? Wyatt said goodbye to him, then called down the hallway to Laura. The old arthritic dalmatian came out of his parents' room and groaned her way down the hall. Wyatt hugged her; she had taught him how to swim two summers ago. Today she smelled of burlap and dirt. She was so old, she was almost earth again.

Carrying his suitcase and passing Gretel's room, he heard his sister say, "Where you going?"

"I'm leaving."

"Again? Oh yeah, sure you are." Her door was open wide enough so that he could see how she was reading in front of the mirror, her preferred location, checking her face to find out if she was any prettier now than she had been five minutes ago. Wyatt had told her several times that he was going to run away, and she had had two reactions: gleeful ("Good idea. Why don't you leave *right now?*") and skeptical ("You'll get about as far as the driveway"). But now he had outsmarted her: he was actually doing it, taking off, and he wouldn't have to see her anymore, her poisoned smile or her curly hair that made him want to shout or throw stones at her.

The house was a trilevel, the first one ever built in Five

Oaks, and the way the rooms were arranged, like a series of randomly connected L's, allowed Wyatt to get to the back door without being seen by his parents. His father, an architect, would be in the basement anyway, working on some carpentry project or other, and his mother would be in the kitchen, making one of her gloomy stews while she talked on the telephone. He would miss them, he thought, but he wouldn't miss them very much.

He grabbed the knob on the back door with his free hand and flung it open. Standing in the doorway, he felt the rain spattering down on his face. He had always liked the paraphernalia of storms: hail, lightning, darkness, thunder. Last fall when his friend Harry Peet had told him that *he,* sometimes, hid under the dining-room table during storms, Wyatt hadn't believed it. He had opened his mouth, not in fake disbelief, the way his sister did it, but in real disbelief, right there on the playground.

"But it's a show," Wyatt had said. "Storms are. You got to watch it or you miss it."

He was running now, with his suitcase, past the backyard tire swing and the old sandbox nobody used anymore, a puddle of water already in the center near his rusting steam shovel. He felt his shirt getting sopped. His shoes made a kind of sick, gluey sound in the perfectly mowed grass. If he made it to the woods behind the house, he would be safe. He would live there. His parents wouldn't find him. He was safe anyway: his mother and father wouldn't *bother* looking for him. They noticed him about as much as the cat did, maybe less, because he was the one who usually fed the cat.

In front of him the woods smiled open, smelling of pine trees and decaying grass, and the rain pattered on the dry leaves like inhuman whispering. At the edge of the woods he turned around. He thought he should look at the house one last time. He would never see it again, after all. As he raised his eyes, the crow cawed again, even more irritable now.

The house appeared to be the same as ever, a mess of boxes and angles and windows. Once again he felt ashamed of living in the only modern house in town, as if his parents couldn't stand to live in a house that looked like a real house, the sort of structure that everyone else lived in. This one might be a Lego construction, a home for aliens.

His sister was staring out of her window at him, having dragged herself away from the mirror. Her elbows were propped up on the windowsill and her head rested in her hands, and Wyatt thought that she would at least bother to wave, but she didn't. She was pretty in a particularly annoying way: her blond hair and even face gave a phony impression of kindness. He had just started to notice this. At Christmas, his relatives all said, "Gretel, you look so *sweet*," while she smiled that awful creepy smile of hers, and they dolloped out the presents in her direction. She was watching him now, the queen of I-don't-care, with a blank expression she used on him most of the time, as if she were practicing to be a ghost, or an only child. He decided to wave at her, and when he did, she waved back by flicking her hand out at the side of her face, a casual gesture that could be mistaken for an effort to rearrange her hair, and she could somehow fit in a wave, along with that, without making trouble for herself.

To hell with them, he thought, and the words, terrible to him, made him feel brave and almost grown up. As he turned and pushed himself past a hawthorn bush on the edge of their property, catching his pants, he remembered that he had left behind his baseball mitt. Also his transistor radio and his pocket piece of purple fluorite. But he wasn't about to go back; he could see everybody laughing when he opened the door and crept back into the house with his leaking suitcase and his wet hair hanging down his forehead.

He turned one last time and ran into the woods.

In the basement, Wyatt's father, Eugene, was bent over his worktable. To the side was a small unfinished contraption with several boards and something like a roof, birdhouse-size, but which, he had told his children, was *not* a birdhouse. Whatever it was, they would have to guess. Not a doghouse, not a rat trap, not a rabbit hutch . . . not anything, not yet. The pieces of cut pine were set up in neat piles behind him, and a preliminary drawing for certain parts of this object had been taped to the worktable.

A short, compact man, with fine hair just starting to gray, and a face deeply and prematurely lined, Eugene habitually gave himself a good deal of credit. He had just reached for his bottle of Jack Daniel's and was pouring himself a drink into a Dixie Cup. He drank on weekends, all weekend, but not during the week. Drinking lifted his mood, made him feel like an old-fashioned dirigible, floating over everything. No one he knew had figured out how he could drink this way, with ironic restraint. It was not the norm in Five Oaks or anywhere else. He was a man proud of his moods and of his control over them. If he drank, his drinking would be part of a system, a system that he had first invented and then put into play, and it would work for him, this system, but for no one else.

Pens and pencils filled his shirt pocket.

He was not, as it happened, working at this moment. He was sipping whiskey, and his hand was over his heart as he stared toward the north wall, where he had hung his tools on pegs: hammer, screwdriver, pliers, all in their proper places over the outlines he had drawn with felt pens. His wife, Jeanne, had told him that he was the sort of man who was made content by the organization of objects, as opposed to ideas, and it was true. But right now, inside his chest, and then down near the spine, was a new object, out of place: a bright blazing star. What was a star doing in his chest? He took another sip of Jack Daniel's. It was probably a case of heartburn. He couldn't say exactly that it hurt, because pain was dark, the pressure of a shadow, and this, whatever it was, was extremely bright, like a spotlight. No: this thing in his chest made him feel as if someone had thrown a lariat around him, and he was being hauled in.

With his hand over his heart, he smiled quickly for his own benefit; he sometimes could improve his moods by smiling to himself, he was that transparent. He turned his gaze to look at the basement's wallpaper pattern of antique clocks, all of them showing the same time: 3:30. In this basement, thanks to the wallpaper, it was always 3:30. Wyatt and Gretel called this the 3:30 room. The wallpaper had been his wife's idea, and he hadn't bothered to object to it. Now he liked it. He liked it that it would always be midafternoon here, especially now, when there was a star in his chest where his heart, and then his liver, should be.

He reached down and opened the thought-drawer. The little pieces of white paper inside trembled like strips of packing excelsior. He had been scribbling thoughts and depositing them in the drawer for years, ever since Gretel had been born, and he had come down here when he couldn't sleep, anxious with parental responsibilities. By now the drawer was nearly filled. Soon it would overflow with thoughts. He took out a pen, wrote down "Stars don't belong in the body; it should always be pitch-dark in there" on a slip of paper, and dropped it in. He pulled out a thought at random: "Sunlight in July: blank and powerful and rather dull. Dull people and children

are always happy during the summer. I myself am unde-
cided."

This thought now struck him as too simple and certainly
unpleasant in its snobbery, and he tore it up. He reached in
and drew out another thought. This one was underlined, so
he must have meant it when he thought of it.

> Spent part of the morning talking to a subcontractor
> about practical matters. A great relief from speculation. I
> shouldn't bother worrying over the big questions. They
> just disturb me.

He put that thought back. He didn't feel like having any
thoughts now; the star in his chest was shining too hotly and
brightly. Feeling like a solar system, he walked past Wyatt's
crayon portrait of him, labeled "My daddy by WYATT," in
which he was smiling a jagged child-surrealist Crayola grin, a
kind of stick-figure hilarity he wanted to feel for his son's
benefit, but usually had to fake, and he arrived at the Ping-
Pong table. Near the paddles, Gretel had left her toy nurse's
set scattered. Next to a yellow plastic hypodermic needle and
a bottle filled with tongue depressors was a genuine stethoscope she had purchased at a local medical supply store with
her own money. Leaning against the Ping-Pong table, he
picked up the stethoscope and felt its peculiar rubbery tubes.
Gretel was twelve and used to enjoy playing nurse. Looking
around—what was this thing doing here on the Ping-Pong
table?—he put the listening devices into his ears and placed
the stethoscope's diaphragm inside his shirt, over his chest at
exactly the point where the star was radiating its light outward.

He listened. Through the rubber tubes came the sounds
of a pulsating, moiling and roaring bump and flow, a thick

muscular fleshy thumping halfway between the sounds of a pumping station and a stamping plant. The chaos of the noise from his chest made his forehead break out in a light sweat. His chest sounded industrial and mechanical to him. I have not paid attention, he thought, to this before, this noise.

He walked to the window and gazed out at the rain, the stethoscope flapping against his chest. Blood and muscle, and the unreliable human fuses and tissue. He liked rain in September, its calm gray pattering. In the wet trees beyond his yard he thought he saw something, some small object, moving through them.

"Daddy?" Gretel, looking half awake, was standing on the other side of the Ping-Pong table. She liked to come into rooms silently, to creep around and suddenly materialize behind him; it was one of her special talents. "Daddy, what are you doing with my stethoscope?"

"I'm listening to my heart."

"How come?"

"Because it's there. I never heard it before. Here I am, at my age, and I never heard the beating of my heart before. Thump thump. Thumpthumpthump."

"That's the systolic and diastolic flow you're hearing," she said, struggling not to look smug. She picked up a Ping-Pong paddle. "Want to play?"

The star wouldn't permit it. He could feel solar flares rising into his shoulders and arms. "No, kiddo, I don't think so."

"Want to listen to *my* heart?"

He gazed at his daughter for a moment. Then he said, "No, I don't think so. Not today. But there is something I *will* listen to."

"What?"

"Your head. I'll listen to your thoughts."

"You can't hear thoughts." She was smiling.

"Oh, yes, I can." He placed the diaphragm on top of his daughter's head and listened. All he heard was the rustle of her hair. "Your thoughts sound like a field of crickets. I hear your schemes. You're planning on going roller skating tomorrow." From outside came a brief flash of light and, a second later, thunder. "You're thinking about that book you're reading—"

"Maybe."

"And you're thinking about Wyatt."

"Am not." She removed the stethoscope from her head. "What am I thinking about him?"

He smiled and shrugged. "That he's a pest. All sisters have sour thoughts about their little brothers. Say, let's go try this on him. Let's find out *his* thoughts."

"I don't—"

But Eugene was already headed up the stairs. He felt better already. The star was gone. When he reached Wyatt's room, the door was closed, and Eugene knocked, but when no one answered, he went inside and saw that the bed had been made neatly, the lights left off, the toys put away. The map of the New York City subway system was pinned to the wall above his bed; Eugene had brought the map back after a business trip, and Wyatt had promptly memorized many of the stops. Nothing was out of place. It didn't look like a boy's room at all. It was as if a maid service had come here and straightened up. Eugene felt a shiver travel up his back, along his spine. Gretel stood in the hallway, watching him.

"Gretel, where's your brother?"

She waited for five seconds. Then she said, "He ran away."

"Again? Where?"

"To the woods. He took something with him."

"What?"

"His suitcase this time, the blue one. He took some clothes. He left a note."

"Where?"

"On his dresser. Over there." She pointed.

Eugene had made that dresser, with its four drawers, a few months after his son was born, and he could still feel the maple and pine under his hands, a love he felt for his son transferring itself to the wood. Next to a plastic comb was a small piece of paper on which his son had written, "Goodbuy and see you in a few years, signed Wyatt."

"Good God."

"He says you never do anything with him." She spoke these words plainly, like a court reporter, almost without interest. "He said *you're* always in the basement and don't notice him at all."

"Where'd you say he went? When was this?"

"Out there. Five minutes ago. He said he was going to maybe live in the woods or go to Aunt Ellen's house or something. He said he had had it."

"Christ Almighty. Didn't he notice the storm?"

"Daddy, you know how he likes storms."

"Jeanne!" He was shouting now, in the direction of where he thought his wife might be. "Jeanne!"

Wyatt came to a clearing and heaved his suitcase over a fence. For a hundred feet ahead of him was a flat green meadow where the neighbors' horses, Simon and Lennie, sometimes grazed, and over to his right was a salt lick, a pinkish-colored one-foot-high block with a single depression in the center. Carrying his suitcase, and feeling his clothes clinging to him, he felt—now that he had actually escaped from the house where all they ever said was "No"—that he could do anything he wanted to do, everything he *had* wanted to do. He bent down and lightly touched his tongue to the salt lick. It tasted of salt and horses and swamp gas. He licked at it again. He had always wanted to do this; now he could. The horses were watching him and raised their large heads in a gesture of horse-interest.

Wyatt waved, picked up his suitcase, and started across the meadow.

Because they—his parents—had lied to him, had said they would buy him a rock tumbler for his agates, and they hadn't; and because they had left one time for New York without him or saying much about it, when they knew he wanted to ride the subways, and they had left Mrs. Connolly, with the warts on her face, in charge of the house, and of him, humming her hymns and listening to her radio, the more-Jesus-power-per-hour station, WJCP; and because he was sent to his room when he threw food at his sister, but she had figured out how to throw it back at him, especially Jell-O, without being caught; because his mother often stared unhappily at the ceiling; and because his father sat and sat without any reason in the 3:30 room in the basement on weekends, building furniture or playing boogie-woogie on the piano and laughing for no reason by himself all alone but so you could hear it anywhere in the house; because he drank that Jack Daniel's and got happy but wouldn't share the joke; and because now when Wyatt walked through the rooms of the house his father had designed no one really noticed that he was there; because they had had him and then forgotten about him; and because no one had really bothered to love him except his Aunt Ellen, he was leaving. He had left. That's why he had taken off for parts unknown. They'd notice he was gone in about a week. It felt good even though it felt stupid to be doing this. His cousin Cyril, who did brave stupid things, would be proud of him.

Except for his aunt, he didn't really like adults and hated the idea of becoming one.

Lightning struck something behind him, and he felt and smelled the air breaking apart and sizzling, and the thunder took up residence in his brain and echoed through it, barking. Wyatt laughed. He had once asked his Aunt Ellen, when she was in one of her fortune-telling moods, if he would ever be hit by lightning, and his aunt had crossed her heart and said, no, he would always be safe from that, but he should watch out for women and lawyers, in that order.

When he turned around, he saw a tree that had been split in half, with part of the trunk separated and dangling like a wishbone. He should have made a wish. He made one now: he wished never to become an adult like the adults that were adults now.

The suitcase was heavy, and he put it down. It hurt his arm a little. He held one arm out and then the other, and then both, and he swirled around in the rain until he was dizzy, his face held up against the sky, which had lowered by now to his height, to exactly where he was. The sky covered him. It was like a face on his face. He was so dizzy that he stepped in some horse dung and then fell.

Jeanne, Wyatt's mother, had put on her raincoat and rain bonnet and was checking around the trees in the backyard and calling her son's name, for the sake of appearances. She watched Eugene and Gretel rush down into the brush and woods in the back of the house toward the meadow and the park at the edge of town. The rain and lightning frightened her, but not her son's leaving. Children ran away, and then they came back. They all took themselves so seriously, and adults, like Eugene, who was half child anyway, should not pretend that the theatrics were real. It was part of growing up. She herself had often felt like running away when she was a child, and then, a few times, as a young woman, after she had been married. It was called acting out, as she knew very well, and it was a form of giving in to yourself. She hadn't run away, much as she'd wanted to. Most people don't; at least most women didn't. Jeanne had lain in bed, waiting for the sun to rise, and it always did, bringing another day in which she was the same person in the same place. You could learn to live with most things, and, after a while, pain didn't make any difference. Anger made no difference, either. She had not felt like running away for years, though she did sometimes wish to board a ship and sail away and never come back. She worried, now, about Wyatt's getting a cold. But he would return, and probably be better for the experience. As she stood near the sandbox, contemplating the rusting steam shovel half submerged in a puddle, she imagined herself as an old lady, sitting in a front room, baby-sitting her grandchildren, or walking around a large city admiring the statuary. Yes: the day was turning out well, despite the rain.

The star in his chest had reappeared in his arms, where it burned with an unexpectedly soaring light, and Eugene stopped for a moment to catch his breath and to wait for the sensation to pass.

He caught his pants on a bush, and noticed, near some rocks, a patch of wild blueberries that he had missed in his July excursions back here. Now he looked down the hill, past a stream next to which his daughter stood, transfixed by the water or by her broken image in it. She did love to look at herself in objects that reflected her. She had an idea of herself, as they used to say. It was quite consuming, this idea. She would probably marry one of those men with faces like mirrors, Gatsby-men, poisonous and charming. In the distance he saw a rabbit shivering under a pine tree. He aimed his voice toward the bottom of the hill and shouted his son's name.

Gretel said, "Daddy, he's not here. I want to go home." Her knees trembled underneath her raincoat. Thunder frightened her.

"Okay. You go back. I'll do this."

She turned and ran toward the house, kicking up mud and loose grass. "Tell him hi when you see him," she shouted over her shoulder, as if Eugene were going on some vacation. Eugene looked back to see her; in the distance, through the trees, near the top of the hill where the meadow began, Jeanne was standing, looking down toward him. She would not be impressed by any of this. He knew his wife: for her, any form of desperation was suspect.

Some of this land belonged to one of his neighbors, a man who owned horses, and Eugene noticed that two of the horses were outside their fences, apparently having jumped them. The horses were neglected, perhaps abused; he turned away.

Another bolt of lightning struck behind him, and Eugene felt the air seared into ozone on either side of him. Retroactively, he jumped. Thor's bolts—if one hit him, it would probably be a quick death. The shock of the noise made his heart thump. The star burning in his chest wasn't his heart, he knew, because he had had his heart recently checked, and he'd been given a good report. Still trotting along, feeling his hair slicked down by the rain, he found himself thinking about the two horses left out here, loose, jittery, alarmed by the weather.

In the distance a few lights from Five Oaks blinked through the apple and pine trees swaying in the wind. Under his feet, fallen apples were mixed in with the first autumn leaves. Eugene lost his footing and fell, his hand landing on an apple. He bit into the apple—pleasantly tart, a living substance—and saw, through the wet lenses of his glasses, his son, sitting under a tree in the near distance, his suitcase open, his clothes in tiny neat piles, and his night-light set up on the ground, its cord dangling away loosely.

"Wyatt!" he called, just as thunder broke through again, and his words were swallowed up in the tympanic rumble.

Wyatt didn't mind the rain. What he hadn't figured on was the shivering, or that his new pair of Keds tennis shoes would get soaked. Maybe it wasn't such a good idea, living in the woods. Even with his clothes laid out, it'd be cold at night, and his teeth would chatter, and if there was anything he hated, it was chattering teeth. Wyatt thought of his Aunt Ellen's house and of how she kept fires going in the living room through most of the fall and winter. He couldn't walk that far. But he couldn't walk back, either. He'd have to stay here and figure out how not to shiver.

"Wyatt!" The air had breathed his name, using his father's voice. The air knew he was out here. He wanted to shout back at it.

He turned and saw his father running toward him, his hair, what there was of it, slicked down over his forehead, a stethoscope around his neck, for some reason, and rain covering his glasses, so that Wyatt couldn't see his eyes. He ran and ran, but in the manner that adults do, so that it wasn't rushed. His approach took a long time. His father's arms were out, came near; they scooped him up. The stethoscope pressed against him now, after the arms had reached around him and lifted him, and he felt his father's cold lips press against his cheek, and he was being gathered up now, in this one speeded-up gesture, collected in his father's arms. It felt as though it had happened several times. He smelled the usual weekend whiskey on his father's breath, and a wet saggy furry smell from his father's wool shirt. Slow and rapidly, one minute he was by himself and then suddenly here was his father. He huddled against him. He loved his father at moments like this, when his father loved him, and he was glad he had run away so that his father had had to chase after him, claim him, and hug him.

"Hi, Daddy," he said. "How come you've got that doctor's thing around your neck?" He knew he wouldn't be carried like this much longer. He was eight years old. His father would let him down, his arms would weaken, his soaking tennis shoes would make contact with the wet high grass as his father tilted him, feet first, toward the earth.

"Wyatt, you're a wild one. And you're too heavy," his father said. "Pack up your things and we'll go back together." Then he said, "You gave me a scare."

He ran toward his son unable to see clearly where he was going—the rain had dribbled all over his glasses and smeared them—and his arms were extended involuntarily toward Wyatt, who was sitting under a tree and only now, just now, moving the line of his vision up toward his father's uncontrolled progress toward him. With the propulsion given by the hill and the storm, Eugene was running faster than he knew how to run, so that when he reached Wyatt, instead of simply taking his hand, he felt the physical force convert itself into emotional exuberance, and he put his arms under Wyatt and picked him up, and in that moment, the star in his chest, almost a supernova by now, blew apart into planets and planetary dust and debris, floating through his body. The pressure disappeared, as did the pain. Eugene suppressed a groan and lowered his lips to Wyatt's cheek, and Wyatt exhaled on him a child's breath smelling of peaches and chocolate. "Hi, Daddy," he said, as if he'd been having an adventure of a minor, weekend kind, like hide-and-seek. "How come you've got that doctor's thing around your neck?"

Just playing games, Eugene thought, just like you. His son was too heavy, and he lowered him to the ground, where he would stay. He had wanted to carry him all the way back to the house, but it was not permitted. "Wyatt, you're a wild one. And you're too heavy," he said, before telling him to pack up his things.

Wyatt put his night-light and his clothes into his suitcase and snapped the locks on it; then, carrying it in his left hand, his right hand in his father's, he walked through the apple orchard, up the hill, toward his house. Two weeks later, at work, Eugene let out a quiet yelp of surprise while sitting at his drafting table—he had been designing a gift shop to be built downtown—and he drove himself over to the hospital to be examined. They found nothing wrong with him and sent him home.

For years, after the funeral three months later and the distribution of his father's possessions—including the strange contraption Eugene had never finished, which was not a birdhouse and had not, in fact, become anything—Wyatt would remember the water dripping down on the lenses of his father's glasses. How could he see anything, with glasses smeared like that? How did he know how to walk when he couldn't tell where he was going? He must have known how to walk through the blur. And what he also remembered, along with the glasses, was his father's hand, how wet and chilly it was, as it held on to his own hand, as if his father had come to him from underwater and from very far down, where it must have been unendurably cold.

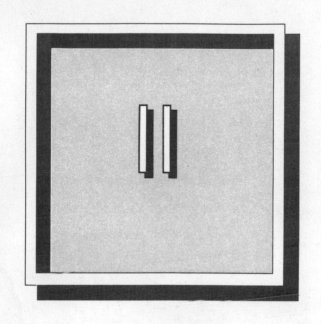

T hat morning, riding in a friend's car on a small expedition to buy some grapefruit, Susan had been involved in a traffic accident. Her roommate, Lara, who'd been driving, had reached down for a pack of cigarettes on the floor, between her purse and a tote bag, and she had taken her eyes off the road just long enough to hit the back of a Buick at an intersection. Because Lara's car was small and foreign, its front hood and fender had been mangled, and the radiator had caved in, dribbling fluid on the pavement. But no one had been hurt, despite all the noise and the shattered glass. Susan had a small bruise from the shoulder belt, and her glasses had flown off her head, though they hadn't broken, and she imagined her neck would be sore from the whiplash for a few days. But it was just an accident. Nothing serious had ever happened to her. Nothing ever had, nothing ever would. She wouldn't be hurt until she was dead.

That afternoon, working at her job in the college library, and pushing the green book cart with the squeaky right front wheel through the basement storage area, where the old books smelled like death-by-paper, she was thinking of how her life was probably going to be one of those boredom-tragedies that only could interest other victims of boredom-tragedy. Despite her athletic abilities and her talents in stage design, and her skills as a magician, she would end up moldering like one of these books, or getting herself laid in the backseats of taxicabs out of sheer ennui, like Emma Bovary, whose life story she had just read in her English lit class. Or she would spend her long futile housewife days overspending her credit limit at Lord & Taylor. At least she had escaped from Duluth, where her parents still stubbornly lived.

But no: she *wouldn't* let that happen, no boredom-tragedy for her, no lifetime of casseroles. She would spend her life being fierce and final and absolute, like a goddess who was five feet five, had a ponytail and a high B average. She wouldn't follow laws. She would lay down the laws. She was imagining which particular decrees she would decree—the ones everybody had neglected to post until now—as she replaced a volume of Macaulay's essays on the shelf, when she looked over to the side and saw this guy sitting slouched at a study-desk. He was sketching something in pencil, she couldn't tell what. He had taken off his shoes and socks. He had an orphan look, quiet and turned-in. He was sort of beautiful.

She was annoyed at him for attracting her and for sitting there in his bare feet and not studying and just sketching; also, he hadn't noticed her, as she squeaked her cart around, re-shelving Montaigne and Heidegger; he hadn't even looked. She could tell from the vacant feeling on her back that he hadn't bothered to glance up. Why not? She felt competitive: she was more beautiful than he was. Where had this guy been hiding himself? Holbein College was so small that you saw everybody eventually, but she didn't recognize *him* from any-where.

"These are the reserve stacks," she said loudly, to a book. "You're supposed to have a pass to be down here."

"I have a pass," he said, his eyes not leaving his sketch pad.

She pushed the cart down the hall to the elevator, *er er er,* God, she hated wheels that needed oil. She didn't turn, she didn't need to, now that she felt his gaze at last resting on her. Probably she had won that one. There had been a guy-smell in the air, a light pleasant musk of sweat and muscle, and she hadn't even cared, though it *had* added a trace of life down there, underwater with all those books.

The next time she'd seen him she had been on her way to the corner mom-and-pop store to buy some tea bags, the caffeinated kind to keep her wired so that she could finish her midterm paper on the geopolitics of Kenya. Almost by acci-dent, she'd looked up—actually, she'd been noticing the split broken cubist shapes of fallen autumn leaves—and had seen him, barefoot again, this time sitting on the sloped roof of a college apartment building, almost invisible up there, still drawing. This guy drew. Draw or die, maybe that was it. The sun was behind his hair and shone through it, an unfair advantage, she thought.

"Don't you ever study?" she called, and he smiled and waved, or seemed to smile; the expression on his face was distant and illegible. She resented it that he wasn't, right now, preparing to write a tedious term paper on an important subject. Furthermore, he was precariously balanced and might fall. He could lose his purchase on the roof and tumble, breaking several bones, but she was not in the mother business and would not warn him. "What're you doing up there?" she asked, although she knew, and, for answer, he tore off the oversized drawing paper he was working on and let it go. It seesawed on the wind, back and forth, fluttering downward, first on one side of the street and then the other, landing by a fire hydrant. She crossed the street to get it. She realized belatedly that it was the first move she had made in his direction.

In pencil: the buildings and trees of the campus, sketched with a tight obsessive precision, like an architectural drawing, admirable on first look but a bit dry, somehow, on the second, as if the guy didn't have enough soul heat in him to draw the trees so that they had heat, too. Standing there in her jeans slit open at the knee and knowing that he was watching her, she recognized how much attention he had paid to the shadows of the trees on the lawn, more to the shadows than to the trees themselves. The drawing was very fussy about those shadows, Grant Woodish and Midwestern. He didn't seem to inhabit the objects he drew—she wasn't ignorant, she'd taken drawing classes, she knew the difference—so much as stand outside and stare at them. Something was missing—the human, for example. Some artists knew how to make that absence work for them, but he wasn't one of them.

She rolled it up. "Thanks," she shouted. He waved; he had started on something else. One of those won't-give-you-the-time-of-day types, she thought, momentarily distracted by his indifference. But he *had* given her this drawing, floated it to her. She passed it on to her roommate, Lara, who, when Susan came in, was talking on the telephone to her insurance agent. Lara liked the drawing and asked about its source. Susan lied and said she had done it herself. It went up on Lara's bedroom wall, across from a color poster of a fluffy rabbit.

Having planned on a double major in theater and art, she thought she might get a job in set design, an occupation her mother and father in Duluth had said was not an occupation at all, but only an idea, one of those ideas that did not exist in the world but only in Susan's head. They had complimented her on the speed and accuracy of her typing and said she might be a good secretary or court stenographer. But on a high school field trip she had once seen a production of a Strindberg play, and she had been transported out of herself by the sensual dreaminess of the staging. She wanted to be lost like that and to design the styles of those illusions. She didn't happen to think that most of life was reality anyway; she thought most of it was illusion, and it was important to make the illusions as accurate as possible. She thought she might be wrong about this, but the odds—the odds favoring illusion—were all on her side.

She knew she was from nowhere and wondered how she might turn that to her advantage.

She bit her fingernails and was afraid of her own vulnerability and tried to cover it with energy and humor, when she could get access to them. At least she laughed easily. She thought her laughter was her best side. At times she felt a sense of total exposure, especially when she had made a foolish generalization, and she felt naked in her ignorance. But even ignorance could be turned to your advantage, too, if you knew how to be knowingly and benevolently ignorant. Some people thought they were full but were actually empty, mostly men, and they were easy to encounter and easy to leave. The others were full—of ideas or information or feeling or inclinations—and thought themselves empty. They were the hard ones to find, to keep. Those she could stay interested in. She had the idea that there existed in the world virtues that made a human life bearable: one was humility, the other was modesty, and if she had known how to evoke them in others, she would have. She would have prayed for them if she had believed in prayer. Although she had rarely witnessed those virtues, they were the only ones she trusted.

Knowing that she wasn't an individual quite yet—she sometimes felt like a telephone that worked, but never took any incoming or outgoing calls—she also knew that she hadn't loved anyone so far, in her life, or been loved, and this knowledge kept her alert. She had slept with three boys in high school. She had not succeeded in loving any of them. Whenever they had looked at her, they never got beyond her skin; they were as self-absorbed and as restless as chimpanzees and had the same wide-eyed expressions. They were not affectionate but used affection to persuade her to do what they wanted her to do. They belched, even in bed. They seemed fast and desperate and absentminded and short of wind. They drove old cars with bad mufflers. They had good skin and used expensive soap. They kept their track shoes hanging on nails on the walls of their bedrooms, next to the posters of businessmen disguised as rock 'n' roll desperadoes and above their piles of comic books and sports magazines. Good-natured and a bit muddled about where their feelings were—their feelings lacked shadings and seemed monochromatic, yes-or-no, up or down to match their sexual moods—they would, she knew, collapse quickly into a stodgy settled domesticity: brown sofas and pole lamps. She had something else in mind for herself but didn't know quite what.

So when she saw him again, this time in an empty classroom near the theater building, shoes on this time, and studying, she went right up to him and stood there, until he looked up.

"I liked your picture," she said. "Thanks."

Instead of smiling back, or responding immediately, he did something amazing, at least in her experience: he waited, gazed at her, and said nothing for several moments. He waited! His eyes were a pale blue behind his wire-frame glasses and took her in, vacuumed her right out of herself, and she thought that if he didn't say something quickly, she would have to turn around and leave, go down that sterile fluorescent academic hallway, to an afternoon of distraction and sleepless attention to trivia.

But then he said, "Thank you. I'm Wyatt." He held out his hand and she shook it. She had a sudden crazy notion—she knew it was unbalanced the moment she had it—that she wanted to marry this guy. Then, an instant later, it wasn't a desire so much as a piece of knowledge, a perfect pitch of foresight. "Want to sit down and talk?" he asked.

"I have to go to a class."

"Too bad."

She intended to make a polite comment, something flippant or funny, but all that came out of her mouth was, "Who are you? Where have you been?"

He held his breath and gazed at the floor. "I'm a transfer student. I haven't been here long."

"What's your major?"

He pointed his index finger and touched her hand, there, where it met the wrist, one of those soul-points, and he knew where it was. "No. Let's not have this conversation now," he said. That was fine with her; she had felt light-headed from the intimacy of his gesture. Leaning back, but not confidently, not in the cocky way boys usually leaned back in chairs, to survey and evaluate, he invited her over to his apartment for lunch the following day, and she nodded. He gave her an address. She turned around and left before asking him about the time—she had the right not to ask, and besides, people ate lunch around noon, and that was when she'd show up. She wanted to show him her back, as she walked away from him.

When she arrived, he had already made the sandwiches—chicken salad—and laid them out on the kitchen table for her, next to a bowl of fruit. He met her at the door, his pet white rat, whom he introduced as Lily, peeking out from under his shirt collar at her. The rat rode around on his shoulders like a parrot whenever he was in the apartment, he told Susan, and when he was studying, the rat slept in a cigar box, where her nest was. Susan found it disconcerting to be watched by this rat while she ate Wyatt's sandwiches and apples and drank his iced tea, its little pink eyes following her suspiciously and, she thought, possessively. Was she actually competing with a rat? Well, he said, he'd raised this animal almost from birth, hand-fed her and trained her. She was affectionate and was good company. "And she's clean," he said, as if this were unusual in a companion, and vitally important.

"What do your parents think of this rat?" she asked. "Do they like her?"

"My father is dead," Wyatt said, suddenly turning toward the window, "and my mother is insane."

"Everybody's mother is insane."

"No. That's not true," he said, aiming himself at Susan

with some intensity. "They may be odd, but they're not manic-depressed, and she really is."

"Where does she live?"

"She's in a halfway house."

"Do you have any brothers or sisters?"

"I have a sister named Gretel," Wyatt said. "I don't like her."

"Is there anyone you *do* like?"

"I have an aunt," he said, "named Ellen. She mostly raised me. She was my father's sister. She was sort of my mother. I loved her all right. And my cousin, Cyril. He's sort of like my brother. I have quite a few sort-of relatives."

"Where is he now?"

"In jail. For drunk driving."

"No, I mean: where? What town?"

"A place called Five Oaks."

"Oh, I think I've been there," she said. "Gone past it. On the freeway. Haven't actually been *in* it."

"That's wise. It takes nerve to live in a city like that."

Because she didn't like the direction of the conversation, all those cul-de-sacs and dead ends, she asked, "What's your major?"

"Economics and art. I wanted to be a painter, but my aunt said I should learn how to do accounting. I've majored in almost everything by now. Maybe I'll still be a painter some-day."

On the walls were portraits, one in pencil, another in oil. The oddity of both was that the face was not visible, only the shadow on a wall cast by the sitting subject. The wall and the shadow had been drawn with great care. "They're quite unusual." She nodded toward them. "All those shadows."

"I do shadows," he said. "Some people cast shadows. Some don't."

"So I see."

"What about you?" he asked, picking up the dishes and taking them to the sink, the rat riding on his shoulders. "Tell me everything about you."

She told him what there was to say about herself and about Duluth and her family; it took a bit over two minutes.

"That's very interesting," he said, managing to convey that her background wasn't interesting, but that *she* still was, that she was somehow more compelling and more important than the elements that had given rise to her. She loved watching him walk around the kitchen in his jeans and sweatshirt. He could do that all day and it would be fine with her. She wasn't sure anymore that she was more beautiful than he was. She'd never known someone like this: his stillness. Had she encountered it before, a young man with an inner life? Give him to the Believe-It-or-Not museum, along with a photograph of his eyes and his feathery blond hair.

He was standing by the sink, his back to her, rinsing the dishes. "I was just wondering if you would go to bed with me."

"Now?"

"That's what I was thinking." He dried his hands on a dishtowel and turned so that he could smile at her. That deliberation of his again. "I know we've just met. But it's what I want to do, so I thought I'd just ask. I like you. You're very pretty, but it's more than that, you seem really *awake*. I'm attracted to you. I see you, and it's like I feel something in my stomach. End of speech."

"End of speech." She waited. "I don't know," she said, although she did. "It's pretty early."

He seemed puzzled, then laughed. "Oh, you mean: between us. This. Not in the day. You probably think I'm cheap," he said, "asking the way I have. But I don't do this, not usually." He kept his eyes on her. His blond hair tasseled down to his shoulders. She liked it that he could ask, straight-forwardly, without being particularly urgent or embarrassed, or, for that matter, particularly anything. He just asked.

"I have a class at three-thirty."

For some reason, he smiled at that. "There's time." He touched her on the wrist again. "Let me show you some-thing."

He took her into his bedroom, put the rat down into her nest, and then waved his hand at the walls. Above the bed, attached with adhesive tape, was a New York City subway map. On the bedside table was a small lamp, almost a night-light, with figures painted on the sides, mostly flaked off. She thought she might be mistaken, but they had the appearance of Scottie dogs, those figures. What sort of guy would keep a night-light like that around? On the side, in the corner of the room, was some contraption or other, some meaningless as-semblage of wood. "What's that?" she asked.

"I don't know," he said. "My father was making it, but he never finished it."

"Why a subway map?"

"Because," he said, "I've always had it. Ask me about where the stops are. Ask me about any one of the trains."

This was certainly new, this variety of come-on; she had already agreed to what he had asked for, and, besides, she wanted to lie down with him and wasn't inclined to waste time talking about subway stops. "You must love New York," she said.

"Go ahead," he told her. "Ask me what's north of Sev-enty-seventh Street on the Lexington Avenue line. Go ahead. Ask."

He was standing there, leaning against his desk, every-thing in its place: pencils and pens in a glass vase to the left, typewriter in the center, papers and pads to the right. She kicked off her shoes and went over to him and kissed him and, as she did, reached under his sweatshirt and put her hand on his chest, exactly where she wanted it to be. His hands fell to her back and her hip. His mouth tasted of peaches and something else, chocolate, maybe. After a moment she let him loose.

"Eighty-sixth Street," he said, smiling. "Both the local *and* the express. Is that how they kiss in Duluth? It's nice."

"Yes." She felt a sting of anger. "No. That's how *I* kiss. They don't kiss much in Duluth, except when they have to. It's not a community noted for that." Her hand was moving toward his waist, taking its slow pleasure with him. He was slender and articulated.

"Sorry," he said, his hand trailing around her back.

"Oh, that's all right." She took his glasses off and touched his eyelids with her thumb, one of *his* soul-points. She wanted her emptiness to be filled with his emptiness. "Let's lie down now. Make love to me, all right? Since you want to."

He didn't pull down the shade in his bedroom; he said that no one would see. The sun shone through the window onto the wall above the bed, and Susan felt pleased to be able to work up a bit of a sweat in October, with the leaves starting to turn outside, and all that. Seeing his body naked made her heart thump, and she made herself calm, she made herself leafy. She gave him a breath of herself. What she got back from him was darker, some root and shadow: exactly what she had needed that afternoon. He paid attention to her and said she was beautiful, and she knew she was, just then, at exactly that moment.

Afterwards, glancing with half-closed eyes toward the subway map, she inspected her memory and couldn't find a

time when she had ever felt better. She heard Lily scratching
in the pencil box, the ticking of Wyatt's bedside alarm clock,
the whisking of their feet underneath the sheet. "Tell me
about your mother," she said, touching him on the chin:
nothing between them now except skin, the length of his
flesh touching hers, intimacy, after all, but it was almost as if
he flinched. He said nothing. On the floor the sun made an
odd trapezoidal pattern.

"Okay," she said, sitting up. "Watch this." After a nice
sunny afternoon bump you didn't *have* to be lethargic, there
was no rule. "Here's something you didn't know I could do."
She put her hand to his ear, brushed away the hair, and did
her trick with a quarter, which she had picked up on his desk
and tucked underneath the pillow.

"What's that?"

"It's a quarter."

"Where'd you get it?"

"I pulled it," she said, "out of your ear."

"No, you didn't."

"Of course I did. I used to practice magic tricks. Give me
that quarter."

He dropped it into her palm. She was sitting up. She put
her hands behind her back. "It's not up my sleeve. I'm not
wearing sleeves. I'm not wearing anything." After holding
out her hands for inspection, she touched his ear again, and, it
seemed, removed the quarter.

"Yeah, yeah," he said, though he was smiling. She pulled
the quarter out of his various parts—he couldn't get enough
of this particular trick—and then, at three-ten, she rose and
dressed. He didn't move. Now he was surveying her. She felt
a pronouncement coming on from him. Then it came.
"You're beautiful," he said, "and you're kind of simple." He
was lying on the bed, as if the presence of his nakedness,

partially in sunlight, one arm turned under his head, gave him the right to say such things. Long after they were married, she would still remember that remark, that word, "simple," also his posture that day, and as much as she came to love him, she could never forgive him for it. She felt slapped, and knew vaguely that he meant well, it was a compliment of sorts, but that she had somehow entered a new country where everybody was going to hurt everybody else disproportionately because they were lovers now, and she knew they were going to be married, although *he* probably didn't know that yet. They were going to create and hurt.

"That's a terrible thing to say," she said, leaning against his dresser.

"It's not meant . . . I guess I should have said something else."

"Yes."

"Something about your brown eyes," he said, raising his hand to her eyelids. "How bright they are." Then, and very quickly, he said, "I can't talk about my mother right now." The *non sequitur* caught her off balance.

"I've got to go," she said. "Call me."

Then she didn't see him. He didn't call, and she supposed that he had disappeared down the rabbit hole, wherever it was men got themselves to when you had pierced their armor and they were feeling bloody and loose inside. She went to classes; she studied; she cooked her dinners and complained about him to Lara, who nodded across the dining-room table and blew out cigarette smoke with rich expressive contempt. Susan thought Wyatt would turn up somewhere, abashed. She had caressed his eyelids. She had seen how that had gotten to him. What convinced her about his interest in conservation of matter was the night-light. He must have had it when he was a kid, and if so, he didn't give up things easily. A scavenger and holder.

On some nights she didn't wear her nightgown, wanting the feel of the sheets against her skin. By now she was convinced, on the recent evidence, that she wouldn't die of boredom-tragedy after all, though longing might just do it instead. She imagined him walking around this room. She whisked her foot against the sheet, just to hear it. Jesus, what a sound. It made her crazy.

She stayed awake. Two words, "always" and "never," kept running in circles through her mind. Often they were attached to his name: "Wyatt always . . ." or "Wyatt never . . ." He always or never does what? Every time she gazed down into her thoughts, they looked like clichés. Goddamn him.

She hated her previous life.

She felt she was trying to tear herself away from herself.

What she felt wasn't longing after all, she decided, after checking herself; it was homesickness. Homesickness was what happened when you went to bed with someone and *then* fell in love. Most of the previous generations had started with the romantic feelings and then ended with the sex, and what came between the two was longing. When love followed sex, as it had with her, the expressions of their bodies together was that of a mutual arrival, and now she was out on her own again, homesick. She'd never felt that emotion before, not for her parents, not for her actual home—only for him.

On a Thursday night, she ran across the dark soccer field to the field house before it closed. At this time of day, the gymnastics equipment was out on the mats, and anyone could use it. She'd always been able to outbalance anyone. She could walk without ever slipping on railroad tracks, across the tops of fences, on swaying tree branches. She felt as though an invisible line through her backbone held her upright. She had to test her balance now. She often came over here to relax to work on the beam, unfettered by the nagging of a coach. In high school she had earned a letter as a diver, but she had given it up after a year because she didn't like falling into water day after day.

Never had she felt so distracted by listlessness, not even by a last year's case of mono. The sensation was almost like inhaling the wrong kind of air—too much helium, for example—in the wrong outdoors, under the wrong sky.

Wearing her leotards, she had worked up to backflips, elbow stands and handstands, hand walks and turns, and dismounts. Simple: all right, she would make it pretty damn simple.

As she was working on the beam, she saw Wyatt on the field-house track, running. He was a good but not a natural runner, muscled for strength but not speed. What annoyed her about seeing him was that her heart began thumping again. With some sense of relief, she noticed that Wyatt's physical timing was a bit jerky, like a car engine a hair out of tune, with odd bits of waste motion, particularly in his shoulders. But his running had an interesting desperation to it, which she was pleased to observe—she imagined herself the cause of this desperation—like a hamster galloping in its wheel. As he rounded the track near her, she caught his eye and waved.

They had something to say to each other; however, she would do this first. She would give him a good dose of herself, of her grace. She would pit her grace against his speed, his refusal to call. Barefoot now herself, she walked, arms out, fingers slightly raised like a dancer's, across the beam; then she pivoted on the ball of her right foot. She saw the beam ahead of her as a ray of logic, as a line, as a geometry to which she had a relation, a magical connection, as she did to the stage. It *was* a stage, the balance beam, the narrowest one in existence. Feeling almost endless resources of power in herself, she bent over, grasped the beam, and stood on her hands, a line of gravity passing through her palms, up through her arms and shoulders, across her back, splitting and dispersing up her legs through her feet and disappearing into the air. She pivoted on her hands so that she was facing the other direction. She heard Wyatt's breathing. She had mastered him: he had stopped running to watch her.

It occurred to her, standing nearly upside down on her hands on the balance beam, that she didn't know Wyatt's last name.

She lowered herself to the beam, one leg down, the other forward. She glanced over and saw that he had started running again in that graceless style of his, apparently more crazed than before, his fists clenched. What was the matter with him? Hadn't he seen yet the inevitability of their lives together? Maybe he was being stubborn and male and obtuse.

She tumbled backward, then turned herself sideways and extended both legs along the beam, in splits, bending down. This wasn't as easy as it had been a year ago. Even so, it seemed almost too easy. She could tell by his panting that he had stopped after doing two circuits again and was watching her. Well, Orpheus had lost everything by stopping to look. They couldn't help it, those men in the myths she had studied: they peered out from behind clamorous branches. They raped and then changed their partners or were changed themselves into trees or birds or dogs. . . .

She brought herself to her feet, did several single hops, then, her hardest move, a forward somersault, followed by a dismount, almost into his lap. Of course he was still rooted there in his damp T-shirt and his headband, beads of sweat dripping down his forehead and clinging to his eyebrows, even the eyelashes wet with tiny droplets, above the blue eyes with their hungry look. She could see his body again and felt a pocket of sensual remembrance as she looked at his legs, but he would have to speak now, or the hole he had poked in her life wouldn't be healed over anytime soon.

He opened his mouth, and it came out quietly: "That's beautiful."

"Thank you."

"It's controlled. And strong. It's sort of perfect."

"Simple," she said. "It's meant to be simple, Wyatt. That's the idea behind it."

"All right," he agreed. "Yes. Simple. I'm sorry. It's that, too."

"You've been all right?" she asked, wiping her brow, grabbing her towel off the floor.

"Me? I've been kind of out of it. Distracted—that's what I've been. I've been in love, actually.'

"Oh, have you?"

"Yes." He had his hands folded crosswise, the palms tucked in his underarms, an odd protective posture, she thought. "And the thing is," he said, "it's weird, it's like impulse shopping, and I'm trying to convince myself that I'm wrong about . . . you, but—"

"We hardly know each other," she said. "We had an afternoon."

"You're lying, aren't you?" he said. "You're just lying to me. I can tell. I know you, Susan. I spent an hour or two with you, and I know you already, as well as you know yourself. It's not the particulars I know. But it's like I know your blood and your bone and your heart. I *know* them."

"What are you saying? I have to go."

He reached out and held her lightly on the arm just above the elbow. What he said came out in a hoarse near-whisper. "Jesus, we're going to be married, aren't we? I mean, it's so obvious. Isn't it obvious to you? I've been having dreams about it. We could, like, get separated and decide not to, and we still would. Get married, I mean. Can't you feel that? Don't you *know?*"

She was looking at the floor, the mat, the wooden slats.

"I've been trying to resist it," he said. "I mean, I thought a person could *decide.*"

"Oh, a person can," she said, looking at him.

"The others, maybe they can. But I don't think we can." On his face was a sort of outer-space, astronaut look—the expression of someone who has just returned from Venus or Mars. "I feel sort of cheated, even. No choices."

"This is just infatuation," she said, thinking maybe it was.

"No, it isn't. It's precise. It's very knowledgeable."

"What's your last name?" she asked, bemused by his body, by his visible arousal.

"Palmer." Other students were running on the track near them, the relentless squeak of their shoes, their petty decisions, their fitness, their whims, the smell of the foam mat, while they, Wyatt and Susan, were having *this,* this space-age conversation, or whatever it was, what the hell was it? "You're Corvick. Susan Corvick. I looked you up," he said.

"Palmer?" she said. "Like the Palmer method? Like handwriting?"

"That's it," he said. "You want it?"

"Don't I get to think about it?"

"I suppose so. Yeah, sure, of course you do. You'd *better* think about it. You might as well try to. And you'd better live with me for a while. You'll have to meet some people, too.

49

My mother and my aunt and my cousin. Anyway, let's take showers and meet outside in a while, okay?''

She nodded.

She woke up scared next to him that night, the darkness triangulated above her, the sounds of traffic outside making ominous moans of tires on pavement, a radio in some other apartment floating Bruce Springsteen through the hallway and, dimly, into this room. The dream from which she had awakened had been terrible and without content: no images, no narrative, no symbols. Nothing but pure feeling, claustrophobia and love somehow jammed together in one condition, without a name, another one of those feelings they never had a label for. She woke with her face in her hands. Wyatt's arms were around her, his legs pressed next to her, and she felt as if she had been painfully given birth to, by herself. She'd lost her usual sense of calm, and humor; she'd been exiled from rest, if not from dreams. She guessed that he wasn't sleeping, either. "Are you?" she asked, and he said, "No." How could he be? She went to his closet and pulled out the first shirt she found, with cut-off sleeves and a skull-and-crossbones and the word DIE underneath it. It didn't seem much like him, that shirt, so she put it on and got back into bed. He felt the shirt, then moved his hands underneath it, somewhere near where the skull was, and rested them there, against her breasts, and she moved back against him: everything was serious now, she had to pay attention, damn it, he *had* done this to her, even if he wasn't responsible, exactly, for these feelings. They didn't smile anymore when they made love.

He was whispering her thoughts to her. She didn't like it, that he could do that, pull her thoughts out of the air, but he could, and there was no arguing with it.

And then she was experiencing joy and oppression simultaneously, and she wondered: All right, when does *this* one end? All he could do was respond to her; with all her force she was pulling him into her body.

She felt awake all the time and she didn't like it and she wanted her innocence back, but it was no use even thinking about it.

He had a tentativeness, a way of stopping and looking up into the air as if he were examining the sentence he was about to say, that touched her, because she had never known a man her age who was scrupulous about words. Inside his apartment he had arranged most of his possessions neatly, and she wasn't sure whether she liked this compulsive orderliness in a man—it seemed somehow superstitious to her—but finally decided that she did. One evening he came in, carrying a rose for her. They put it into an empty bottle of 7-Up, where it was visible from the bed, like a lamp. When he laughed, he closed his eyes. He said he had once drowned and come back from the dead, but that he didn't remember how it happened, exactly. Someday he would find out. He had the mildness of a man who has grown used to women, lived with them a long time, and who liked to have them around. He was conscious: that was it. He seemed to be a conscious man, a rarity, in her experience, conscious of whatever he did. He read books with his legs crossed at the ankle and his head propped on his left arm, elbow on the desk, in a pool of light. His skin smelled of Ivory soap. They talked about everything, all their interests and ambitions; at odd fugitive times she felt, when murmuring her love to him, as if she were talking to herself.

Of all the subjects they discussed, the only one he would not elaborate on was his family. "You'll have to see them for yourself," he said, meaning his mother, cousin, and aunt. He once said, out of the blue, that he was an orphan, or always felt like one, and then went back to his reading. He had a trick of naming the capitals of all fifty states in order, and, on command, would. She hoped he would give up this trick as he grew older. Sometimes when they made love, his hair trailed over her, and she could feel the tautness of his legs against her, the thigh muscles and the hard bulging of his calves. His tongue was careful and slow and curious. She once screamed softly when she was fantasizing about him and he was coming into her. She hadn't known how far away from herself she could travel and wasn't sure she could come back.

Somehow even his sweat was familiar. She was puzzled by the way he could fill all of herself with him, but being puzzled had nothing to do with the tense energy of their lovemaking; it was one of those small-time emotions she had given up.

She wondered about his ambitions, beyond his ambition to love her forever, as he claimed. Probably he should be defined, so that she could define him to others, if they asked, as they would, as they always did. He said he wanted to be a painter—he was getting ready to paint her portrait—but that he might have to settle for some kind of desk job first. All the details she told him about herself, he remembered. He liked to put his ear on her chest and listen to the beating of her heart, the systolic and diastolic flow.

She had never been so close to a human being, and, now that she was, she couldn't be sure that she understood it—his tongue and penis and hands and even his soul were always *there,* where *she* had once been—but then she fought back, making herself occupy him, for a change. She became more aggressive with him and pushed him away and let him know when she desired him. Slowly a sense of her own power made itself clear to her, and she regained her composure.

She thought up metaphors: I'm the body, he's the jacket;

I'm the water, he's the air; I'm the boat, he's the oar . . .

He didn't bring himself into her so much as harbor himself in her. He was even in her brain, taking up valuable space. When she wanted to remember demography tables, the relative fertility of different population groups, all she could think about was him, that feeling, and she wanted him resting himself against her, and then that was all she wanted.

He seemed to love women, and he seemed to love her, and she couldn't quite believe it. Her roommate (now, quickly, her former roommate, Lara) said, as Susan was moving her meager possessions over to Wyatt's apartment, that it was all a mistake and that she'd been hypnotized by his dull surprise, his little cobra rising out of the jar. Jesus, she'd been nursing *that* metaphor a long time. It didn't have a trace of spontaneity. The line had been delivered from where Lara sat steeping herself in envy and malice at the kitchen table, the cigarette lit in the ashtray, smoke rising acridly while dinner burned on the stove, as it was supposed to, as was planned. She was three months older than Susan and pretended to wisdom, an annoying trait in someone so angry and solitary.

Susan stopped in the doorway, carrying a chair. "A cobra? Rising out of a *jar?* Have you looked at his hands, for Chrissake? Have you heard him talk?" She bent down, triumphant and ashamed. "I never heard anybody whisper so much as he does. Lara, he loves me. I'm sorry. I hadn't expected it, okay?" Lara was turning into a traffic-accident personality, and it wasn't fun to watch, but maybe someday she'd get lucky and have one of those Enlightenment relationships where both people were rational and honest and straightforward, and they discussed every move before and after they made it. What fun, the world of decisions, and how distant, how impossible.

She wouldn't carry anything of Susan's into Wyatt's car,

though she eyed him every minute, keeping up an odd audi-enceless patter about the weather, first, and then faucet wash-ers and the difficulty of finding roommates these days.

But she had a look on her face, and Susan recognized it and forgave her.

Objects of some interest were arriving in Susan's dreams, and she did her best to pay no attention to them: the waves of Lake Superior breaking against the harbor walls in Duluth; and a dog, a sort of mongrel, on fire, walking through a backyard she did not recognize. She woke out of that dream, and Wyatt rubbed her back to help her return to sleep.

In his blue-gray portrait of her, he left her out of the picture and painted her shadow instead, lighting her with a single-source spotlight, against a flat off-white wall with folded curtains on either side. When she finally saw what he had done, she decided that the figure in the painting was clearly her own and that probably the profile was hers as well, because she recognized it. The painting was saying something else about her, or about Wyatt. What did this shadow express? That she wasn't *there,* or that she was getting up to go? She asked Wyatt about it, but he just shrugged. He said he didn't know what it meant, he had just painted it.

Sitting in the blare of incandescence, she had asked him again about his family, particularly his mother, but all he would say was that a few years ago she had given up on the meaning of things and had moved into a halfway house. "She's lucid," he said, then added, somewhat mysteriously, "but not so you can understand her, the way other people are understood. I mean, she makes up words. You have to know how to listen to her."

A few weeks later, when Susan asked Wyatt what his

father had looked like, he left, then returned into the room where she was studying, carrying a pencil sketch, which he handed to her.

"Here," he said. "That's what."

Line by line: the face of a man named Eugene, an architect, leaning back, perhaps against a pillow or the upper edge of a sofa. His eyes, obscured in the sketch by glasses whose lenses appeared to be wet or streaked, were set in a face that expressed bewildered intelligence and sadness, and Susan had the idea, which passed like a quick wind, that he was sad because he was dead. He looked a bit like Wyatt himself, except for the hair, which was shorter, though Wyatt's glasses were very much like these, in the picture.

While she was looking at his father, Wyatt asked her whether she wanted to get married before or after she had met his mother, and Susan, without thinking, said, before.

They were married in March, in the city hall, with one witness. They'd told no one. Susan thought there was no one worth telling, and that this was the first true event of her life, and the past had grown irrelevant, and, in her case, childish.

She didn't know what she had hit, or what had hit her, and she didn't care.

He had seen her three times, and when she came to his apartment, the fourth time, after he had invited her there, he knew, watching her eat a chicken salad sandwich, with her elbows on the table, that he was going to have a bad case of love-cramp for her, because she kept interrupting what she was saying to laugh. She even laughed with her mouth open, so you could see the food in there, if you cared to. He had a thing for laughing women. He had probably gotten it from his aunt, who laughed frequently and inappropriately. This one, this Susan, walked like a dancer, proud, apparently, to be upright, and he could sense the animal in her, right under the human veneer, but all the same it was the noisy laughing that did it.

Any woman who laughed like that had strength and sanity. For the time being, at least, she had more sanity than life itself did. Wyatt knew this was a serious lunch because the rat scratched nervously at his shoulders and pulled at his hair. It had a suspicious, ratlike intelligence, and disliked all women who sat down to eat at the table.

When Susan extracted a coin from his ear after making love to him, Wyatt was finished: he wanted to move right into her, into her bones and blood, at exactly that moment. He wanted to take full possession of her. He wanted to move out of the house of himself and into whatever she had to offer him.

She resisted sadness, to exactly the degree that he invited it. She said "Guess what?" often at the beginning of her sentences. She touched him on the eyelids and told him about her parents and stage design—how their house in Duluth was the setting for the wrong kind of play, the kind of play where you had to be a dutiful daughter—and after a while he leaned back and meant to compliment her on her simplicity, but the sentence came out wrong.

"Simple," he had said, as if she were so beautiful anyone could see it. *Simple* like anything that was obviously true, but she had apparently thought: Simple, like dirt; simple, like slow and dull.

His use of the word had annoyed her so much that she had dressed and taken herself off in the direction of the sociology class that she claimed she was enrolled in. He'd been hoping that she would stay in his bed for a few days, blow off her classes and their data-heaps, until they both settled down for a lifetime, which would, after all, solve everything.

Because he was obsessive, impulsive, and fell in love easily, he had become methodical, hoping to resist his own emotions, and his notepad lists and cleanliness and fastidiousness about random things had helped to organize him, up until he had met this woman, this Susan. He was one of those men— he thought of himself this way—who took women more seriously than they liked to be taken: he was the problem, and they were the solution, with the result that he tended to be charming without meaning to be. His was an unintentional charm, having to do with the quietly appreciative way he looked directly into their faces, and it ended up making many of the women he had known feel cornered. Susan's roommate, Lara, had recognized that quality in him immediately, and she had glowered at him from the kitchen table, as she smoked and drank coffee, in an acid of pure longing and resentment. He had that effect; he recognized it, having seen it before.

He couldn't think of a reason not to marry her. The plan was to love her forever and then, somehow, become a good citizen. But he *had* always been a good citizen. Cyril, his cousin, hadn't been, and his mother certainly hadn't been, and his aunt, Ellen, was a question, but he, Wyatt, had been exemplary. Soon he would have to get a serious job, once he had graduated from Holbein. That was how it would work.

They were married in a room smelling of varnish and floor wax, and official documents growing musty in the filing cabinets.

Wyatt couldn't believe his good luck: this ecstatically beautiful human being had agreed to marry him, without meeting his mother or any other members of his family.

• • •

Susan didn't want to inform her own parents by telephone, so, using her fountain pen, she wrote them a two-page letter about the marriage, ending with the line "You're not likely to understand what I've done, but I am happy, and I hope you will wish me well and be happy for me." She wrote the letter at her desk naked. Wyatt thought that her nakedness probably made her feel fierce, full of animal power that would defeat parental conventionality. Of course they would feel that he had stolen her away, but he and Susan were husband and wife now, undressed at breakfast, undressed at dinner, drugged out on each other's bodies, absolutes. They felt like giants of desire, pleased happy monsters digging into pay dirt. The world had gotten very small, compared to them. Whatever they wanted now, they could get.

When Susan showed this letter to Wyatt, he said, "They'll be jealous and angry."

"Jealous? Jealous of what?" She was sitting cross-legged in the chair, her glasses on, and wearing a Detroit Tigers cap she had picked off Wyatt's closet shelf, the glasses and the cap intensifying the effect of her nudity, as did her wedding ring.

"This. This part about being happier than you've ever been in your life. They won't like that. That's criticism. They'll be annoyed."

"Oh, let them be." The rat, very much in a snit since the wedding, peered out from its cigar-box bed, chewing on a food pellet. It was adjusting, but slowly. "I don't care if they're annoyed. They'll manage."

"We'll see if they do."

She sent the letter. Her mother called on a Saturday morning when Susan was still in bed, with Wyatt next to her. He'd been tonguing the little hairs on her upper thighs when the phone rang. Susan's mother was teary but brave, and polite in a new way, Susan said, cupping the receiver so she could do a color commentary on her mother to Wyatt. Wyatt moved up so that his ear was next to Susan's, and they could both hear her mother.

"Your father," Susan's mother said, "wanted to give you away. He wanted to walk down the aisle with you and give you away to your young man. He's heartbroken. Although I must say that he's bearing up quite well."

Susan cupped the mouthpiece again. "She's brutalizing me with her clichés," she whispered to Wyatt. "I gave myself away," Susan said, sitting up. "I did it by myself."

"Where is this Wyatt?" her mother asked.

"At this very minute? Right next to me. We're here in bed."

"I suppose he's listening in to everything I say."

"I suppose he is."

"Hello, Wyatt," Susan's mother said, over long distance. "How do you do?"

"Fine, thank you. And yourself?"

"Oh, for heaven's sake. I'm not going to respond to a question like that."

"Why not?" Susan asked. "It's a typical question."

"What's his family like? What does he *do?* That's what your father wants to know. Your father thinks we'll be supporting both of you until the end of recorded time."

"Don't worry," Wyatt broke in. "I'm very respectable." He was, however, feeling up Susan at that moment, hoping for a giggle, but she shoved his hand away.

"Respectable? You'll be respectable when you have a job, Wyatt." Well, he thought, after all she was Susan's mother, and they all learned how to do this routine in mother school, all except *his* mother, who'd never learned any of that. He found his mother-in-law's stiff probity somehow reassuring.

"We'd love to meet him, this Wyatt. Will that be soon, do you think? Or do we need to come down to see you?"

"Oh, you'll meet him, all right," Susan said, "but we're awfully busy just now. Exams are coming up."

"And how soon will you be less busy?"

"Summer. He's going to be working as a janitor in a hospital near here, and I've signed up as a part-time secretary. Maybe we'll have a week, somewhere in there."

"Very nice. Well, you could at least send a photograph. Just don't make it one of those photo-booth photographs. I hate those. They make everyone look criminal."

"All right. We'll get something else. Something flattering and uncriminal."

"I don't think"—her voice turned energetically angry—"that what you're doing is very grown-up *at all*."

"I know," Susan said. "There are so few grown-ups around these days, you hardly know how to act."

Wyatt sat back. He'd never heard a sentence like that from Susan before. Marriage had given her a language, maybe what they used to call a tongue; he felt, with some surprise, that this language included eloquent anger. Where had that come from? From the ecstasy they'd been sharing? Where was the anger in all that? Possibly in the certainty and the gravity of their feelings. It wasn't his doing, but *their* doing, and it was their first offspring.

Her mother made a sharp inhaling sound. "I hadn't known you to be so obstinate. You seem to have become quite opinionated all of a sudden. I suppose," she added reflectively, "that love does that. Well, cheers and good luck to you both. I expect you'll need it."

Because she had no photographs of Wyatt, she decided to send them a drawing. He didn't want to pose for it, but she insisted that he sit in a chair under a reading lamp. She didn't have his skill for draftmanship, but she was still better at portraiture than he was because she could capture the spirit behind the face. She couldn't get his collar right, however—he often wore shirts that didn't appear to match his personality—so she told him to take his shirt off and to sit under the light so that his face was lit from the left-hand side. The picture she sent her parents, the second one she drew, showed him looking toward the floor, his glasses on, lips parted, and, below the face, his bare shoulders.

"Oh, they won't like that," Wyatt said.

Whether they liked it or not, they never said. They didn't acknowledge receiving Susan's drawing of her new husband; she never found out whether they thought the picture was art, or a vulgar display of a new possession, or some other thing, some artifact.

They weren't emotionally violent people, so they didn't curse her, or engage in public displays of anger, but they did cast her off. They flew down, spent a day with Wyatt and Susan, tensely filling their time in restaurants and a nearby mall, where they bought Wyatt and Susan a coffeepot. They smiled through clenched teeth all day, and Susan's father ate candy bars, starting with Reese's Peanut Butter Cups in the morning and moving on to M&M's, which he kept hidden in his coat pocket, throughout the warm afternoon. Wyatt had never seen an adult eat so much candy. Just watching his father-in-law fish out treats from his pocket and toss them back surreptitiously gave Wyatt a headache. On the next day, with a great deal of mutual relief, they flew home to Duluth, and that was the last that Wyatt saw of them.

In late June, he said, one evening while he was washing the dishes, "Now you have to meet mine," and she nodded, without asking him what he meant by using the possessive pronoun, and he knew she was nodding without even turning around to check.

He'd warned her about them, and she had told him that it didn't matter: he could have had any kind of family he pleased, bugs or aristocrats, it made no difference to her. Time had started with *him,* she claimed, and all the time before that was just wasted time—it was just personal, the way parents are: personal and eventually irrelevant.

"It's not quite like that," Wyatt told her. "My mother travels great distances in her mind. Sometimes she takes people along with her. You'll see."

Susan shrugged.

Together they drove north in Wyatt's rusting Chevy Malibu toward Five Oaks. As they hurried along the freeway toward the open, vacant spaces of central Michigan, Wyatt felt the landscape invading him, drawing him outward and downward. The cornfields, the silos, and all the exposed desolation of the farmland made him think of his family, and more particularly of his mother, and he thought: *I belong here, I didn't really leave,* and he saw in his mind's eye his father running down a hillside, a stethoscope flapping on his chest, to fetch him back.

The halfway house was outside of town and therefore located in no one's backyard, and inside this formidably unimaginative ex-farmhouse, built right on the ground, his mother's room was located upstairs and toward the back, where its west window caught the afternoon sun, which Jeanne preferred to the morning sun, claiming that the two of them were different. Wyatt had called ahead, and Jeanne had sounded excited and pleased and temporarily balanced, willfully sane, like a delicate, mad actress playing a Donna Reed part with great concentration and difficulty.

Lucille, who managed the house, called upstairs when

they arrived, and Wyatt heard his mother call back, from behind her bedroom door, "Yes, I'm here."

After knocking, Wyatt opened the door. He was holding Susan's hand tightly. His mother stood by the window, and then, remembering herself, sat down. Her hair, dirty blond like Wyatt's but mixed slightly with gray, was pulled back in a tight bun, and her face had a quiet and composed expression, but her expression meant nothing: you could only tell about the condition of her soul from her eyes, which, today, were interplanetary, he thought. Cosmic dust. Neutron stars.

His mind always associated too quickly when he was in a room with his mother.

"Mother," he said. He went up to her and kissed her on the cheek, and she pursed her lips and kissed the air near his face. Then he gestured toward Susan. "Here's Susan," he said. "We're married now."

"Oh, well, I know *that,*" Jeanne said, with a laugh. "Come over here, sweetie, so I can see you." She held out her hand, and Susan reached for it. Jeanne stared up for a long time into Susan's face. "My goodness," Jeanne said, "what a sweet beautiful woman you are. How lucky for you both. You're quite descorbitant—you know that, don't you?"

"What's that?" Susan asked. "That word?"

"My mother makes up words," Wyatt said, his hands in his pockets, fingering the keys.

"I *don't* make them up. They're just there. I catch them in my net. Anyone can see how you're a womanly animal, Susan. Any fool. Well, now, if you're my daughter-in-law, you should give me a little kiss, I think. A confirmation." Susan bent down and kissed Jeanne on the cheek. "Yes," Jeanne said. "That was nice." Then she shivered. "I miss kisses, you know," she said to the room. "It's impossible to get kisses if you're crazy. So I end up kissing the air. And of course that looks nuts." She reached out for Susan's hand again. "Do you like to kiss?"

"Very much."

"Well, thank goodness." After a pause, she said, "People should be married. Well, I don't mean married, I mean thirled. Lying down and standing together and kissing and wondering when you're going to get home for dinner. Do you like my room?"

"It's fine," Susan said. "Very sunny."

"Yes," Jeanne said. "Actually it's not a room, it's a stateroom. You know that my husband died?" Susan nodded. Wyatt was standing back, leaning against the wall near the door, trying not to tilt the photograph of himself and Gretel hanging there. "Eugene. Jeanne and Eugene. I wish our names had been more different than they were. I wish I could remember being kissed by him. I don't. They fill you so full of medications here that you can't remember neighborhood things, not a bit of the curiosita." She put her head in the cup of her hand. "I've been in the gray."

"The gray?"

"Well, *you* know. Don't be refractory." Her mouth began working silently, then stopped. "How I love the gray. But then you have to come back, and you're always on the wrong side of the window. Do you love Wyatt, Susan?"

"Yes, very much."

"Thank God for that. It must be nice to be so young and to be able to touch someone for no reason at all. You see, I had a trouble," Jeanne said, arranging herself in the chair. "I can even explain it, because it's something that I know. When his father"—pointing a finger toward Wyatt—"died, or rather didn't go on living, it loosened me. Women aren't supposed to think that, but sometimes they do. I became debundled. I just drifted out to sea. That was the trouble. And

I suppose I might have been *cured,* you know, renormalized, except that what they do to you leaves you right out here in the middle of the water, because they can do everything except love you. They *did* try to start my motors, but my motors just wouldn't start. So I'm the Queen Jeanne out here in the middle of the Atlantic and I have three decks—first, second, and third class—and I always thought there'd be parties out on these voyages, but no. Ever see someone coming out of the fog and going back in? That was me."

She had taken a piece of Kleenex from a box on the windowsill and was twirling it around her fingers. It was breaking apart, as she talked, and small shreds were falling on the floor.

"The ocean is a prison, too," she said, looking directly at Susan. "All the mad men, they put them out into pastures and playing fields, but the women, they put us on these ocean liners, just drifting. They drift us. Sometimes a trade wind takes me toward land. I'm so close, I can even see you now, right this minute."

"Good," Susan said. "I'm right here."

"You're a little *triste,*" Jeanne said, reaching up with her index finger and touching Susan near the eye, "right in that place. Yes, I can see you." Her hand dropped again. Wyatt noticed, through the window, two squirrels chasing each other on the lawn. They reminded him of his thoughts, in this room, circling and nonprogressive. He imagined he heard a bell from down the hall, and as he bent down in order to hear it better, the sun emerged from behind a cloud, and the rays of light came through the window and fell on Jeanne's face.

"Oh, yes, hello. Present and accounted for," she said, closing her eyes and facing the sun. All at once she said, "Wyatt, you ran away."

Wyatt nodded.

"You ran away and didn't come back, and then *I* did. Or did you drown? Maybe you did that, too. I can never remember."

"I came back, Mother. I didn't drown. Here I am."

"So they say. So they all say. And now you've married this mermaid. But what I want to know is, are you really Wyatt, or are you that actor they found?"

"He's the real Wyatt," Susan said. Then she kneeled down in front of Wyatt's mother and put her hands into Jeanne's hands. Her arms were spread on Jeanne's lap, and she looked up into Jeanne's face. "Wyatt, leave us alone for a minute. I want to talk to your mother. Just go outside for a sec, okay, love? Please?"

He went outside to the hallway, smelling the cigarette smoke, not wanting to leave Susan with his mother, but feeling that he had no choice.

When Susan reappeared, she said, "We can go now. Don't tell her goodbye. Do that some other time."

"What did you do to her? What did you say?"

"It was between women. I can't tell you."

"Give me a hint."

"It was private."

"A little hint? After all, she's my mother."

Susan stopped outside the Chevy Malibu and leaned against the passenger-side door. "Here's what I'll say." She draped her arms over Wyatt's shoulders; he'd been standing there to open the door for her. He liked to open doors. "I told her that I'd love her, and then I did a magic trick for her, and then she said something to me that I won't repeat. She's okay, Wyatt. You shouldn't be so grumpy about her. I like it that she's a little nuts. I like it better than the sanity of those two relatives of mine in Duluth."

He started the car. He couldn't imagine what his mother

and his wife had said to each other. Who would ask the questions? Who would pretend to answer?

To get to the visitors' area of the county jail, Wyatt and Susan had to go through a metal detector, which shrilled with electronic alarm at the presence of Wyatt's car keys. He left them behind, at the gate, in a little white plastic bin. He thought he had gotten lucky, however, because it was visiting day, and his cousin Cyril might be in a good mood, good enough, at least, to make a social effort in Susan's direction.

"Drunk driving," Wyatt had explained, about Cyril. "He has a tendency to drive while drunk."

Through the thick Plexiglas, on the intercom phone, Wyatt introduced Cyril to Susan; Cyril apologized for being behind bars, said hi, and asked Susan if she had an opinion about R. Stan Drabble and R/Q Dynamics. She said she didn't. He scratched his arms and said *he* sure had an opinion. Would she like to hear it?

Susan didn't respond, and Cyril appeared to forget what he had been talking about. He gazed with undisguised interest at Susan's breasts—Wyatt didn't think that Cyril had done more than glance at her face—and then claimed he had written a song about the county lockup. "It's called 'Dirty Mattress Blues,' " he said, "and it's about lying down but not sleeping, because I can't sleep." Even through the Plexiglas barrier, even over the phone intercom, Wyatt thought he could smell Cyril's bad breath. "Are you a singer?" he asked Susan. "Then you'll appreciate this song." He sang a few bars and grinned at her, and she grinned back. She asked him about himself, and Cyril launched into his autobiography.

After ten minutes, Wyatt took the phone and said, "Well, we'll be seeing you, Cyril."

Cyril gestured at Susan. Through the phone intercom, he said, "She's a nice lady and a nice piece of tail, though I shouldn't speak that way about your wife. It's just that I always did speak that way. But, hell, congratulations. You got yourself a wife and I got extended jail time. Pretty good for a drowned man. By the way, you been to see your mom? You said hello to Queen Jeanne?"

"Drowned? I'm not drowned. I'm here."

"You are definitely drowned. Definitely drowned. I can see the bubbles rising, right there, right out of your drowned mouth." Cyril pointed a dirty index finger in the direction of Wyatt's face. "Many happy returns, pal. Go visit your mom."

"I did that, Cyril," Wyatt said, before hanging up the intercom phone.

In the car, leaning back, Susan said, "So, that was your cousin?"

"That was him."

"You like him?"

"It's not a question of liking."

"What's it a question of?"

"Family. He's like a brother, sort of."

"Ah." She inhaled. "So you once said. A brother. So it's complicated. This is a funny town. I think I liked your mother better. I bet he called me a nice piece of ass, when you were talking to him. I could read his lips. Is that what he called me?"

"No," Wyatt told her. "That's not what he said."

"You're lying," she told him, "but I don't care, right now. Okay, who is it we're going to see next? Your Aunt Ellen? The one who raised you?"

"Yes. And then we're done."

• • •

They found Ellen out in her garden, watering her tomatoes. Wyatt had forgotten how pudgy she had become, so that she seemed to be more dimpled than ever, and not only in her face, but in her hands. Her hair flew up and around in all directions, and Wyatt thought, for a moment, that she looked a bit like a bowling ball. To be hugged by her was to be enveloped in flesh; she hugged Susan before being introduced to her, and Susan looked pleased and surprised. "I'm Ellen Palmer," Wyatt's aunt said, "and you must be Susan. Come on inside. We're going to have to talk. How smart of you both just to go off to city hall and get married. All those dreadful church nuptials! They're so tiresome I could scream. Vows, vows, vows. The wretched platitudes of love. You'd think people would get tired of vows, wouldn't you?"

"Ellen plays the organ at weddings," Wyatt explained. "She gets paid."

"Not enough, I don't. I want to play Bach, and they want me to play Barry Manilow. Tell me *that* isn't punishment. I haven't got the stomach to eat the canapés at the reception, after that. Well, come on in."

The house needed a coat of paint; the lawn needed mowing; and, inside, the living-room floor was covered with newspapers, magazines, and books. Over the entire room hung the smell of paper. Wyatt was used to it but wasn't sure what Susan would think about it.

"I'm not much of a housekeeper," Ellen said, bringing in some iced tea from the kitchen. She didn't waddle yet, Wyatt thought, but if she kept putting on weight, she soon would. "Here, have some of this." After pouring glasses for Wyatt and herself, she returned and clinked her glass against Susan's.

"Here's to you, Beauty," she said. "Now let's sit down and explain ourselves."

Susan explained: her parents, how she and Wyatt met, her magic tricks, her interest in set design, and her ability to balance. She explained everything in five minutes, while Ellen sat back and listened.

"That's fine," Ellen said. "I like the magic part, and the others. Could you do a handstand, right here for me?"

Susan put aside her iced tea, reached forward, and, in one of the few clear spaces in the living room, stood on her hands.

"Thank you. That's quite wonderful. I think you're wonderful. You're lucky, Wyatt, but then you always were." Wyatt nodded. "You're probably wondering why this house is full of paper, Susan. You're too polite to admit it. It's what I call the evidence. I'm writing a book. Isn't that funny? A middle-aged lady like me writing a book. But I am. A William Blake sort of book. Tigers of wrath and so on."

"Excuse me?"

"I'll explain later," Ellen said. "Not now, not until I know you a little better. So: what did you think of your mother-in-law? What did you think of Jeanne?"

"I liked her," Susan said. "She's all right. She was sort of sweet."

"Yes, she is." Ellen nodded. "Poor thing, all that ocean-liner business. And did you see Cyril? He's locked up, but it's visiting day today."

"We saw him," Wyatt said. "He said the same thing to me that my mother said. He said I drowned. So did she. I never drowned. What's that about?"

"Oh, I'll tell you someday. It's a long story. We don't have time for it now. I guess you don't remember. Well, why would you. Listen, Susan, I want to tell you something."

Ellen leaned forward, her elbows on her thighs. "This boy, your husband, is a treasure. His sister, Gretel, she's something else, but this one is a find, and you be sure to love him, all right?"

Susan nodded.

Ellen turned toward Wyatt. "Sonny, what're you planning to do once you graduate?"

Wyatt shook his head. "Don't know."

"Reason I asked," Ellen continued, "is that Hugh Welch, out there at Bruckner Buick, told me that he's heard they're holding an assistant's job to the city manager for you, as long as you can do some accounting and write sentences for the grant proposals they've got to have written. This city isn't thriving, but it's getting bigger, and they need someone over there who'll do the paperwork. Someone with a manic-depressive mother and a cousin in jail, and who wants to be conventional, and I think that's you. A red-tape sort of fellow, newly married and in want of a job. You interested, in a year or so?"

"I don't know. I don't know about coming back."

"Well, you want a job, you give me a call, all right?"

"Okay."

"Of course, people should do what they *want* to do, but they don't often have the chance, or the sense, either, especially right after they're married. Well, listen. You two go on home now. You've seen enough of me for one day. You'll see me again, plenty of times. And, Susan, don't you take Cyril or Jeanne too badly. They're all right."

"I know."

"No, you *don't* know, but they are. And what you don't know is that he"—she pointed her thumb toward Wyatt—"he's his father's child. He's Eugene's. I'm almost the only one that knows that. Now you two take off."

She hugged them both and then eased them toward the door.

They had stopped at a Dairy Queen, on the way back, and Susan was eating a Peanut Buster Parfait, when she looked up at Wyatt and said, "You're going to end up back in that town."

"I am?"

She dipped her spoon in the ice cream. "Oh yes. With a family like that one, sure you are. You're going to go back there and get a job and pretend to be ordinary for a while. That'll be interesting." She smiled, and flicked some ice cream at him.

"No, I'm not." He wiped it off his forehead. "I won't."

Overhead, an airplane was crossing the bowl of the sky, and Wyatt shielded his eyes to see it. Somewhere behind them a dog was barking furiously, and he heard the chattering of insects. Susan flipped some ice cream at him again. Of course she was right: he *would* move back here, and pretend to be ordinary, for her sake, for theirs, for his own.

4

The salesman who sold them their house said
that in any other city a young couple like themselves would
probably have the purchasing power to buy only a starter
condominium whereas, *here* . . . and he pointed at their front
lawn, where a single Rainbird sprinkler sprayed out water
over a few patches of grass and what Susan had called "starter
mud" when she first saw it. The house that faced all this
starter mud was in a subdivision that backed up against a dairy

farm, and the house's particular design, used in similar subdivisions all over the country, the salesman said, was called the Glencoe. Wyatt had no idea why that name had been chosen; the design had nothing to do with Scotland, so far as he could see. It was a three-bedroom ranch, and Wyatt thought it was horrifically nondescript, down to and including what was labeled the family room, but Susan said, well, you had to live *somewhere,* and was he expecting Xanadu, this time? Or maybe a *palace,* on his income, with gold-inlaid duck faucets? She had cultivated a talent—he hadn't known she had one— for irony, while he himself seemed to be cultivating a particular tone of earnestness, the sort of tone you needed to get by day after day pushing papers around city hall. She said he was now about twenty percent Rotarian and that the numbers were rising every day, but it was all right: he'd get to about twenty-five percent and then stop. Rotarians didn't make slow crazy love, the way he did.

Their neighbor was a Mr. Needleman, retired, and not much given to conversation, though he did have an inclination to look out his back window at Wyatt and Susan when they were busy with one thing and another in their yard. Susan was teaching Wyatt how to stand on his hands. She claimed it was easy: all you needed was strength and balance. He had the strength but lacked the balance, and he said that he would only take lessons from her at night, under the light of the moon.

Under the light of the moon, then, in late spring and early summer, Susan held up Wyatt's legs as he walked upside down around the backyard, and Mr. Needleman silently observed their activities. On those occasions when Mr. Needleman had spoken to either of them, he had ignored their names and simply said "You kids," as in "You kids might keep it a little quieter," or, in one of his better moments,

"You kids have a nice lawn there. Remember to keep watering it, or it'll look like blind hell."

On the night when Wyatt finally managed to walk on his hands by himself, they had decided, he and Susan, to make love somewhere on the lawn, in a spot out of range of Mr. Needleman. Clouds obscured the moon and the stars, and the grass on Wyatt's back felt prickly and sensual. Looking up into the black emptiness of the sky, he saw nothing except Susan, enjoying herself and trying her best to keep her voice down—she was sometimes noisy during their lovemaking—so as not to awaken Mr. Needleman.

That same month, they had bought a white rabbit named Fred. The rabbit was meant to replace Lily, the rat, who had died soon after they had all moved to Five Oaks. Fred had no personality and lived in a hutch Wyatt had built in the backyard; when the mood struck Wyatt and Susan, they brought Fred inside, for socializing. Fred was closer to Susan than to Wyatt. She pulled him out of hats at children's birthday parties, where she was employed to do her magic act. Fred always looked slightly surprised when he emerged from the hat, and his expression of annoyed bewilderment delighted the children. Susan had put an ad in the paper, and, being the town's sole magician, she had received more requests than she could fill.

She had had to order, from a magic-supply warehouse, trick rings, an exploding handkerchief, a top hat with two compartments inside, and a Coke bottle with a false bottom in it. Children didn't like card tricks, though they did like it when quarters appeared in their ears. Susan earned twenty-five dollars per birthday. Her show wouldn't have amounted to much, however, if it hadn't been for Fred, and his constant surprise and annoyance at being pulled out of Susan's hat.

After a few months, Susan said that there was a limited

future in magic: she was starting to see the same kids at these birthday parties, and one or two boys, who knew the tricks, were learning how to heckle her. She said that she was going to organize a kids' gymnastics group down at the city recreational center.

Mr. Needleman did not like Fred and claimed that it was against some city ordinance or other to keep rabbits around the house. "You kids," he said, standing in their driveway and gazing off at nothing in particular, and apparently trying to think of an accusation that would fit, "can't just keep any animal around your house in a cage." Wyatt didn't like to pull rank on his neighbor but was forced to say that he *knew* all the city ordinances, and there were none restricting the possession of rabbits, "particularly," Wyatt emphasized, "for professional purposes." Susan had pulled Fred, one Saturday morning, out of a hat for Mr. Needleman's benefit, and the old man had smiled, though it had seemed to be an effort. Wyatt had said later that you could almost hear his mouth muscles creaking.

Mr. Needleman had spent his life as an airline dietitian, planning in-flight meals. Susan said that that explained everything.

They owned a tree, too, a maple, planted for some reason by the developer, and it stood six feet high in the backyard, and after Susan became pregnant, three months after she stopped taking the pill, Wyatt planted three more trees, a crabapple and an ash in the front yard and a linden in the back. On the night when his daughter Christina was born, Wyatt came home, four hours after the delivery, and lay down in his backyard on the spot where he and Susan had once made love, and he gazed toward the white-pin light of stars transfixed in place above him. He told himself that he was a lucky man, the luckiest man he knew. The stars, looking back, had

as usual nothing to say, but he felt sure that they were interested in the way that he now qualified as a father and as an
adult, having survived, somehow, the wreck of his family. He
wondered if Mr. Needleman could see him; if he could,
Wyatt thought he would wave at him, or throw some snow at
him, or make an obscene gesture in his direction, but Mr.
Needleman didn't seem to be watching, and Wyatt rose from
the ground and dusted the snow off his trousers and went
inside.

The next morning, after visiting Susan and Christina in
the hospital, he drove over to the city's recreational center to
play basketball, to work up a sweat, and it was odd how his
jump shot and his lay-up had improved. He played in an
ecstasy of sweat and aggression. He thought he had become,
for at least a day or two, untouchable, unbeatable, almost
airborne.

His classmates from Five Oaks High had either disappeared out of town, or gone down various drains, or were
working intermittent dumb jobs. He knew of only a handful
who had stayed afloat or were actually doing better than their
parents had. Nearly all of them had gingerly taken that first
step downward. The ones he still knew came over sometimes
on Saturday or Sunday afternoons, and he and Susan would
pour the beer, tell stories, talk about the past and the future,
stand on their hands, and display Fred. These get-togethers
lasted until after Christina's birth; somehow, and for some
reason, Wyatt's old friends from high school didn't care to
come around, with a baby in the house. They didn't want to
bring their wives and girlfriends to see the baby. They didn't
say why, but Wyatt could see—he hadn't known about it
until then—that his friends were frightened of infants and

their lifelong demands. That would change when they had kids of their own, but for now they looked like deer, caught in someone's headlights.

One or two of his classmates, he had heard, had become investors. Investors? From Five Oaks? The idea seemed preposterous, but he had been told all this by Harold, his incompetent but friendly barber; one of the more anonymous members of his high school class, Jerry Schwartzwalder, had gone to Minnesota and somehow made a tidy bundle, and was promising to return to Five Oaks, and bring that bundle with him, Harold claimed, as he haphazardly cut Wyatt's hair.

On the walls of their house, Wyatt and Susan had hung posters of paintings by Bonnard and Vermeer, artists of quietly ecstatic familial order. Wyatt himself had tried to paint a new still life—a wooden chair, a table, a few flowers, and a butter knife—but it lacked what his paintings had always lacked, and after a month he threw it out.

After Christina was born, Susan organized a child's gymnastics class, just as she said she would, with fifteen children in the first group. She brought Christina down in a stroller, and for an hour, every other day during the summer, and on Saturdays and Wednesday nights during the winter, she taught them to tumble, balance, and climb. Wyatt came over to watch out of sheer astonishment and pride.

He had made himself into a model bureaucrat, good at writing up forms, reading regulations, knowing when to ask the city attorney a question and when to leave him alone. He fit in. He was learning how to hide information from the city council and the mayor. He had never been quarrelsome and seemed to be able to tell most people what they wanted to hear; when he had bad news to give to someone, he suggested just the right amount of distress by wrinkling his brow. He had a small office close to the coffee machine, near the office for special events run by a woman named Alyse Schneider. It all seemed to be going according to some sort of plan.

But still: there was Cyril. Upon being released from jail, Cyril had rented an upstairs apartment in a house where, downstairs, a beauty parlor, The Magic Mirror, happened to be located. But he didn't like the smell of the permanent-wave lotions, or the Van de Graaf generator sound of the hair dryers, so he moved into an apartment in the Oak Motel, recently converted for permanent tenants. He considered himself temporarily unemployable; besides, there were no jobs, and everyone knew it. He survived on assistance payments, food stamps, and money that Wyatt brought him in an envelope every two weeks, on Saturday morning. Wyatt couldn't spare the money, but Cyril was family, and that was that.

The motel was located on Frummage Avenue, which started north of town at the city dump—now called the municipal landfill—and which entered the city, going past Cyril's apartment, then headed south toward the water treatment plant, and every time Wyatt took the street, eventually stopping underneath the flaking and faded OAK MOTEL sign, with its permanently mispainted NO VACANCY in pink letters mixed with the gray discoloration on the metal where the neon tubing had once been, he had a feeling of light-headedness, but it felt good, a bit like an adventure, because that was the way Cyril usually felt, apparently, both depressed and dangerous at the same time.

On this particular morning, when Wyatt knocked, Cyril yelled at him to come in, it was open. Pasted or glued on the door was a small card with the name BIRTHDAY printed on it. Cyril had recently changed, though not legally, his last name from Wilson, his mother's family name, to Birthday. He had told Wyatt that family names were irrelevant to him, and, besides, he had always liked birthdays. He had liked them so much, in fact, that he wanted to *be* a birthday, and now he was.

Wearing his boxer shorts and a T-shirt, Cyril was standing near his hot plate, rubbing his unshaven chin as he stared sourly at the saucepan. His hair had a stand-up look, and, as usual, he gave off his customary air of despondency and bad humor.

"Oh, it's you," Cyril said. "I was hoping for the playmate of the month. I guess you're not it."

"No. How're you doing, Cyril?"

"I ask for Bo Derek and I get Ward Cleaver." Cyril was picking at something inside his ear, using a paper clip.

Wyatt removed two books, *Grand Prix Limericks* and *How to Pick Up Girls!*, from a chair and sat down. He coughed twice. The air in here was personalized and unhealthy in an indefinable way. It smelled of fish oil and something that made Wyatt think of a mattress that had been doused with beer. Next to Wyatt, the Statue of Liberty souvenir ashtray was filled with the butts from Cyril's unfiltered mentholated cigarettes.

"What's new, Cy?"

"You. You're new. You are exactly what is happening to me right now." He went into the bathroom, and Wyatt could hear him yawning.

"I mean besides me."

"Want a cigarette?" Cyril emerged from the bathroom, holding out a pack of Kools. Aiming himself in Wyatt's direction, he shot off one of his unpleasant smiles.

"No, thanks."

"Too early, huh?" Cyril lit up and blew smoke toward

the hot plate. "Gets *me* started, anyhow. Coffee and cigarettes. Now all I need is a wife, a home, and a job, and maybe
twenty-six thousand dollars in the bank, and I'd have a chance
at being just like everybody else." He nodded, as if he agreed
with himself. Wyatt noticed that the tattoo on Cyril's arm was
beginning to fade. You could hardly read the name there
anymore, but Wyatt knew what it said: *Angie,* over a heart.
Cyril had been the sensation of Five Oaks High when he'd
gotten the tattoo in Saginaw, on his eighteenth birthday.
Wyatt remembered Angie, too: how she walked down the
hallways of the school, so close to Cyril they seemed jammed
into each other, her hand stuck into the back pocket of Cyril's
jeans. Before her, there'd been another one named Mandy.
"Can't figure out why I can't get this water to boil," Cyril
muttered. "You want a beer? I'd serve you some tea if I had
hot water, but seeing as I don't, I can't."

The sun fought its way past Cyril's curtain and made an ax
pattern on Cyril's stained bedsheets. Wyatt tried to think of
something cheerful to say.

"Susan says to say hello. Christina's doing fine. She actually walked a few steps. Everybody wants to see you."

Cyril had dropped himself into a beanbag chair and was
looking puzzled. "They want to see me? Christina does? She's
a sweet child." Christina, to Wyatt's astonishment, was always happy to see Cyril and would stick her fingers in his
mouth and laugh in his face. Cyril sometimes had that effect.

Wyatt took the envelope with Cyril's money out of his
jacket pocket and placed it on the table next to the chair.
Cyril saw him do it. Neither of the two men said anything
while this action occurred. Cyril had never thanked him, that
Wyatt could remember. It was just something that happened
between them.

"So," Wyatt said, trying not to inhale the air. "Anything turned up for you lately?"

With difficulty, Cyril pulled himself out of the beanbag chair—its seams, Wyatt noticed, were beginning to split, and polyester beans were beginning to spill out onto the floor—and walked over to the window and raised the shade. Sunlight fell all over him brutally. If anybody had been outside, that person would have seen Cyril in his underwear, but no one was, or would be. Behind the Oak Motel was a vacant warehouse fronted by an empty parking lot. "Oh, sure. I got this new thing figured out."

"What new thing is that?"

"You going to take my new idea and steal it?"

"No, Cyril, I'm not."

"Well, it ain't taking bottles for the refund, Wyatt. That's not what it is."

"What is it?"

Cyril breathed out, and Wyatt could smell it, halfway across the room, but it wasn't Cyril's breath, that smell, it was his soul, and Wyatt could hardly stand it. "How come," Cyril asked, "it's always me that's the topic of conversation between us? Me, an old bag of black sheep. How come it isn't you?"

"I don't know," Wyatt said. "I'm not very noticeable. I was just asking about your new thing."

"Oh yeah." Cyril walked over to the saucepan and examined it. "Cousin, the water is hot, at last. What they call the miracle of electricity. They got the little bubbles in there on the floor of the saucepan. Did I believe I heard you say you wanted tea?"

"Sure," Wyatt said. He watched as Cyril picked up a Styrofoam McDonald's coffee cup, poured water into it, then dropped a used dried brown teabag from the sink into it. He handed it to Wyatt.

"Bottom's up," Cyril said, "like they say in the movies."

The water smelled faintly of kerosene. Wyatt touched his lips to the water, pretended to swallow, then smiled. "Like they say. Thanks, Cyril." He sat back, and the chair's cushion let out an exhalation that sounded like breathing in intensive care. "Cyril," Wyatt said, remembering the times he and his cousin had played together as children, "do you remember that time we went down to that place, it was somewhere near the river, and they had some radio promotion or something, and somebody drowned? I must've been about six. Do you remember that? I remember you called me a drowned man. So did my mother."

"Jeanne did? When was that?"

"When Susan met her."

"It was you who drowned, Wy. That's how I remember it. That's all I remember. Anyway, screw the past. Do you want to hear about my money-making idea or not?"

"Damn it, Cyril. This is *me* talking to you. Why d'you have to get like that? You don't have to get all irritated and everything."

"Yes, I do. Besides, I'm talking. I'm being Mr. Good Host. I'm standing here moving my mouth around the syllables. And as I remember, I just poured the tea. What the hell else do you want?" He blew out some cigarette smoke. "I'm making a social effort here when in other respects I wouldn't mind being left alone. You were the one went to finishing school, not me, pal."

"All right, all right."

"I'm not selling drugs. No fucking way."

"I didn't say you were."

"I'm living deep down inside the ordinary, same as you,

only it's more disgusting, the way I do it, because the ordinary is punishing me here, but I'm okay as long as I don't complain. When I complain, it all gets worse, because I say it aloud and then it happens. You follow me?"

"I think so."

"If there was a job to take in this town, I'd take it. But there isn't so I don't. Getting the companies to come is your department. Anyway, you want to hear my money-making idea?"

"Sure."

"Basements."

"Basements?"

"Absolutely. All over town there's people with basements, right?"

"Right."

"And all those basements are dirty and filthy and filled with refuse and garbage, am I correct again?"

"I guess so."

"So what I do is, I go around, I knock, I say, 'Lady, you want this shit in your basement cleaned out? Well that is what I am here to do, at your service, Mr. Cy's Basement Cleaning Agency.' "

"You'll have to get a permit to dump at the landfill. There are a couple of other permits you might have to get."

Cyril breathed out a sigh, and Wyatt thought of how rarely he had ever heard Cyril do that: he wasn't the sighing type—passive poetic breaths had always irritated Cyril, and he had preferred braying laughter or one sample from his inventory of offensive behavior—but when Wyatt looked at him now, he saw that a particle of Cyril's energy seemed to be gone, and in its place was a kind of feckless confusion, a woundedness. Cyril had never minded hard work as long as he had been needed, but no one had needed him, or had said so, in a long time. Cyril had been stranded, orphaned, in adulthood, in the land of the grown-up. He had the natural unluckiness of those who had never cared about money.

He held his hand out, the gesture of a beggar in the street.

"Oh, my cousin Wyatt, he'll take care of that. So: what do you think of my idea?"

"It doesn't sound much like you. You really want to do that?"

"No, I don't *really* want to do that, what I really want to do is lie on the beach in beautiful downtown Honolulu, but seeing as how I am the recipient of fate and am streamlined for failure in America, I got to do something, and that is what I thought of. I'm tired of watching *Bowling for Dollars* and *American Gladiators*. So what do you think?"

Wyatt stood up and put his cup of kerosene-flavored tea on the television set, whose rabbit ears were broken and drooped down toward the floor. "Well, I think, if you're going to have relations with the public, you shouldn't sound so bitter. And I think everyone in this part of the city knows you, Cyril. They might not let you past the front door. Well, maybe they will."

"I've thought of that. I'm going to get insured and certified."

"No one will insure you."

"Well, I know that, too," Cyril said calmly, picking up a stained white T-shirt, and twisting it at its sides as if he were wringing out a wet towel, until it became knotted, at which point he threw it at the wall; then, not waiting for longer than a second or two, he walked over to the window and began to pound his fist against the glass. The normal, the expected thing, for Cyril, would have been at this moment to send his fist through the glass, and Wyatt waited motionless for this to happen, the calm Cyril-like logic of destruction, from A to B and arriving at last at C, where things always broke or were ruined or injured, and the cops or the doctors arrived and started to write down nouns, verbs, and adjectives on pads of paper, and Cyril looked sheepish, and was sometimes taken away. He would be able to hold up his fist, with the shards of glass stuck in the heel, the blood as a kind of trophy, and Wyatt would do his best to look shocked by Cyril's latest act of ruination. By now, Cyril's anger had a certain clocklike regularity. And did he, Wyatt, enjoy seeing it? He wondered about that. He thought probably he did. But instead of putting his fist through the glass, Cyril stopped, turned around, and smiled.

"Oh, I don't know," he said, suddenly calm. "Maybe they'll let me in anyway, all the ladies of the house. Who knows. I got to start a business, I got to be an entrepreneur one way or the other, or else I'll be one of those famous homeless people they got now, living inside a cardboard box and getting on the television news, being famous and living on oatmeal cookies and dog food. Hey, let's go for a drive. You bring your car?"

"Yes."

"See," Cyril announced, putting his hand on his chest, "what I just did, was, I suddenly thought of you, and I put myself in your place, the way this book I read advised me to do, this book that tells you how to stop being a shithead, if you are one, and I imagined me as you, like I was saying, and I thought, Cyril, you asshole, you really want to start the day doing another crazy-ass fuck-up thing? No. You do not want to do that. So I am soaking in the cosmic calm that comes down to us from the skies, this book says, from the cosmic radiation background, and I look at you, Mr. Solid Citizen, and I get all calm, like a chicken that you take out of the freezer, you know, frozen solid? That's how I am, right at this moment. You couldn't heat me up with a buzz saw. Wyatt, you're a good man, don't get me wrong. And I'd be a good man too if I could figure out the trick to it. You ever think about God? Your Aunt Ellen says I should, not the God they got, but the other one, the God they don't have. That's hers. Well, never mind. I'm getting all excited. Let's go for a drive in your car. I could just look around and pretend I was the scenery."

Slumped down on his side of the car, looking out morosely at the passing parade of two-story houses, Cyril said, "Even on a nice day there's nowhere to go in this city. You notice that? How the weather don't make no difference in the things to do?" When Wyatt didn't answer, Cyril said, "And another thing. If you were doing your job, would everything be for sale? I don't think so. Look at this. Everybody wants to get out of this city."

Spread out in front of them was the grid of homes that made up what was sometimes called the west side of town, and the two visible blocks created, in the Saturday-morning sun, a Norman Rockwell effect, with pleasant-seeming colonials and Tudors and bric-a-brac Gothics, except that on each side of the street, decorating the lush green lawns, were FOR SALE signs, and nearly all the houses needed one or two coats of paint.

"Five of them," Cyril said. "Five of these fine houses for sale."

"Well, it's a depressed area. It's hard to find work."

"*You're* living out there in the Glencoe, I noticed. So why don't you find some new businesses and bring them here? That's your *job,* man."

"That's not my job. The Chamber of Commerce does

that. I just do odds and ends in the city government."

"Well, you should make it your job."

"I try. We all try, Cyril."

"I notice the warehouses are closed up. Why don't you fly one of those billionaire inscrutables in from the mysterious East, and let him buy up the whole goddamn town? I hear they're buying up the moon next month."

"The Japanese? I don't think they want to live in this city."

"Can't say as I blame them. Besides, they could have the whole city for about twenty-nine ninety-five. One of the blue-light specials. You want a small city? We got one right here. But no: nobody wants to buy us. Let's go to the river. I can't stand these neighborhoods with all these picture-postcard families in them."

"What's at the river?"

"Water flowing past. That's something." He waited. "Besides, I'm your personal cross to bear, am I right? So you have to take me to the river." Cyril laughed almost soundlessly, a wheeze like *nhuh nhuh nhuh,* a marijuana laugh.

"You don't take a cross to the river," Wyatt said. "You take it up a hill."

"This one you take to the river."

They drove into a shaded parking area bordered by willows on one side and tall pines on the other. Behind them were two benches and an old picnic table, where Wyatt had taken Susan, when they first moved up here, and as they had eaten their sandwiches, he had looked down at the table and seen, gouged there, the name TRACY, carved by him eight or nine years ago. Ahead of them, now, the river broadened out to create the effect of a lake, and the slow drifting current was so nearly imperceptible this time of the year that the town had dumped some sand on the pretense that it was a swimming beach, though they had not hired a lifeguard, not yet. There was some suspicion that the current was too fast for swimming: lawsuits. About a dozen mallard ducks were sleeping on the sand or quacking in a subdued manner under the dock. Another group of them were swimming out in the water.

Cyril pulled himself out of the car and clumped down toward the sand, trying to light up a cigarette as he went, and Wyatt heard a string of obscenities as Cyril's matches flared and went out. Not all the weeds had been cut back here, and Wyatt felt dried burdocks nestling into his pants. Then at last Cyril had his cigarette lit, and Wyatt smelled the smoke and heard Cyril coughing happily as he looked out over the water toward the canoe livery on the other side of the river, where the canoes were stacked up on their trestles.

Cyril's gaze moved over toward the ducks. "Wish I had my shotgun," he said. "I'd have some duck dinner. Some nice bar-be-cue duck."

"Cyril, these ducks are *sitting.*"

"That's the only kind of duck I've ever got." Cyril rubbed his chin violently; his eyes were meanly squinting, and Wyatt heard the river say, *Who is this guy?* "Even the sitting ducks, they sort of get away from me. I stand around, and I watch my life, you know, and it's like I can't even grab that. Do you know what I'm talking about? You don't know what I'm talking about. I keep chasing my life, my very own goddamn life, and I don't have it yet. It just isn't there. It's ahead of me or something. You wouldn't know. You've got a life of your own. It's right there in your wallet."

Wyatt was looking around for a stone to skip. He glanced down, as the sun came out from behind a cloud, and he thought of his mother, and he saw his own shadow bend down and grab a flat smooth stone, but his own hand threw the stone out over the water, where it skipped, five, six, seven times before sinking out of sight.

Cyril sat on the dock and took a long puff. Out here, in the autumn sunlight, he looked halfway used-up, the way James Dean might have looked if he hadn't been handsome and had had no luck. Well, James Dean hadn't had any luck either: he had died. Cyril leaned back and tilted his head so that his face was aimed at the sky. He exhaled, and the cigarette smoke rose in a straight plume. "I'm more than you think I am."

"No, you're not," Wyatt said. "You don't know what I think."

"I've always known what you think, Cousin. Always have, always will." He looked through the slats of the dock. "You ever pat one of these ducks?" He pointed at the mallards with his cigarette.

"No, Cyril, I have not."

"These ducks, they don't like to be petted," Cyril said, giving Wyatt one of his sour smiles. "They just like to sit there and get fat. They don't give a shit, and then when it gets cold, they fly to West Palm Beach. They got the life." Cyril uprighted himself, walked down to the beach, and began to approach the ducks. Wyatt didn't like the way Cyril was walking: he had stubbed out his Kool in the sand and was stooped over with his arms bent and his hands held out in a slightly predatory manner. "Come to Papa," Cyril said, wagging his index finger at them.

"Cyril, what're you doing?" Wyatt breathed in, having gauged Cyril's intentions. The day had taken on an aura of pleasant strangeness, the way it tended to do when he was with his cousin. He looked up at the roadway and the parking lot to see whether any of the local police might be watching them. He couldn't see any.

"A chicken in every pot, a duck on every hot plate," Cyril said, creeping toward a sleeping male, whose eyes, suddenly, opened, and took in Cyril. The duck gave out an alarmed quack and began to waddle toward the water. "Come to Papa," Cyril said, a bit more loudly, but still unconvincingly, and in what was apparently an effort to persuade the ducks that he himself had birdlike ambitions, Cyril began to waddle a bit, dipping from side to side, but it failed: Cyril looked nothing like a duck. He looked entirely like himself.

They were flapping their wings now, getting out of his way, the sagest ones flying up toward another part of the river.

Wyatt had moved backward, away from Cyril. He was trying not to laugh, but he *was* laughing, enjoying Cyril's show the way Cyril probably meant it to be enjoyed.

Cyril was now standing at the edge of the water and had leaned down and actually managed to grab a particularly sleepy female by the leg. She began a frantic quacking at the moment that Cyril got his two hands around her. Wyatt could see that Cyril's hand was scrabbling upwards toward the duck's neck, to wring it, but the duck bit Cyril on the arm before he could grab her head. Her wings flapped, and the duck took immediate flight. Cyril let out an explosive obscenity and stepped into the water, a hungry and crazed look on his face.

"Go get her, Cyril," Wyatt called. "Show her who's boss."

Cyril had lunged into the water, his arms flailing, the entire force of his rage directed against the ducks that remained. He was up to his knees and was heading further out, and Wyatt noticed, now, some autumn leaves drifting downstream, past Cyril. How little you could do for people! And why should you? Cyril wanted to be a show, and he was, and Wyatt laughed as he picked up a stone to throw at someone or something, and then let it drop. But Cyril, a force of nature, was wading around in the water, going further out, getting his clothes soaked, holding his arms out like a crazy man, quacking insanely, an imitation so bad that not even the dumbest duck, a retarded duck, would be convinced, would come over to Cyril's side, to have its neck wrung and to be boiled in a pot in the Oak Motel.

With all the birds swimming away, rather calmly now, toward the center of the lake, Cyril stood, quiet at last, up to his waist in water, and he turned there and looked toward Wyatt, and with a smile that had lost its sour edge, an actual happy smile with no apology to it, that suggested he had been pretending all along, doing a little pantomime, he said, "Well, nothing for me that time." He reached into his pocket and lit a cigarette.

"Guess not." Wyatt grinned. He felt happy. It was a great day. "Let's go home, Cyril." As Wyatt walked, his shadow walked underneath him, toward the water's edge.

"Okay. I guess that's a good idea."

On the way back to the Oak Motel, Cyril seemed to be falling asleep. As he began to snore, his side of the windshield gradually fogged up. The mist on the glass seemed to be forming into the pattern of a boiling pot, and, standing over it, some sort of hooded figure, like Cyril next to his hot plate. Wyatt turned on the blower and the image disappeared.

Instantly Cyril woke up and said, "What's so wonderful about making forty thousand dollars a year?"

"Nothing. I didn't say it was. I didn't say anything about forty thousand dollars."

"Maybe it was a hundred thousand."

"You were dreaming, Cyril."

He rubbed his eyes and patted his shirt for his cigarettes. "Forty thousand dollars? I must've been."

When they reached the Oak Motel, Cyril opened the door and poured himself out. Wyatt had put the car into reverse when Cyril leaned in and said, "Remember me to Susan. And Christina, too." His breath smelled of swamp water and mentholated cigarettes.

"I will."

"Don't forsake me."

"Excuse me?"

"You heard me. You think I'm some kind of entertainment. Don't leave me behind here, Wyatt. Get me out of here."

"Out of what? The motel?"

"Naw," Cyril said, turning around. "Everything. This life. All of it."

•

After seeing Cyril, Wyatt thought his own house had a let's-get-down-to-business quality, an effect of predictable corners and department-store furniture and faded drapes, a house like any other, designed for invisibility. But its architectural dutifulness pleased him, its quality of camouflage, its democratic plain style. All the same, the memory of Cyril, his screwed-up childlike presence, inserted a note into the living room for Wyatt, like F-sharp over F, a distant painful dissonance, so that he had a sudden headache taking root at the base of his skull, and branching up toward his forehead and back toward his neck, a headache like a tree, sprouting, as in springtime, blossoms along its length, blossoms in this case of pain. He looked over toward the kitchen, where Susan was preparing sandwiches, walking around the playpen.

"How's the bad penny?" Susan asked. "Still out of jail?" He noticed her wrists, their slender gracefulness.

"Still out."

"Any plans?"

"Oh, he has plans. Basements."

"Ah. Basements. Cleaning them out, I imagine."

"That's what he said."

She closed her eyes for a moment, a habit of hers when she was exasperated. Then she ran her hand through her hair. "Would you let that man into any house you owned? And did you give him that money again?"

"Sure. And yes."

"We can't afford that, Wyatt. Damn it, we can't. He's a creep. He looks like a rapist."

"No, he doesn't. Lay off him. He's just a grown-up kid."

"To whom? Not to me. And you go telling me that he's innocent and a child and all that sort of thing. He's sort of vile. He gives off a noise."

"Well, I can't hear it," he lied. His headache had in fact reached a level of intensity and purity. "I like him. He's fun. End of discussion. When's lunch?"

"Lunch is soon. Who's Jerry Schwartzwalder?"

"I don't know. Yes, I do. He was in high school with me. Why?"

"He called while you were out."

"What did he want?"

"Business. He said it was business." She put down her knife with a particularly delicate gesture—now that she was older, Susan had acquired, along with her irony, a certain fastidiousness—and she turned toward Wyatt a look that lasted a split second. He saw it and understood it immediately.

Her expressions weren't casual. She thought about them before she cast them. She had a touch of aristocracy in her taste for premeditation, and she assumed he would understand it: this mixture of anger and love and impatience, that he had made himself just slightly smaller than she had thought he was when she had fallen so heavily and unguardedly in love with him; now he was taking business calls from little commercial men with unpleasant voices, on a Saturday.

He walked over to the playpen and picked up Christina and held her soft heat against his chest. She was awake, her brown hair twirled at the top of her head, and when he touched it, he realized that the skin in his fingertips was so roughened by adulthood that he could hardly feel her hair at all, it was so fine. Perhaps Susan could still feel it.

Carrying her down to the basement, he opened the thought-drawer and pulled out two of his father's slips of paper. There were so many, he still hadn't read all of them. Christina pointed and made a questioning noise, and Wyatt said, "Paper things," as he picked them out.

A streetlight, still on at sunrise this
morning, in fog, made me happy all day. A
streetlight! The odd moods of objects.

On the second slip of paper, however, were only two words.

life grief

Wyatt dropped the slips of paper back into the drawer, hoisted Christina onto his shoulders, and carried her upstairs, where the sandwiches were waiting.

efore their daughter had begun to toddle around the house, Wyatt and Susan had taken Christina for rides in the car, to ease her colic. Past the county roads, where even the mailboxes were rusty, Wyatt had accelerated over a series of hills shaggy with scruffy pines. Sometimes Susan fell asleep, with her head on Wyatt's shoulder, before Christina did. He knew the street system in town by heart, but he was pleased to know almost nothing about the roads out here—

where they went, what they connected to. He had often driven out to the isolated western end of the county as a teenager, soaked in beer, joy-driven, but in those days he hadn't bothered to look out the windows at anything except the road. Only the road mattered: how it loved him, and lay down in front of him.

But now he was curious about houses and open fields, barns so rotted that they tilted, and farm equipment left out to gather rain and snow.

One August evening, with Christina asleep in the backseat, Wyatt had come to an intersection with a dirt road he had never heard of called Emerald Trail. Having stopped the car, feeling pleasantly lost, he peered through the half-dark. Coltrane's *Live at Birdland* wailed softly from the tape machine, "I Want to Talk About You," the song was, and at the return of the theme, Wyatt heard the crack of a baseball bat. Christina's head leaned to the left against the Saf-T-Seat padding. Leaving the motor running—the exhaust was tuned pink to the taillights and to the music's heat—he looked north and made out, in the woolly dusk, that some people were playing softball.

"Let's go see," Susan said.

They left the car, shutting the doors quietly. Except for this softball field, they were surrounded by farmland, and a woman was at bat, but in the poor light she kept missing the ball, fanning it. She was very young; they all were, and they played as if they were cushioned on beer. At last she connected. The center fielder ran out, his head up. After throwing the ball back, the fielder waved toward Wyatt and Susan as if inviting them into the game. Wyatt waved in return and strolled back to the car, Susan's hand in his. "Too bad," she said. "I was always good at second base and at shortstop."

On another occasion, driving Christina around, again at

twilight—these events always seemed to happen at twilight—but with Susan out with the rabbit at a birthday party, he had seen, halfway out to nowhere, a grown man dressed up in an engineer's outfit chugging around the yard to the side of his house, seated in a waist-high model steam railroad train on an oval track. Behind him, near the front door, his wife was pruning the roses, oblivious. A marriage.

And Wyatt had seen a wedding going on at a rest stop off the main highway, everyone wearing a Hawaiian shirt, including the minister. He drove past that, as he had driven past a kite seemingly pasted to the dome of the sky. He couldn't see the string. How was that possible, a kite suspended in the air, without an anchor?

He suspected that if he had brought Susan along, he wouldn't have seen these things. They were meant for him. Besides, after the baby had arrived Susan wanted her time alone in the house.

One Friday evening, with Christina gurgling happily in the back, Wyatt had stopped to observe a fight, five miles out of town, between two young men. They were in a front yard, no other houses nearby. Both men were in jeans. One wore a T-shirt; the other was bare-chested. The fighting was close and silent and brutal. The old manual violence: did neither one own a gun? And apparently they hadn't been taught how to box—they were just going at it. They would stand near to each other, hitting wherever they could, jabs and uppercuts and blows to the midsection, and then separate, and spit blood onto the lawn. They didn't seem to want to kill each other. They would pause for breath, swear, and then come together again, their fists up, moving in.

It had to be about a woman; that was how it looked. The one in the T-shirt was taller, with a longer reach, and his short blond hair stood up with sweat. The shorter bare-chested one appeared to be stronger, more muscular, but his nose and mouth were bleeding, the flow dripping down off his chin like a red goatee. His eyebrow was cut. All the same, he stood there, planted, and Wyatt thought that with that strength he might bring the taller one down. But a knockdown wasn't the point either, not exactly. They were just fighting to hurt.

Dim, on the other side of the house's front window: a woman's face: Wyatt saw it at last, peering out. She had dark stringy unwashed hair, and an overbite, and she was smoking a cigarette, held in the hand cradling her elbow, the other hand at her cheek. The coal of her cigarette glowed when she inhaled.

Christina cried, a baby squall, and the two men stopped, glanced toward Wyatt's car parked on the dirt road, and then went back to their work.

He wanted to see the fight to the end, but now he wanted to get home. After he returned to the house and had put Christina to bed, he hurried toward their bedroom, dropping his trousers and discarding his socks in the hall outside the doorway. When Susan saw him, from where she was lying under the sheet, she asked him where he'd been and what he'd seen; instead of answering her, he pulled the sheet back and began kissing her with his shirt still on, but she was adept, and was good with buttons, as she was with coins, and handkerchiefs. He tore himself away from her only long enough to take off his shorts. Then he was reaching for her. "Jesus," she said, brokenly now, getting her breath, "what brought this on? What did you see?"

"It's you, it's just you, I love you," he said, and at least that part of it was true. He wasn't slow this time; he slammed into her.

.   .   .

The next morning, he was still tired. At work, his business was paper: checking figures on it for city maintenance expenses, writing words on it for government grants that, to his astonishment, actually were granted. He was convinced, at first, that he was utterly incompetent for this job, a seemingly jolly and at times darkly thoughtful college-kid impostor in a suit. Then he learned how to talk loudly to other men and how to hide information when necessary, and he didn't feel like a college kid anymore, but instead like a standard-issue bureaucrat with a bad haircut, the sort of person his cousin Cyril had never liked. He learned how to move into the shade of the city manager's melancholy, how to take comfort in it, how to say "I'll take care of it," and then how to improvise some patchwork solution. He learned how to boom out facts and figures to the city council members that they were unable to refute. He learned about where the money came from and where it went, its exciting Protestant predictability.

He thought he had an undemanding job, close to being weightless—hard hack work, reams of paper, hours at computer screens, with mosquito-size results. The only people who really noticed such results were the usual town maniacs, whose hobby it was to keep surveillance on the city government. They were strange men and women with peppermint breath and pictures of humiliated ancestors up on their walls. He didn't have the sort of job that anyone would call rewarding, but, these days, who did? This job was about sewers and snowplowing and money, but it did help to make the town habitable and fiscally coherent, and it put him in an office on the sixth floor, where he could position his father's half-finished contraption on top of one of the file cabinets.

Because the city manager had been trained as an engineer, Wyatt did more of the figure-and-word work not delegated to one of the city commissioners. It kept him busy, but he felt like a man whose mission in life is to search through the streets for twigs shaped like specific insect species: demanding but almost meaningless tasks. He took great care over anthills and particles of dust; at least, that was how it felt at the end of the day.

What he really wanted to do, when his mind drifted, was to talk to Alyse Schneider, who worked in the office next to his, where she had a job in the recreation department, coordinating and planning events that were supposed to enhance the city's image, that lost cause—why they had put her up here, next to him, was a continuing mystery—and, as a sort of pastime, Wyatt wanted to fall in love with her and make her fall in love with him, just to see what would happen. He allowed himself this much: to be drawn in Alyse's direction. She had a boyfriend she neither loved nor liked, she was smart and funny, and, without being exactly beautiful, she caused in him a teasing charge of sexual uneasiness. He could see her if he moved his chair out three feet behind his desk so that his office doorway lined up with hers. From his office window, Wyatt had a view of the lake. Alyse had a view of the warehouse district. She seemed to like her drab vista. She called it "my so-called view." With her, it was all like that: "my so-called office," "my so-called desk," "my so-called life." Wyatt liked her morose humor. Discontent in women interested him; it gave him a conversational opening, a place to plant his seeds of compassion.

In her way, she reminded him of Cyril.

"Is this Wyatt Palmer?"

The voice on the telephone was both familiar and brusque.

"Yes. Who's this?"

"Jerry Schwartzwalder. Remember me?"

"Sure. Jerry. Of course. Are you kidding? Five Oaks High. It's been . . . what? Six years? Sure, I remember you. I even remember that Dodge you drove around. That was one bad car."

He remembered Schwartzwalder's car better than he remembered Schwartzwalder. The car was beaten and rusty but even with its junkyard appearance it had more character than its owner, a pale kid who usually sat by the classroom window, saying nothing, biting on his pencils and leaving teeth marks, a nondescript guy, a second-stringer. Apparently he hadn't been thinking about sports or girls: he'd been thinking about money. Here, on the phone, he was now.

"Oh yeah, that Dodge. What a piece of junk. I heard you were in the city government. An assistant to the city manager. Jesus, you know, I never thought you'd go back to that town, once you left it, but here you are, a big muck." There was a displeasing heartiness in Schwartzwalder's voice, an audible insincerity. "Have I got that right?"

"That's it."

Wyatt heard scribbling or scratching in the background, and the chattering of what he took to be a fax machine. Jerry Schwartzwalder's voice itself had a new quality that he didn't recognize from a few years ago, but Wyatt couldn't think of an adjective to describe it. Maybe, he thought, his mother had a word for characterizing hearty insincerity; he just couldn't think of it right now.

"I want to have lunch with you, Wyatt."

"Sure. Great."

"I have a business proposition."

"Terrific."

"You know I've had some success lately."

"So I've heard."

"Nothing like bringing some of that success home, right?"

"Nothing like it."

"Especially to a place that needs it, like our fair city, our pathetic hometown."

"Absolutely." He didn't like to agree to that word "pathetic" but Schwartzwalder had to be kept on the line. He had turned into an investment opportunity. "What's on your mind, Jerry?"

"Let's save it for lunch. Where do people eat downtown? They don't still pull sandwiches out of the sewers, do they?"

"Not anymore. There's a place called Chez Steak now. Let's go there."

"Perfect. Day after tomorrow, noon?"

Wyatt crossed out a meeting in his schedule book. "Perfect."

That night, he checked the yearbook. Underneath the photograph of Jerry Schwartzwalder smiling toward the upper right-hand corner of the athletic equipment room, where the photographer had set up his camera and lights—he had an expression of here-we-go optimism on his thin anxious face—were the accumulated credits.

Jerry Schwartzwalder
"Garf"
Service Committee, Debate, Art Club, Science Club,
Swimming
"Or else I have not reckoned with it."
—Shakespeare

Garf? Wyatt didn't remember anyone ever calling Schwartzwalder "Garf," and he hadn't remembered that he had ever competed in any sport. And that Shakespeare quotation. What the hell did *it* mean? He had heard that the year-book committee had made up quotations and attributed them to famous authors; maybe this was one.

A kid who sat by the window, but not exactly a day-dreamer. Never grew his hair long. A pencil-chewer. Had a girlfriend, but Wyatt couldn't remember who she had been or what she had looked like. Hadn't ever been taunted though—hadn't been gay, or a nerd, or a mess. What *had* he been?

And then Wyatt remembered—it wasn't even senior year, it had been a year or two before that—outside of biology lab, Schwartzwalder had dropped a couple of his note-books and textbooks in the hall, and Wyatt had helped him pick some of the papers up, while all around them the other students passed and blinked and went on, and Schwartzwalder had said, "Hey, thanks a lot, Wyatt. You're a good guy."

You're a good guy.

The restaurant smelled of bloody meat and salad dressing. Wyatt had parked himself in a corner underneath one of the lights, so that if there were documents, they'd be legible. The back of his knee itched from poison ivy. He'd spoken to his boss about this meeting but had said that he didn't think anything would come of it.

Into this universe of business attire and subdued conversations about money and lawsuits, Jerry Schwartzwalder appeared, wearing a three-piece suit and a necktie with a splash of tropical fruit colors, and Wyatt knew, from the tie alone, that in the years since they had graduated, Schwartzwalder had acquired money and, with the money, an attitude about it. His face had a curiously bland and cheerful expression: it reminded Wyatt of an emcee on a local game show, where the prizes were small, and overpraised.

They shook hands. "I'll bet you've started drinking already," Schwartzwalder said, although Wyatt hadn't. The only drinks on the table were water glasses. "I'll have a martini," Schwartzwalder announced. The waiter had not appeared, and Wyatt didn't know for whom the order was intended. "I wonder if they know how to make them here."

"I don't know," Wyatt said, shifting without meaning to into a mode of apology. "I've never ordered one. How are you, Jerry? It's good to see you."

"The best way, of course, is to do it with the gin already chilled," Schwartzwalder said, patting the tablecloth lengthwise as if it were a dog that wanted a bit of affection. "And if they put ice into it, well, I'll just walk right out of here. I'd rather sit at the A&W drinking the root beer. How about you?"

That sounded like a good idea to Wyatt, but he was careful not to say so. He put his hand in his pocket, wanting the tactile reassurance of gum and loose change, as Schwartzwalder began to ask about their classmates from high school. Anita Penn. Warren Atwater. Sheryl Jo Klinghart. Nancy Aspen. Terri Broderick. Nate Fleischmann. Tracy Vold. Cammie Skow. Wyatt saw them sometimes, and said so, and reported on their doings; he admitted that he kept on distant and vague friendships with some of them by telephone. But theirs had been a large class, he didn't know what had happened to all of them.

"Oh, sure you do," Schwartzwalder said. By this time Schwartzwalder's martini had arrived, and, as he sipped it, Wyatt held on to a dime in his pocket, for luck. He himself had ordered a Bloody Mary. He thought that some sort of hard liquor was probably the requirement here. Schwartzwalder swallowed, shrugged, and said, "Good enough. Makes the rotten dead sit right up. Hell, Wyatt," he said, suddenly vehemently merry, "you knew *all* those people, you were so damn popular, right there in the middle of everything."

"It didn't look like the middle to me," Wyatt said. "I was just trying to get through it."

"Well sure it was the middle," Schwartzwalder told him, with a bluff heartiness belied somewhat by a pained smile on his face that seemed almost painted there. "Hell yes it was the middle. Do you know what happened to that girl, Carole Esterbach?"

"No," Wyatt said. "I don't think so. I don't remember her."

Schwartzwalder leaned forward. "She was stuck-up, a tease," he said, overpronouncing the consonants, "and a real mess in the backseat of a car. You don't remember her? She was in my social studies class. She sat across the aisle from me. I can still remember how she crossed and uncrossed her legs. There we were, talking about the Bill of Rights, and she was just doing that thing with her legs."

"Did you ever take her out?"

"Girls always liked *you*," Schwartzwalder said. "I used to watch you. You didn't know I was watching, but I was. Some girl or other was always talking to you. You had the secret."

"I don't think there's a secret."

"Of course there's a secret."

"Well, you got to *like* them, Jerry." Wyatt thought that maybe it was time to use first names. "But that's all over now. You're married, right?"

"Yeah, I'm married, but that's different. That's an arrangement." Another martini had appeared in front of him. "What did you mean about liking?"

"Well, ah," and Wyatt tried to laugh. "You know: you have to sort of get into what women do, be part of it. Enjoy their company. And love them. You know what I mean."

"You got to like the pussy show they put on when you're

hot and lovesick and all they want to talk about is 'commitment' and 'caring' and 'pledging' and 'promises'? What's to like?"

"That's not it," Wyatt said, a little desperately. "For example, human things. I mean," and he paused because he didn't know exactly how to say it, "even the small things. All I ever did was take an interest. It wasn't much. I listened a lot, I guess, and then I just *liked* them, Jerry, a whole lot more than I liked men. They're not limited the way we are." Suddenly it felt like ninth grade.

"Aw, I get it."

"Get what?"

"You're a convert. They converted you."

"Excuse me?"

"The woman-religion. They got you. Well, okay. Not me, yet. But you, well, I guess it was bound to happen. Oh right," and Schwartzwalder laughed and patted the tablecloth again. "All that piety about let's treat them all as if they were goddesses, because maybe they think they are?"

"Right." Wyatt looked up: on the other side of the room was a red glowing EXIT sign, and he gazed at it for a moment with longing.

"Well, forget it," Schwartzwalder said. "You were always talking to them and holding hands with them and I always wanted to know what you knew, but I never asked. It doesn't matter because it was all just sex anyway. Yeah, I'm married." Schwartzwalder took another sip from his drink and seemed to slump backwards. "I'm incredibly happily married. I even have kids. Two daughters. If it weren't for my kids, I'd feel so lonely at home, I'd be one of those guys who goes into a McDonald's and starts spraying the patrons with bullets."

"You said you were happily married."

"Yeah, but you have to be successful first," he said, peering at the menu through his horn-rimmed glasses. "I've no-ticed they won't get interested in you unless you're successful. Of course now, I got to admit that I sometimes lie awake nights, thinking of all those girls in our class and how they ignored me and thought I was nothing. I mean, Jesus, I had a car, and a lot of guys *didn't have cars*. It's hard getting over not having love or being in love when you really wanted it and couldn't get it. Ha ha. God, it made me desperate. I read books, trying to figure it out. There was a secret and I didn't know it. What do they serve here for lunch? Tell me about your wife, Wyatt. Tell me about what you settled for. I'll bet you're incredibly happy. Let me in on the secret. I wouldn't ask except we were in school together. And don't let me forget: I've got a business proposition to make."

Wyatt looked at the celery in his Bloody Mary. He couldn't remember having so many conversational cues, or miscues, lobbed in so many directions at once; it was like standing in the middle of rush-hour traffic. He looked over at Schwartzwalder and wondered why the sideliners and bench-warmers who usually became nice people had not become nice, in this one case. He was puzzled about how to argue with someone who was now leaning back, raising his glass, and saying, "To life! All whip and no carrot, right?"

Wyatt felt himself raising his glass. "To life," he repeated, feeling peeved and dismal. "I think some of it is carrot."

"Money and golf," Schwartzwalder said, laughing and showing his small malformed teeth. "And love, if and when you can get it. There's the carrot. And, of course," he added, "the kids and the family. That's the *big* carrot. Well, enough of philosophy. Let's order something to eat."

The room seemed to rearrange its objects into a perfect duplicate of itself as Wyatt searched for something on the menu that he thought he might enjoy. Food, in these times, had become the clearest indication of someone's identity-theme. Well, there were always the virtuous and unrewarding salads. Meanwhile, Schwartzwalder was talking about how much he hated and loved Five Oaks, and Wyatt knew he should be listening very, very carefully but found he could not.

> *Steak sandwich, mash potatoes, gravy*..................$6.99
> *Fried halibut steak with slaw and choice of bread*....$9.50
> *House specialty: chicken 'n' a basket*....................$7.55

How could people eat such things, put them in their mouths, chew, and then swallow? It was part of one's job to come to a place like this and consume nourishment, then reach into one's wallet and pay cash money or hand over a credit card. He struggled to refocus on what Jerry was saying.

". . . you were my hero," Schwartzwalder announced, more loudly than he should have, and Wyatt felt his stomach lurch. After the waitress took their order, Schwartzwalder continued. "And not just because you picked up my papers that one day in the hallway. I admired you. You had character. The girls draped all over you, and you, the only kid in the class with a crazy mother, excuse me, that's a terrible thing to say and I'm sorry. It just popped out, but anyway you came out more sane than any of us."

"My aunt raised me," Wyatt said, calmly considering whether he ought to punch Schwartzwalder in the face, probably now, no, five seconds ago, no, half an hour ago, but the moment, whenever it had been, had passed, and he was listening, and nodding, as if the conversation they were having was perfectly normal and within the bounds of human decency. He waited in a state of painful attention.

"There was a story going around," Schwartzwalder said, sticking his fork with some violence into his pork chop and slicing the meat with precision, "that you drowned once. Have I got that right? Another skeleton in your closet. I heard that in a couple places."

"Well, I wouldn't call it that. Besides, I don't remember anything about it."

"The drowned man. Funny how that story stuck. Don't remember now where I heard it, but I heard it. Want to see my kids?" Wyatt nodded. On his plate were some deep-fried shrimp he had mistakenly ordered; he couldn't remember why. Suddenly he was staring at baby pictures: two children with bright blond hair.

"Aren't they a couple of sweetie pies? You bet they are. Who'd've thought of it: me, a father? Unbelievable! But listen, I'll tell you, I'm a good father. I love them but I'm strict, and Carmella, that's my wife, she's strict too. They don't get away with anything. And that's why I'm here, too, having lunch. Because we aren't going to raise those two kids in any criminal-ruined urban stinkhole. I want to raise them right, and of course, that's why I thought of our humble place of origin here, Five Oaks. Now you tell me, Wyatt, why should I move my family into this town, and if you can tell me that, I want to know what advantages there are to building a plant here, a little manufacturing plant, for my company."

"Now?"

"Of course, now. That's why I'm here. That's what I want to hear from you."

When Wyatt looked up, he saw Schwartzwalder, all affability gone, staring back at him quietly and almost coldly, with just a glimmer of amusement on his face, and Wyatt saw that his former classmate had set this meeting up to watch him squirm. The recording mechanism had been switched to *on* in Schwartzwalder's head. It was all business now, and Wyatt had been batted around so that he'd be slightly disoriented just before his pitch. But that maneuver wouldn't work; he wouldn't let it work.

Raising himself an inch to simulate confidence and the certainty that underlies that confidence, Wyatt went into his act: he talked about the Opportunity Group, an association of businessmen and lawyers from the Chamber of Commerce who could help to expedite the red tape involved in setting up a manufacturing base; he talked permits and regulations and loans, making them all seem easy, if you knew how to go about it; and then he began his Traditional American Values speech, locating all those values, one by one, in the leafy residential streets and bustling neighborhoods of Five Oaks. He neglected his fried shrimp and watched Schwartzwalder consume his pork chop, salad, and martinis. His former class-mate kept his eyes fixed on his food while Wyatt talked. Occasionally he nodded.

The air in the restaurant smelled like a Xerox machine, all of a sudden, but Wyatt talked on, despite the way the dishes, and the cutlery, were staring, amazed, at his performance. He painted Norman Rockwell children, freckled and ponytailed, in the air in front of them both: scampering off to school, delivering newspapers, respecting their elders . . .

"Cut it out," Schwartzwalder said politely and affably, swallowing the last of what was left on his plate, and smiling in a hip let-us-not-fool-ourselves manner. He had used a piece of bread to mop up the sauce, so there wasn't any evidence of food, except for the solitary bone, there in front of him. "For Christ's sake, you haven't even asked me what we're making."

"That's not my concern. I just assumed you'd tell me."

"Of course it's your concern. You just wouldn't know what they are, what *it* is, even if I told you. It's very technical. They're made out of plastic and other substances they don't talk about until you get to graduate-school chemistry, and then, well, it's more like an initiation ceremony, like you're meeting a new virus that doesn't care for human beings so awfully much. Anyway, it's got a long name." Schwartz-walder said it, and Wyatt realized he wouldn't remember the name of this compound unless he saw it written down, if then. "We stand to make a lot of money on this thing. It's got uses in those little tiny pumps they're putting in bodies now, and in waterproofing, and in the process of converting natural fibers into more plasticlike chemical structures that retain their original appearance but don't degrade through time. We make some of these products, and we process others. I could use some coffee. What was the name, did you say, of the woman you married?"

"Susan."

"I don't remember any Susan in our class."

"I met her in college."

"Didn't you want to be an artist, I thought? You were always drawing and painting."

"I wasn't good enough."

"Right. I know that feeling. Susan . . . and you say you have a daughter?"

"Christina."

"You like raising her here?"

"Very much. I . . . I drive her around at night, just so she can see it."

"See the town."

"Right."

"This town going to cause any trouble for us if we make a little dirt?"

"Excuse me?"

Schwartzwalder seemed to sit up; he had an appearance of great alertness. "You know, after the permits and the EPA and the DNR and OSHA and the regulators, after all that, are you guys going to start whining and wringing your hands if we spill a little hoohah on the floor? We've got some VOCs, some volatile organic compounds they call them, and they can be pesky and produce airborne toxins now and then."

"I don't think so. Are you talking about discharge permits? Site studies?"

"There's always a little hoohah spilled," Schwartzwalder said, reaching for his water glass. "Different towns and cities have different personalities when it comes to the hoohah. Well, let's say there's some trichloroethylene down there. I sure as hell don't want to suddenly hear a lot of mothers yelling at me because they think I'm making their kids stupid because of the air or the groundwater, or because the woodchucks are suddenly speaking Albanian or something."

Wyatt was about to make a reassuring pleasantry in Schwartzwalder's direction, and then he thought better of it. He let a little air pocket of silence hang there between them for a moment. Something in the discussion had made him feel the ghost presence of courtrooms and litigation. "We'll want to be careful," he said.

"You know what they say about eggs and omelets," Schwartzwalder said.

"Yes, I do."

"First you break the eggs, but then, it's a *nice* omelet, in this case. We're saving lives with this material, this chemically weird compound, and these pumps we're making . . . and the jobs. I'll bet that you personally know a whole raft of people around here who could use a job. Benefits, retirement, the whole enchilada. That's the way it is, most places now. Anyhow, that's part of the omelet, too. Kind of a jobs-and-product omelet."

"Yes." Cyril working. Cyril getting a paycheck.

"Hey, pal, I'm glad you're so agreeable." Schwartzwalder reached over and patted Wyatt's arm. "Because we really *wanted* to move here, and what we needed really was a kind of green light, and I feel now that we've gotten that green light, from you and from others—well, I mean, I *did* talk to the mayor—but it was you, I mean, really *you* I wanted to talk to, to get the green light to go one hundred percent. Because, after all, the bottom line is omelets. And I mean, if we make a *real* mess, I'll buy a gallon of orthobenzyl parachlorophenol and drink it."

"Well, I don't—"

"Christ." Schwartzwalder began laughing and shaking his head. "I remember one time walking down the stairway and seeing you and some girl in the foyer, you know, near the east doors out to the parking lot, and you two were kissing, this was right after lunch, and her hands were all over you, and it made me feel so awful and lonely, me, an outcast from love, and I thought, well, Jesus, that guy has got everything: people love him without him even *doing* anything, and here I am, and I just felt like moaning into the sky, or moving to another planet. You had everything, all that happiness-equipment, and here *I* was, Garf-the-weasel, but, hell, I'd show them, and so here we are now, having lunch. Sometimes I think my whole life is a revenge for high school."

"Appearances are deceiving, aren't they?"

Schwartzwalder was still shaking his head, but he was gazing carefully at Wyatt, a steady unblinking look.

"No, they're not." Schwartzwalder held his arm out and glanced at his watch, but it wasn't an effort to find out what time it was; it was more a little pantomime to show off the watch. "People say they are, but they aren't."

"Oh, sometimes they are. You take me. I wasn't always happy."

"Yeah, but you were *sometimes*. *You* weren't noticing other people, were you? I bet you weren't. That's the difference. You always part your hair that way?"

"Which way?"

"The way," Schwartzwalder said, "that you have it parted now."

"I don't know. I think so."

"Seems to me it used to be parted on the other side."

"Maybe. I don't remember."

"The way you got your hands clasped there on the table, it's almost like you're praying."

"Jerry, I don't see what my hands—"

"Well, it's what I said. It's funny. I'd like some coffee. You ever get to New York City? You once told me you wanted to. It looks like you're saying grace, when you sit like that."

"It's just what a person does when he sits and listens after a meal."

"Well, from over here, it looks funny. It looks . . . *pious.*"

"No, I don't think so."

"Well, it looks like it."

"You want me to *un*clasp my hands, is that what you're saying?"

"Hell, no."

They sat there for a moment, staring off in separate directions.

"This is good news," Wyatt said, "about your locating a new plant in Five Oaks. It's really terrific for all of us."

"I can't get over," Schwartzwalder said, "how you look with your hands clasped like that."

"Come on, Jerry."

He laughed again. "I just can't get over it."

"Jerry, would it be better if I unclasped my hands? Would that solve it?"

"I'm sure it would."

"This is weird."

"Well, maybe so."

At that moment, Wyatt had the sensation—part idea, part pure feeling—that he was in the foreground of a scene, behind which large gears were about to mesh and turn, bodies rise and fall, souls given and exchanged, and that he was in the presence of someone who was both businesslike and whimsical, and the water glass was calling to him *Don't give way,* and it all had to do with whether he kept his hands clasped together, there in front of him, or whether he pulled them apart.

"Well, it's almost time to get back."

"Yes. Exactly right."

Wyatt pulled his hands apart, and Schwartzwalder smiled, a large wide unfriendly smile full of promise and degradation, and he said, "I've already paid the tab. The fair city doesn't have to pay for this. It's all taken care of."

That evening, he put Christina in the Saf-T-Seat and drove through the early twilight over to his aunt's house. She was as much his mother as his aunt, and he didn't have to call. Anyway, he knew she would be home, bent over behind the house over a bean plant—he knew such things—and that was where he found her. He had carried Christina, burping and calm, with him on his shoulder, and when she turned around to see him, she said, "I like to see you that way." She kissed them both. "Let's go inside."

Following her, he said, "Isn't it late to be in a garden?"

A handkerchief hung out of the back pocket of her trousers. "In the day, or the year, or my life? You were never much of a gardener, were you?" She stopped and touched his free hand. "How's Cyril?"

"Kind of unemployed."

"That's Cyril." She opened the door for him, and he smelled the faintly dry and acid scent of rooms filled with old papers. The living room was piled high on the south wall with newspapers, magazines, and Ellen's old copies of the Modern Library Giants. It was all evidence, Wyatt knew, for the Bible she claimed to be writing. "Want a beer?" She made a vague gesture in the direction of the refrigerator. Wyatt shook his head. "The baby's being awfully quiet."

"It's her adventure hour."

"Ah. That's nicely regulated." She half sat and half fell into a chair. "You were always attracted to regulation and sanity, kiddo. Maybe too much. Maybe because of Jeanne. But there was always a lot of hunger for the other thing in this family and I guess you just didn't get it."

"How's your Bible coming along?"

"Oh, all right. It's not so easy, writing a Bible. Just try it."

Christina had turned her head on Wyatt's shoulder and was now sleeping against him.

"Ellen," he asked, "what's this about my drowning? I can't remember it. Everybody says I drowned. I mean, here I am. People keep talking about it and I can't remember it. Cyril mentioned it, and this guy today mentioned it, as if everyone knew it. I can't remember what they're talking about, and you never told me."

She was in a position in the chair that Wyatt thought might be called pseudo-relaxed, and now she bent to take off her shoes, and as she did, some garden dirt fell out of them onto the worn brown cushions.

"What difference does it make, since you're alive?"

"I just want to know, Ma."

"Don't call me your ma. That's Jeanne."

His aunt pushed herself back up into a standing position and went toward the window, although she couldn't get close enough to it to get a good view because the evidence had been piled up near the wall underneath it. "Oh, all right," she said. "But I'm going to tell it my way, and you shouldn't stop me. If Christina stops me, well, that's different. But I won't tell this story as if it's just a story, because it's something else."

"What is it?"

"You listen and then you tell me." She turned around to face him. "Are you comfortable? You should be, to start, because this is about you."

"I'm comfortable."

"Good." She pointed suddenly at him, but the effect was disconcerting because she wasn't looking at him. "This is about you but it's also about money and drowning. You don't remember the money, do you?"

"No."

"I didn't think so. That's what happened. You were about six or seven when this occurred, and there'd been a recession, no one was doing too well . . ."

You were about six or seven when this occurred, and there'd been a recession, no one was doing too well, not even the squirrels, as they used to say, or the raccoons at the city dump: no one. I think some harmonically bad energy was in the air. It was like the feeling you have just before a war starts; it's that calm you feel before you go and do something you shouldn't, the way I had, a year or two before, marrying that garage mechanic I hardly knew because he had a nice diving catch on a baseball diamond and could fix my muffler and had good teeth. Remember him? We were married for all of five months. That was before your father died and your mother bought a ticket on that ocean liner she's still riding on, and the summer weather was bad, too, "tantrum weather," your Great-Aunt Hattie used to call it. Businesses were failing, as they tend to do in this town. You've heard about prosperity in those times, but I don't remember any. People were scratching their heads and looking up into the sky for a sign.

You'd go downtown. Everything was for sale, including the churches. Well, they're always for sale, of course, you can buy a church anytime you want to. They had double-coupon days at the IGA, and the Our Own Hardware was selling nails off-price, a bad sign. No one was begging, or lying down in the streets, but I remember a sort of absented look people had. The assassinations had done that, of course, and then the war in Southeast Asia, and the crooks in high office, so that if you said you were an American, you were beginning to have to define what you meant by that.

Anyway, it took the starch out of people, and we had a tractor-parts factory that closed, and a milk-processing plant that closed and relocated in Saginaw. Barry Hanfield just shut down his stepladder factory and retired to Fort Myers, with his third wife, the one who played the flute right in front of people at parties. The biggest employer got to be the county prison. Anyway, the other businesses were mostly all gone, and the men and women here didn't know what hit them. This is not a city where people know how to use leisure time. You give them a chance to think, they get scared.

And when that happens, what they'll do is, they'll just *leave*. They'll pack their bags and drive straight for Los Angeles, a mistake of course, I don't have to tell you that, because they think a suntan is the answer for worry. It must be that unemployment looks better with a beachball and an umbrella.

In those days I had gotten used to the idea of not being married, at least not for long, which suited me fine and which was just as well, once I had to start taking care of you and Gretel up here, though that was a couple of years later. And it was later too that no one could handle Cyril, and he was staying with me part of the time, I guess I was everyone's part-time parent, and of course I loved him too much, with the result that he was already starting to act like the sweet little maniac he eventually turned out to be. The thing about Cyril was, he was a clown and he knew it. He loved to make me laugh. He'd put on magic acts, and he was learning to juggle tennis balls while he whistled patriotic tunes like "The Stars and Stripes Forever" through the gap in his teeth. That's pretty impressive in a preadolescent child. It's hard not to love a boy who wants to put on a show. I'm talking as a woman now. You see what I mean.

As for me, I was selling encyclopedias and giving piano lessons and working as a secretary for a few hours a week, and teaching one section of French at the high school, and those collected activities were enough to help me get by. I did a bit of everything. I played the organ on Sunday at First Presbyterian and rehearsed the choir on Thursday nights. I wrote for the paper sometimes. I boarded dogs when families were out of town. What I liked about this was that nobody could say *what* I did, my occupation was pretty much undefinable, and so was I, and I liked it that way.

"Well," they'd say, "that's just Ellen, she's an *artiste*," if they even knew the word, and probably most of them didn't. None of that stunted-lives stuff, though. Nothing stunted my life. I always thought I was something. Really something. And, as it turns out, I am.

But anyway. That summer Cyril was living with me, over there in the back room, empty then, before I had started to collect the evidence. You were about six, I think, and you came around on your red bicycle with the training wheels to see him.

And there was another boy, named Donald, who lived just down the street, and this is the important part, the part about Donald, because I didn't like him at all. He was pretty much Cyril's age. He had hair parted so far over on the left side that it looked like he was wearing a toupee; it had an odd swirl and it stood up in back. He had a mean face and a voice too low for a child. He was one of those boys with his hands in his fists all the time, pounding whatever was close to see if it would give way. I like trouble in boys, and scuffling, because it comes to them naturally, but I didn't like him. Cyril's mischief was always sweet, and it still is, and it's my weakness to say that, but it's true. But not this Donald. He'd always be giving you an *estimating* look when he saw you to see how much he could get away with. I'd think of the silver candlesticks and how he wanted to walk away with them under his shirt or tucked inside his jeans. He was one of those "Yes, Miss Palmer, no, Miss Palmer" types. A politician, was how I thought of him at first. I never saw the child that looked so calculating and smug as this one.

If I had had children of my own, I might have thought differently about him, but I doubt it. His parents were ordinary working people, and he had a perfectly nice younger sister. But this one, this Donald, he measured you, he was cold and narrow, and he schemed.

It's hard to tell the difference between mischief, the sort of roughhouse that boys do anyway, and what he did. I'll give you an example. He'd write threatening notes and leave them around the house, and he'd be there when you'd pick one up and read it. I guess it made him happy to see you getting upset. What the hell sort of thing is that for a ten-year-old kid to be doing? He dug a pit once in his backyard and covered it over with twigs and leaves, and then he put a Hershey bar on top of the leaves to watch his sister walk over to it and fall into this hole up to her waist. Cyril was there. He says Donald didn't laugh, didn't even smile. He just watched, all eyes.

He never sang, never hummed. He'd watch when I played the piano, but it was an empty look and it'd make your hair stand up. I'd be playing Chopin, an étude, Schumann or Rachmaninoff, and he'd just look like an arrival from another planet. Then he'd walk off. Couldn't hear a note of it. Well, one day I sat down to play and found somebody had poured a bucket of sand into the piano. It took me a month to get it out, and it never sounded the same. There were birds dead on the lawn around here; I didn't know how he did that. How do you kill a bluebird without shooting it? There was a young tree in back of the house, toward the start of the woods, and he pulled the bark off, I think to see how it would die. That was the sort of thing he was interested in. Death. It absorbed him.

The easy part is to say that he was bad, or to say how bad he was. That's what people do, and it's just not interesting. He's dead now anyway. What good does it do? That's the story I'm telling. The hard part is to say that he was still a child, and he'd been wounded and he had come out that way, and someone should have, I don't know, held him and read to him . . . what *do* you do for a sick soul, anyway? In a child, I mean.

.   .   .

So what happened was, as I said, the city wasn't thriving, and of course that meant that few of the retail stores could afford to buy commercial time on the radio station, WFOM. The station had almost no advertising revenue, and they conceived this idea, this promotion. It was quite an idea. It tells you a lot about us, the way it worked out.

The idea was this. The radio station said they had fifteen hundred and thirty-nine dollars in cash they had hidden, they said, somewhere in town. This town, Five Oaks. They said it was in different denominations, and it was packed inside a rubber band and then put in an envelope and maybe put into a box, too. I don't remember. It was a long time ago. You were supposed to listen in to the radio to get the clues about where they'd hidden the money. Well, I'm not an outsider. I was listening, and I still remember one of the damn clues.

> Not where it's too high,
> But near where it's wet—
> Get under the wood
> And you'll be all set.

Everybody was getting up early in the morning, just as if they had real work to do, to listen to Big Bob O'Leary, the morning announcer. He wouldn't tell you when he was going to do his clues, so you had to sit through his morning wake-up cowbell ringing, the march around the backyard, then the commercials for rodent poisoning—they had more farmers listening in those days—and dish soap and DeKalb hybrid seed corn, then the songs played by Percy Faith and Mantovani and 101 Strings and the Voices of Walter Schumann. What the hell did they think they were doing, down at that station, beaming out this trash? Myself, I always liked the radio for baseball and weather reports, not this. Anyhow, maybe about midmorning, if he felt like it, Big Bob would give the city of Five Oaks another clue about where the money was hidden.

It was interesting, what would happen then. You'd go downtown, to the main streets, and you'd see people—this was at first—I mean actual people kind of sneaking around on their tennis shoes as if they were taking a stroll, getting some fresh air, looking in windows and inspecting the sidewalks. Then, and I admit I did this too, I never said I wasn't one of them, you'd see them going down in the direction of the lakefront park, where there were benches and a bandstand and picnic tables and the municipal docks.

It was all genteel at first. I remember seeing this fellow, Bill Evenson, a fat man with his hair combed over his bald spot, something fat men should never do, a carpenter with no work that spring, crawling around the base of the bandstand, peering inside the wood slats, looking for that money. I didn't know Bill very well. I knew him well enough to know he had a sense of humor, sometimes a nasty one, but at least he had it. I just sat on the park bench and watched him dragging that potbelly around.

I watched him pulling out several boards so that he could get underneath that thing, and then I saw him crawl inside. There was a racket, as he pushed and pulled the boards. I think he knocked a few onto the grass. Then he came crawling back into the light of day, blinking like a mole. Did I mention he had a snout? And I watched him walk away, not looking back at the wood he had broken and the hole he had made, not even brushing off his shirtfront. But he was a carpenter. He *could* have fixed it, if he had wanted to.

I don't remember if they said they had hidden it on public property. I think the radio station was interested in a certain amount of regulated chaos.

So then you'd see people with their stepladders out in front of the stores, climbing up to check the tops of the neon signs. I saw a distant cousin of mine, David Bardwell, climbing the municipal watertower, which was against the law, but he took that risk. In broad daylight, there was my cousin, fifty-two years old, gray-haired, wheezing his way up that steel ladder, his wife below, scared and egging him on. There were children creeping along the gutters and housewives standing in the flowerbeds of the public parks, pushing the flowers aside gently and then a little more firmly until the flowers just didn't stand up again.

You'd turn on Big Bob in the morning. "Well, good morning," he'd shout, and ring his cowbell. He'd give a clue. Something about water. Well, I went down to the water. I knew what would happen. Somebody, I think it was Harry Benson and his wife, Alice, they got down to the swimming raft at the public beach. She was rowing, and he had a crowbar. He pulled out a board, then another one. It hadn't been made very well. When that didn't work, Harry took off his clothes and jumped into the water and swam under the raft to see if the money was there.

It was just like people were swarming around, angry bees. We had a police force, but there wasn't much lawbreaking to speak of except for drunk driving and fistfights down by the taverns, and what the police decided was, they'd just sit back and watch this. They saw what was going on. It was something the town was doing to itself. They weren't going to interfere. They got a few calls. They said they didn't know what laws were being broken, except occasional destruction of public property, and they'd do something about that.

But it was like a secret. People didn't want other towns, other cities, to know. The WFOM signal didn't travel far, and people weren't talking much. They knew what they were doing, and they didn't want it to be news. We were alone with ourselves.

So one morning I was on my way down to the public schools, and I passed the lakeside park, and I looked to my left, in the morning light, and there was the bandstand, destroyed, just a pile of lumber now, and then, some distance past it, the old gazebo, that was rubble too. You'd think the station would stop their promotion at that point, wouldn't you? That's what you'd think. But by then the whole city, or I mean really the town, was listening to the radio, which was what the station wanted, and after all, *they* hadn't torn down the bandstand, some wrongdoer had. They weren't responsible.

From here on, the worst happened at night. You'd drive around in the morning and there were the front boards, the siding, of the used-car-lot office pulled out, and the vinyl siding of the east wall of the retirement home removed, and then the front sign of Bacon Drug pulled off and the painted wood and broken neon tubing lying there on the sidewalk. All over, materials chopped and in pieces. That was when the businesses began calling the station, threatening to sue, and they had lawyers screaming about proximate cause and I don't know what all. I don't remember how they ended up, those suits. This destruction went on for two weeks. Big Bob loved it.

And I'll tell you something. I think some people in town loved it, too. It was a fever, that's what it was.

I think, if you had given them enough time, they would have pulled apart the whole town, left it as little pieces of kindling wood.

·   ·   ·

This is where you come in.

The kids loved it as much as the adults did. No, they loved it more. I never saw so many children outside. They were tearing up the playgrounds and tearing up the front lawns and the porches. Anything they could pull at, they'd pull, see if it would give way.

This is what you don't remember.

I saw you and Cyril and that Donald boy, the one I just told you about, going around on your bicycles. Your training wheels were still on, I remember that, and you sort of tagged along behind them. You were prowling around places, the nooks and crannies that kids can fit in, looking for that fifteen hundred and thirty-nine dollars. But what were you going to do with it, any of you? *There* was the mystery. What was there ever to buy, around here?

So anyway, it was Saturday, early June, in the afternoon, and I was working in my garden here, when Cyril comes dashing up pell-mell on his bicycle, and he's screaming and screaming. He's all soaked. He says you're lying dead on the beach, and Donald's gone, too. I felt my hair turning gray in a split second and then I asked him to at least explain where you were, so I could drive down and find you. On the beach, on the beach, he screams. So I get into my car and drive like sixty with him down there.

I parked off the road and ran to the beach area. There you were. But you were alive. You weren't dead at all. You were sitting on the sand, looking a little white, all wet. But there wasn't any Donald. Where was Donald? I shouted. Then I looked out to the middle of the lake. Cyril was talking as fast as a child can talk, at you and at me. He said you or he or somebody had found the money in a recess under the boat dock, but to get it, you fell off first, and then he did, and then

Donald jumped in, and you sank, and this Donald got you, this awful little boy, and pulled you to shore, and pushed on your chest until the water came out of your lungs into your mouth and then dribbling in a flow down your cheek into the sand. Well, I mean, I figured that out later, he wasn't shouting those details at me right then.

That was when Cyril had left you here to get me. He thought you were dead. So where was this Donald, who saved you? And where was the money you boys found?

I looked out, in the middle of the river, what we called the bay. And way out there, I saw him.

By that time he wasn't much more than a pale arm sticking up from the water. He was that far. In his hands I could see he had something. Of course it was the money. He had fifteen hundred and thirty-nine dollars in cash, and he had swum out to the middle of the bay where nobody could steal it from him. That's why he had swum out there. To get the money away from everybody else, including Cyril. He must have thought Cyril was chasing him.

My Lord and all the sweet gods: there he was, this child, holding on to that money, and drowning. Waving and drowning, dying and happy, not even knowing he was drowning, probably, he was so happy he had found that cash. I must have shouted and screamed, I don't remember anymore. Because then all you could see was his arm just a bit above the water's surface, and the edge, the sleeve, of the green shirt that he wore. I was shouting, seeing that arm, staying up over the waves.

That was when I stole the rowboat. I ran up onto the dock and untied this AlumaCraft they had there, don't know whose it was, awash in lures and leader line and hooks and wet matches and empty cigarette packs and bilge water. And I started to row out there, but two other people had spotted that boy, I don't know how, and I saw their boats going out, too.

And even as I was in that boat, rowing those oars—and they squeaked, too, damn them—I thought this terrible thought: Well isn't it a nice day, sunny and mild, the days don't get much better than this.

The other two boats got there first. Bill Evenson was in one and I don't remember the other fellow except he used to have a shop in town repairing television sets, and I think he was a Congregationalist, and he always wore what they call a porkpie hat. They had stalled their boats out and thrown down the anchors, for all the good it would do, and Bill, I'll give him credit, had taken off his shoes and started diving into the water where Donald was, because right up there, right on the surface of the lake water, just like markers, were all those wet twenty-dollar bills, gotten loose, floating as fancy as you please.

That was when I took off my shoes. I took off my shoes and my blouse and I jumped in, because, although you don't know this, I am one fine swimmer, I could have been a lifeguard if they had hired girl lifeguards when I was a girl, but of course they didn't; they hired boys. I dove down into that river water. It was brown, this water, thick and muddy because it didn't flow much here. It collected grit. So you couldn't see much once you were five feet under, it all just blurred out.

And every time I came up to the surface, this television repair man asked me, Did you find him? Is he there? Sounding worried, as he gathered that wet money into his hands off the surface of the lake. Is he there? he asked. That poor boy.

He was there, all right. He was down there among the fishes, and when I was diving I saw Bill Evenson hauling him up, pulling up this boy in a green shirt. Through the light the sun casts down through brown river water this live man and this dead boy came up to the surface where the sun was shining on them both, and I thought, oh, that brown water was just the exact color of grief. That's actually what I thought, and those are the words I thought it in.

That boy's face broke the surface, and I hadn't liked him, but he had saved you, Wyatt, and now here he was, pale and all finished.

We lifted him up out of the water, arms and legs, and into Bill's boat. The boat I stole was drifting down the river, not that I cared, with my blouse and shoes in it. The Congregationalist was sitting about ten feet away in his boat a little bewildered about how he should look now that he had collected fifteen hundred and thirty-nine dollars and seen a drowned boy pulled up out of the water and tumbled in over the gunwales. Bill was in the boat first, and he went to work with artificial respiration in the way they did in those days, pushing on the back and lifting the arms. They didn't do mouth-to-mouth; maybe people just didn't know.

You know, by this time I wasn't crying or anything. I was watching this, because I knew that boy had passed on, and it was still a fair, warm day, there was a spirit in the air, and I had seen something important and terrible, it had just clarified me, seeing that boy waving as he drowned with all that money.

I'm not going to linger over telling you any more of that scene. The boy was dead. We took him in. He went from water to ashes.

No one wanted to talk about this. It hardly got into the newspapers, although it did. A very secret little story, for this community, all alone with ourselves.

You and Cyril were sitting on the beach, shivering. Warm and sunny as it was, your lips were blue. Why no one thought to throw a towel around you, I'll never know. You caught cold after this. You got a fever and some kind of child's pneumonia, and you were sick and hot for a couple of weeks, and that's one reason why I think you don't remember anything about it, why you're sitting here in front of me asking me a question like this.

I came by your bed sometimes. Your mother was taking care of you, and your father sat with you and read to you, as you were getting better, from *Treasure Island* and *Kidnapped,* but I was there, too, and I was thinking as hard as I could. I'd stare at that Scottie dog night-light of yours, and I'd think, not about you, exactly, because I knew you would be all right. You would be healthy in your own time. No, it wasn't you I was thinking about, though I loved you and was watching over you. It was God I was thinking about.

It had been the drowning of that boy, that Donald, that started me. I thought: Everything they've said about God is wrong. It is factually incorrect. Or it was true of the God we once had, but that God is certainly gone, and we have another one now, a god that nobody is talking about. This one is *interested* in everything and is making sure that everything happens over and over again. This one has always been here, maybe—the god that has always been here, that is almost unspeakable, the one who never left, and it's time to tell the truth about that god. The god of pure curiosity, who doesn't love us, but who watches us, day after day.

That was when I decided to write a Bible. It was that drowning that did it.

7

Wyatt had developed a habit, which he was now trying to break, of tapping the west window of his office three times before sitting down at his desk to begin work in the morning. He had to have a cup of coffee on the right side of his desk and his legal-sized yellow note pads on the left. At meetings, he preferred to sit facing the door. Windowless rooms caused him trouble. In such places he found it hard to breathe, as if tight chains circled his chest. Chaos and its twin sister claustrophobia waited for him down some of these hallways and past a few of these cubicles, but for the time being he was stronger than they were. On some mornings chaos looked like paper clips, and on other mornings claustrophobia had the appearance of pencil sharpeners or rolls of computer paper. Sunlight helped. Having a wife and daughter whom he loved helped. Having a mother who happened to be *his* particular mother did not help, nor did it help that he could see the wide part of the river from his office window where that person, Donald, his forgotten apparent playmate, had gone under the water for the last time.

If only people were competent! The world was run, he had recently discovered, by approximations, rules of thumb, and half steps. Or at least this city was. The building inspectors sort of knew what they were doing and the tax assessors sort of knew what they were doing and the water-treatment people sort of knew what they were doing, but if they *actually* knew what they were doing, and did it *exactly,* he would have known by now. He would have seen the evidence. Most of the time they were half asleep, chatting about the weather.

When he mentioned all this to Susan, at the end of the day, she told him he had apparently grown up, at last. He asked her why tall buildings simply didn't fall down, given the wide variety of incompetence and approximations in the world, and she said that occasionally they did, and he could certainly worry about it if that was how he wanted to spend his time, but what was he going to read to Christina at bedtime, this evening? And would he run out first, and get a quart of skim milk, please?

Did the sun, traveling through the empty reaches of space, follow rules of thumb? He didn't think so. And what would Schwartzwalder do, once he brought into town his plant manufacturing its odd little compound and products, if some of it spilled on the floor? What did he mean, "make a little dirt"? Wyatt had the feeling that the laws of chemical composition weren't rules of thumb, they were laws, but that the remedies for the damages they caused were the products of guesswork initiated in panic states.

It wasn't his business to be a pessimist. He was paid to fix and to arrange, and to look on the bright side, the side where improvement was always possible, where congratulations were always in order, and were in fact coming to him from the mayor and the city manager, both of whom were delighted that they had hired someone who had been in Schwartzwalder's high school class; and letters and permits were flowing toward Schwartzwalder, whose business would soon, everyone said, be established and booming.

Susan had become quieter. Wyatt thought that they were happy together, but on some days he caught her studying him when she thought he wasn't looking. And she had started a new hobby, during those moments when her time wasn't taken up by Christina, or gymnastics, or magic. She was making miniature stage sets in the basement, with Fred, the rabbit, sitting behind her and watching her, sets like Joseph Cornell boxes, but she said there was a trick to them, and she wouldn't let him see them, just yet. She said she loved him, and he could tell that she meant it by the way that she looked at him: he sometimes took naps on the sofa, and when he woke up, there she was, sitting across the room from him, studying him, and smiling.

Often in the morning, he thought: *I should be happy*. And then he thought: *I am happy. I am. I am. Damn it, I'm a happy man*.

He could tell when Alyse was standing in his office doorway from the perfume she wore, a scent that seemed a mixture of sweat and strawberries; late in the afternoon, he could sense she was there without having to turn around. She gave off the peculiar strength of presence that unhappy women sometimes radiate. He could feel her from fifty feet away. He could feel her presence there on the skin of his back. He liked it, that feeling.

"Do you think anger is a failure of character?"

"Hi, Alyse." He turned around. She was rubbing the back of her ankle with the toe of her shoe. "Do I think anger is a failure? A failure of what, did you say?"

"It was just a question. Congratulations on the Schwartz-walder thing."

"Thanks." She had been working, he knew, on a Renais-sance Festival—knights, jousting, lutes and madrigal singers, ladies in flowing gowns—for the following summer in the central city park, the fourth annual such festival, arranging for someone to book the musicians and sign contracts with jug-glers, and she was often short-tempered when asked about it, so he did not ask. "Have you been getting angry lately? Why don't you sit down?"

She made her way toward one of his four chairs. "I've always meant to inquire," she said, pointing, "what's that thing on top of the file cabinet?"

"Something my father made. I don't know what it is."

She nodded. She sat with her hand at the side of her head as she stared out of the window. When she looked back at Wyatt, she let her eyes lock into his, and he let it happen. She was a bit like a traffic accident: you couldn't *not* look.

"Oh," he said.

"I yelled at him last night," she said, referring to Dennis, her boyfriend. "I swore. I even threw something at him, but I missed his face."

"What was it?"

"An ashtray, I think," she said, looking glum. "It should've been larger, and I might have hit him. Next time, a potted plant."

"What'd he do?"

"You don't want to hear this."

"Sure I do. It's the end of the day."

"You'll think I'm irrational."

"No, I won't."

"You'll take his side. All men are alike. They band together. They're like pack animals."

"Try me."

"You want to hear this?"

"Yes. Only tell me one thing: with all the incompetent people loose in the world, why don't buildings fall down? Why don't the bridges give way?"

"Oh, they do," she said, "they do, sometimes, haven't you noticed?" And he saw that she was trying, lightly, to seduce him with the cool draft of her unhappiness. Her discontent was making a nice fitted match with his own restlessness, and, after all, he *had* been interested in her, at first as a sort of hobby, a distraction. "No one knows how to do anything correctly. So you've noticed?"

"Yes, I have," he said. He had also noticed a small heartbreakingly beautiful wisp of gray hair just behind her right temple. "Yes." He decided to let the day wind down to disaster at its own speed. Alyse went over to his father's contraption on the file cabinet and touched her fingers to it.

"Odd," she said. "This isn't anything." The late-afternoon sun cast its light over her, and her shadow was thin and quietly unmoving, there on the floor. She leaned back against his window. "These damn Renaissance Festivals," she said, "are the worst part of my job. I don't get the appeal."

"Knights," he said. "Shining armor. Damsels, being rescued, that sort of thing. No industrial revolution yet."

"No, wait," she said, holding up her hand. "All right. Once upon a time, the world was covered with forests and dragons, and there were plagues, of course, but *these* plagues had no explanation and didn't make you morally responsible if you got them. People were in a minority compared to everything. There was more of everything than there were people. So when you, for example, went out in your armor on your steed and you fell in love with some damsel, it *stuck,* you follow me here? Anyway, what I mean is that love, what made it big and important and spiritual, and murder, what made *it* terrible, all depended on there not being many people around. If people are scarce, you love somebody because that person's all you're likely to get, and the person is precious, pure gold. You see? It was sort of supply-and-demand. That's why we had humanists. Plagues produced humanism. People were scarce and valuable and lovable. It was a seller's market."

She took a breath and reached over to Wyatt's desk for a pencil. "Alyse, do you want to talk about Dennis?" Wyatt asked. "We can, it's okay, we can go out for a drink."

She was toying with the pencil. "I *am* talking about Dennis." She was keeping her equanimity, her cheerful tone, but she was staring at the floor, and her eyes seemed too bright. "But now," she said, "in the Age of the Renaissance Festival, you're not scarce, and neither am I. I'm nobody special and that goes for you, too. So, if you're using market theory in regard to humans, people are getting divorces and murdering each other enthusiastically for the same reason: supply. There's a big supply of the human being, so it's just passé to get interested and to stay interested in one of them. So here's Dennis. He's gone all the time, he makes those phone calls. Sometimes he shows up, like last night. He takes off his clothes—I don't even know what time this is—and he's giving off an odor of unfaithfulness. I am in bed arranging my attitude toward all this. I am much too cool to throw a rolling pin at him. I don't even own a rolling pin. I don't bake. I go to bakeries. No: I don't even go to bakeries, I go to the bakery section of the supermarket. So anyway here he is, and I'm wondering what happened to serial monogamy, so I turn to him and ask him where he's been, because you have to start a fight according to certain rules if it's going to be really satisfying, and then he says *he* has a theory. God. Everybody has a theory these days.

"He says, and he's sitting up now, not nearly as drunk as I was hoping he'd be, in fact not drunk at all, propping his head on his arm in that way that some guys have in bed that just really breaks my heart, that he loves me but that love shouldn't be dependency. That when people talk about love what they usually mean is dependency. He doesn't want me to depend on *him,* is what he means. And he doesn't want to depend on *me,* either. Well, you know, I didn't want to be crying during this scene, but, like, at least temporarily, I couldn't help it. So I asked him about all those things he said once, like how he loved me, how I was the most beautiful woman ever, how just the image of me walking got him through the day, how he'd love me until the collapse of time, and he said, and I quote, 'I meant it when I said it.' "

She smiled and pointed the pencil at Wyatt. "That was when I threw the ashtray at him."

"You get him?"

"Glanced off his shoulder."

"You were in bed at this time?"

"Hell, no. I was pacing and crying."

"Where was he?"

"He was up, too, sitting in his favorite chair." She was still smiling, as if all of this constituted an amusing anecdote at the end of the day. "Usually," Alyse said, "I'd tell all this to a girlfriend, I don't know why I'm telling you. Maybe because you're a man and you can give me insight into their creepy ways."

Wyatt shrugged. He thought it was the only safe gesture he knew.

"There are too many women around," Alyse said. "Men, too. Now, if I were a tree, it'd be different. Trees are scarce. Scarce and necessary. So trees are what he actually and genuinely loves. He's a nature lover, for God's sake. I don't leave more than a trace with him, nothing much more than a little bruise on his shoulder."

"Did he leave?"

"Oh, he left, but his *things* are still around, so he'll be back." She waited. "There's something I didn't tell you. The awful part."

"What part is that?"

"The part after I threw the ashtray at him and was crying and slapped him and hit him. This is the part just before he left. It's the disgraceful part. This is the part I'm ashamed of."

"Oh," Wyatt said. "You went to bed with him."

"It was evil and disgusting. There were ashes in the bed, from the ashtray. Talk about sex being meaningless. Pleasure can sometimes be so irrelevant to everything. But we did it. We smelled like a couple of cats. It was the opposite of quality time."

Wyatt sat in his chair. He was feeling a little tired by now. The sun's light from his west window had acquired a sinister orange sunset hue.

"So I'm feeling like giving you a little quiz, Wyatt. Think you're up to it?"

"A quiz."

"Right. Here it is. Would you like to, oh, an hour or so

from now, go with me for a drink, then go off to the Best Western in Harrisonville? We could stay there until at least seven. Feel a little like a rebel? This is a quiz, now. You'd get home a little late. That's all."

"Alyse—"

"—For example," she said. "There's been some attraction around this office. Don't think I haven't noticed. I can stare at your hands—I . . . anyway. So, according to this, what we do, because we want to and because it's part of what people are doing now, this new antihumanist thing, is, we go down there, and you take your—no, excuse me, *I* take *your* clothes off, and you take my clothes off, and maybe we slow-dance for a while right there on the polyester rug with the TV on to one of those cable channels, and then we lean against the flocked wallpaper, and you kiss me just the way you've wanted to. We make love. It's not ideological because we haven't made any promises and we haven't said, 'I meant it when I said it.' We have our little physical explosions and then we go home. How about it, sailor? I could make you happy for a couple of hours, and, with some luck and technique, vice versa."

He let the quiet hang in the air, the muffled sounds of traffic coming from the streets below, before he said, "I don't think so, Alyse. No, I don't think so." He rose and went over to where she was still standing and put his hand on her shoulder. "I don't just want to be a player in your revenge fantasy."

"I *knew* you'd say that!" She moved away from him and back toward the doorway, which she had been careful to shut. "You guys. You guys are always bonding and telepathically agreeing about everything. Pack animals. And you just think I'm a sexual scofflaw. You'd do it if I were a tree."

"No."

"What is it then?"

"What is what?"

"A woman doesn't repeat her invitation. A woman doesn't have to explain. She doesn't even have to *clarify.*"

He stood up. "That's not it. I'm attracted to you, Alyse. You're beautiful. I even imagined doing just what you proposed we do. I'd like to . . . I'd like to kiss my way up your legs. But that's not the point."

She groaned very quietly. Then she lowered her head and put it in her hands, and she kept that position for an unsettling moment. Then she said, "If that's not the point, what is?"

"It's late, Alyse. I have to go."

She was shaking her head. "Jesus." She laughed again. *"I* feel like *I* want to cause a little trouble, and nobody lets me. You guys feel like *you* want to cause a little trouble, and *everybody* lets you do it. All right, skip it." She had her hand on the doorknob, but then she turned around to look at him. "You know, Wednesdays are my worst days. On Wednesdays I always feel like a sexual time bomb."

"Don't you understand?" he asked suddenly. "I want to. But what I want doesn't matter so much anymore."

"Oh, right," she said. "You're running that family of yours, your little business, your lemonade stand."

"Yes."

She reached into her pocket and pulled out a coin. "Here's a nickel, Wyatt." She tossed it toward him, and it landed on his desk. "Here's a nickel says that you're going to call me, some afternoon, some evening, sometime." The nickel landed near a pile of papers; the third President had a tiny bemused look on his face. "Give me a call when you get serious about what you want, just pick up that phone, and then I'll decide whether I say yes or no. You'll get desperate. You'll get desperate for a little desperate love. And this nickel says you *will* call."

•   •   •

After she had left the office, Wyatt sat and listened to the ventilator go on and off. By the time he had arrived home, it was dinnertime, just spaghetti, but Susan had bought a red wine he liked, and she opened the bottle and served it to him with a flourish.

$\int$omewhere, somehow, Cyril had acquired a truck.

A Jeep, it had a blue door on the driver's side and a reddish-brown door on the passenger's side, and the rest of it, where there was metal, wore a pond-green color that Wyatt had seen on the houses of the poor but never on trucks. The sounds from under its hood were terrible. Wyatt, who knew little about the mechanical operations of cars but was certain about what he did know, thought that the truck's fan belt was loose and its tappets were bad, and he had doubts about the clutch. Whenever Cyril shifted gears, there was a moment of high mechanical violence, a grinding and clashing as Cyril shoved the shift lever into second or third. Such noises made Wyatt wonder if Cyril bothered to use the clutch at all or had resolved somehow to do without it.

The first time he had seen his cousin in this vehicle, Wyatt had been emerging from Bacon Drug around lunchtime (headache, aspirin). Clutching his bottle of pills and stepping out onto the sidewalk, he saw the truck go by on Second Avenue, right in front of him, a rocking chair oscillating in the truck bed as if a fretful ghost were sitting in it. Next to the chair was the ugliest lamp Wyatt could remember seeing, a tall thing with a punched-in lampshade on which had been painted circus-motif faces of clowns, lions, and dancing bears. Near the lamp was a dresser, its drawers half open, and some lady's clothing, turned to rags, hanging out. And next to the dresser was a mattress standing on its side, stained with secretions. It was all very junky and domestic.

The lettering on the side and the back of the truck said BIG TIME HAULING. Wyatt stared, stupefied, as the truck happened in front of him. Cyril was supposed to be a charity case, not an entrepreneur. The light turned green, Cyril's hand went up to wave, and the truck rumbled, lurched, and ground its way forward, the rocking chair still furiously unsettled. On the back of the truck, Wyatt saw, under the company title, Cyril's phone number.

When he called Cyril that evening, his cousin explained that he was tired of sitting around on his butt all day and he had decided to get on with his life. This was a capitalist country, right? Wyatt admitted that he thought, yes, it was, but his cousin went right on, as if he hadn't agreed, and said that he,

Cyril, had been inspired by how everyone in Eastern Europe was going into business and out of the mind-numbing shit-for-brains Communist ridiculousness.

"Remember how I said I was going to clean out people's basements?" Cyril asked. Wyatt made a noise of assent. "Well, that's what I'm doing. I put an ad in the paper, and I started to get calls right away."

"Cyril, where'd you get the money for the ad? And for the truck?"

"I borrowed it. That was easy. I have investors. You want to be one? You almost are one already. Listen, you're good with words. Do you think it's the right company name? I decided to call it Big Time Hauling because I thought I should lay it on the line and let everyone know where I'm coming from. Image is important. Large is important. I have a couple of other ideas."

"What ideas would those be?"

"Don't get like that. Well, for starters, I thought of Easy Ace Hauling. I thought of it because it's kind of romantic and lonesome, like me."

"What's your other idea?"

"Headless Horseman Hauling. I like it because it's got all those aitches. It's what do they call it?"

"Alliterative."

"Right."

"I wouldn't use it. It sounds criminal."

"Okay," Cyril said. "I already agreed with you before you said that. Then there was Easy Rider Hauling. That was my other idea, but it was bad, because I don't ride a Harley. But anyway, for now, I'm Mr. Big Time, I get out, I'm in the open air, and I clean up basements and I haul it all away."

"Where do you haul it to?"

"That's my secret. Actually, I've got some permits. Yes.

You ought to know about that. I take some of it to the land-fill."

"What about the rest of it?"

"The rest of it? Well, that's a professional matter I don't care to divulge."

"You can tell *me.*"

"Wyatt, of all the last people I would tell, you're the lastest." Cyril waited, and when Wyatt didn't respond, he said, "I've been getting religion. There's this guy—you can buy his books—fellow by the name of R. Stan Drabble, and he's got this system called R/Q Dynamics where you start to take responsibility for yourself to increase the R-power in your life enhancement complex. The R-power is like the life force, only it's passive, unlike the Q-power, which is active, and you got to balance them off or else there's hell to pay. In the countries of the world with, you know, big debts and office buildings they never finish constructing, there's a lot of R-power. But you take a place like Japan. That's totally Q-power, that place. They don't need crystals or taking naps. Did you know there's no word for *mañana* in the Japanese language? That's just a sample of what this guy Drabble says. He says like alcoholism is a mix-up of Q- and R-power. What an idea! You want to borrow the books? I've got *Unthinkable Things* right here."

"I don't think so."

"Too bad. You could fix yourself in about a week."

At dinner, Wyatt couldn't eat. He didn't feel interested in food. When Susan asked him what the matter was, he said he didn't like the idea of Cyril going into business. It made him uneasy, Cyril going into people's houses and hauling away their trash, and he wanted to know where Cyril was dumping it. He said he didn't like Cyril's efforts to improve himself

with self-help books. Besides, hauling and disposal was supposed to be regulated, and you couldn't, for example, just
dump asbestos tile in the landfill, you had to—

"You liked to have him dependent on you," Susan said,
sitting back and sipping her wine. "You liked that, sugar."

"No, I didn't."

Susan took Christina into her lap and bounced her. Christina's hair was so fine, it stayed up in the air and floated for a
microsecond, as if weightless.

"Oh yes," she said. "A woman knows." She smiled, and
Wyatt wondered if some remnant of Alyse's invitation to him
remained, visible somehow in its erotic reach, perhaps on his
face. But no: Susan was talking about the future: how, for
example, the town needed a center for gymnastics training for
little kids, and how she was the perfect person to do that; and
how her stage-set boxes in the basement were progressing
wonderfully and perfectly; and how, soon, it would be time
for them to think about having one more child, and what did
he think of that?

Yes, he wanted to be a father again, he wanted to be a
father forever, and, holding Christina with one arm—she had
come around to his side of the table—he reached forward to
grasp Susan's hand, which was, for some reason, so cold that it
made him flinch, but almost invisibly, so that she didn't notice, and he smiled back at her, a sign of agreement. All these
responsibilities: it was as easy as falling down a mountain.

"You should let Cyril help himself," Susan said. "We've
got our own lives to lead. If he wants to do something on his
own, well, let him."

When Wyatt tapped at Cyril's front door at the Oak
Motel—cash, this time, and not a check, rolled in his pocket
and surrounded by a rubber band—he heard a woman's voice

answering. "It's open, you didn't have to knock." It hadn't been open, but he opened it now, although he thought he might have the wrong room. He pushed the door wide and saw that Cyril's apartment was filled and cluttered with cast-off objects: near the dining area was a grandfather clock, ticking, but with a coat hanger on the dial where the hands should have been. Next to it was the same circus-clown-motif lamp he had seen in Cyril's truck. On the sofa were several radios and typewriters and telephones, one of the radios so old that it appeared to have been manufactured from Bakelite. There was a television set cabinet with no picture tube, and there were piles of shoes and signs near the window: PLEASE DON'T SPIT ON THE FLOOR and ALL EMPLOYEES MUST WASH HANDS and DO NOT SPEAK TO DRIVER WHILE THE BUS IS IN MOTION. In the center of all this, sitting on the bed painting her toenails with one hand and smoking a cigarette with the other, was a young woman Wyatt had not met before. Her hair was piled up and teased in a Frederick's of Hollywood way—"Big Hair" was the phrase the Sunday supplement employed for this style—and she displayed junk jewelry rings on several of her fingers and wore pink shorts and a Def Leppard T-shirt. Wyatt thought that, in this woman, Cyril had finally met his match.

"Who're you? You come for something?"

"Wyatt. Wyatt Palmer, Cyril's cousin."

"Oh, right." She stopped and glanced up to get a good look at him. She took the cigarette out of her mouth and picked off some tobacco from her tongue. "I know who you are. You're Mr. Saint."

"I was looking for Cyril."

"Cyril, he's not here. I'm not real sure where Cyril is, but you can bet he's *somewhere*. He's dependable that way."

"I don't believe I've made your acquaintance," Wyatt said.

"I don't believe you have. I'm Pooh."

"How do you do." Wyatt made an awkward hand wave, not wanting to upset the bottle of nail polish on the bed by shaking her hand. "Pooh?"

"Yeah. You know. Like Winnie-the-Pooh. The bear? Christopher Robin and all that shit."

"Right. I just hadn't heard it before on a woman."

"Or probably on a man, either. Well, of course it wasn't no name my parents gave me to start with, it's the simplified one. My real name that no one calls me is Priscilla, which I thought was sort of pretty but which my ex, I mean my ex-ex, thought was frumpy, and he wanted something more *Playboy* Playmate–sounding, so he came up with Pooh, 'cause he said it was cuddly. Do you think it sounds like a Playmate?" She tapped her front teeth with her fingernails. "Cyril does. He says it sounds just like one of those girls you meet on the beach at Malibu that invites you up to her beach house after you play volleyball with her or otherwise get acquainted."

"Cyril's never been to Malibu."

"Well, I know *that*," she said contemptuously, capping the bottle and blowing a stream of air on the cotton between her toes. "But he has been, in his mind." She walked to the bathroom, her head held high. Whatever else Pooh was, she comported herself like a queen. She closed the bathroom door, and in the middle of the sound of flowing water, she said, "What're you here for?"

"I sort of came to see Cyril."

"With the money?"

"How'd you know?"

"I'm from around here. Cyril told me about that, but we don't have to take any more of it unless you're so committed to leaving it that you can't help yourself." She was still shouting from inside the bathroom. "You can see how fine we're doing." She came out of the bathroom, the toilet flushing behind her, and she stopped in the middle of the living room, as she fastened the clasp of her shorts. "In fact, we're going to move."

"Move? Move where?"

"We're moving *up*. We're like a success story. We're both into R/Q Dynamics. You want to sit down? I guess with all the money you've given Cyril, I should give you a soda. You like diet Dr Pepper? I think we got some."

"No thanks."

"Don't mind if *I* do." She opened the refrigerator door and peered in. Cold mist cascaded down from the freezer compartment. "It helps my digestion, and if I drink enough of it I get ideas faster than Einstein. Besides, it has prunes in it, did you know that? The secret to Dr Pepper is the prunes." After finding a can she lowered herself onto a scratched antique-looking chair with one back leg missing, so that she had to balance. She turned a puzzled expression in Wyatt's direction. "I met him . . . Cyril? Did you ask me how we met?"

"I guess I did."

"Well, my ex, I mean my *recent* ex, that's Todd, had gnawed through his leash and left me with his creepy stash of junkola, which is why I wanted to get rid of it in the worst way. This was Saturday morning. That's the best morning for starting a new life. Man first landed on the moon on Saturday. Even though it wasn't Saturday on the moon. The moon has a different calendar. Anyway, that was when I saw your cousin's ad. The rest is history."

As Wyatt listened to her, he continued to survey the room. She asked him if he played golf. This question came to him so unexpectedly that he nodded without taking his eyes off a particularly abused chest of drawers lying flat on its back near the door. "Help me with that wastebasket, then," she said. She had put on a pair of flip-flops and was carrying a golf bag out through the back door, having pointed to a bucket that, Wyatt now saw, had over a hundred golf balls in it.

When he picked it up, he revised his estimate: this wastebasket held several hundred, maybe a thousand golf balls, most of them in bad shape, their brand names worn off, their sides gouged and cut. "You coming?" she called. Why was she suddenly giving him orders? Wyatt put his arms around the wastebasket as if embracing it, and, after lifting it with his legs rather than his back, as the Sunday Supplement column on health said you should lift heavy objects, he carried it out to the backyard.

"There's a nice piece of grass behind these warehouses," Pooh said, carrying her clubs. "Cy already took out a chair. We been using it to practice our swings." After following Pooh for what seemed to be half an hour, Wyatt came to a patch of grass. It sloped down slightly for about fifty feet. At the edge of the lawn, one tree stood, a spindly silver maple. Beyond this maple stretched the ocean of a farmer's field, plowed up and probably planted, though Wyatt couldn't tell with what—it was too early in the season. Off in the distance, a mile or so away, stood a silo, a barn, and a farmhouse. This city might be expanding, he thought, but the farms still bordered it on every side.

"That's good," she said, pointing to a place on the lawn near a yellow tee. "Right there." Then she gestured toward an aluminum chair where he could sit. "I *think* that chair is working, but only if you fold it out right. If you fold it out wrong, gangbusters. Do you mind sitting and watching? I can let you have a turn in a minute."

"No, I don't mind."

"These here are a new set of clubs which Cyril found

recently, which I haven't played with since I haven't practiced in years now, unless you count last week, but Cyril wants me to be better, and I wanted that before he did. Cyril says they're my size, that's all I know."

Wyatt sat. She was very commanding. For several minutes he watched, bewildered and impressed, as she practiced hitting golf balls.

She had a hard, gutsy swing, with a follow-through, but she often didn't face the ball directly, with the result that she would get good distance but with a severe slice every second or third shot. She would watch the ball, shading her eyes, and blow a pink bubble. Then methodically she would put another ball on the tee. There seemed to be no end to the supply of balls. It was a very large wastebasket. Wyatt asked her where Cyril had found all those balls, and when she said that he had just *found* them, maybe it was behind a bowling alley, Wyatt decided to go in for that Dr Pepper. When he opened the refrigerator door, he saw that two boxes of postdated print film, and another box, a jumbo supply of lubricated condoms, were stashed on the same shelf as the Dr Pepper, just above some graying hamburger under cellophane from the IGA.

Back in his aluminum folding chair, Wyatt watched the golf balls sail out into the open field, one after another. He liked the easy mechanical *thwack* as Pooh drove the balls off into the distance. She missed occasionally. The ball would spin or dribble down the lawn and stop a few feet away from the silver maple. But then she would recover her form, and off they went, disappearing into the distance and the dirt. Wyatt sipped at his Dr Pepper and belched. Pooh smiled. Off went another ball. This one hit the silver maple right in the trunk and seemed to lodge there, jammed somehow through the pure force of Pooh's drive. Pooh cursed, violently and inventively, one hand on her hip, chewing her bubble gum angrily. She put another ball on the tee. This one lifted up, as if carried on a zephyr, and vanished in the hazy agricultural distance.

Where was the day going? Wyatt couldn't remember what he had come here to do, and then he did remember and put it out of his mind. "What's going to happen," he asked, "when the owner of that land finds his field covered with golf balls?"

"Simple," Pooh said. "If he plays golf, he picks them up. He's grateful. If he doesn't, he doesn't." She didn't bother looking at him. She worked on her stance, wiggling her hips sportively. Off went another ball. The wastebasket was still at least three-quarters full. "And he'll have walnut trees."

"Excuse me?"

"Well I heard somewhere," Pooh told him quietly, as if imparting a secret, "that golf balls have walnuts in them there at the center, to give them bounce. So if they, like, fall apart after wind and storms and rain, that farmer'll have a grove of walnut trees right there in his field. Lucky him."

"Well, yes," Wyatt said. "But I don't think it's walnuts, Pooh. I don't think that's right."

"I didn't say I knew *exactly*. I said that's what I *heard*."

"It's liquid. A lot of rubber and liquid inside."

"That's in some of them."

"Yes."

"And in the rest, it's walnuts. You want to do this? I guess I'm hogging things here."

"Okay."

Wyatt lowered his can of Dr Pepper to the grass and took his turn. Pooh sat down in his chair, removed a pair of pink-framed dark glasses from the pocket of her shorts, and began to watch. After several drives, Wyatt heard her say, "You're too stiff, Chico. You don't follow through like you should.

But you got a nice stroke there. You look like Cyril, from the back. Family resemblance." She raised her eyebrows at him, over the glasses.

"You're looking at me from the front."

"But, like I say, from the back, you look like him."

"Where'd you say Cyril was?" A ball sailed up and broke several leaves off the silver maple as it flew through; they fluttered down slowly on the lawn.

"Did I say? I don't think so. He's out cleaning or collecting stuff, or selling it down at Saginaw or Bay City. He doesn't always tell me. Saturday morning, which this is, is a big business day for him. You know: with people wanting to buy and sell and *dump*."

"Right." A perfect swing: out went the ball, toward that barn. Broadside. "Do you clean basements, too?"

"Shit, no. I wouldn't do that work for a million years. I hate basements. They give me asthma and make me sneeze uncontrollably."

"So what do you do?"

"I like how you say that." She sipped from Wyatt's Dr Pepper, still chewing her gum, and as soon as she swallowed, she blew another bubble, a big one. Wyatt admired her skill. "What do I do? Is this an investigation? What the hell, I'll tell you. I work part-time in a dry cleaner, and I'm a contact-paper decorator."

"I've never heard of that."

"Lots of people haven't. I'll save you the trouble of asking. I'm Nu-Floor. That's how I go by, that name. Anyway, suppose you're tired of your floor and you want a new one, but, like for example, you don't want the new current linoleum, because the current fashions in linoleum are for shit?"

"Right." He swung and connected. The ball flew out straight.

"So you call me. And I come over with my samples of contact paper, and together me and you settle on a new look for your floor or the fridge or the cupboards, and then I get it and lay it, the contact paper. You got to lay it right or it looks like a total loss. I help you choose the paper, and then I lay it down, is what I'm saying. I help you with the good taste, and then I do the actual work. I put a plastic coating layer for protection on top of the contact paper, even though it's contact paper, too, only it's plastic. You following me on this?"

"That's quite a job."

"It's very specialized work."

"Do you have a lot of business?"

"You'd be surprised," she said, getting up and taking the club out of Wyatt's hand. He assumed that this meant that his turn was over, and he returned to the folding chair. Pooh fired the golf balls into the field, and now Wyatt watched in silence, waiting for Cyril to come back.

When he finally showed up, only a few balls remained in the wastebasket. Cyril was sweaty, and his forehead was streaked with purple grime. "Hey," he said. "I guess you two have met." He was carrying a beer, and after watching Pooh hit two balls out into the field, he said, "Come on. Both of you. I need some help."

Wyatt asked where, and Cyril took him around in front and pointed to the truck. Its cargo bed was piled high with the halves of things: the broken upper half of a painting showing a waterfall, the broken half of a bookshelf, and half of a television set, another cabinet with a missing picture tube, and inside the screen, a headless Bert—or perhaps Ernie, Wyatt could never keep them straight. Stuffed in near the front and blocking the driver's vision of traffic behind him was a refrigerator, its door removed, its cooling coils exposed and stretched out behind it. Beside the refrigerator, propped up for balance, was a declothed sofa standing on its side, several springs lollygagging out. Pressed against the sofa were four barrels. In front of the barrels, a taxidermist's stuffed squirrel, its mouth open, silently chattering. There were open boxes and board games: Clue, Careers, Monopoly, Chutes and Ladders, and one that Wyatt had never seen before, Mr. Ree. Play money, mostly fifties and hundreds, was scattered all over the truck. There was the barrel of a rifle and a textbook on anatomy, open to show the ligaments of the knee. There were copies of *My Friend Flicka* and two of the Oz books, and scratched-up phonograph records without their sleeves: "The Piano Magic of George Shearing" and "Lester Lanin Plays Jerome Kern" were the only two whose labels Wyatt read. An open book of a piano score—the preludes of Rachmaninoff—was wedged inside a drawer also filled with used-up tubes of Mary Kay cosmetics and campaign buttons: I LIKE IKE and WE'RE MADLY FOR ADLAI and ADLAI AND ESTES IN '56. Wyatt reached in and drew those out. They were worth something. He put them into his pocket. There was a Howdy-Doody throw rug and a transparent screen from a Super Winky Dink Set. There were the remains of a ship in a bottle, smashed to smithereens, and a rubber toy Bowie knife. There was a picture frame, coming apart, inside which was a portrait of, probably, someone's grandfather, looking rather cross. A large table with only one leg was sleeping with a collection of broken rain gutters painted blue. A rusted Radio Flyer wagon carried an unclothed crybaby doll with no legs. Matching outhouse salt-and-pepper shakers rolled back and forth in a glass souvenir-of-the-Everglades ashtray, circled by a Rima the Bird Girl lampshade. There was part of a card table. There was an old telephone. A broken toaster and several ripped window shades were crammed in near a cracked welding gun and a rotting fence post.

Wyatt couldn't stop looking at it, this pile of objects, and underneath them, the shadows of things left behind, and the more he looked at it, the more light-headed he became. Things, too, could die. Here they were.

"Wyatt! Are you coming or not?"

"Where're you going?" Cyril and Pooh were already in the cab, Pooh jammed up next to Cyril, her leg aligned with his.

"Come see."

He got in the truck, stashing himself beside Pooh. Cyril ground the gearshift into first, and they lurched deafeningly forward.

In one pocket, the Adlai and Ike buttons; in the other, $200 in small denominations. He wasn't sure that Cyril needed it anymore. He asked where they were going again, and Cyril nodded this time. "Can you keep a secret?"

"Depends."

"Well, you got your regulated landfills, right? You got to get a permit for those, and the permits are real expensive, okay? Forty dollars for one *single* dump. So what does that mean? It means everybody who's got something to dump finds out about let's call it the black market dump, and that's where I'm taking you."

They had crossed the city limits and were in the township, passing alongside a creek draining into wetlands a mile or so up. Here the road was bordered by reeds, and Wyatt, over the heaving sounds of the truck, heard the cries of redwing black-birds. After another eight minutes, they were outside the township, and Cyril had taken some turns that Wyatt wasn't familiar with, and the road had turned to dirt. This dirt road branched off into two other roads, both narrow, and Cyril turned left.

"Where are we?"

"What d'you mean, 'Where are we'?" Cyril reached down to flick on the radio, but no sound came out, although the dial went on. It was one of those silent radios. "We are where we are."

"No. I mean, what's the name of this road."

"It hasn't got a name. They never bothered naming it. This road," Cyril said, with a philosophical pull at his ear, "is totally anonymous."

The truck, in first gear again, was heading through a forest of small thin jack pine. The road had no shoulders and only two narrow tracks. Wyatt had never been down this direction before. He had tried to get lost, but never like this. Here the trees, as they grew larger, arched in a canopy overhead, and their branches brushed the top of the cab with a fingernails-on-slate screeching. The light was darker here—the trees, now, were a mixture of maple and poplar—and the branches seemed to have scabs on them. Then the trees gave way to a small meadow, three acres or so, where the grass appeared to have smallpox, gray withered fencing at the south border, a barn to the north. Then, more forest: the truck plunged noisily into it.

"This is a long way to dump this stuff, Cyril. A *long* way."

"Yeah, well, you know how they say the customer is king."

Wyatt didn't get it and stared at the road, which began to make a few dips, and he noticed a ditch expanding into a ravine on the right-hand side. Shaded by poplar and silver maple and pine, the ground cover consisted of a mix of ferns and mayapples and a few wildflowers. He thought he detected in the air a smell of forest growth. The truck heaved suddenly to the left, down another makeshift road, even more badly maintained than the one they'd been on.

Now the bushes were scratching the sides of the truck, and Wyatt had to pull his arm inside the window. This road was pockmarked with holes and centerline grass growth. It wasn't much more than a cattle track. They eased their way on a slightly elevated rise between what seemed to be two swamps, went into another forest, came out, and slowed down when the ravine appeared again, this time on the left. Cyril put the truck into four-wheel drive.

They were backing up to the ravine. After Wyatt had jumped down from the cab, he saw that the road they had been on continued forward into the trees, but part of it, in the direction Cyril was going, in back, veered off onto a Y that stopped at the edge of a drop-off.

Wyatt went over to the lip of the ravine and looked down. Cyril and Pooh were already shoveling and throwing the contents of the truck into the ravine, and the junk was clattering down in an avalanche of other similar waste. There was a small pinkish-white cloud of waste-dust that rose up from it. It smelled of clotted plumbing.

"Hey," Cyril said. "Give us some help."

The ravine extended toward the north, out of his line of sight, but below him its floor was covered with broken furniture, barrels, battery cases, tires and inner tubes, empty paint cans and cans of oil and emptied bags of herbicides; and ceiling tile and old shingles, and a white dusty cottony substance he couldn't identify; and pieces of what he guessed were electrical transformers, the kind he'd seen at the top of light poles; and then, off to the left, where the truck was, more barrels— he didn't care to count them—some painted on the sides with large orange X's and some with M's and F's or R's, a few with skull-and-crossbones. Near these were assorted plastic containers. The ravine was covered on both sides, though not yet filled. It was a river. It flowed downward. The refuse had been scattered so far that Wyatt couldn't see the end of it.

"Help us," Cyril called.

Out of sight somewhere a bird was singing, and the song seemed wrong and incurious to him.

The ravine made him think of a painting, but not a painting that he himself could have conceived of or completed. You'd almost have to be Italian to paint this.

"God damn it," Cyril called.

Wyatt hoisted himself up into the truck and began to push and shove the rest of the load onto the clattering pile. With Cyril's help he lifted up the edge of one of the barrels, heard something sloshing around inside it, and rolled it off the truck down into the ravine.

"This is a secret place," Cyril said, taking a breath from his work. "You have to be a secret person to know about this place."

"Not *that* secret," Wyatt said. "Look at all that stuff. Lots of people must know." He found that his voice had suddenly changed, roughened, for some reason, and dropped lower, as if he had instantly gone through a second stage of puberty. Looking at the ravine, his eyes stung, and the inside of his nostrils felt as if someone had set a match to them. "It's not that secret if it's filling up."

"You got a point," Cyril said, throwing the board games, one by one, downward. Some of the play money lifted itself into the air and fluttered back into the truck. "I guess it's one of those secrets that everyone knows about."

"Cyril, you could be arrested for this." Wyatt threw some pieces of furniture off the truck and uncovered a dented bowling ball that bounced happily down toward a barrel. "This is totally illegal."

"Who's going to arrest me? Who's going to know? Who's going to *care?* Answer that, Mr. Answer Man. People've been dumping here a couple of years and it's like a fraternity or something, you find out about it and you keep your mouth shut, and everybody is happy. I've seen off-duty cops out here, cleaning out. So it's like a *family,* and that's why I brought *you.*"

When they were finished, Wyatt took one last look around before getting back into the cab. One of Pooh's feet was bleeding, and Cyril said, "You should've worn shoes out here instead of those flip-flops." She took a Band-Aid out of her purse and stretched it over the cut.

As they started up, Wyatt leaned against the door, mechanically raising and lowering the window. His mind shuttled into and out of blankness. It was a bit like the sensation of falling asleep. At last he said, "Cyril, whose land is that?"

"Isn't anybody's."

"Tax-default land, you mean?"

"That's what they say." He waited, shifted the truck, and grinned at his cousin. "You guys in city hall: every single regulation you think up, every single permit you charge us for to try to keep things clean and aboveboard, well, you're just creating another black-market dump like that. We'll beat you every time."

"What direction does the water drain?"

"Excuse me?"

"I mean, when it rains, and the rainwater and the chemicals sink through the topsoil and the clay, where does it flow?"

"How should I know? It flows down, that's where it flows. The water doesn't tell me. They don't print that in the paper. And I sure as hell don't ask."

"You don't have to worry anyway," Pooh said suddenly.

"First of all, it's way out of town, and, second, sand and clay filters everything, so when you drink the water, it's clear and clean."

Wyatt shook his head. "Jesus."

"Well, it *is.*"

"Where'd you read that, some comic book?"

"Hey," Cyril said, warningly.

"Of course not." Pooh tilted her head back and rubbed her neck. "There was a thing about water on *Earth World*. The science of hydrology. It's on public TV."

"Public TV? *They've* suddenly got an answer for everything? You can't build houses anywhere near this place, or drill for water, and it's dropping poison into the water table. Anybody can see that."

"Well," Pooh said, more quietly, "nobody lives out there."

"You know," Cyril said, his voice artificially steady, "you can't tell me just what about everything, on account of you used to bring me potato money on Saturday morning. You don't dictate to me. You don't tell Pooh and me what's what."

Branches scraping the truck again, a grinding downshift into first: and the truck jarring itself over dirt. To Wyatt the air in the truck smelled of discarded and fugitive chemicals, a high sharp dangerous odor, and he sat up.

"Well, damn it, Cyril, think about what you're *doing*. It's shameful. You got to be careful about how you throw things out. Things when they're thrown out, they like to make people sick. That's the revenge they have."

"Where? So where are all these people getting sick?"

Wyatt felt himself dropping into the preludes of rage. "Where? Everywhere. Who's *not* sick? Look around, for

Christ's sake. Smell the air. You don't have to be a woman or pregnant anymore to have morning sickness—anybody can have it. And it's thanks to people like you, buddy. Is this what you've been learning from your self-help guy, Mr. What's-his-name, Mr. R/Q Dynamics?"

Cyril braked, and the truck shuddered.

"Out."

"Excuse me?"

Cyril flipped his thumb toward the back. "Out."

"You're not serious."

"The fuck I'm not."

"You're throwing me out of the truck?"

"Believe it."

"This must mean that you don't want the money I brought you."

"Out."

For a moment, Wyatt didn't move. "To hell with you, Cyril."

"Out of my fucking truck."

Pooh closed her eyes. "How come guys when they get angry use that word so much?"

"Stay out of this. And you," he looked at Wyatt again, "get out before I open that fucking door and pull you out."

"Cyril, you'll be sorry, and I'll make you sorry."

"I think maybe I'll count to three."

"You're a damn ungrateful lowlife lout, and you live like a pig."

"One."

"I *walk* back?"

"Two."

"Uh, Cyril," Pooh said, touching Cyril's shirt sleeve. "He's got that money with him. Just to mention it."

"Shut the fuck up."

They all sat there for a moment, and Pooh bent down and turned on the radio. Immediately—perhaps the bouncing had repaired it—Johnny Mathis's voice came slithering out, singing some slow ballad Wyatt didn't recognize.

"Three." Cyril opened his door and was on his way over to the passenger-side door when Wyatt got out and stood, trying to control himself, his hands clenching in his pockets, at the edge of the dirt track.

"The thing is," Wyatt said slowly, "I think I'd really like to punch you once in the face, just to see what it was like."

"You never could do that, I could always take you, always. You're just a little pasty-faced bureaucrat could never handle himself in a real fight, and this here's no exception."

Cyril stood on the other side of the truck bed, glaring at Wyatt, and Wyatt thought: This is about the money, it was always about the money and nothing else. "Cyril," he said, "you're going to be sorry about this later, and I can make you sorry."

"Hell, you've done it." He turned around and spat into the ditch. "I'll apologize later when they've given me a chance to get calm. We'll see. You can't insult Pooh. And you don't know anything about me and my situation. You're just like the rest, sitting in their easy chairs and yammering at me. That's you. You can just fucking walk home and think about that, every step you take, and how you're nothing to me." The door slammed, and the truck rattled and ground its way off into the distance.

He hiked along the road for an hour. Along the way he discovered on the road a Budweiser bottle cap, a quarter, and a cigar stub. He kept the quarter. After reaching another dirt road, Wyatt was picked up by a teenage boy, a bandanna around his long hair, driving a huge old oil-burning Oldsmobile that had been in the sun for so long that it seemed to have no particular color at all. Weights for barbells clanked in the backseat. The boy was freakishly muscular in the way some teenagers seemed to be now, and Wyatt asked him how he got that way, if he used steroids for example, and the kid said, sure, of course he did, but he had it under control. He said it was for football and to look good and to maybe get a job as a bouncer, because he didn't mind getting into fights. Fights were the essence of sport, he said. Wyatt decided to change the subject. Who owns the land back there? he asked, pointing in the direction from which they'd come, and the kid said the county did, he thought, way back there, and the reason he'd been around here was that his girlfriend lived on a farm down there. Wyatt asked what township it was, and the kid said it was Harrisonville, at least he thought so. When the kid asked Wyatt why he was walking along the road by himself, Wyatt told him he'd argued with his cousin about something, and his cousin had thrown him out of his truck. Oh yeah, the kid said, that's why I get myself pumped up, so nobody ever throws me out of a truck or nothing. The strong survive, the boy said, nodding his head. They're the ones that ride in the truck.

But the steroids, they're bad for you, Wyatt said, and the kid laughed and shook his head and blinked. I don't care, he said. I want to be good and mean looking and die young. I don't care about it if I check out of Hotel Life early. Who wants to be old? he asked. Who wants that? Who wants years of watching TV? No thanks. Dying young was cool if you died when you were still good-looking.

He dropped Wyatt off in front of Cyril's apartment, where Wyatt's car was parked. Despite his muscles, the kid was quite obliging. He said he knew where Wyatt could get some steroids, if he wanted them to improve himself. He said his name was Jeff Holsapple, and when he shook Wyatt's hand, he smiled, showing his white teeth: he looked almost like an all-American, but not quite.

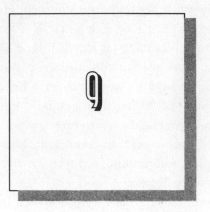

9

She had a pair of yellow socks that she had bought at Woolworth's on sale for eighty-nine cents, and on those occasions when she needed cheering up, she would open the drawer and look at them, their bright color nestled there, and she would think that her moods could hardly be considered important if they could be improved so easily.

The large, important experiences having no apparent place in her life, she took whatever pleasures and satisfactions she could get from the small experiences that she could claim as her own. During the few months that she had been married, she had felt intruded upon: Harry Davis, who was otherwise quite companionable, had brought his mechanic's grease and sand to her bed and prowled around her kitchen at night and somehow filled her house with himself. He wanted her life to be bigger than it was, with him in it. Worse, when she took walks in the evening, as she had done all her life, he followed her. He seemed to think that she needed protection, or that it was wrong for a woman to leave her husband after dark. He would call to her from behind, "Ellen! I'm here, wait up!" and her refusal even to turn around probably was what decided him to seek an annulment. She had had this habit of solitude, and nothing, not even a man calling to her, could cause her to break it.

Ellen didn't miss him but was glad when he visited, and she was pleased, almost in spite of herself, when he telephoned her every week to chat. She liked to serve him dinner now and then, the chicken in Parmesan cream sauce he enjoyed. She had admired the way he looked on a softball diamond, diving for a catch, and, after all, his untroubled geniality was something of a rarity in men. She didn't blame him for quitting the marriage right away. But she seldom thought about him once he was gone.

Nor did she miss her father, not an atom of him. She had not loved him for his black patrician beard, his reading of the Bible and Luther aloud at the dinner table, his renunciation of farming for carpentry and home repair in town. He had been a silent man, one of those rural men living in the law, clothed in wordlessness and emotional refusals and stoicism. He listened to his orders from God, and he nodded yes or no. His heart he had hidden away like a stone in a forest. No one could find it. But he knew where it was. He contemplated it, his heart, but no one could have it except God, his only collaborator.

And Ellen did not miss her mother, despite the love she could summon at her memory; her mother had agreed to that marriage. Her mother had made a bargain with the black-bearded man to live in silence and lovelessness and Scripture. They exchanged glances of iron and fire over the dinner table and across the seemingly still spaces of the living room. It had been one of those marriages where the worst is to be tolerated and endured, and hatred burns steadily like a pilot light. They did not converse. They muttered comments and corrections to each other. Anger summoned their bodies and surrounded their nearest possessions. Because of her husband, Ellen's mother grew to loathe all men for their obdurate silence and rigidity. Their laws were bad enough—and they were always making the laws—but their willfulness was worse. They hammered and plowed and drilled.

Her father's stony reciprocal contempt for women was visited upon his face when he looked at them, a look he also cast upon dogs. At the spectacle of womanly sociability he turned away, but he could not find a fortress safe from their terrible capacity to attract. Families were impossible without women, and, after all, he was a man, had been young once, and helpless in his desires. It was written in the law that he should feel that way.

They had been a remnant of the married couples who had first settled here, but she had seen many others like them, out in public: the men glaring straight ahead, the women looking at the ground, the total absence of conversation, and, instead, the monosyllabic directives, the adjectives boiled in oil.

No, she didn't miss either of her parents, but in her weaker moments, she felt the absence of her brother, Eugene, whom she had loved. All right, she missed him, and she could admit that sentimentalism to herself. She had brought him up, lavished the love on him her parents could not provide, and tried to make him as fierce as she herself was. It hadn't worked. Six years younger than Ellen, he was a sweet-faced child with a sorry cowlick and eyes so open that it was a cause for worry. He was all "Yes, ma'am" and "No, sir." He put his toys away every night in labeled boxes. By the age of seven, he made his bed dutifully every morning. From their father he learned carpentry and the dovetailing of materials. He sat by the old man's side in the shed under the one sixty-watt bulb showering glare as he made tables and chairs, the terrible instruments of domesticity, and the boy waited and watched and hoped for a good word, a humble compliment, to make its way toward him. If that word ever came, if Eugene ever received it, Ellen never knew.

She did her best to make him a bad boy. She saw how it would be if she didn't. She gave him a whoopee cushion and a joy buzzer, and she pulled his chair out from under him when no one was looking, and he fell to the linoleum tile. She made him stay out late and dress badly in dirt and rags, the way boys should dress, and she tried to make him unafraid of anger. One summer evening, when he was eleven years old, upstairs, she taught him the word "damn." She taught him how to say it correctly, in two syllables. She knew worse words, the powerful ones, but thought they were too awful to teach to a little brother his age.

She taught Eugene how to go barefoot and how to ride a bicycle with no hands and how to break windows with stones when no one was looking. She taught him how to honk a horn. She explained in detail what two people do in bed, and why, once she knew. She had been pleased to be known as a bad wild girl in high school, subject to her parents useless fury, even though she had been bad with only two boys, both of whom she had loved. One of them smelled of hay, the other of seashells. Love, she thought, was no effort at all. She might have become pregnant; she refused to care. But she didn't bear children, not then or ever. She could have lavished her disgrace proudly on the town and on her parents—she had planned out in detail how she would refuse to go away and instead display her blooming pregnancy on the main streets—but the days passed, and her periods came in their moony orderly way. Conception and disgrace somehow eluded her.

Her brother passed uneasily into adolescence. A gentle and dutiful kid, he surrounded himself with animals as cushions against the difficulties of hormones and pubic hair. On his shelf he had a goldfish bowl with two goldfish swimming blankly around. He owned two yellow parakeets purchased from S. S. Kresge, a dog that followed him everywhere, and for a brief period, a pet opossum he had found as a baby, half dead in the yard, and which he had nursed back to an opossum's limited lucidity. But the animal was bad-tempered, and one night Eugene opened the cage and let him shamble away.

Even when he was fifteen, Eugene would escape from the silence of the house by standing in the yard, out in the snow, his hand extended with birdseed in the palm, waiting for chickadees to swoop down and perch on the edge of his glove, fluttering, picking at the seeds. Against all of Ellen's expectations, the birds came and returned. They trusted him. It was a bad sign, she thought.

Learning carpentry and design and silence from his father, and submission from his mother, he had, of course, Ellen thought, terrible taste in women. He didn't like them wild and sexy and loud and beautiful. He liked the tame ones. Those were the ones he brought home, once he was in college, and after his father died and Eugene had gone on to architecture school, those were the ones he sometimes brought up to Five Oaks, where he'd introduce them to his mother and to Ellen. By this time Ellen was living by herself on the north side, having suffered two years at the university before deciding that she could learn more by herself. She wore the uniform of her bohemianism—a beret and flannel shirts and jeans—both summer and winter. She subscribed to *Partisan Review* and read it. By herself, getting from day to day, she read Simone Weil and Sartre and de Beauvoir in French. She was making herself over, fixing herself up, repairing the damage done by her provincialism, until, she thought, there would be no sign of any wound anyone had inflicted on her.

Her brother, meanwhile, brought home these drab little women with bad posture. They chirped, just as his birds had. The worst one, named Ruth, with frighteningly white skin, dressed in prim cotton dresses and sat like Little Miss Muffet. She parted her hair in the middle and pulled it behind, pinned in the back, as if a woman's hair were some sort of disgrace. She talked sewing and recipes. Ellen couldn't stand her. It was all she could do not to make a scene.

After this Ruth, Jeanne was almost a relief. For one thing, she had a vice: she smoked cigarettes—Eugene took them up, too, so his sister knew he was actually in love this time—and sometimes, when she spoke, her eyes flashed, and passion entered her voice. She had a physical presence, breasts and legs she was apparently not ashamed of, and she walked with her head up, the first woman Eugene had ever taken home who did.

It wasn't until years later, after Eugene and Jeanne had married, and Wyatt and Gretel had been born, that Ellen, who thought of herself as a perceptive woman, noticed an anomalous quality about Jeanne that she had somehow missed. Jeanne never asked questions and could not make

ordinary conversation. It was beyond her. She wasn't reciprocal in anything. Conversation, the back-and-forth flow of
ideas and responses, simply didn't take with her. She would sit
or stand and make statements, her ankles crossed, not caring
whether anyone responded to her statements or not, and then
drift off, sometimes leaving the room, and sometimes just
sinking into herself. She didn't make eye contact. Ellen never
saw Jeanne touch her brother in an affectionate way. She
seemed to live in a parallel universe. She knew what was
occurring in this universe, but it didn't seem to affect her
much. Her real life glimmered and settled in the parallel universe, where no one here could reach her. She was the absen-
tee landlord of her own body and mind.

They all went to a picnic once, near the river. It was a hot
day, and Jeanne wore a sunhat, saying that sunlight disagreed
with her and beat her spirit down. Ellen noticed that when
Jeanne pulled the sandwiches out of the basket, she cocked
her head as if listening for some traceries of sound. At first
Ellen thought Jeanne heard birds calling, but, no: this conversation was going on inside, echoing in the cave.

Ellen in those days was traveling down to Bay City to see
her lover, a man who operated an earth-moving machine,
and with whom she had little in common except for the
shared energy of their affair and an ability to laugh easily. She
could never depend on the conversation, but she could always
depend on the sex, on his odd, subtle lightness with her, as if
that was the only extended conversation they would ever
have. One time in bed with him she told him that he had a
calling for this, for making love, and although she knew it
would make him insufferable, she couldn't help saying it, and
he laughed. It was as if he gave her pleasure without much of
any effort on his part. She would be too easy for him, and he
would lose interest in her, and he did.

Around this time, Eugene took up solitary drinking, basement drinking, but drinking of a kind that was supposed to be
impossible: utterly controlled, like the utterly controlled man
he had grown to be, on weekends, all day and all evening,
Saturdays and Sundays, but lightly, sip after sip of Jack Daniel's, so that he didn't become actively drunk but instead ce-
mented himself in a condition of mild intoxication hour after
hour. He would sit in the basement of the house he had
designed for himself and his family, in a room with a pattern
of clocks, all showing the same time, 3:30. Ellen would drop
in and find him there, smoking and drinking and humming to
himself, a new version of the old patriarch, and she would ask
him, "What on earth are you doing, hiding down here?" He
would get up, all smiles, and move her gently toward the
hallway, and then pantomime closing a door.

The children occupied themselves any way they could.

His houses, the ones he could see in his head and sometimes drew as a hobby, on speculation, were beautiful elegant
things, in the style of Eugene's hero, Frank Lloyd Wright—
spare, with an effect of nudity and simplicity, a kind of Prairie
School in his own style. He planned into them a quality of
camouflage: they would blend into the wooded lot so cun-
ningly that you would not see the building in front of you
until you were almost upon it. Eugene lived by such principles of disguise and disappearance. But one afternoon Ellen
was prowling around in his basement and found his thought-
drawer. She'd opened it up, looking for a screwdriver, and
there they were, those little strips of paper.

Heaven: one dies and meets God who has
enlarged all your good qualities by $1/5$.
If you've been good or loving or generous,
this being is more good or loving or generous

than you are, by 20%.
Hell: the same, but the vices are now surpassed
and you're confronted by somebody who looks like
you but is crueler and meaner than you are, and
bigger, also by 20%.

The drawer was beginning to fill with these slips of paper, just as the drawer next to it was beginning to fill with designs for unbuilt houses. To get an income, Eugene designed gift shops and gas stations, and, as the city spread outward, shopping centers and golf clubhouses and stinking pink palazzos. His best creations stayed in the basement.

She couldn't do anything with her brother, she had decided. But after Wyatt had almost drowned as a result of that idiotic radio promotion, Ellen thought she might be able to help *him* along. Gretel possessed fire and beauty and vanity in about equal measure and needed no one's help. She would manage very well: the world was constructed in order to house people like her. But not Wyatt—whatever help she could give him, he would take.

Cyril had started hanging around by this time, having been given up on by his mother, Ellen's good-time cousin, Rhonda. Of course he was a tricky fellow, but he wasn't a nasty piece of work, and maybe he would save Wyatt from the wretchedness of becoming dutiful and a good citizen. Cyril and Wyatt had gone around together with that other boy, that Donald, who *was* a nasty piece of work. And then Donald had died, and she had witnessed it. Sometimes, gathering the evidence, Ellen would remember it, those hours and evenings after the drowning.

She had found her rowboat, the one she had stolen, a few hundred feet down the river tangled in some trees, and she had rowed it back to the dock she had taken it from, her clothes soaking. On the sand the boy's drowned body was now surrounded by interested outsiders. Wyatt was there, too, and Cyril as well, their teeth chattering in shock. There was a sheriff. There were questions.

Late that night, with Wyatt home, and Ellen herself dressed in dry clothes, she returned to the boat dock to stare at the river where earlier in the day, in the midst of the perfected weather, she had seen that child go down. Something was going to come to her. She didn't know what. She sat on the dock until after midnight, when she was stiff and could hardly stand, and the stars reflected their dim light in the form of broken constellations on the lapping water.

She waited. Because nothing came to her, and she was beginning to fall asleep, she gave it up and resolved to come back the next night. Nothing came to her that night, either, so she brought herself back to that same spot a third night, and then a fourth.

On the fifth night, sitting on the dock, staring out at the water, a slight drizzle just beginning, Ellen became consciously aware around one-thirty—she had looked at her watch—that someone was behind her, sitting or standing, she couldn't tell which. She turned and saw nothing. She was waiting alone on this dock. Nothing visible, at any rate, nothing the eye might see. Fixing her gaze back on the water, she felt again the presence behind her, waiting patiently.

The moon was reflected on the body of the river, finger-touched by drizzle. Who are you? she asked.

She heard no answer to that question, nor could she think of one.

Are you young? Or old?

Silence like a wind drifted in parallel waves through whatever was there.

Why are you behind me? Why don't you present yourself in front of me? You are supposed to appear before me.

Supposed to? Where does it say? she wondered. No, she would not be told in sentences. Whatever she would discover would arrive, if it came, as a specific feeling.

What gender are you? She tried to feel if the presence behind her registered on her back as male or female. Men, when they crept up behind you, had a distinct feeling of wool and grease and cut wood; and women, behind you, felt like secrets and leaves and almost sweet, like perfume. But, of course, you could be wrong, turning around, expecting one thing and finding another. But this was neither man nor woman.

Then why are you here?

The only words she heard, the only ones that would come to her that night or the nights that followed, fell into her mind like mild stones falling down a hillside that was infinitely high, whose top could not be seen: *Because I have an interest.*

An interest in what?

Behind her, the presence gave her its silence, its particular vacancy, of parallel waves flowing through some sort of grid.

Oh, Ellen thought, beginning now to shiver, and the goose bumps rising on her arms, you're interested in everything, aren't you? You don't care what happens.

Watching and waiting, just as she did. She didn't have an accurate feeling of *it waited,* or *it waits.* Whatever was behind her wasn't an *it* or a *he* or a *she.* This was a *waiting,* a *watching,* even *an interest,* without a pronoun, and nameless otherwise.

Ellen stood up. She turned around. The presence moved around behind her, so she would have, so she would always have, this *watching* at her back.

Once inside her house again, she opened a yellow notebook near the telephone and wrote, *Everything written about*

God is wrong. She put her pen back into the drawer, confident that she would write a new book before the end of her life and that she would live to complete it. Then she went to bed and slept for ten hours without dreams.

The next morning, she wrote: *The world exists because God is curious about it*.

Months later, she heard from Eugene that Wyatt had pretended to run away, repeatedly. Eugene insisted that Wyatt meant none of it. At first he hadn't even bothered to pack. She knew because Wyatt had called her one Monday morning in the middle of summer.

"Well, hello, sweetie," she said. "Guess what. I found a rock out in the yard I thought you'd be interested in. You like rocks. This one, when you hold it up to the sun, you see rainbow colors in it. Do you know why that is? I don't think I do."

"No," he said. "I never figured that out. Like glass that's cut in the light?"

"Yes."

"Or like gasoline or oil in rowboat water?"

"Yes. I wonder how that happens?"

"Nobody knows," Wyatt told her. "It's a big mystery."

"Good. I like that."

They waited in amiable quietness.

"I'm going to run away," Wyatt said suddenly.

"Oh, good. Where?"

"Well, I was thinking, your house."

"Over here? Well, that's fine. But I'm a mess, you know. You really want to live with your old aunt?"

"You aren't that old, are you? You don't seem old."

"Compared to some humans, I'm old. What seems old to you?"

"Well," Wyatt said, "my daddy seems old."

"He's younger than I am."

"Oh." Wyatt waited. "So I thought I'd come and live with you for a while. Is that okay?"

"Oh sure. Love to have you. It's small over here, but big enough for us."

"That's what I thought," he said excitedly. "I won't bring much stuff. Just anything I can pack."

"That won't be a bother. Now why'd you say you were leaving?"

"I don't like it here."

"Why not?"

"I don't know," he said. "I just don't."

"Maybe you should give them a chance."

"I have. But my dad sits in the basement all the time, building stuff, and writing, and Mom talks to herself."

"She does?"

"Yeah. So I was thinking, maybe I could come over to your place tomorrow. To stay, I mean."

"Well, I'd love to have you. Maybe you should talk about it to your parents, though."

"Really? I don't think they'd like it."

"Well, ponder it. Discuss it."

"*Discuss* it?"

"You know. Sit down and talk about it."

"They don't talk about much."

"Not even at dinner?"

"My mom turns on the phonograph so loud with the dinner music that you can't hear anything, so nobody says much."

"Oh." Ellen recovered her mood and said, "Well, try talking to them anyway. And if that doesn't work, you could always get mad at them."

"Get mad?" This time there was a real silence, a genuine one. "Do I have to feel mad first?" Wyatt asked.

"Usually. That's usually how it works. You feel mad, and then you get mad, and then you start yelling."

"Oh." He inhaled. "Gretel does that. I thought I'd just run away instead and live with you."

"Why, Wyatt?"

" 'Cause you love me."

"That's true." She tried not to make too much of the moment. Children always noticed when you impregnated the pauses. "Well, then, maybe I'll see you tomorrow."

"Okay."

He didn't come. Perhaps the weather was wrong or the distance too far, but he never made it, nor did he make it that rainy day in the fall—she heard about this later, from him— when he had packed his suitcase and escaped during a thunderstorm, and his father had chased him and found him; but he had had his wish, though probably not in the way he had intended it, because when their father had died and their mother had started to lose her senses, Wyatt and Gretel, through the wisdom of the court, and Ellen's own efforts, were moved, toys and nursing equipment and clothes and all, temporarily and then semipermanently into Ellen's house, upland from the river. Gretel set herself up in the basement, and Wyatt moved himself into the back room near the kitchen on the first floor, where Ellen had started to accumulate the evidence. When Cyril moved in (Rhonda, Cyril's mother, had asked Ellen to take him for a few weeks while she searched for a job in Las Vegas—she left two hundred dollars for any expenses that Cyril might incur), Ellen saw that she would have to give up her evening walks for a few years.

She suspected that she had no talent for raising children,

but as long as there was enough money—and there had been, from the sale of Eugene's house, at least a sufficiency—she would do her best to supply everything else. The only lasting annoyance was that she happened, still, to be angry at Eugene for slipping out of this life as quietly as he had slipped into it. It was a failure of temperament, Eugene's placidity, and she had never trained him to shed it. Certainly Jeanne had never tried to adapt him to the realities, a job for which she was remarkably ill equipped anyway. In the aftermath of Eugene's death, she had been conveyed, first, to the Upper Peninsula, where she was settled among other distraughts and her brain jolted with therapeutic electricity, and then she had been transported back to a halfway house on the east side of Five Oaks, where Ellen brought the children over to see her on Sundays.

For the first visit, Jeanne said that she had made sand-wiches, so Ellen dressed up the children—she left Cyril back in the house—and brought them over. She was hoping that the whole experience, by being duplicated every Sunday, might be brought in under some subspecies of what might be considered normal. Jeanne hadn't come to the door, but after they rang the bell, they heard her sing out "Come in!" in a cheerful and unearthly voice, and they found her in the living room, sitting alone in a straight-backed chair underneath a poster on the wall of a barn in snow. The house's supervisor introduced herself from a doorway in the back hallway and then disappeared.

"How you two have grown," Jeanne said, smiling. She raised herself with what seemed to be a mechanical, rather than a physical, difficulty and approached her children to hug them. "I'm so happy to see you both," Jeanne said at last. "A mother misses her children, and she feels zarklike if they're not around."

"*Zark*like?" Gretel said, drawing back. "What's that?"

"Oh, vaguely solitary," Jeanne said, with her hand in her hair, and a social smile on her face. "Gretel," Jeanne continued, sitting down again, "you're pretty. You're all dressed up. I never thought I'd be the sort of mother that a daughter would have to dress up for."

"I guess you are," Gretel said.

"I guess so. Your hair . . . it's lighter than I remember it. Have you been dyeing it?"

"I've been outside," Gretel said, sitting down on the sofa and looking away from her mother, toward the window. "It's been bleaching out."

"I've been bleaching out, too," Jeanne said, in a manner that Ellen thought was studiously calm. "I've been taking walks and doing a bit of birdwatching. Saw an indigo bunting the other day. You should try it, birdwatching, I mean. You know, I want to take care of you both, the two of you, and I *think* I will, but, for just now, I don't think I can, because I'm not resilient. Every once or so often I pass a whole day in zonal disaptitude. Have you been taking care of yourselves? I try to take care of myself, but it's awfully hard, and I don't always succeed. I worry that you're not dressing warmly enough. Wyatt, you always used to go outside without your coat on. You caught colds. I hope that Ellen is watching after that."

"Oh, I have been."

"Good. With all this snow . . ." She stared at her shoes. From somewhere upstairs, there was a peal of laughter, followed by a long string of coughs. A truck rumbled by on the street, and when Ellen next looked out of the window, a sparrow was perched on a branch, and the branch was swinging back and forth, but the snow on the branch did not falter. No: that wasn't the word. It didn't *fall off,* or *disperse.*

"What's that?" Gretel asked. She was pointing toward the side table next to Jeanne's chair.

"This?" Jeanne picked up a little ceramic dog in a crouching position. "This is Don Quixote. Only he seems to be missing his spear." She put the dog back.

"How do you like this place, Mom?" Wyatt was standing in the middle of the room, a few feet away from his mother, his fingers knitted together at waist level.

"But Sancho Panza," his mother said, gazing toward Wyatt. "I wonder where he's rounded himself to. Me? Oh, well, I spend entirely too much of the day watching television—plots, plots, *plots!*—but that's what you do if the ocean liner doesn't brusk itself into port, and this one certainly doesn't. Wyatt, how have your grades been? Have you been working hard? When they tell you to learn geography," she laughed, "for God's sake learn geography!"

"Yes, I've been working hard."

"He's a very good student," Ellen said, as brightly as she could.

"The key is in study," Jeanne said. "Come closer, Wyatt, so I can see you better."

He took two steps toward her.

"Oh, yes, I can see now. You *have* been studying. You have that bookmark expression, right there in your eyes." She reached out for his hand. "You feel of seaweed, though." She let go of Wyatt's hand.

Ellen had been watching this scene from near the front of the room, and as it went on, she perceived, more strongly than she had before, the presence of that God at her back, that principle of curiosity, letting this scene happen in exactly this way. *Because I have an interest.* And Ellen thought, Oh, nonsense, why don't you ever learn anything? Why do you have to witness scenes like this over and over again?

Wyatt had backed away from his mother. On his face was an expression of mingled alarm and hopefulness. He was reaching into his pocket. "Mom," he said, "I brought you something."

"Oh, how wonderful. What did you bring me?"

"This." He held it out, a polished agate.

"Oh," she said, looking at it but not taking it, "how beautiful. How did you polish it?"

"I earned some money, and Aunt Ellen loaned me the rest, and we bought a rock tumbler."

"Where did you get the stone?"

"The last time we went up to Lake Superior. Remember?"

"Yes," Jeanne said. She closed her eyes and tilted her head back. "Your father was still alive. It was the four of us, wasn't it? North of Duluth, that beach."

Wyatt smiled. Ellen glanced at Gretel; she could see from Gretel's expression that she thought that her mother's previous dissociation must have been a hoax, some kind of joking.

"Remember how many flies there were?" Wyatt asked, clinging, Ellen guessed, to the normality of this memory. "Black flies that bit."

"Yes," his mother said, nodding. "I do. We all had bites. Didn't you, Gretel?"

"I don't remember."

"Well, I'm sure you did." All at once Jeanne rose to her feet, and Ellen felt herself suddenly go on a physical alert. Standing, Jeanne looked at Wyatt, then at Gretel, her head twisting like some kind of isolated human lighthouse, and before Ellen could decide whether she should stop her, Jeanne rushed over to her son, took the agate from him, and hugged him.

"There," Jeanne said, raising her head and speaking to the

ceiling. "That's done. Now you." And in the same rushed manner, she hurried over to Gretel, tilted herself down toward her, and hugged her while Gretel was still sitting in her chair. "Now that's done, too," she said. She returned to her own straight-backed chair. "Ellen," she said, "you don't get a hug, because you're my sister-in-law and not my child. I have that relative-who-is-also-a-friend feeling with you." The expression on her face brightened. "Love can be such a chore, can't it?" She glanced toward the front door and the entryway. "Any moment now something will be coming in through that door, and it won't be me!" She laughed hopelessly. "This is so hard."

No one said anything. "This is so hard," Jeanne repeated. "I can hear myself, and it sounds so awful, so crazy." She held her hand toward Wyatt before raising it up, as if she were holding the air on an invisible tray just above her head. "I don't mean to sound this way to you. But if you want to sound right, I mean the way mothers are supposed to sound, you have to have the sentences." She shook her head; in her hands she was fingering the agate that Wyatt had given her. "And I don't have the sentences. All the sentences they give me to say are so terrible. But they're the only ones I have. I'd like to have some of my own ideas, but none of my ideas belong to me."

" 'They,' Jeanne?" Ellen asked. "What 'they' is this?"

"Why, just 'they.' The ones who write the sentences. You don't think you write your sentences, do you?"

"Of course I do," Ellen said.

"Well, that's crevartious," Jeanne said, "because someone is writing this sentence at this very moment and giving it to me to say, and I wish I had another sentence, but I don't, and that's that, isn't it?" She smiled dreamily. "And that's who the 'they' is."

Ellen came over to her sister-in-law and squatted in front of her and took her hands in her own hands. "Jeanne," she said. "It's Ellen. *I'm* Ellen, *I'm* speaking now, and I'm here with your children, and we all love you, and you're going to be fine, I know it. And you'll write your own sentences, and you'll be back with us, just the way you were."

"That's a phrase, isn't it?" Jeanne said. "What they call a cliché. Well, maybe you're right, Ellen."

"Of course I'm right."

"This is so hard, doing this in front of my children." She released one of her hands and began to fan her face with it. "It's funny how difficult everything is when you can't be spontaneous anymore, except to be crazy, I mean." She laughed again.

In the silence that followed, Wyatt walked into the kitchen, and his sister stood up and stared through the east window, tapping the windowsill and pulling at the ropes that connected to the window weights. They made a hollow thumping sound inside the wall as they knocked against the wood.

"Let's have lunch," Jeanne said. "I made sandwiches."

As they ate, Ellen felt the presence of God, that random curiosity about everything, watching the scene from some closed protected space behind her.

They had never again given Jeanne custody of her children. For weeks at a time, she would come back to Five Oaks and stay restlessly in the halfway house, working at small tasks and reading the essays of John Stuart Mill, whom she claimed to love, until the pretense of ordinary life was too much for her. One Sunday evening she told Ellen, who had come by for a visit, that she could imitate ordinary behavior adequately for about three months, and then the strain was just too much for her. She said she was a boiler in which the steam built up. "And that's when I explode," she said. They would find her running outside, barefoot, screaming and laughing. She would have to be returned to the state hospital for a review of her medications.

Jeanne didn't think it had anything to do with medications. She claimed she had somehow been placed on an ocean liner that had lost its way at sea. They had run out of fuel and now drifted here and there with the tides. Sometimes someone spotted land, but it was far away, and the ocean currents took them back out into the great spaces of vague empty sky and water. The liner was huge; her stateroom resembled a house. Also on the liner was this town, and other towns. Roads, even. Families, houses, and green lawns that had to be mowed in summer and raked in the fall. Perhaps the ship contained the entire Midwest. But to forget that they were on a ship was a soul error, and almost everyone *had* forgotten. "Don't you see," she said confidently, "how we're drifting out here? If there were a hand on the tiller, we'd certainly know by now. You can feel the drift, can't you, down in your soul? The vague movement of everything?"

Ellen said that she could not feel that.

Someone had done this to her, Jeanne claimed. Someone invisible, and she thought it was a man. "You mean Eugene?" Ellen asked.

"No, of course not. Eugene died. He did his best, but he's gone. This is different. This is someone I can't see, but I know he's there. I don't know his name. He won't tell me. He gives me thoughts and makes me say these things. I've begged him to let me go, but he won't do that. He says he might, someday, but not now. So that's why things have turned out the way they have."

•   •   •

Ellen watched apprehensively as the children grew. She had no feeling for parenthood, for rules or discipline, and all the books claimed that improvisation in parenting brought on seething resentment and ultimate disaster. All the same, improvisation was what the children got. She bought a slightly larger house with an upstairs room for Gretel, across the hall from Cyril's room, and down the sloping hallway from Wyatt's room, and her own. The house was badly built—a farmer, in the 1890s, had taken too much pride in his own carpentry skills—with support beams that sagged and doorways that slanted so crookedly that you had to shave off the tops of the doors just so they'd close, but its purchase price had been reasonable, and its ugliness suited Ellen just fine.

She did develop a habit of repeating some phrases over and over in a loud voice, so that Wyatt, Gretel, and Cyril would know that there were some principles in the world to live by. "Have some adventures!" she'd say at breakfast and dinner. It was good advice for Wyatt but not for Cyril. "Avoid irony! Share beautiful things!" Gretel never listened to that one. "Don't kill anything in your nature!" "No excuses! Take responsibility!" After hearing these phrases repeated so often, the children, teenagers by then, came up with their own, and Ellen was never sure if she was being mocked or not. "Don't waste food!" Wyatt would declaim loudly, at the dinner table, and Gretel would point her fork at Wyatt and say, "Never leave hair in the bathtub! Always clean up after yourself!"

Without meaning to, she felt that she had turned morality into a sporting event for them.

But as Wyatt grew, he seemed, to Ellen's pleasure and astonishment, to be a sweet and kindhearted kid. He worked in the hardware store, painted canvases on weekends, and

brought his girlfriends home to meet his aunt. He was devoted to these girls, and he fell in love easily. He was one of
those boys who was not only attracted to young women but
who loved them as well. Girls loved how he loved them, and
they swarmed around him, putting their hands in his long
hair, and making offers to cook for him and to mend his
socks. He had a girl named Tracy his junior year and another
named Carrie his senior year, and Carrie, in particular, all but
moved in with him. The house was full of noise and laughter
and shouting and lovemaking and chatter. Ellen hadn't meant
to nurture so much uproar, but there it was. These young
women Wyatt sought out were proud and strong-willed—
what Ellen noticed about them first was the way they stood, as
straight as soldiers, and a particular way of looking around a
room without fear—and it seemed that perhaps there was,
after all, cause for optimism in what had happened between
the sexes, at least in this one respect, that perhaps the young
men and women liked each other more than they had in her
father's generation. No more angry stoicism, or prideful
unexpressed resentment.

Gretel grew up to be shockingly beautiful and smart. She
had no vague edges. She was impatient, angry, and scientific.
She wasn't likable, and she didn't care that she wasn't. She
dressed in severe clothes and was immune to opinion. Love
seemed to make no impression upon her. She sailed through
college and medical school, where she specialized in pediat-
rics, and she moved out to Seattle, where she was taken by
surprise one day by her feelings for the father of one of her
patients, a six-year-old boy. She easily drew this man into an
affair and away from his wife, and they were married eighteen
months later, after his divorce was final. Ellen couldn't bring
herself to disapprove, exactly, but she didn't like the way it
had happened. She was certain that she had forgotten to tell

Gretel some important piece of information by which to guide her conduct, but she couldn't for the life of her think of what that information was.

As for Cyril, he hadn't grown up at all. He was always trouble, and, for that reason, along with his showmanship and worthlessness, she loved him—it was her terrible secret—best of all. His life had so far been a series of misadventures, but she had never detected in Cyril's offenses any maliciousness, just irresponsibility and a sprinkling of mindlessness. She knew she hadn't been a good, strict parent with Cyril, but she had no idea what good strict parenting looked like or how it was done. Her own parents had muddied those waters irremediably.

This God behind her seemed especially curious about Cyril.

She thought she had done the best she could. She didn't blame herself for anything. At night, now, she sometimes felt that Wyatt was about to break away from his own life and do something unusual, the sort of thing you might tell about in a story, but, try as she might to locate his future on the ceiling of her bedroom, she could not see it there becoming visible. She wanted to pray for the souls of Wyatt and Gretel and Cyril, and for the lacerated soul of Jeanne, but she did not know how to do that. Instead, she would rise out of bed, turn on one light, and open her drawer. Inside the drawer were her socks. She would take out one pair, the eighty-nine-cent pair she had bought on sale at Woolworth's, and admire the yellow color. You didn't expect to find yellows like that at the dime store, but there they were, Matisse-bright, pure joy in a simple thing. One simple color was her happiness at three in the morning, and after holding the socks in her hand for a moment she would put them back, exactly in place, flick the switch on the bedside light, and try to fall back to sleep, that presence always at her back, watching her toss and turn, perpetually curious.

10

From a west-facing hallway window on the tenth floor of the city hall building, close to a standing ashtray, Wyatt could see, in the distance, Schwartzwalder's plant going up on the east end of an industrial park, on the other side of which was a new two-hundred-unit condominium complex called Maple Meadows. Through the winter and on into spring, he had been helping Schwartzwalder's people with the issuance of the water and land permits; he had recommended lawyers and subcontractors; and Schwartzwalder had taken much of Wyatt's advice. His tone toward Wyatt could be chummy one moment, businesslike the next, and sometimes, disconcertingly, both at once. Now Wyatt could begin to see the results: WaldChem, a rectangular building constructed on top of a slab, with corrugated exterior windowless gray walls.

In a business call to Wyatt on a Tuesday when the sun hadn't appeared all day, Schwartzwalder stopped himself in the middle of a sentence and then said, "I owe you. You've been going out of your way to make all this happen. Don't get me wrong: I'm grateful. You got any favors you want done that I can do?"

And Wyatt, at his desk, looking at his shoes on the floor, said, "Hire my cousin. His name's Cyril Wilson."

"To do what?"

"Sweeping. Maintenance. Anything you've got for him."

Wyatt heard the scratching of a pencil at the other end of the line. "If he applies, consider it done," Schwartzwalder said.

A week later, on a Sunday afternoon, Wyatt took his mother out in the car for a drive. Christina was in back, along for the ride. His mother was now wearing hats with wide brims that seemed to express everything or nothing, and in deep winter she had taken to wearing a reddish-brown overcoat whose female-cardinal color would have looked acceptably muted on anyone else but on her, he thought, looked insane. On the way out to the countryside, he drove her past the new WaldChem plant. They hadn't spoken very much until then. She had always failed in the tactics of small talk.

Now she satisfied herself with commentary concerning the music from the radio, or with broken dead-end mutterings that circled back on herself.

"See that?" Wyatt asked, pointing at what everyone called the no-nonsense exterior of WaldChem, highlighted by its yellow logo of a test tube over a flame. "I helped to build that place. I helped make it possible."

His mother gazed in the direction in which his finger was aimed. Then she said, "Ah. Life at a discount."

"It's a manufacturing plant, not a discount store."

She sat up and inspected him. "This is one of your I-know-what's-best-for-you-in-the-long-run-and-that's-why-everything-absolutely-everything-has-to-be-so-ugly-now-ideas, yes?"

"Well, I wouldn't call it that, Mother. It's not an idea."

"Of course you wouldn't. Of course it's not."

"We're creating jobs."

"Wyatt, you're so corilineal I can't stand it sometimes."

"Please don't make up words. I hate that. All those word-heaps of yours, I never know what you're talking about."

"No," she said, reaching into her purse for her dark glasses. After she put on the glasses, she began to apply some lipstick that matched her overcoat. "No, you never do."

Wyatt didn't want to talk to Cyril, so he called his cousin midmorning on a weekday, hoping to get Pooh, but instead he got Cyril's answering machine.

"This is Big Time Hauling and I'm Cyril Wilson and please leave a message after the tone."

Wyatt took a breath and said, "Listen, Cyril, this is Wyatt. It's a lucky thing I'm not still mad at you because of that thing that happened last fall, because if I were, I wouldn't be talking to you. Now listen. This is serious. I got a job lined up for you over there at that new plant they've built in that industrial park, and it's called WaldChem. They've already opened an office in one part of the building, or they . . . no, I just remembered, they have a trailer outside, that's where the hiring is. They haven't finished hiring, not exactly, but they'll hire *you* because I asked them to. You go over there. Tell them who you are. They're planning to hire you. Do this. They've got benefits, Cyril, and you'd really have to be more of a . . . you'd have to be crazy to pass this up. Go over there today, because they—"

He heard a high piercing bell or siren or wail from Cyril's machine. His time was up.

"We hired your cousin," Schwartzwalder said, two weeks later. He called regularly now. Apparently he enjoyed using up Wyatt's time with these phone calls. He had spent half an hour on a business day discussing recipes for venison. "This guy's an obvious risk, but because of you, we hired him. He's on probation, only he doesn't know that."

"To do what?"

"Cleaning. Maintenance. Just what you said."

"Thank you."

"You are welcome. You are very magnificently welcome. Happy to pay you back, Wyatt. You've been a brick."

He waited to get a thank-you call from Cyril. He wondered if Cyril had forgotten his phone number or misplaced it somehow. The man bore grudges, but only short-term ones; he wasn't disciplined enough to hold them for very long. Sooner or later Cyril would call.

It wasn't until he saw Pooh, thirty feet away in the infant-clothes section of Putnam's Department Store, fingering the infant overalls and wearing a BABY ON BOARD T-shirt, with an arrow pointing downward, that he figured out why Cyril had taken the job, and, possibly, why he hadn't thanked him.

"By the way," Schwartzwalder said over the phone, another afternoon, when the snow was falling in thick, late-winter, movie-sized flakes, and Schwartzwalder was using his winter voice, a soothing coldness in it somewhere. "You know about my house?"

"Your house? No, what about it?"

"Well, I know you've never been over, but it's on Jellison Road. Ring any bells?"

"No," Wyatt said. "The bells are silent."

"I found out who designed it originally. Solarium in the back, pillars and driveway fountain and the high style in the front. Any bells now?"

"My father," Wyatt said. "My father designed that house."

"Bingo. We're living inside your father's design. Love the solarium. Love the details. Great design. Great house."

"Yes." He did not say: My father hated that place. He was under orders to design it exactly that way. A house, he had said, for Mr. and Mrs. Daffy Duck and the Duck children. "Congratulations, Jerry."

"Great house," he repeated. "The wife and kids love it." He cleared his throat, as he tended to do before a pronouncement. "This is one great town."

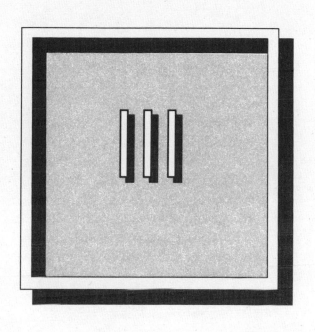

11

Wyatt had been warned about the behavior of two- and three-year-olds but not, he thought, warned sufficiently about their abilities to make relentless demands. Christina could be imperious, and she screamed and made threats and was implacable. At times she reminded him of Hitler. She marched around the house, strutted, and howled for what she wanted. She said thank you only when ordered to do so. Her behavior seemed to have nothing to do with innocence.

Wyatt wanted to know who she really was beneath all that impulsiveness and the half-human, half-animal mode she presented to the world, but, finally, she seemed to be only and completely the daughter of Susan and himself, a fierce tiger girl who, when she laughed, often laughed so hard she fell down.

On weekends he took her to the hardware store, or over to the park or the bandstand. As she rode on his shoulders, she would call out, "Daddy, what's this?" and he would see her pointing toward an electrical transformer or a billboard for a substance-abuse clinic. She pulled at the hair on his head and shouted, "Daddy, go that way." She had constant opinions about animals and objects smaller than she was: They were the soldiers, and she was the general.

Wyatt thought she was dangerous and beautiful, and she reminded him of his sister, Gretel, who had required twenty-nine years of living before she could love another human being.

He had grown attached to the activity of bedtime reading. He didn't care that much whether his daughter liked it or not, curled up, as she usually was, next to her stuffed penguin. Reading *Goodnight, Moon,* his favorite, he admired the cow, the resourceful mouse, the gradual diminishing of the light in the rabbits' living room until only the coals in the fireplace radiated a rusty glow.

"Goodnight, face," he would say in bed, to his wife, kissing it. "Goodnight, hands." Sometimes he progressed as far down as her knees before she accused him of sexual cuteness, of being a sort of human genre painting. "Just make love to me, why can't you?" she would say, and then, more irritably, "We're still interesting when we take off our clothes. We don't need gimmicks." And he would think: Gimmicks—

what's the problem, why not? He had noticed that even their orgasms had become terribly calm.

He missed Cyril. He wanted Cyril to call. He would not call Cyril himself.

On weekends, during the times when he had once visited Cyril and given him money, he took Christina to the neighborhood playground, where he sat on the benches and watched. The place was well equipped, especially with small horses on heavy springs so that children Christina's size could occupy themselves without getting bashed by flying metal. Wyatt watched his child frolicking, charging, knocking over other children, heading somewhere else. Usually no one was hurt, and no one cried. When he saw a newspaper drifting across the playground carried by the wind, he thought: Yes, right, I should visit my mother.

He didn't like to visit her too often with Christina. He worried about the aftereffects.

The playground made him restless. The children on the swings were like pendulums on a giant clock. The minutes and hours passed, but the children never noticed; only their parents did. With mild shock he realized that he was giving his time away to Christina and that, after all, was what parents did. One child fell and howled, and all the other children turned to look, though without sympathy. The sun rose and descended in the sky, whether anyone saw it or not, and then the day had concluded, and the pigeons waddled around at his feet because he looked, he thought, exactly like a statue.

After running after his daughter, circling her and catching her, he returned to his bench and closed his eyes. Above the shouts of the children were the intermittent warnings and encouragements of their parents, and then, as the day folded

up, the sounds of the children's names as they were being
called in. To his right a mother called for Holly, and to his
left, a few moments later, a father called for Ben. Flower
names were coming back: Violet was on the swings, and Rose
had been digging an open-pit mine in the sandbox. Daphne
had been playing with her friend Jason on the teeter-totter.

A last ray of burning rusty light glanced off the monkey
bars, where Wyatt remembered playing, himself, as a kid. The
bars had for some reason been painted a glossy swimming-
pool blue, and Wyatt listened for the call-in of the boys who
were hanging by their knees, and the names were all of heroes
and kings: David and Hector—Hector dangled near the top,
making a sputtering motorboat sound—played together on
one tier, and, beneath them, Arthur and Alexander and Mark
were quarreling about some mutant turtle cards being traded
back and forth.

But not all of the names were familiar. One little girl in a
bright blue outfit was Reesha, and a boy with a cap too small
for his head was, apparently, Roylston. Wyatt thought he
heard Amos being called. Was that possible? What about the
names that made children old as soon as the names were given
out, names like Ezra and Charity, Nehemiah and Dolores?
People became superstitious about certain names during particular eras: Wyatt couldn't remember meeting a single Flora
at any time in his life, though he had known twenty Johns, a
dozen Julies, with no other apparent resemblance among
them. Cyril had been the only Cyril he had ever known. He'd
never met a Loring, and he was the only Wyatt he knew, and
had suffered for it. All through junior high, he had been
Wyatt Earp and sometimes just Urpy. He remembered his
elementary school, with the virtue-names. In his first-grade
class there had been a Joy and a Comfort, and a boy who for
some reason had been Rock. Cartoon names had disappeared,

however: no more Cicero or Petunia or Bugs.

All the children were being called in. Their names rose from the sidelines from the parental chorus—Julio and Taneesha and Barry—and they were gathered up, including Christina.

When he arrived home, he bathed her, astonished by how much grime her body could attract to itself. It was like a blotter. In the tub, she played with her busybox. She didn't notice him scrubbing her back. He couldn't be sure whether she really noticed him at all.

At one-thirty he rose out of bed, ate six cookies in the kitchen, and, after picking up a book of matches, went down to the basement.

He smelled mustiness and mildew. He resolved to buy a dehumidifier. Walking past the Ping-Pong table and the basement alcove with its three chairs and TV, he entered the smallest space in the house, the cubicle where his workbench was, and the tools and the cabinets. To his left were the small eerie rooms inside boxes with which Susan was beginning to occupy her time. She had them out in the open now, where he could see them.

To his right was the large file drawer. He opened it and pulled out four of his father's thoughts.

Trees are holy and don't look like anything except trees.

The dead are very dogmatic about their
empty authority.

I never did see the point in Las Vegas
and no one ever bothered to explain it to me.

Dwight Eisenhower would have failed at simple
tasks, such as teaching high school English or math.
He never explained anything competently.
Military men never do.

He had an ashtray, which he had once taken from a bowl-ing alley. A bowling ball was painted in the inside cup of the ashtray, and the thoughts burned neatly there, on top of the bowling ball. By dropping the ashes of the thoughts into his metal wastebasket, Wyatt was able to burn half the thoughts, after reading them, in forty minutes: he checked his watch.

Nature *loves* a vacuum.

Stars don't belong in the body; it should
always be pitch-dark in there.

Saying goodbye twice: a sign of real friendship.

The odd static energy to be loved by someone
who is not married with one of those alarming smiles
and all the interesting energy of obsession—but I want
her anyway.

He stared at that one a long time before burning it. They had to go, all of them; they weighed on him, not with what they said—not until now—but with their presence. When the drawer was opened, they trembled like living things, paper organisms suddenly exposed to light, his father's secret life, which was no one's business now except Wyatt's. Or was it even his? Who was supposed to read these sentences and make sense out of them? It certainly wasn't for others to discover all those slips of paper with scribbled ideas and half-ideas and whims tucked away down there in a basement drawer. Ellen had kept the papers for Wyatt and had passed them on to him when he'd moved into this house. She claimed she had never read them, but she had probably lied: he recognized statements from her conversation here, in his father's handwriting.

By reading them, remembering them, and burning them to ash, he would keep them safe, hidden away in his mind, like a keepsake.

The second night, just as he was finishing up the task of setting fire to the last remaining slips of paper, a shrill scream began upstairs. The sound went straight into his bones. He ran up the basement stairs toward the noise in the back hall-way, where the smoke detector had been set off: it wailed steadily straight into his face until he pried off its lid and pulled out its battery, leaving the wires dangling. In his boxer shorts, wearing his glasses, Wyatt felt himself shaking. He tried to control his hands by pressing them against his thighs, and then he squatted, fingering the nine-volt battery. The last few thoughts he had burned had been about love, somebody who had been loved, someone who did not seem to be his mother.

"Wyatt, what is it?" Susan called, half asleep, from the bedroom.

"Just changing the battery," he said. "It's okay."

"Come back to bed."

He returned to the basement, wrote "Wait for me" on a slip of paper, put it into an envelope, and addressed it. After he had turned off all the lights and climbed into bed, he felt Susan turning him over. Her skin was hot and dry, and she seemed to be in a hurry. He felt her hands in his hair and her lips moving over his face and chest, and she said, "I had a dream about you," and she took him quickly into herself and began a lapping motion over him.

From her inwardness, and the expression on her face when she opened her eyes and gazed down at him, he knew she was pregnant again and that this was her way of telling him.

12

"What's Maple Meadows?"

Wyatt shrugged and opened a beer. Spring, and the end of another day of demanding pointless work at which he was becoming highly skilled: he felt sloppy and hot and out-of-tune. He sat down in the kitchen to watch Susan stirring onions in a pan. Her other hand was propped awkwardly in the small of her back, a pregnancy posture. "It's a condominium complex," he said. "One of those new ones. Why?"

"I'll tell you in a second." She sneezed. "Damn it," she said, "I sneezed right onto the food. Can onions pass on germs if you're browning them? I don't think so."

"I don't think so, either. Here. Let me do that." He carried his beer over to the stove and pushed her lightly away, after taking the fork out of her hand. Instantly his eyes watered. He had always enjoyed the sensation of watery eyes, false weeping; it never began with feelings but it always brought them on, but right at the level where they could be controlled. "Why are we browning these onions?"

"Because your cousin Cyril called," she said. She obviously enjoyed the look on his face when he turned around to stare at her. "He was almost apologetic. Said he had been bad-tempered. And he's living in a place called Maple Meadows, and he's married now to that Pooh person, and they've got a baby. He said something over the telephone about bygones being bygones, although the way he said it, you had to guess that that was what he meant. Anyway, we're invited over on Saturday, and I think they're serving hot dogs. Hot dogs were implied. I guess we need to get a baby present."

"So. They had their baby? Boy or girl?"

"Otis. A boy. Otis, like the elevator. Otis Cyril Wilson. Not what you'd call a pretty name, but I bet it's not a pretty baby. That's wicked. I shouldn't have said that. He tells me they named him after the singer, what's his name, Otis Redding. What're we going to get them?"

The onions were beginning to sizzle in the preburn stage, and he could hear Christina yelling for something in her room. He reached around for the beer, found it, and took a long swig. He wanted to paint Susan in her late pregnancy, a nude, maybe, with a candle in front of her belly, like one of those Georges de La Tour portraits, but he doubted either one of them had the time for it, and she would probably think that even the idea was tactless—a nude pregnant woman holding a candle.

"You want to pose for me?" He wiped his eyes with a dishtowel. "I've been thinking of doing your portrait. And not just your shadow this time. As a pregnant woman." He took another sip of beer. "You would look so terrific."

"Are you *listening* to me, Wyatt? Cyril and Pooh invited us over. What the hell are we going to get them?"

Standing at his front door, Cyril was almost unrecognizable. He was wearing a white shirt and gray pants with a crease, and his former wild-man haircut had been tamed into a Secretary of the Treasury look, and he gave off a powerful odor of cheap drugstore cologne, of sweetened almonds. But when he grinned, his life-of-riot expression, it was the old Cyril, and Wyatt couldn't help himself: he threw himself forward and gave his cousin a hug.

"Don't give me no kisses," Cyril said gruffly. "It hasn't got that far yet, and it won't."

"Them two are like brothers," Pooh observed, holding Otis and smiling in Susan's direction, her smile fading for a split second at the sight of Susan's pregnancy. "Aren't you a house, though? I don't recollect your telling me."

"Well, I don't think I said." Christina was staring up at the pink bubble emerging from Pooh's mouth, which Otis was trying to pop. Wyatt reached over to touch Otis's hand, and the baby grasped his index finger tightly.

"Hey," he said, "this boy's a strong baby."

"You got yourself a nephew there," Cyril said. He coughed as he lit up a cigarette. "If you and me aren't brothers, then I don't know what you can put in that category except Martians, right? Okay, so we didn't talk on speaking terms there for a few months. I guess it was my fault. That's

what brothers do: argue and sulk. All we did was have ourselves a sulking contest, and I decided to give it to him, after
the fact of him getting me that job." He flicked his head in the
direction of the WaldChem plant, visible to the north, on the
other side of the Maple Meadows access road. "Besides, you
got to see our place because of our new seriousness, me being
a paid employee and all. Come in, you guys. You got to see
what reformed human beings live inside when they get hit
smack in the face with the American Dream. Watch out for
that door there. It sometimes sticks."

They took off their shoes in the front hallway. The white
StainMaster carpeting came up to Wyatt's ankles, and, between Cyril's cigarette smoke and cologne, Wyatt thought he
smelled formaldehyde and particle board. On one side of the
living room, facing the two chairs and the sofa, was a book-
case, on whose top shelf were volumes by R. Stan Drabble:
The Science of Psychic Balance, *The Ancient Source of Power in
You*, *Mastering Your Inner Victim*, *I Know How to Make You
Happy*, and *No Upper Limit to Success*. Sitting-dalmation book-
ends kept the books upright. Cyril extended his right arm and
made a master-of-ceremonies arc toward the room and the
back window. "How about this?" Susan and Pooh had already stepped into the kitchen, where, Wyatt could see,
Susan was lightly putting her fingers to Otis's face. Christina
had turned on the TV set and was already lost in whatever she
was watching.

On the wall just above the TV set was a framed picture of
a man in a business suit. "Who's that?" Wyatt asked. He
hadn't recognized him.

"Let me give you the tour." Cyril was marching up the
stairs. At the top, once Wyatt arrived, he made his grand
gesture again. "*Voilà* the bedrooms, ours over there, and this

one here for Otis." Wyatt was beginning to get a headache from all the white walls and the neatness. Cyril and Pooh's bed had been made so neatly that it might have been in an army barracks; there was no inspection it would not have passed. All the clothes were put away. Next to the bed was a table, a box of tissues, and a clock radio. Above the bed was a painting of a sunset over waves crashing on a visually impossible sandy beach. The whole room looked more like a model home or a stage set than a place where Cyril might live. "Listen," Cyril said. "I'm real sorry I gave you such a hard time in my truck way back when. I was just being a goof-off."

"That's all right. We were both pretty fucked-up that day."

"You shouldn't use that word."

"What?"

"The word you used. The f-word."

"You mean 'fucked'?"

"Yeah. That's the one."

"Cyril, what's gotten into you?"

"I've been reading. You're looking at a new Cyril. I owe it to R/Q Dynamics. I can recommend it. They improved me. Every time you use the f-word, you lower yourself. It's an obscenity. It's the devil in your mind choosing your vocabulary."

"Aw, come on, Cyril. That isn't you. You used that word a million times."

"Yeah. And look where it got me. Come on downstairs." He stubbed out his cigarette in an ashtray next to the bed, then headed down in front of Wyatt, who was beginning to feel that either he or his cousin wasn't there anymore.

In the kitchen, Cyril asked, "Want a cola?"

"Actually, I'd like a beer."

"Sorry. We don't drink. Alcohol just plays living hell

with your alpha and your beta receptors. I'm the expert in that."

Wyatt drank the cola Cyril handed him. "But you still smoke."

"Yeah. I tried quitting that one but I couldn't. Anyway, it takes away the smell of the job. They got smells in that Wald-Chem plant you never smelled in your life because they never was human or animal smells. They are not of this planet, the things they make in there. But, like you say, they pay me, and I work hard, and if I keep working hard, maybe I get promoted. You want to see the basement, my man?"

In the basement: the washer-dryer, the furnace, the water heater, the washtubs, the wires and beams and the pipes, the circuit-breaker box, and the windows. There was one back door leading out to the tiny enclosed backyard. Wyatt asked Cyril where all his stuff was, and Cyril said there wasn't any— he'd thrown it all out, he said, his face full of pride—and he went back upstairs. Wyatt felt himself ready to shout: everything was new here. The house was new, the baby was new, and even Cyril himself was new. There was no sign of the old Cyril at all, except for the cigarettes. Where had he taken himself to? Wyatt trudged upstairs to the kitchen, where Susan and Pooh were laying out plates for the hot dogs and the potato salad and the cola.

During the dessert of Jell-O and Reddi Wip, Wyatt asked Pooh if she was still a contact-paper decorator, and she said, "Of course not. That was for amateurs." She opened her nursing bra, and Otis reached toward her nipple. Wyatt looked over toward Susan, her hands clasped under her belly, and then toward Pooh and Cyril, and he felt himself spinning backwards, moving far away, but when he turned toward Cyril, he saw for a moment an expression on Cyril's face, a brief split second of skepticism, like the false movement of an actor who has suddenly had a break in concentration and fallen momentarily out of the part he is playing. It made Wyatt smile with pure happiness, seeing it, but Cyril turned away to cough, as if he wanted to pretend it hadn't happened.

"See the lawn?" Cyril asked. "I even bought a lawn mower."

They gave Cyril and Pooh their presents after the meal. The politeness was so thick on both sides that Wyatt couldn't tell what anyone was thinking, and in his gloom he announced loudly and with false heartiness that now they had to go.

Cyril appeared to be relieved and stood up immediately. "Well, you come back soon. We won't argue anytime ever again about anything. That I can promise you."

"He's turned into a robot," Wyatt said in the car. "Damn his politeness."

"He's not a robot. He just cleaned himself up."

"Cleaned himself up? He's not there. Cyril is *gone*."

"Pooh says it's because he doesn't drink."

"That wasn't Cyril, that was a pod. A polite conservative go-getting pod."

She snuggled next to him. "You just wanted a private cause."

"That's not it."

"Oh, it isn't? I think it is. I think Cyril was a little colony you supported, and you liked it. You thought his failure made him an individual. And a dependent."

He shook his head. "No. No. It wasn't the dependency I liked. He was such a mess. He was disreputable. He was fun. Cyril isn't fun anymore." He felt himself clenching his jaw muscles. "Who was that person in that picture on the wall above the TV set, anyway?"

"I asked Pooh. It's a picture of R. Stan Drabble."

"R/Q Dynamics. You know, I couldn't breathe in there. But Otis was nice."

"Otis was beautiful."

"*You* like babies."

"I liked him." She inhaled. "But it's true. I *do* like babies."

"They're going to raise him to be an accountant."

"What did you want, Wyatt?" She sat up and hit him twice, lightly, on the arm. "Did you want him back in jail? Taking money from you? Getting into drugs or whatever? Wandering the streets? Your own little private fuck-up fantasy?"

"Don't talk that way in front of Christina," he said.

"You see? Now *you* sound like him. Don't forget: you helped him get that job. You helped bring those jobs here. I don't see what your problem is."

"He used to be fun," Wyatt said. "I want him back."

Wyatt thought maybe he could do a nude portrait of Susan in her pregnancy, without her having to pose for him, and he did manage to sketch in her face—she had let her hair fall down over her shoulders, and he caught in her expression one of her characteristic moods of untroubled introspection—but he found he couldn't recognize in what he was drawing the breasts and torso of his wife. With her pregnancy, her proportions had changed to such a degree that his hands could be surprised when he rested them on her skin at night; also, his maniacal precision was unsuited to the portrait of a woman in her eighth month.

But his real difficulty was that it was no one's business how her body looked, not even, or particularly, his own; it was too private a matter for any art.

In his portrait, before he gave it up, Susan's face rested above a body of sketched-in, tentative charcoal lines.

Alyse had stood in his doorway and said, "Wait for you? How long?" and he had his hands open, and out, and she had turned quickly and neatly and walked back to her office.

Susan had been working on one of her miniature rooms—a motel lobby with a dusty indifferent chair and one table with a tiny permanently closed magazine, and, on the other side of the room, near the fox-and-hounds picture, a tiny unplugged vacuum cleaner—when the contractions began. This time the labor eased its way through the breathing exercises, which worked this time, as they had not before, with Christina's birth. Throughout the first four hours she seemed to Wyatt to be in a state of painful exaltation. She had a look on her face of excited extremity, and it embarrassed him, because he had seen that expression many times before, when they had made love together, and it was how she gazed at him just before she closed her eyes.

It was the opposite of anonymity: he was *known* to her, at these moments, every one of his defects and virtues, every hair, every gesture. He was comprehended by that look.

In the delivery room, she yelped twice as the baby was emerging, and Wyatt, for just a moment, thought of apologizing for her, and then was ashamed of himself.

From between Susan's legs Wyatt saw the face of his father brought into the air and light of the delivery room. For two days the baby had a curiously middle-aged facial contour even when asleep, of world-weariness, a ghost remnant of some other life. After a week, he lost that aura and became himself.

All the same, they named him Eugene.

13

The first time Ellen knew that Cyril wasn't himself came at the middle of August, when she saw him in the
poultry barn at the Five Oaks County Fair. He was leaning on
a railing in front of several cages of Wyandotte hens and was
coughing into the sleeve of his army surplus shirt. Ellen had
planted herself across the aisle, observing a prize-winning
Rhode Island Red—its first-place ribbon had been tacked to

the table just underneath its cage—and she was puzzling over the odd combination of arrogance and stupidity on its face. She wouldn't have given *this* chicken a prize, herself, she was thinking, when she looked above and past its cage and saw a tall pale slender man whose loud liquid hacking rose audibly over the clucking and crowing. After a moment, Ellen recognized the man as Cyril.

His skin had whitened, and he appeared to have gone on a diet, the wrong kind, sold by one of those TV salesmen wearing glasses and a white smock. Pooh and the new baby, Otis, weren't with him, and he was standing all by himself, on a Friday afternoon, feigning an interest in pullets but actually coughing, here in this place smelling of cement and feed and dung. On his face was a preoccupied inward-turning expression made shadowy by the glaring overhead barn light bulbs.

Ellen bestirred herself, and after giving the Rhode Island Red a judgmental frown, she turned a corner around the roosters and Muscovy ducks and made her way toward Cyril. Standing on his left, she watched him for five seconds before she tugged at his sleeve.

"Hey, handsome," she said. "You got any chewing gum?" Before he could turn toward her, she had hugged him in her domineering-aunt manner, a style she thought he was used to. With herself pressed against him—the hug was sincere, but she also wanted to feel how thin he was, and she didn't like what she felt—she could detect his ribs against his jacket. Next to her right ear she could hear his breath, a shallow snuffle.

By the time she had pulled herself away from him, he had transformed himself: on his face was the widest of grins, and what she thought had been his pale complexion had somehow colored, so that his face had bloomed into a halfway shade of pink. Not the picture of health, exactly, but better. "Hey, doll," he said, holding both her hands. "You wanna go dancin'?"

"Sure. Where?"

"Naw. I was just kidding." Now it was his turn to look at her. Bird admirers milled around them. "How're you doin'? Added a few pounds here and there, I see. How come you don't visit us no more? You haven't seen us since Otis was born. I guess you're too busy making those goor-may dinners of yours, am I right?" He pinched a modest bulge at her waist.

She slapped his hand away. "My life keeps me occupied just fine." She reached for his elbow and piloted him out of the poultry barn onto the path outside, muddy from last night's rain. Rains always fell on state and county fairs. It was some sort of law. "I haven't visited because you and that Pooh of yours haven't invited me, and single people don't go where they're not invited. They're sensitive about such things. And by the way, I may have gained weight, but you look like something the cat *and* the dog dragged in. What's happened to you? You quit eating or something?"

Cyril shaded his eyes against the late-afternoon sun. "Ellen, you want to go to the sheep barn or to the hogs? I saw the cattle already. Some great-looking Holsteins here, big guys, you should check this prize beef. And how about the pigs? You seen the pigs?"

"No."

"So let's go."

"I don't like pigs. They always sound as if they're speaking Swedish."

"These ones don't speak Swedish. These ones are Americans. These pigs speak the native tongue."

He took off, without her having agreed to it. Frightened and annoyed, she followed him, making her way around a family, the daughter licking a Slurpee, that had blocked her view of Cyril's narrow back.

Here and there in the pig barn, some of the teenaged boys whose pigs these were sat on rickety chairs in the stalls near their animals, while others cleaned out the straw. The rest sat close to the east door, muttering and laughing. The sight of farm boys with their stand-up hair, noisy settledness, and habit of conversing with their animals, always struck Ellen in the heart. It was so brief, this moment of male sweetness before the donning of the armor.

"Listen," Cyril said, pointing toward a grunting sow. "Hear that? What does that sound like to you?"

"Like an after-dinner speech at the Rotary Club."

"Well, exactly what I'm saying. These pigs speak American."

"Let's go see the sheep," Ellen said. "They have interesting ways."

"I see sheep every day. Oh yeah, speaking of sheep: how's your Bible going? You made it up to the Flood yet, or all those begats? How about a Savior? You got one of those? How's all your, what d'you call it, evidence?"

"Don't criticize my hobby. Besides, there isn't going to be a Flood," Ellen said. "And as for the evidence, there's always plenty of that." She peered at him. "For example, you. How come you're here, Cyril? Why aren't you at your job?"

"It's a day off. County Fair day, is what it is." She knew he was lying. He was almost her son, so she could tell. She had to press charges against him.

"Cyril, you don't look so hot. What's the matter with you?"

"Me and Pooh've been on a diet. That's how come. You want a teddy bear? I'll win you a prize, and you can put it in your Bible. Come on."

221

He was grinning now, his old soul-of-the-party trickster look. After pulling her toward the midway area and a shooting gallery—where, because Cyril always had been a dead shot, he won for her a huge white fuzzy teddy bear with WALDO stitched on its front—he acted the part of a healthy man. Standing under the awning, his cheekbones protruding on this side of the pellet rifle, he methodically and swiftly pinged down the moving ducks, the sitting ducks, the twirling corncob pipes, the jeering briefly visible clowns, the tugboats, and the little cars; and, watching him, Ellen, without knowing how she knew, knew he was dying.

Then they argued. Cyril, waving his arms and grinning again so that his skull seemed visible at all points, insisted that he buy her a ticket for the Barrel of Monkeys, a ride that twirled you around, turned you sideways, and then dropped the floor out from under your feet. Ellen found the prospect of this experience unappealing. Nor was she particularly interested in the other rides—the Alpine Snake, the Scrambler, the Mexican Hat Dance, and the Mixmaster—despite Cyril's praise for them. She admitted that the Haunted House, with its little cars and mechanical screams, was more to her taste. Having extracted this agreement from her, Cyril strode off to the ticket booth, leaving her next to the cotton-candy concession.

Dinnertime, and all the couples and children arriving in the sticky and humid air smelling of sugar syrup: she turned toward the west, the sun behind a thin sheeting of clouds, and let a heartlessly brief north breeze blow on her face. As she stood with her eyes closed, letting the cool air pass, she smelled again the scent of the animals in their barns close by, the paint-and-metal of the tractors on Machinery Hill, and the sticky sweetness of the recreational food being sold behind her. The mechanical arm of the cotton-candy machine whirled and oscillated simultaneously, spreading the pink silky fluff out into the air and then collecting it. A high school couple walked by, talking of Jesus. The boy's arm was around his girl's waist, and her hand was stuffed into the back pocket of his jeans. They had the blank stunned look of lovers, and Ellen felt herself begin to cry, little sobbing angry gulps lifting out of her chest into her throat and watering her eyes. Instantly she composed herself, was Ellen again, watching the couples loitering hand in hand, the sooty men and straggling nagging older women on their way toward places she had already been to. The cotton-candy machine's arms whirled and spun. She watched the fairgoers pass, their faces lit with expectancy of having a moderately good time and being cheated out of a reasonable amount of money.

Everybody is so stupid here, she said in her heart. I can't stand it. They let everything happen to them, and then they just don't complain for a minute.

"Here," Cyril said, creeping up next to her and waving a string of tickets in her face. "Time to take you on some thrill rides. You ain't never had enough thrills, lady."

"I have had too many goddamn thrills, Cyril, for one lifetime, I'm here to tell you."

"Well, it's time for another thrill then. With me. Come on—"

Suddenly he broke out into a series of liquid coughs, half coughs, half spasms. He bent over and dropped the ride tickets into the dirt. He put his hands on his knees and propped himself there, while Ellen glanced quickly at the fairgoers to see if anyone looked, even a bit, like a health-care professional, as people called them now. She retrieved the tickets, reached around Cyril, and guided him back toward the pig barn, outside of which was a water fountain. Cyril continued to cough just inside the front entryway, and Ellen saw one of the pigs lift itself up from its straw to observe Cyril, the origin of the noise.

This pig, Ellen thought, knows exactly what's going on.

When Cyril had finished, and had wiped the water from his eyes with his sleeve, he said, "Bronchitis. I got a little touch of walking bronchitis." He patted his chest with his index finger. His face was bright red. "Haven't been able to shake it. Guess I should've cut out those cigarettes a long time ago, right?" He said this sentence between in-sucks of breath.

"Cyril, that's no bronchitis." She was helplessly patting him on the back.

"Phlegm. Phlegm is all it is. Don't pay it no mind." He went for a drink of water, and when he came back, he said, "Okay. Which one of these here rides are we gonna do first?"

"We aren't going to do any rides at all. We're taking you home."

He shook his head and took the tickets out of her hand. "You buy the tickets, you take the ride. That's how it is."

"Don't feel like it," she said.

"You're pooping the party. Don't you start queening it now all over me."

"I'm *not* queening it," she said. "I'm fifty-nine years old. I don't have to sit down in a threatening chair if I don't care to."

"Well," Cyril said, rubbing his chin, "since you're so *careful* and everything, you come along and watch me, make sure I don't die on one of these gizmos."

Off he went, striding like a man whose masculinity is at stake, in the direction of the Mexican Hat Dance. A fair employee who looked like a gangster took Cyril's tickets and put him, alone, on a car before lowering the safety bar. Cyril's car was connected to a central octopus arm that lifted him, spun him around, and dropped him, while a metal loudspeaker played "La Cucaracha" performed by an orchestra of, it seemed, tinfoil instruments played by scorpions. Cyril endured the fun with a tight determined smile.

When he was out again, standing unsteadily but still smiling that same smile, he said, "Now we take you into the Haunted House."

"Now we don't take me anywhere. What in the living hell are you *doing* here, Cyril? You aren't answering a single one of my questions."

"You're a fool, Ellen," he said, his gaze gliding over her. "You're an old woman and a fool. And you're spoiling my fun. That's a fact."

She felt herself clenching her fists. "Don't you talk that way to me, you dumb son of a bitch. Don't you go on. The only fool here is two feet away, and it's looking me in the face."

"All right, all right."

They stood there, staring at anything within sight. "I'm sorry," she said at last. "You're such a dope, you get me upset. You're my boy, that's all. You want some popcorn?"

"Naw." He was fingering the tickets with one hand and had taken out his comb and was parting his Secretary of the Treasury slicked-down hair with the other. "Listen," he said, "I just always did this. I always came to these places, these fairs. There was always fun here. Still is."

The sun, having embarked toward the horizon, gave her no hope, and in the air a dispiriting scent of caramel corn and burning leaves blew past her. Couples covered with ragged clothes and dust mingled interchangeably in the public spaces in front of and behind her.

"There isn't any fun here now," she said.

"Sure, there is," he said, in his old voice. "There's always fun." He took her hand and led her toward the Haunted House, where he gave eight tickets to a roustabout with a screaming-eagle tattoo on his biceps and who smelled of brine. Cyril and Ellen sat themselves down on a cart; the roustabout lowered the safety bar over them; and the cart started up over its track with a noise like a broken starter motor. It lurched toward a set of double doors, banged into them, and flew into darkness.

The mechanical terror of the Haunted House was oddly comforting. The little cart swung around on its tracks past poorly recorded screams, skulls lit with flickering orange bulbs, and tattered ghosts made of something between plastic and vinyl. They dropped down wearily on metal rods. Well, Ellen thought, I guess it's a job like any other, frightening people. Someone sobbed. She clutched her bear, the one with WALDO stitched on it. A bat on a wire swooped past her, sounding like the compressor on her refrigerator, but there was, somewhere far in back of her, and yet almost inside her head, a chirping bird, a real one, an actual bird trapped in the Haunted House. The cart clunked and clattered its way into a cobweb drawn over two doors. The doors parted, but their cart still advanced in jovial artificial darkness. What a funny ride, she thought gloomily, as they turned past a weary dancing skeleton. She saw the double doors leading out—light was seeping from underneath them—and she heard a big, male laugh from a loudspeaker, a boomingly unbenign ho-ho-ho, and that did at last give her a bit of a start, that laughter, because she had heard men laugh like that in her presence at meetings, at parties, everywhere.

The cart made one last turn, away from the exit doors. A few more skulls and monsters groaned their way into visibility and then sank back gratefully into unemployment. Well, she thought, for four tickets it's not bad. Then she turned to see

Cyril: his eyes were closed, and he was smiling. She saw, in the bawling half-light, his calm happiness at being in the dark, at not being looked at, and she reached out for his hand.

She was afraid his skin would be cold. But no: it was still warm, and Cyril turned his face toward her, opened his eyes, and smiled his little-devil smile as the cart banged its way out into the dusk.

14

On a Monday morning in February, having ar-
rived so early that almost no one else was in the building,
Wyatt was standing in his office doorway and feeling sullen
about his drab curtains and gray wallpaper. They were cheap.
They gave the wrong impression, sent the wrong signal. I
may be a bureaucrat, he thought, but if I'm going to work
here for another . . . well, for x period of time, I need to fix
this place up.

A halfhearted blizzard blew tiny white snow-filings against the window. With the darkness of the storm outside, and his office lights on, he saw his reflection in the window, snow swirling in Brownian motion over his own face, and the image startled him.

The next day, he carried in one of Susan's studies for a domestic stage-set box, the one of the hotel lobby done in browns and dark forest greens. It wasn't meant to be in the easy sinister style of Hopper, a cliché anyway, she had said, but more interesting, like something by Reginald Marsh. Where had she heard of *him?* Maybe she'd been reading. Wyatt didn't get the part about the room being sinister: he thought the painting was comforting, all those overstuffed chairs, that empty space, those clean ashtrays painted in with a few strokes.

Oh, well, she said, holding Eugene, who was asleep, that's because you're the sort of man who likes hotel lobbies. That's the sort of man you've turned into. Not that I mind. It's just a fact.

He brought in a rug from New York Carpet World and put it under his desk. Near the window, he put up a framed map of the New York City subway system. Alyse would come in and quiz him playfully about the stops; she never stumped him. He thought he would have to load a gun and point it at himself before he would know why Alyse wanted him, but he enjoyed flirting with her, and it passed the time.

He was beginning to feel competent. He couldn't help it: he had filled out so many forms and spoken and shouted to so many subcontractors and stooges in governmental regulatory agencies that he now believed that not just anyone could do what he did. He would stand at the window during his coffee breaks and watch the pedestrians scurrying along the sidewalks, and a slow steady feeling of I'm-in-charge would steal over him.

Month by month the population of the city was growing. Everyone was pleased with his work. Per capita income was up, probably—all their surveys were informal. The new businesses—WaldChem, CMB Inventory Systems, ElectroServ —were "magnetizing," as they liked to say, workers and managers into the city. The city storm and sanitary sewers would soon be overloaded, and crime, too, was creeping upward in its slow and stately manner. With the urban omelet, a few broken eggs. But there wasn't much he didn't have under personal control, his family, his job, his flirtations. That was what a good job and a marriage were for, to turn obsession into productivity.

Just before lunchtime, he was standing on a chair. The door was closed, and no one would see him. The tops of the curtains needed adjusting. His mind slipped into some thought of his son, and he lost his balance. As he fell, his arms windmilling, he knocked against the side of his desk before he dropped to the floor.

In the middle of the pain, lying on the rug from New York Carpet World, he wondered if Alyse had heard him fall and would come running into the room and kiss him where it hurt. He groaned. Pain and fantasy were a terrible combination. He touched his suit to check for rips. He couldn't find any, though he thought for a moment that they must be there, invisible. As he stood, he felt an odd wobbling pain on his right side, just above the hip. Probably just a bruise, he thought, touching it.

His knees were shaking. He walked around the room, and the pain in his side flared up like a lighted match. He looked down several floors at the sidewalk and saw a woman wearing a yellow hat, and at the sight of her he felt the pain diminish.

For that moment, he was pleased to be himself and no one else.

The phone rang. It was Cyril, whom he hadn't seen or talked to in months, since his cousin had gone straight. His voice had a rough edge. "So," he said, "how come you haven't called me?"

"Why should I call you? You're doing okay."

"I'm your cousin. I'm almost your brother. That's something."

"Well, you haven't called me, either."

"That's true. That's always true. You always say the true thing." Cyril waited. "But this is different. You're not checking up on me."

"Why should I? You're Mr. Respectable. You're Mr. Family Man."

"You mean you didn't hear about me?"

"Heard what?"

"I'm sick."

"With what?"

"The biggest one they got, that's what. I got cancer."

The woman in the yellow hat had turned a corner; Wyatt couldn't see her anymore. The pain in his side flared up again, then died away. "What did you say?" Wyatt asked, and then what Cyril had told him finally registered in his mind, and it was as if some magnetic charge coursed through him, reversing the direction of his poles. "What?" he said. "Where? What did you say?"

"You heard me," Cyril said, a thoughtful expression in his voice. "The Big Casino."

"Where?"

"It's lung cancer. It's in the lungs, all over the tubulets or whatever they call them. Also, it's spread into those places that're hard to pronounce."

"Aw fuck." Wyatt sat in his chair, and it let out a wheeze.

"Don't use that word," Cyril said.

"All right." A migraine headache instantly struck Wyatt, electricity tearing through a leaf, and departed as quickly as it had come. He felt as if random electrical charges were firing through his office. "What're they going to do for it?"

"They aren't going to do anything."

"No, I mean, like, chemotherapy and radiation, or what?"

"They aren't going to do anything."

"What do you mean, 'They aren't going to do anything'?"

"It's real advanced. So I told them, forget it. They're not going to experiment on me like some monkey."

"What does that mean?"

"It means," Cyril said patiently, "that they can delay the conclusion of this thing but they can't stop it."

"How do you know? You're no doctor."

"Doctors. Millionaires in smocks. You trust those buzzards?"

"Jesus, Cyril."

"I was thinking," Cyril said. "I was thinking I should take you out to lunch."

"When? What? What're you talking about, lunch? You seem awfully cheerful, Cyril. I mean, my God."

"I was always a cheerful guy. I'm not cheerful now but I'm determined. Therefore I am okay."

"You're not okay, Cyril, you're dying." He said it, then was sorry he had said it.

"Well, I know, but I got an attitude about it."

"What attitude is that?"

"I'll explain at lunch. Where should we meet?"

"You're talking about today? Well, all right. I can miss a

meeting. You want to go to Chez Steak?"

"That place? That businessman's hangout? If you say so. I'll see you there . . . how soon? Twenty minutes?"

"All right. I don't know, Cyril. I just fell off a chair. My head's sort of out of joint, and I don't have—"

"Yeah, right. You can be a bad boy for once. Be late for everything this afternoon, why don't you? I got some things to tell you."

"What kinds of things?"

Cyril coughed. "Twenty minutes," he said.

On his way to the table, groping through the broiled-meat aroma and half-lit passageways of the restaurant, Wyatt felt the pain in his side again—this time it was like a rubber pitchfork, a kind of jokey pain—and he stopped for a moment to steady himself against the salad bar. He looked down through the transparent sneeze guard into the trays. He recognized the cottage cheese, the onions, the lettuce, bacon bits, chick peas, and—what were those? seeds of some kind?—but the other foods he didn't recognize at all: one bowl seemed to contain pencil erasers; another, small nails and screws fried in deep fat; a third, imitation pearls.

A waitress with deep brown eyes smiled a sexy smile in his direction, meant for him generically as a customer but not specifically as an individual. The hostess was pulling out his chair for him and handing him a large laminated lunch menu. He needed a drink. Leaning toward him, her perfume poking a hole in his thoughts with the aromatic promise of a late-afternoon assignation she might have with someone else but not with him, she took his order for a Scotch-rocks and disappeared into the red-meat dark. Wyatt's thoughts were floating like little helium balloons just above his head. He scanned the menu. Meat and more meat, veal, three scoops of potatoes, with a tasty gravy made of flour and bouillon cubes for $8.45.

What do I hear for this human being? Going, going, gone. . . .

He put down the laminated menu, feeling his fingers glide over several sticky residues of food or human extrusion on the tablecloth. He peered across the dark at a table on the other side of the aisle. A young man sat slumped there, his index finger hooked down into his water glass, stirring the ice cubes around. He was wearing a black turtleneck shirt and blue jeans, and now, suddenly, he turned slowly to gaze in Wyatt's direction, his head pivoting like a closed-circuit camera in a bank, and after they exchanged glances, the young man raised his eyebrows: a question. Yes? Or no?

Wyatt tried to turn away. I'm being cruised? Here in Chez Steak? What does that mean? Does it mean anything? Where's Cyril? He concentrated on the menu. To his present knowledge, there had never been anything on this menu he had wanted to eat. He felt the young man's eyes on him. Do I look gay? Is that it? Where's my goddamn drink? My cousin is dying and someone in this restaurant is trying to stare into my soul where *no* one has a right to look, not even me, and—

The lights appeared to flicker. The first stop on the A train south of Seventy-second Street is Fifty-ninth, Wyatt thought, in an effort to calm himself. He looked up, after his menu had briefly blacked out, but now the lights were steady again, apparently, but the young man across the aisle had vanished, as if he'd never been slouched there with his inappropriate prettiness and his raised eyebrows and his sympathy. A Scotch on the rocks was located near Wyatt's right hand, and he reached out for it gratefully, and took a drink, and closed his eyes, and when he opened them again, there was Cyril, standing in front of him, grinning.

He looked like walking death. He hadn't just lost weight,

he had disposed of the mass of his body somewhere, and his shell had sauntered in on two legs and stood amused at the shock registering on Wyatt's face.

"Cyril."

"You look surprised."

"I *am* surprised."

"Can I sit down?"

"Well, sure." Wyatt pulled back the chair next to him.

"No, I think I'll sit across from you, over here, where I can see you."

Once seated, Cyril smirked and leaned back. "So. How do I look?"

"Jesus, Cyril."

"That's what I thought. Not so hot, huh?"

"Not so hot."

"Compared to how I feel, how I look is not so bad. But it's not actually painful, not *painful* painful, more like something's wrong, it's a strangeness-feeling, you know? Helluva deal."

Wyatt tried not to stare. He groped for something to say and found his mind empty of sentences. Erasers were busily at work. Outside, it would still be snowing. Weeks and weeks of snow had been intent on covering up everything. "How's Pooh? How's Otis?"

"Well, now," Cyril said, sticking his finger into the water glass in exactly the way the young now-vanished man across the aisle had done, stirring the drinking water, "that's the one thing I can't get used to. My boy hasn't grown up and already I miss him. I miss his future. He's a little heartbreaker. Bet you thought you'd never hear me say such things."

"Hmm."

Cyril sat up. "Can you believe this? Me? Sick? It's too weird to be realistic. Fucking-A."

"I always thought reality was pretty weird. And I thought you didn't swear anymore."

"It's not swearing exactly. It's more like taking an oath." He took his finger out of his water glass and sucked it, closing his eyes when he swallowed. "But you're right. I said I wouldn't do it, and I should stick to that. Did you order anything?"

Wyatt shook his head, then picked up his Scotch and rattled the ice cubes in it.

"Let's have a feast here." Cyril raised his arm to the waitress, an action that sent him off into a fit of coughing. He bent over and brought a handkerchief to his mouth, and when he was finished, he tucked the handkerchief away before Wyatt could see it.

"Cyril."

"What?"

His cousin was looking at him now, an incongruously relaxed expression showing past the gauntness, and Wyatt felt the lights flicker in the restaurant as he groped for the correct sentence to throw into the yawning and possibly hungry void. "Cyril, I don't know how to talk about any of this."

"Yeah, well." He tapped the table. "Two men, right?"

"Huh?"

"Two men talking."

"What about it?" Wyatt asked.

"Well, you know how, well, anyway, Pooh says that men can't talk."

"About what?"

"Pain and death and love and that sort of thing."

"She says that?"

"Yeah. That's what she says."

"How is she?"

"She's sort of upset." His trace of a smile disappeared. "She's not feeling so hot herself. Otis keeps her pretty busy."

"Cyril, have you got any insurance?"

"On my life? You better believe it. I have got my white trash ass insured up to here. I started work at WaldChem, I took everything I could get. If Pooh don't spend it all in one place, she and Otis'll have it made."

"I guess." Wyatt took a long emptying slug of his Scotch. "Are you in pain?"

"I explained this to you already."

"Oh. Right. So, are you scared?"

Cyril nodded. "You bet."

Wyatt nodded in agreement, and they sat there, listening to the Muzak, as the lights began to flicker again. "I don't know if men can talk or not."

"Wyatt, brother, I would like to discuss with you what men can't do—that'd take a book the size of the Sears catalogue—but I got what they call an agenda with me."

"Yeah? What's your agenda?"

"Where's the waitress? I can't do my waitress without . . . no, I mean I can't do my agenda unless the waitress, she comes over here and takes my order, because we're going to do a feast, you know? That's plan number one, plan A."

"What's plan number two?"

"I am going to explain to you about WaldChem. Which is run by your buddy."

"What about WaldChem?"

He looked at Wyatt. "It's how come I'm dying. It's about how come they killed me."

"You're still here."

"Don't be a goof. Not for long, I'm not. That's what I am about to explain this to you."

· · ·

He ordered the roast beef luncheon plate for himself with the French onion soup on the side and the Chez Side Salad, and before Wyatt could order for himself, Cyril, in his most commanding manner, ordered the Veal Oscar for his cousin with the soup of the day, cream of cauliflower. "We must have the Too Chez dessert, when we're ready," he told the waitress. "And the best beer you got, like St. Pauli Girl or that other one they make over there, Hitler Brau or something, I don't remember the name."

The waitress shrugged and walked over to the kitchen.

"They live in a strange twilight world, these service people," Cyril said, "but she's got a nice ass on her all the same." This sentence seemed to tire him out, and he sat back in his chair and said nothing. To cheer him up, Wyatt—feeling a bit tired himself just now and bothered by the bruise in his side—told Cyril that he remembered one of his girlfriends, one that Cyril had gone out with when he was fifteen, who worked as a carhop at the Smack Drive-in: Mandy, her name was, and she had looked a lot like this waitress.

"Yeah," Cyril said. "She used to say we were immortal. I thought she meant 'immoral' but I was wrong. Well I guess we weren't immortal after all. She had a ponytail and she'd yell when we were, like, having intimacies. She was the first girl I loved that I could tell her that. About love, I mean. She used to suck on my fingers. I carved her name on my forearm with a kitchen knife, so it'd scar there. I was fifteen years old. It was my midlife crisis."

"What happened to her?"

Cyril shrugged. "She moved away. You don't know what happens to people. They don't even know what happens to them."

He hadn't opened his eyes during all this time, and even

though he was speaking, he was now leaning forward as if taking a nap, so that when the waitress brought their food, he appeared to be asleep. Cyril smelled the dishes and opened his eyes partway.

"Smells good," Cyril said, just above a whisper. "I'm just not sure I'm hungry."

"You don't feel hungry? I thought you ordered all this."

"I did that. It feels different now."

"How does it feel?"

"Like I got this bar around my chest. This iron bar that it keeps me from breathing almost."

"You don't mind if I eat?"

"That's the idea. You go ahead. Maybe I'll just take a little catnap."

And as Wyatt watched, Cyril slept. "Cyril," he said, under his breath, but Cyril didn't awaken. Wyatt glanced around the restaurant. Across the aisle, the young man had returned and was gazing steadily and a bit quizzically now in Wyatt's direction. Suddenly, from behind a wall, there erupted the sound of a tray loaded with dishes, glasses, and flatware crashing to the floor, followed by the higher frequencies of glass breaking and the high, momentary cry of the waitress. Two fat men on the other side of the dining area began to applaud.

"Dig in," Cyril said, his eyes still closed. "Chow down."

"You're awake."

"Of course I'm awake."

"But your eyes are closed."

"You ever closed your eyes when you were awake?"

"I seem to remember a few times."

"Well, that's what we're talking about here. My eyes are closed but my mind is open. You just go ahead and eat your Veal Oscar that you got there. Lucky that your lunch wasn't on that tray. You'd be eating off the floor right now. You'd be late for all those important appointments you got."

"They can wait."

"That's the spirit," Cyril said, opening his eyes to look briefly at Wyatt. "You know, I still got that scar."

"The Mandy scar?"

"Right. That one. But it's fading. What it was, though, I wanted to be branded with her name on my hide. Like a steer. If they'd had one of those red-hot iron brands, I'd've taken that, a permanent love ID. You aren't eating."

Wyatt had dabbed at his salad but so far had been unable to launch the meat on his plate into his mouth. It had a slightly fleshy appearance.

"You seen Aunt Ellen?"

"Not just lately," Wyatt said.

"She's up there at the house carrying on with her Bible and getting angrier every day at God, and right now she's about to let Him have it."

"She doesn't think He's a Him, she thinks He's an It."

"Whatever. My getting this malignancy is the last straw, in her opinion. She's got a grudge against the Powers That Be. But it's not the gods that did this to me. That's where she's wrong. She always stuck her head in a bag on that one. It's something else."

Wyatt pushed the food around on his plate to give the impression that some of it had been interfered with. "What is it?" he asked.

"That's what I'm about to tell you," Cyril said. "It's like I'm the messenger that's come with the news of the battle. I got the wound, too, so I'm the proof." He coughed again into his handkerchief.

"What? What is it?"

"Good. I was just seeing if you were paying attention."

"I'm paying attention."

"Good," Cyril said. Wyatt looked across the aisle. The young man had disappeared again. Maybe he was an angel visiting from the celestial ranks. "I don't know all the things they make at work. I mean, they don't tell *us*. It's, like, secret? These things, they look like worms, the plastics, and the others, they're like rhomboids. Of course I just clean up. All the messes they make, when they're pouring things into containers, I mop up afterwards and suchlike."

Cyril opened his eyes and reached out for a fork. He picked it up and pointed the tines toward Wyatt. "Anyway, you go in the plant in the morning. The place smells like something died in there, but not something from Earth, something dead from Mars. The only thing I ever smelled that was like that was a Big Mac. This smell, it hits you and hurts you, it burns in your nostrils, and you get dizzy. You get dizzy right away, smelling this smell. But you figure, well, I'm *working,* right? I'm just an American, and I got this rare thing, an American job. What the hell, I was dizzy all the time in high school, but that was from the beer and the cigarettes and the all-night fun.

"So anyway, you go to work and get dizzy. Then you start coughing. The women, they've been sort of coughing more than the men, but most of them, they only cough while they're in the place, and, see, nobody's complaining because everybody's been unemployed so long around here that they don't want to mess anything up. You're not eating."

"Yes, I am," Wyatt said, trying to laugh. He took a big bite of veal.

"That's better. This is a celebration it's supposed to be. We got carte blanched. So anyway, the last couple of months there's this other thing they got going in the plant you haven't heard about, back to the story I was telling."

"What's that?"

"Pink fog. You go in there, and the air's okay for part of the morning, and then, on some days, depending on what they're making, the air starts to turn this sort of pink color, it'd be pretty if it was anywhere else, and they got masks if you want to wear them. Other days the air's got this yellow color, and on some days, it's worse. It's goddamn *blue*. I've heard of blue sky but I never heard of blue air until now. The girls've been saying it's part of the material mix that goes in when you make the mold, but all I know is, I've been breathing it."

"This is illegal," Wyatt said. "You should call OSHA."

"You're silly and you're a bureaucrat and you're naive," Cyril said. "I haven't even told you about the drains and the discharges and the barrels we send down to Mexico, where they like you to dispose of things, on account of it's their major income, using their country as a dump."

"The EPA supervises all that," Wyatt said. "This is all controlled. There are laws."

"Fool," Cyril said. "You think everybody's got dignity and ethics and all that stuff. That's just you. That's what you've got. Nobody else has got it. This is modern life we're talking about now. We're TV babies. It's cut-and-run time, pal, brother."

"Listen, Cyril," Wyatt said. He was trying to focus all his attention on the question he was about to ask, and he was concentrating on the gaunt figure of Cyril so that Cyril could answer him clearly. He wasn't sure that he would ever get a chance like this again. "Are you saying that they made you sick? Is that what you're telling me? And that they're making other people sick?"

"That's right," Cyril said. "They killed me. I am dead right now."

"And the others?"

"The other workers? They feel lousy too, only they aren't saying much, on account of their wages are good. And you know how it is with whistle-blowers. I ain't no whistle-blower, buddy. Those people get their houses bombed, and their cars pushed off the road and all that other fine American fun."

"So what do you want me to do?"

The air in Chez Steak all at once stopped circulating, and the lights flickered, as they had all through lunch, but this time almost as if they were twinkling, like Christmas lights, and when Wyatt turned to look at the other patrons of the restaurant, their forks, holding their food, appeared to be suspended in their hands, just like one of those science-fiction stories where time stops for a moment: but it *does* stop, Wyatt thought, it does stop every now and then, everyone knows that, and you yourself can move *inside* your body, but your body can't move. The body stays immobilized while inside it the spirit whirls and whirls and whirls.

"What do you want me to do?"

Cyril smirked, with his eyes closed. "Whatever you can," he said.

Then he began coughing again, rumbling phlegmy coughs, minute after minute, so that people stared, and he took himself off into the bathroom. When he came back, he stopped in the aisle and seemed about ready to fall against one of the tables until Wyatt rushed to his feet to help him. "I paid the bill," Cyril said. "I finally did it. I bought you a meal. In return. For all. Those times. You gave me. Money." His eyes were streaming with tears from the coughing.

He could not drive—he said he felt a little faint—so Wyatt drove him home.

For three days, the pain in Wyatt's side fluttered and flickered. The bruise, at first an angry purple blot, had felt like a reminder, what they called a *nagging* pain, but its persistent message was trivial: it reminded him only that he had fallen from a chair. The last time he noticed it, he had been watching the weather segment on the six-o'clock news. There had been a high-pressure system over Montana marked

244

by a circled H and a blue patch, and just as the weatherman
pointed toward South Dakota, Wyatt felt a last touch of pain
above his hip. After five minutes, as the weather gave way to
basketball scores, the sensation had passed.

At night he left his bed and walked to the living room.
There, sitting on the floor, he stared toward the coals in the
fireplace. He thought about Cyril, or he tried to think about
Cyril. Sometimes his thinking failed altogether and he found
himself doing push-ups instead. His feelings were formless,
anarchic.

On some nights Susan joined him. They were both so
sleepy, tired out from feeding, bathing, and putting the children to bed, that they dozed against each other. She asked
him how he felt. He said he didn't know, exactly—sometimes all right and sometimes terrible. She asked him what he
was going to do. He didn't know. She asked him what he
thought his responsibilities were toward Cyril. He had no
idea even how to begin thinking about the matter, and admitted it.

And yet here he was, fitfully awake in the living room.
Sitting in back of him, Susan put her arms around him, strok-
ing the flat of her hand against his chest, leaning her head
against his back. Or he would sit behind her, massaging her
neck and bare arms, until the motions of comfort gave way to
the motions of love. In his tiredness and perplexity, the almost
formal predictability of desire seemed lawful, orderly, and
sustaining; but she had become one world, and he had
become another, and he couldn't begin to say what separated
and identified them.

"Do you still think I'm simple?" she whispered at him,
and in the dark he shook his head.

. . .

One night, as soon as Christina and Eugene were asleep, Wyatt went into the kitchen and looked up the telephone number of the halfway house where his mother lived. He didn't want to remember the number, so he never did. His fatigue made the kitchen lights seem so bright that he squinted.

Sitting on the kitchen stool, he closed his eyes and thought of the day he had run away from home, and his mother had stayed behind, near the house, understanding but somehow not caring that he had run away. She understood running away better than his father had. She had always wanted to run away from everything. She had never accepted the terms life had offered her: marriage, childbirth, motherhood, a career, success or failure, maturity, gravity, the sky, trees and twigs, sports, penises and vaginas, minds, nation-states, war, banking and commerce. None of it had made the slightest sense to her. She had tried for thirty years to make it make sense, and when it hadn't, she had boarded that ocean liner and sailed away from all of it. She had cast off the lines. You couldn't be insane by choice, but she was.

It was almost possible to love that, he thought, rubbing his eyes with his fists.

He dialed her number. The supervisor called his mother to the phone, and when Jeanne picked up the receiver, she said, "Wyatt," not as a greeting, but as a fact to be acknowledged.

"Hi, Mom. I wanted to talk to you. Are you okay?"

"You never call. I don't mind that," she said, "but it's true."

"I'm sorry. Are you okay?"

"What's okay? If it's okay to be the way I am, then I'm okay."

"Good. You know, you haven't called me, either."

"I don't like voices on the telephone. You know that."

"Why don't you?"

"They sound like the buzzing of insects."

"Is that how I sound?"

"A little. You sound mostly like Wyatt. But there's always that insect . . . housarara." She still made up words when the occasion demanded. She laughed at her neologism. "You wouldn't understand."

"Well, I just might."

"You might? You never did."

"I do now. I'm beginning to. So—do you have any new projects?"

"You might say that. You might say that I'm the frying pan."

"How so?"

"Oh, no particular way. Not specifically, just generally. I'm the frying pan you try to get out of, and you end up in the fire."

"Maybe you're cooking something."

"Certainly. I'm cooking me. I'm cooking the future, too. It's almost done."

He had always felt that it was a mistake to follow up on his mother's overuse of metaphors, so he said, "Nell said you were sewing when I called you to the phone."

"Yes. I put patches on things. Trousers. I was patching a pair of trousers. Not your trousers. I don't know whose. It's better that way. How is your daughter, Wyatt? How is Christina? And how is . . ."

"Eugene."

"Yes. I know his name. It's just hard for me to say it."

"They're both fine. Healthy and happy."

"Good. I love their hair and I love their faces and I love

their hands and I love the way they laugh," his mother said. "How I do love all that in children."

"I love it, too."

"I wonder what they'll turn into."

"You never know."

"Oh yes, you do. I *almost* know, with both of them."

"What is it? What do you know?"

"Well, I wouldn't tell *you*. And you're so . . . I don't know the word." Wyatt held his breath, hoping she wouldn't thrust one of her new coins at him. Here it came. "You're so corilineal."

"What's that?"

"That's when you're so normal, it's strange."

"I'm not like that anymore."

"Since when?" she asked, her tone brightening.

"Since this week. This month."

"What happened to you?"

"I talked to Cyril."

"So? You always talk to Cyril."

"Hasn't he told you?"

"Told me what?"

"Cyril is dying, Ma. He has cancer."

"So does everyone."

"No, Ma, I mean he really has it, he really has cancer. It's not a metaphor. It's in his lungs and everywhere."

This time, in a normal tone of voice, Jeanne said, "No one told me. I'm sorry, Wyatt."

"So am I, Ma. I'm sorry a lot."

"I guess I should see him. What do you do for people who are that sick? I don't remember the conventions. I never did."

"Oh, I guess you could say something." He was briefly annoyed with his mother, that she didn't feel grief and anger appropriately and that she didn't express it at the right moments. "He says that the plant where he works, the Wald-Chem plant, poisoned him. The working conditions."

"Well, then, they probably did. He should know. The poor boy."

"I helped to bring that company here. I'm responsible."

To his surprise, his mother said, "Exactly right."

"And now I . . . I don't know. I've been thinking about you and WaldChem and Cyril and this guy I know who runs it, Jerry Schwartzwalder."

"And now you're the frying pan."

"I guess so." It was a little like talking to the Oracle at Delphi, or like watching a light bulb flicker on and off. "What am I going to do, Ma? Do you have any ideas?"

"You could explode."

"I don't know how. I don't want to do that."

"You could explode someone else. Someone who knows how."

"Why do you always talk in metaphor?"

"Why, metaphor is my meat. Besides, two people walking hand in hand is the only language I know."

"Ma, I just need some practical advice. I thought you might have some."

"Wyatt, when someone's that sick, there's nothing practical you can do."

"I know. But what do I do about Schwartzwalder? About WaldChem?"

"Why do you have to do anything?"

"Because I'm responsible!"

After what seemed to be a long pause, she said, "That's interesting. What you did, you undo. Is that the idea?"

"Something like that."

"Then go to the exploding places."

"Where are they?"

"You'll have to find that out for yourself. Where does this Jerry Schwartzwalder person live, for example?"

"Interesting that you should ask. He lives in that house that Daddy designed, up on the ridge, on Jellison Road. The one with the solarium."

"Ohh." She exhaled heavily, and, it seemed to Wyatt, came back to herself. "That one. That one started pretty, and it ended up terrible. It sent your father down into the 3:30 room, and how he dropped slips of paper into the thought-drawer, when that happened."

Wyatt felt himself giving up. "Well, it's been nice talking to you, Ma."

"I'd burn it down."

"Excuse me?"

"I would set fire to that house."

"That's against the law. I can't do that. They'd be hurt."

"Oh, you could make sure they were in Jamaica or some-where."

"How?"

"Scare them out of town. He'll take his rotten company. No one ever stays anywhere for long, men anyway. How your father hated that house. I'd just set fire to it, if I were you."

"You think so?"

"Wyatt, darling, it's late and I'm tired. I'm a crazy person. Don't pay any attention to me. Talk to your Aunt Ellen. She may have ideas."

"I have to get that company out of town."

"Well, then, burn down his house. Scare him. He'll leave."

"It's odd for you to say that."

"Oh, you think so?"

"Yes."

"Well, it isn't so odd, Wyatt," she said. "It isn't so very odd. Who knows more about terror than me?"

"You don't feel terror, Ma. Do you?"

"Oh, Wyatt, honey, there's terror in the milk, there's terror in the cereal, there's terror in the trees, there's terror in the patches I sew on the pants, there's terror in the sidewalk, and all this terror, Wyatt, this terror talks to me, and how it talks. Long speeches. So who should know more about it than me? Wyatt, go and be a different boy."

She hung up, and he was left in his kitchen, staring at the magnetized letters stuck to the refrigerator—"dog" was spelled at the center—and the stove, and the kitchen clock over the sink, and the dish drainer, and all the other common household things that had once made him so happy, and no longer did.

16

The Friday-morning business meetings with the city manager and his staff often went on for so long that Wyatt could watch the progress of the sun across the sky, as measured by objects within the room that were lit by its rays. At nine o'clock, in winter, the sun angled into the room and brightened the potted plant; then it advanced toward the conference table and illuminated the city manager's head; and by lunchtime it was lighting up a rectangular patch of carpeting.

Wyatt grew familiar with the ceiling tile. One of his coworkers called these meetings "Feasts of Tedium" and said that he could feel his life being drained away minute by minute. Nevertheless, everyone agreed that the meetings were productive; at least, that was the word they used.

Wyatt had spoken privately to the city manager about the WaldChem problem and the city manager had said he would get back to him about it. A week later, after Wyatt had sent him a paper containing their options, the city manager called him into his office.

"Shut the door," he said. He turned the screen of his computer so that it wasn't facing in Wyatt's direction, and he motioned toward a chair. He touched his hair, arranged militantly in parallel rows.

"Wyatt," he said. "Good man. Yes, let's talk. I'm glad you sat down." He leaned back and gazed out his window. "This may be an unpleasant conversation," he said. "I wonder if maybe we should have it outside. The sun's out, and the day seems . . ." He appeared to grope for an adjective, and when he couldn't find it, he exhaled loudly. "It's early morning, and I feel tired already. It's funny when you can't find the right words. Let's take a walk. Come on, my boy. We'll stretch our legs."

He escorted Wyatt to a patch of grass in front of the building, and they stood near a bench in the shade of an oak tree, but neither man sat down. Wyatt liked the city manager, his tiredness and efficiency and harmless irascibility. Underneath his perpetual expression of official exasperation, he had a quality of apparent warmth, even affection, and Wyatt wondered if good fathers were sometimes like that. But he had no idea what good fathers were like. He could hardly remember Eugene, except for a few random images of him.

The city manager lit a cigarette, and Wyatt leaned forward to tell him not to, to stop that, to never do that again; but with great effort, he restrained himself.

"Nice day," the city manager said. "Wish I had time to appreciate it. I got to be back inside in about ten minutes ago." He pointed upward. "Do you know what those clouds are, those wispy ones, what they call mares' tails?"

"No," Wyatt said.

"Cirrus clouds," the city manager said, exhaling. "They're made of ice crystals, and they're the highest clouds in the atmosphere, and they portend rain. I once wanted to be a meteorologist but got sidetracked into this. Into what I do. I got married early, just like yourself. I couldn't go to school any longer, and I had to have a job. We should have another name for these tasks we perform. 'Village officialdom.' How's that?"

Wyatt shook his head and smiled.

"It doesn't sound very noble, does it?" the city manager asked. "It doesn't sound like the kind of work a hero would do. You want to walk down there, end of the block? There's an apple tree just starting to get its buds."

"No," Wyatt said. He sat down on the bench and looked up at the city manager. "I think you should tell me what you're going to tell me."

"All right." The city manager stubbed out the cigarette on the lawn and immediately took another one out of his shirt pocket and lit that. "You have a problem with that little plant your friend Schwartzwalder built out there on Greenwood Road. I know you want me to get behind you and call the EPA and start putting together reports on the VOCs and the benzene spills and notify the state that the on-site waste management guidelines and regulations and licensing restrictions are being violated. And we could get OSHA in here, if one of the workers asked for it. But I'm not going to do it, Wyatt, and if you start something, I won't back you up."

"Why not?" Just to his right, a bird, apparently used to handouts, had landed on the bench, and was watching him.

"Because you don't have a case," the city manager said. "And, right now, the times are against you. It's not that there aren't regulations. There are. You know that. The problem is that, these days, nobody believes in those regulations, at least not the people I talk to every day on the phone. It's mostly a matter of expediency, getting things done. Do you see what I mean?"

"Yes, but—"

"Wait a minute." He held up his hand. "Don't say anything just yet. Let me be a bastard about this for a second before you run off like Don Quixote. You should know what a windmill is before you call it a dragon and start to attack it.

"So far, Wyatt, you're almost the only person in town with a problem with that plant. I'm not hearing about any problem from the people who work there. They haven't complained to the mayor or the council, and they haven't called any of the environmental regulatory agencies. I haven't heard anything from the regulators. I'm not hearing from them because this state has a new right-wing friend-to-business governor, and, more importantly, it has a six-hundred-million-dollar deficit with which it has to deal. That chickadee is looking at you."

Wyatt turned to gaze at the bird, still perched on the other side of the park bench, but when he did, the bird flew off.

"Too bad," the city manager said. "I had some birdseed in my pocket. I sometimes come down here to feed those critters on my way home. We could advance your case, Wyatt, if the times were different, but times have been hard, very hard, lately, and I for one don't want to get a reputation as a whistle-blower here in this city. Listen: you've *got* to have a consensus of social beliefs to do what you intend to do. But last month the issuance of groundwater discharge permits was frozen in this state. That doesn't mean that you can't discharge garden-variety pollutants into the groundwater. It means you just can't have a permit for it. And that's because the licensing bureau that issued those permits has just had its staff cut in half, plus which, the governor is one of those guys they've been making lately in politics, which means that he doesn't want that agency to be too active just now. He'd actually like to gut it, like a fish, only he won't say so. He says he's improving the business climate. I think we all know what that means."

Wyatt stood up. "But we do have a case," he said. "The air is pink in there, and the women have been getting sick, and—"

"I called one of them," the city manager said. "Behind your back. I called one of them I've known a long time. She's terrified she'll lose her job. She won't say anything. She says nobody will say anything. Not in these times. That's what you get when you've got a contracting economy, Wyatt. You get scared people. What'd your grandfather do for a living?"

"He was a farmer, I guess," Wyatt said.

"Mine worked in a coal mine," the city manager said. "Then he went to work in a copper mine, and he had claustrophobia, and he once told my grandmother he was scared every day of his life, but he did it, because he had to. That generation, and the one before, they all did dangerous work, and none of them, not one of them, thought they had a right to complain until unionization allowed them to. I hate to have to explain this to you, Wyatt. You're smarter than I am, probably. And I like you a lot. I mean, kid, you're competent at what you do."

"Thanks," Wyatt said. "But listen, all I want—"

"No, wait a second. You tell me that your cousin is sick. I'm sorry about that. I didn't know him, but I'm sorry anyway. Still and all, I happen to know that, just like me, he smoked cigarettes most of his life, and, who knows, he may have ingested other substances that could be injurious to a person's health, and with that kind of background, you just don't have any case at all against Schwartzwalder's plant, not in this current social climate. Our black-sheep friends the lawyers would arrive on the scene, and I can assure you that there would be litigation that would go on for so long that horses would age and sag and die, watching it. Even if you had a couple more tumors out there, it wouldn't help. If this were a more progressive town or state or county or time, we could do something. But I don't think," he said, taking a last inhale from the cigarette and stubbing it out on the lawn near the butt of the other one, "I don't think that's going to happen *here*. Wyatt, you're upset. But look at all these people walking past us on the sidewalk." He pointed toward them with his thumb.

Wyatt pretended to look. He had seen pedestrians on the sidewalk before.

"Odds and ends of people walking around. What do they want?"

"What do they want? You should ask them," Wyatt said.

"I don't have to. I know what they want. And so do you. They want jobs, houses, money in the bank, families, security. After they want those material things, they want their health. Then they're willing to do a little trading-off for the ethics. But I'd say that they're mostly postethical. Feed the kids first, then worry about how you did it. And the health, well, that's later, too. This is about survival. Do you want to know how I know?"

He put his hand on Wyatt's shoulder and steered him

toward their building. Wyatt's heart had sunk so low during the city manager's talk that he didn't want to look at the sidewalk, he didn't want to look at anything. He raised his head toward the sky and saw the cirrus clouds again.

The city manager saw him do it. "Portents of rain," he said. "Those clouds usually precede low-pressure systems. . . . I was going to tell you how I know what I know. Here's the evidence. I know that health is not a high priority because cigarettes are still being smoked. By me, by others. Federal subsidies are still given to tobacco farmers. Liquor is drunk by the bottleful. People eat candy bars and put butter on their popcorn. They eat fish from streams polluted with chlorinated hydrocarbons. They live under high-voltage electrical wire. They use electric blankets and microwave ovens, they sit one inch away from the color television, and they eat steak with growth hormone in it and apples that've been irradiated. A person moves into a brand-new house these days and the brand-new-house smell you've got there is formaldehyde. They get electrical power from fission rods, and then they throw the fission rods into the briny sea. Trust me, it's not a boom time for health. People don't exactly live in a state of contentment but it's close enough, it's what I call contentmentlike."

"You're a cynic," Wyatt said.

The city manager stopped on the sidewalk. "No. I know what I can do and what I can't do, and knowing the difference keeps me from being crazy." He gazed at Wyatt for a long time; the gaze, Wyatt knew, was about his own mother, and that gaze was the worst thing the city manager had ever done to him. "Let me ask *you* a question."

"All right."

"Do you think people want to start foraging again?"

"I thought," Wyatt said, "that the issue was air quality and water discharge from the WaldChem plant."

"Officially, it's being taken care of. Procedures are in place. Besides, you've got to see it in perspective."

"I don't like this perspective."

"Neither do I," the city manager said. "It's a tragedy."

"Then why not do something?" Wyatt asked.

"Don't you remember your literature classes, Wyatt?" They had entered the building, and the city manager had pressed the elevator button. "Tragedies are inevitable. That's why they're tragedies. You can't stop them from happening." And the city manager smiled his fatherly, kindly smile. He stepped onto the elevator, and the doors closed in front of him before Wyatt remembered to get on with him. For a few moments he had felt rooted to the floor and had been unable to move.

Now, at certain times of day, sitting at his desk, Wyatt felt light-headed. Print swam in front of his eyes, and voices came to him from voice boxes installed in human throats. The voices were muted, or muffled by what seemed to be cotton. And he thought: I'm thinking like my mother. I'm moving off in her direction. If I don't watch it, before very long, I'll be out in the middle of the ocean, with nothing but sky and horizon in all directions.

He decided to call Jerry Schwartzwalder. Schwartzwalder said he was glad to hear from him and suggested a game of racquetball at his health club, which he referred to as "The Hamster Wheel." They set up a time.

Schwartzwalder had to lend him a racket. On the court, Schwartwalder liked to rush the ball. Wyatt preferred to be accurate. It was another one of his habits that he would have to look into. Because he was stronger than his high school classmate, and more conscious of speed and balance, he beat Schwartwalder easily. He wasn't sure that winning in this case was a good idea, but once he began to win, he couldn't stop.

From the racquetball court, they went to the steam room. Through the steam, Wyatt saw the pleasantly bearded face of a high school teacher he knew, Saul Bernstein. Why was he here? Why wasn't he in school? "Hi, Saul," he said. "What's up?"

"Water pipe broke in the high school," Saul said, "so I decided to come here and melt myself down into a puddle." He stood up and left, steam swirling around him.

Steam hissed from the floor vents into the room. It was so thick that Schwartzwalder disappeared in it. As soon as Schwartzwalder had vanished in the steam, Wyatt spoke up. He told Schwartzwalder about his cousin, and about his concerns: the air, the water, all the et cetera that, he thought, had made Cyril sick.

The steam spoke back to him. A voice! A voice surrounded by steam. "Yes, I know," it said. But the deal had been to give his cousin a job, and that's what had happened: he'd been given a job, and he had thrived, in a manner of speaking. The steam said that the bargain would stand. My company, my employees, my responsibility, the voice said.

The bargain would stand. Wyatt breathed in the hot humid air. Sweat dripped down the sides of his head and chest. He felt trapped in the cage of his body and in the sturdier thicker cage of himself. He needed to become someone else, the sort of person who knew what to do at all times. But it was a slow process, becoming someone else, as his mother, for example, knew very well.

He held his hand in front of him in the steam room: he

was pleased to see that it looked like another man's hand, with alien coloring and peculiar wrinkles and curvatures of flesh, and from out of the steam the voice said that it would soon be summer, and they would play golf together.

llen didn't think that in a condominium complex you could plant anything on your front lawn, but Cyril and Pooh had installed a scrawny little apple tree next to their front sidewalk on 2148 Maple Meadows Drive, and when she bicycled down in late March to bring them a loaf of raisin bread she had baked herself, she saw that this tree, with its six halfhearted branches, was beginning to bud. It was a Sunday, one of those gloomy spring weekends before gardening and baseball have started, when the soul is located not near the heart or the head, but somewhere around the knees, and the sky, where the sun has not appeared for days, is the exact color of depression. Carrying the bread past this new tree—Cyril had probably disobeyed some regulation in planting it there—she counted the buds. Six branches, forty-two buds, give or take a few. She sniffed. She couldn't smell apple, but the air *was* thick with mud. Under her feet the old gods were busily dying into a new life.

Ellen had been calling Cyril regularly and had visited a few times, mostly uninvited, to see them all, but she had been invited in this instance for some sort of get-together, and after Cyril met her at the door, leaning on his cane and kissing her with his bad breath, she saw that Wyatt and Susan and their two children were inside as well, sitting on the floor near the picture of R. Stan Drabble. They looked beautiful, of course, those four; looking beautiful was easy for them, no trouble at all. They were in this life to make other people feel envious. Christina had long beautiful hair and intelligent eyes, and their younger one, Eugene, toddling now, had that look of lucky aggression some smart children have. Wyatt and his family had turned out so well that Ellen felt pointless and unnecessary whenever she was near them. Attractive people always made her feel that way.

What surprised her was that Jeanne was here, too.

They must have taken her out of the halfway house for a day visit. She looked a bit bedraggled as she sat in the dining room, mechanically eating butter cookies from a blue glass plate. Ellen kissed her and Jeanne kissed back, absentmindedly, as if she'd forgotten the point of kisses. On her face was an expression of authoritative bewilderment. Ellen watched as Jeanne sat there, eating one cookie after another. After a time, Wyatt came by and leaned down, and the two of them, mother and son, began to mutter together. Having never seen Wyatt listen as an adult to his mother, Ellen wasn't sure what was up. She felt a bit jealous. What could she possibly tell him, that he would want to hear? Whatever it was, he was listening, and nodding.

Otis was wandering around the house with a miniature billiard ball in his mouth. In any other family, he would choke on it, but in this one, he would not. Nevertheless, Ellen swooped down and removed it, and Otis began screaming at her, as she expected him to. Cyril sat in a corner of the living room—Pooh was in the kitchen, wearing an I HATE COOKING apron and preparing a plate of cold cuts—and he seemed to be pleased by all this sociability in his house. He managed to keep smiling. Ellen thought that the smile was a reflex. Otis, still enraged at the loss of his billiard ball, came ramming into his father, and Cyril tried to pick him up but couldn't get him more than two inches off the ground. Then he shook his head.

Ellen dragged a chair over next to him. Otis had raced off somewhere else. Cyril saw Ellen coming and began to scratch his forearm in a friendly manner. His cheekbones were prominent and yellowish. "How does someone like you become so good a father?" she asked.

"By not reading about it," he said. He flashed his alarming smile directly at her. "How are you, Ellen? How's that Bible coming?"

"Just fine."

"You got some pages?"

"I guess it's my business," she said, "how many pages I have. It's my Bible. I never said anybody else had to read it."

"Well, no." He patted her on the knee. "How can you write a Bible without seeing God or anything?"

"And who says I haven't?" She sat up and reached over

for a nacho on the table next to Cyril. She didn't mind his asking. It was better than talking about his health.

"What I was doing here was asking you, you know, in the polite way that I'm trying to figure out how other people do it when they're making conversation."

"All right. I'll tell you," she said. "You listen. That's all you have to do. And don't go around repeating this, all right?"

"All right."

"Give me your hand on it."

Cyril slipped his bony fingers into Ellen's and gave them a good squeeze. She could feel his bones there, right inside the flesh.

She said she didn't know what middle-aged single men heard at night, alone by themselves wherever they lived, but middle-aged single women who live just beyond the housing clusters of cities or towns start to hear things, things that want to have attention paid to them. "You men," she said, "you're like bad radios. You don't pull in many stations." Cyril nodded.

When night came and Ellen sat in her back room, reading the evidence or practicing the piano, she would sometimes perceive voices floating in from the backyard, but if she stopped playing, if the notes ceased, the voices did, too. Only when she made a musical racket did she hear something calling her two octaves above at the overtone level, a sequence of almost-notes played on an instrument they hadn't invented yet in the human realm. These note-voices sounded like a question, rising at the end the way a human voice does, in inquiry.

So. This would have been January. The middle of the week, a clear night, a half-moon, and plenty of snow. She had trundled herself over to the back door and put on her hat and coat and gloves, and walked out into the stillness. The winter moonlight cast every object in silver.

Once she was outside, she couldn't hear anything. She might as well take a walk. Behind her house and the road leading to it was a small forest, a stand of jack pine and scruffy maple trees and some scrub brush—all the advantages of living out of town—and at the edge of the forest lay McIntosh Road. Across from the road were the uncultivated fields owned by Elmer S. Townsend, an ugly stubborn querulous Lutheran she had known since childhood, who now lived condominiumed in Tucson, where he had always belonged. Just up the road, going north, at a crossing, stood a boarded-up church. She could see it in the moonlight, a plain structure built by Swedish farmers toward the end of the last century. They'd been Swedenborgians, and that decaying house of worship was one of the churches of the New Jerusalem.

She'd seen the last of that congregation as a child, those solemn men and women with their hard-and-fast belief in angels. Later, as a young woman, Ellen had taken a few books of Swedenborg out of the public library. She'd always liked homebrewed religion, as long as it kept its dignity. In the midst of all this North American emptiness it helped to believe in something. As it happened, she had been impressed by Swedenborg's unimaginative prose style describing his conversations and congress with angels, and his visits to Heaven and Hell. Hell was Hell, Swedenborg reported, because everyone there had an inflated ego and spent every minute of waking life giving and issuing orders, which of course no one obeyed. Strutting around and self-importance and unconsummated careerism and street crime abounded in Hell, with the result that, Swedenborg claimed, the streets were dirty and the sidewalks unkempt and uncared-for, and the houses gave off a dingy little light, the light of I'm-not-sorry-for-anything, the light of Listen-to-me.

Ellen thought Swedenborg was a sensible man. Of course Hell was peopled by bullies. They'd make each other's lives miserable. That way, you didn't even need eternal fire.

Anyhow, she had walked over to the church and looked inside, but it was just an empty building now vacated by its angels and its spirits of Swedish women and their husbands, those dour couples. She hadn't thought she would find any spirits here, and indeed they were not present. Her boots crunching over the snow, she walked down the road, crossed over into one of Elmer S. Townsend's fields, and took a path that led her toward a pond.

This pond—it had no name that she knew—stretched out about three hundred feet to her right before curving; she couldn't quite see the end of it. She stepped out onto the ice and felt the presence behind her move like a sudden sucking wind downward, underneath her. She wondered if she would see it. It owed her that. But when she looked through the ice, of course she saw nothing.

She came back on three more nights. She waited in the dark. On a Monday night as she approached the pond, she thought she saw children playing there. Their voices sounded like glockenspiels. Their voices rang instead of speaking. It was the same sound she had heard over the music of her playing.

On the next night, in the dark, she felt a hand taking her hand. She did not look down. Very close to her, from underneath the ice, came the sound of bells.

Two nights after that (Ellen said, looking toward the living room, where Wyatt and Susan and Jeanne were watching a basketball game), she'd gone back. She stood vigilantly on that ice, and then the snow began, but the air temperature wasn't cold—about twenty degrees—and she felt warm and patient and unafraid.

"Now comes the hard part," she said, keeping her eyes fixed on Cyril. "Now listen, Cyril, this is what I saw, and don't you repeat it to anyone else."

She had closed her eyes, taken a breath, hearing music from underneath the ice, even though she knew the music was probably in her own head. Everything was outside the body and inside the mind. Everything was in two places at once. She was watching the branches sway in the winter wind, and the branches moved inside her, into the nerve endings that housed the spirit.

So, with her boot, she shoved the snow aside, the snow on the ice of the pond, and she looked down.

Cyril waited. "Okay," he said, "what did you see?"

"I didn't see anything. I saw ice."

"Aw, come on." He held back a cough. "You lead me on all this way? And now you're saying as how your story leads up to this and it's nothing? Where's the Shaggy Dog part?"

"I didn't say there was nothing. I said what I saw was ice. Just plain old ice."

He shook his head. "Ellen, don't play games with me. I don't have the time. Just get to the point."

"You want to hear what I felt?"

"Yeah, yeah. Sure. Give me the feelings."

When she looked down, she felt but did not exactly see a face from underneath the ice, a face that was made of fire several feet under the water, burning there, looking back at her, a boy's face, this was, there and not-there, and it had the shape of that boy, Donald, gazing back at her with all the forced neutrality of the dead.

Not ghosts or spirits would do this, she said, but only me. I was thinking of that boy, so that was the person I saw. He was in my head, so that's why I saw him, but it was him, you remember him, with his hair parted so it looked like a toupee, and that same expression, that blank one, and now he was the representative, the messenger, not saying yes and not saying no. He was as high up the ladder as I would ever get. Then I shivered. You ever seen a face built out of fire, underwater? I don't recommend it. Oh, everything they say about God is wrong, and I knew it. God isn't indifferent, God is curious. Maybe loving-kindness does rule in the realm of the spirits but it sure isn't the rule down here. I don't think God is taking care of us, Cyril, but we are in the presence of the divine curiosity. The main thing is that we're on our own. If that's the face, that fire of the infinite, there's no comfort to be purchased there but the good news is that there's no pain, either.

Cyril leaned back. "That's the story?"

"That's it."

"You gone back there?"

"A few times."

"Did you see him again?"

"Can't say so. Well, you know. I didn't have to. Once is enough."

Cyril leaned back and fished in his pocket and brought out a quarter. "Here," he said. "That's for your story."

She took the quarter without comment and put it into her own pocket. "Thank you."

"That's a hell of a story to tell to a dying man," he chuckled, shaking his head. "You just beat everything I ever heard of. None of that comfort nonsense for you."

"None of that comfort nonsense for me," she repeated.

"And none for you, either, or for Jeanne over there, or Wyatt, or anybody. Just about no comfort anywhere, is my impression. Love, but no comfort. Oh, kiddo," she said, her voice rising, and she suddenly lunged at him, her arms out, trying to hug him but not succeeding, because he was still in his chair, "you know I'd do anything I could for you now, I'd go with you if I could. But I can't."

Cyril nodded, then reached into another pocket. He took two pills out of a prescription bottle and swallowed them. "It's only the pain I mind," he said. "I hate the goddamn pain. Just *hate* it. That, and getting fogged." Then he sat up. "Hey," he said, "I just got an idea." He smiled. "By God, Ellen, you performed a service after all. You gave me an idea. I don't get one of those except maybe once a year in the dark of the moon. Hey, thanks."

"What idea?"

"By God you're a peach. You sure are. You send my cousin over here. Hey, Wyatt!" he shouted, but in fact it was not a shout, just a slight increase in the loudness of his voice. "You come over here. Right exactly here by me."

Ellen watched Cyril rise, in pain, and walk with Wyatt into the kitchen. When Cyril saw her watching him and trying to eavesdrop, he grabbed Wyatt's elbow and piloted him out into the backyard.

The management of Maple Meadows had built a small playground behind Cyril's unit, including a swing set with cement footings and tubular steel, and three seats. Wyatt sat down on one of the swings and Cyril on another.

The day was still heavy, with scudding clouds and two minutes of sun followed by two minutes of overcast: sun, cloud, sun, cloud, in regular succession, as if on a timer. Around the swing set, there was still no grass planted, no sod, just a mixture of dirt, sand, and gravel that had achieved a uniform grayish-brown. The air was thick with the smell of mud and roots.

"I don't remember seeing you in a swing before," Wyatt said. He gripped the chains and swung back and forth, a slow pendulum.

"You're getting your shoes muddy."

Wyatt shrugged. "They're weekend shoes." He looked down at them, as if inspecting the damage.

"Your mother looks okay," Cyril said. "Haven't talked to her in a coon's age."

"Has it been that long?" Wyatt turned to look at Cyril. "Now what was this you were saying about a rowboat?"

"Well, see, I got it figured out."

"What?"

"What I'm going to do."

"What're you talking about?"

"About a month from now," Cyril said, nodding to himself. "About a month."

"For what?"

"Goodbyes and more pain. I'm not about to sit here and turn into one of them victims of modern medicine. There's nothing for me waiting up there except more pain and the morphine and hours of *Geraldo*. I don't want that in the least. I'm going out on my own steam. I want you to be there."

Wyatt stood up immediately. His shoes sank half an inch into the mud. To his right, in the distance, he could see the WaldChem plant.

"What?" He waited. "No. I won't even hear about it."

"You got no choice in the matter."

"Of course I do. Hell, it's illegal. It's murder. Forget it."

"Shut up and listen," Cyril said. "It ain't murder, the way I'm going to do it. Okay. I get everything in order here.

Then, about a month from now, you and me go out rowing on the river, you know, like a pleasant time, where it's real wide and slow. That's all you have to do. Just row the boat. You got to row the boat because I can't. I'm not strong enough. That's all I'm asking you to do."

"You're asking me to do a lot more than that. You might as well ask me for a million dollars. I can't do it. Hell, I *won't* do it."

"Yes, you can. I'm a dying man here. You got to respect my wishes."

"It's murder."

"No, it ain't. I just explained this to you. All I do is fall off the boat and, blipblop, down I go. I never could swim anyway."

"Where'd you get this idea? This is just a *terrible* idea, Cyril."

"It's my idea. I originated it." Cyril was proud of his vocabulary, always had been. "Besides, they all say that drowning's easy."

"Who says this?"

"Everybody that's ever drowned."

"How would they know? They don't come back."

"Of course they do. Don't play ignorant with me. They get revived and suchlike."

"You won't sink."

"I'll take weights along with me or something."

"They'll rule it a suicide."

"No, they won't. We'll have an accident together, you and me."

"If it's a suicide, Pooh and Otis don't get your life insurance."

"It won't be a suicide, it'll be an accident. Nobody ever

suicided by drowning, buddy. It'll be like I fell off a dock or off the side of a boat."

"They'll blame me."

"I'll meet you somewheres," Cyril said. "Nobody'll even know you took me out. Not even Pooh. You'll be invisible. You'll be my last pal. Listen, Wyatt," and then Cyril stopped to cough. When he was finished, his face was white, the lower half, and yellowish, the upper half. "You're my brother, sort of. You got to do this for me, like you had no choice."

"But I do have a choice. My choice is to say no."

"You got to care about me. If you care about me, you got no choice. You can't fight me on this. I'm half angel already."

And that ended it. Wyatt had never heard a sentence like that from Cyril, and when he glanced down at him, he saw Cyril's thick black hair—appearing now slightly too large for his head—and he could see that he would have to do it. He would have to row the boat for Cyril.

18

The morning Cyril planned to drown, with Wyatt's help, was a Saturday, and the day dawned sunny and clear; Wyatt saw how clear it was from his bed, where, for the entire night, he had not slept. His wife's right leg was stretched over his thighs, and at dawn he touched it absentmindedly, thinking that the sun—his enemy—might go away if he willed it to.

He ate his breakfast of Cheerios and an English muffin.

He made toast for Christina. He told Susan that he had some errands to run and that he'd be back just before lunch. Then, in the afternoon, he'd stay around the house and she could take off. She nodded, still only halfway out of sleep.

He drove down through the gratuitous eeriness of the early-morning sunlight, into the downtown area, past the office building where he worked, and then north of the city toward the public-access boat dock and landing. Turning off the main highway, he drove his car down a narrow dirt road, bordered on either side with hawthorns and high grasses— burdock, he thought—that slithered and hissed against the side of the car as he went past them.

He was ready to turn around and leave if anyone else was already at the boat landing, but, no, no one was there. Wyatt parked his car and walked out onto the dock and stared east- ward into the blank stupid shellacked face of the sun. He had arranged with Hugh Welch, the man who had helped him get his job in the first place, to use Hugh's rowboat. He had told Hugh that he just wanted to go out and row, get a little exercise in the spring, and Hugh had agreed, as if he knew exactly what Wyatt meant.

"No problem," Hugh had said. "The boat'll be there in the morning." And there it was, *Noah's Ark,* the words painted in green on the boat's stern, tied up at the dock, just as Hugh had promised it would be. He was better at keeping promises than anyone else Wyatt knew. He hadn't even put a lock on the chain, he was that trusting. "Just put it back when you're done," Hugh had said, in his huge and spontaneous spirit of benevolence. Wyatt felt little grace notes of feeling— blankness, love, forlornness—touching him inside his chest, where the heart was supposed to be, and then moving out toward his fingers. You could have feelings in your fingers, he realized, gazing up and seeing a male cardinal singing *pret-*

tybirdprettybirdprettybird perched on a branch, and gazing down at him. No: the bird did not care about Wyatt, or what he was about to do. He had his own concerns and flew off. Wyatt felt a surge of desolation in the knuckles of his right hand.

Down below him under the dock, and out in front of him, the river, swollen with its late-spring runoff, flowed silently but quite visibly from his left to his right, around a bend and out of sight, southward. Rowing back to this dock would be a bit of an effort. He hadn't expected the river's progress to be this strong, but even that was an advantage, in its way: anyone falling off this dock—anyone claimed to have fallen off this dock—would be, what was the word, *taken,* by the force of the current, down and away.

Cyril was late.

Maybe he would not come.

Thank God: he had changed his mind: he would now die in bed.

But then Wyatt heard the bad-muffler rumbling of Cyril's pickup, Li'l Devil, coming down the dirt road off the county highway, and at last it poked through the foliage crowding against the road before the road widened into the parking lot, where Cyril was now. After parking, he extracted himself slowly, a scrawny shell, supporting himself with a cane.

"There's something in the truck you gotta get," Cyril said, pointing, not even trying out a hello or good morning, but, then, why should he? Wyatt walked past Cyril going the other way, and found on the passenger side of the truck a twenty-five-pound dumbbell. "Just grab it," Cyril said, "and put it over there in the boat."

Wyatt did as he was told. He had never been dutiful—he could never be accused of that—but he could be, as people said, *obliging.* This morning he could be obliging. He picked up the weight and carried it to the rowboat, where Cyril was now sitting, his cane next to him.

"Morning, Cyril."

"Well, yeah, okay." Cyril's face had new lines drawn in it, pain lines probably, and when he smiled Wyatt thought he was seeing a special effect in a movie, it was that artificial. Cyril smiled behind a curtain of flesh that was not smiling itself, but was resisting the smile effort and then finally giving way to it. Wyatt squatted down, laid the dumbbell on the floor of the boat next to a fishhook, and untied *Noah's Ark*. He sat down in the center of the boat—Cyril was at the back—took the oars in his hand, and, as soon as the boat had been propelled into the river's current, an arm's length away from the dock, he began to row toward the middle, where it was deeper and calmer.

"Little breeze," Cyril said.

"Not much."

"I can feel it on my face."

"Hmm." Wyatt felt the pleasurable strain of his back muscles as he pulled the oars. "Where does Pooh think you are?"

"She thinks I took the truck just to get out of the house. Where's Susan think *you* are?" Cyril seemed cold and snugged his jacket tightly around him.

"Driving here and there. Doesn't matter to her. Eugene's sleeping and Christina's watching the Saturday-morning cartoons, so everything's . . ." He didn't know how to finish the sentence.

"Everything was fine."

"Yes. Everything was fine."

Wyatt looked at Cyril. His cousin was wearing, in addition to the jacket, a heavy flannel shirt and heavy boots, to keep him warm, and, maybe, the better to help him sink.

"You said goodbye?"

"I have been saying goodbye for months. That is one thing I don't have to do again, and that's a certainty." Cyril's voice had developed a wet growl.

"What about Otis?"

"What about him?"

"Well, I was just asking."

"Otis'll grow up like I did, without me. I grew up without me and that's what he'll do, too." Cyril lowered his hand into the water and let it lap against the waves. "Cold," he said.

"Well, the ice hasn't been out that long. It's spring, Cyril."

"You got that right." He raised his arm to point. "There's a duck. One of them green-headed ones. Wood duck."

"It's not a wood duck," Wyatt said. "It's a mallard."

"It ain't no mallard, it's a wood duck. Wood ducks've got that green head like that one does."

"Sorry, Cyril. No. It's a mallard. Mallards have green heads, the males do, and wood ducks, they've got brown heads, or something like that, but I know it's not green."

"How come you're all of a sudden the Answer Man?"

"I don't know. It's just not a wood duck, that's all."

"How about if you give it to me? How about if you say, 'Okay, Cyril, it's a wood duck'?" The effort to speak was tiring him out again, Wyatt could see.

"I just changed my mind," Wyatt said, still rowing.

"Good."

"It's a wood duck."

"Thanks." Cyril breathed out. He reached into his pocket, pulled out a pill, and swallowed it. He had been wincing whenever the small waves hit the boat.

"I don't think I missed much of anything," Cyril said, speaking to the floor of the boat.

"No?"

"No. I saw Niagara Falls once, and the Grand Canyon. There was the Taj Mahal, I didn't get there, or Disney World either, but it's too far away. Besides, I saw the pictures."

"I've never been to either of those places," Wyatt said. "I guess I wasn't interested enough in the rides. You hear about them, though. Space Mountain and like that. People waiting in line and then screaming."

"You can't see everything."

"No, you can't. Besides, the pictures they have of it on TV are pretty good."

"Well," Cyril said, "they're good enough. You just gotta decide what you're going to do in life."

"That's right."

"Me, I wanted to get into a little trouble more than I wanted to sight-see."

"Yes."

"I was a man of simple tastes," Cyril said elegiacally.

"Yes."

"Mostly I just wanted pussy."

"You got that."

"Then I wanted to settle down."

"Right."

"You know, a house and family."

"Well, you got that, too."

"I sort of made too much trouble. Sometimes I had a bad temper, you know. Beer can do that. I got mad at you once or twice. I apologize."

"No need to apologize, Cyril. That's okay."

Wyatt rowed for a long time without saying anything. He could feel the sun's warmth on the top of his head, especially where his hair was thinning and a bald spot growing, like an infestation, at the back. Here, away from the dock, the river had widened out to become a lake, and he gazed down into the depths of the pale green water: whorls scudded in the wake behind the oars.

"I've always wondered," Cyril said, almost in a whisper, "when you row, are you moving the water, or are you moving the boat?"

"You're moving the boat."

"But the water moves, too."

"I suppose. A little."

Cyril was hunched over, apparently to keep warm. "I had a lot of questions like that, but what I didn't have enough of was curiosity to get them answered."

"Well, there are always more questions. Just as soon as you get one of them answered, there's another."

"Well sure."

Cyril twisted backward to see how far they had gone. "Houses on the shore're starting to look little and far away."

"Well, we're close to the middle of the bay."

"I never liked that part of the river," Cyril said, "where the current was strong, back there by the boat dock. I always liked it better here, where it was wide, and it didn't seem to be doing nothing. Why don't you row a minute more, why don't you?"

"Sure, Cyril."

He began coughing into a handkerchief, then quickly slipped the handkerchief into his pocket.

"I was just thinking about the worst thing that I ever did."

"What was that?"

"I can't think of it now. I guess I was bad to people. I didn't always mean to be. I'd be sorry right now if I could have been any other way. But I couldn't be any other way except for the way I was."

"I thought R/Q Dynamics helped you out."

"Aw, that shit. R/Q Dynamics was just jiveorama. That guy, R. Stan Drabble, it was just a money-making venture for him. It was all just about getting him rich. Took me a while to see that."

"It helped you straighten out."

"No. I straightened myself out. You helped me. You were my example."

"Don't say that, Cyril."

"Naw, it's true. You had that home and that job and that wife, and every Saturday, just like a clock, there you were, there was Wyatt with his charity money. I got so I hated that so much I *had* to straighten out. I mean, you and me, we were pals, but I didn't want your money anymore. That was why."

"Oh."

"The worst thing I ever did was to slap a woman once."

"Well, that's not so bad, I guess."

"I think it is. I punched her around. I defaced her. I don't think I did it more than once. There are times in my life, when I don't remember them."

"You were okay, Cyril."

"Most of my life, I couldn't help what I did."

"I know."

"There was damage I caused. I'm sorry."

"I think it's all right."

"I had carnal relations with women who didn't especially want to have my naked skin anywheres near theirs."

"Well, that's all past now. That's all in the past."

"It is and it ain't. I take it with me."

"Nobody's perfect."

"That's what they say. Stop the boat."

Wyatt pulled the oars in from the water. He felt a breeze on his face, and the sun still in his hair. The wind brought with it a trace of vegetative-water smell, a slight scent of fish. They were hardly drifting downstream now at all.

"I'll just sit here a minute," Cyril said. He was looking toward shore.

"You sit as long as you want to. You don't have to do this, you know."

"Oh, I'm doing it. You start something, you have to finish it. Besides, I'm sick of the pain and the drugs. I am tired, man. Just plain tired."

"Yes."

"They didn't have to make WaldChem so dangerous, those bastards. They could have made it safer. Well, forget that."

"You smoked, Cyril. You smoked cigarettes all your life."

"Hell, I'm *still* smoking." He pulled a pack out of his flannel shirt pocket and threw it into the water. "There. I just quit."

They sat in the boat together, on Saturday, in the mid-morning sun. Wyatt looked around. He saw no other boats out on the water.

"You know," Cyril said, "I loved this world."

"Yes."

"I did what I wanted to do, but the only problem was, after a while, no one thought I was serious. They just thought I was silly. You know. What I wanted was only to be taken seriously once or twice. Just enough dignity to live was all I needed. It wasn't a totally meaningless life, the life I had, was it?"

"No. No, Cyril, it wasn't. Jesus," Wyatt said, "I'm rowing back."

"No, you aren't." Cyril reached for the oars. "I ordered you. You know I had that right. I mean, it's not my fault that we're here, but we're going through with it, and that is my fault, if you want to blame me."

"No."

"I hope this isn't a hassle."

Wyatt looked at him.

"Put that dumbbell over here."

Wyatt lifted it and placed it near Cyril's feet.

"Well," Cyril said, "guess I'll see you around."

"Right."

"You take care."

"I'll do that."

"Check on Pooh now and then. She doesn't know everything there is to know."

"Definitely."

"Bless me."

"What?"

"Give me a blessing. You know, like people do."

"Okay." Wyatt held his hand up. He didn't know what to say, so he said the first words that came into his head. "I bless you, Cyril. Go in peace. Find rest."

"Thank you. That was the last thing." He leaned forward and patted Wyatt on the back. "Okay, now," he said. He put the cane on the bench next to Wyatt, then stood up. He reached out, as if he were pointing toward some object in the distance, then sat down again.

"I'm such an asshole," he said. "I couldn't do it that time."

"You don't have to do it at all," Wyatt told him. Wyatt's heart was pounding. He looked down at his hands. They were trembling, just a bit.

"Yes, I got to do it. It's the right thing."

"No rush."

"No, I guess not."

They sat for another moment in silence, and then Cyril stood up again.

What happened after that came to Wyatt in a series of images that stood on their own, even at the moment that they were occurring. It was exactly as if he had been sitting in a movie theater in a small town, and the projector's arc lamp burned out frame after frame of film. After Cyril was on his feet, his right leg went out, toward the gunwale, and he must have pushed his weight down, because the boat tipped in that direction. The dumbbell on the floor rolled toward him, and Cyril seemed to lose his balance. He didn't jump into the water; he fell into it. Or at least that was what Wyatt seemed to see: Cyril, halfway between the boat and the lake, suspended in midair, his arms out, the left arm pointing upward, and the right arm pointing south. Then the hole burned through it. It seemed to Wyatt as if Cyril stayed in the air forever, but when he looked again, Cyril was in the water—himself, his shirt, his pants, and his boots—and instead of sinking, he was struggling.

He had sunk below the water's surface, laminated with sun, but he had bobbed up again, so that his face was visible, and he was gasping, possibly from the relentless freezing cold of the water, now that the ice had gone out. His arms flailed in circles, then hit the surface, and sprayed Wyatt, and Wyatt looked down at his cousin, and saw on his face the clarity of desperation, and at that moment Cyril said, "Help me."

Wyatt reached down to pull Cyril back in, but Cyril shook his head, or seemed to shake it, as a dog shakes water off its fur, and he did not reach up to take Wyatt's hand but instead repeated in a voice clogged with phlegm, "Help me."

He meant the weight.

The dumbbell was made of stainless steel or chrome—
something shiny. Wyatt reached down for it, and the sun—
once his friend and now his enemy—reflected off the weight
and made his eyes water. He used to do biceps curls with
weights like this. He picked it up. It was heavy, heavier than
his own life. He brought it over the side of the boat. Cyril's
hands, both of his hands, were now up, and Wyatt let the
weight down, but instead of falling directly into Cyril's hands,
the weight glanced against his cousin's forehead, but, even so,
Wyatt thought he saw Cyril reaching for the weight, both
hands, and then, rapidly, though at the same time frozen for a
moment, he saw Cyril heading downward to the bottom of
the lake, grasping the weight Wyatt had given him. He didn't
go straight down, but at a forty-five-degree angle, a trail of
breath bubbles following him, and his brown boots, the last
set of his possessions to be visible, descending behind him and
with him. And then they were invisible. And at last there was
no trace of Cyril, no bubbles rising to the surface. Nothing
but the sun reflecting off the water, and, in the distance, the
cry of some bird Wyatt couldn't identify.

His heart was thumping irregularly in his chest, and he
was crying, and when the crying rose in intensity, he opened
his eyes and saw a mucus discharge dribbling out of his nose.
He was embarrassed by his own grief, even though no one
could see him. He fell back onto the floor of the boat and
heard waves lapping against the side in a quiet placid frenzy.
He thought he heard the sun, a rattling noise, or an alarm, a
horrible buzzing of sunshine. Then it was quiet: nothing but
the day, and the blue April sky.

He must have blanked out for a moment, because when
he came to, the tears had dried on his face, and whatever had

come out of his mouth and nose was on his cheek. After wiping his face on his sleeve, he leaned over the side of the boat and cupped his hand in the water to drink. Then he made a bowl with his hands and splashed his face, and a sob gripped at his chest. He resisted it. The water tasted of vegetation—it tasted green—and it was so cold that it made his hands feel as if they had been injected with frozen iron.

It was so quiet out here. There was no sign of anything.

But he *felt* somebody or something watching him. He looked around: but no boats were anywhere near him, and no one on the shore would have been able to see what had just happened even if that person had been using binoculars. And why would anyone have bothered to watch two men out in a rowboat on a Saturday morning?

Gazing again at the water, that placid stupid element, Wyatt thought of his cousin down there, rolling and drifting, drifting and rolling. . . . Oh, he could have supported Cyril for years and years, why had Cyril thought he had to get a job and grow up? A split second of blindness and tears, before Wyatt picked up the oars and began to row *Noah's Ark* back toward the public-access boat dock. As he neared the dock, and the river narrowed, the current increased, so that he felt the lapping resistance to the strength in his arms and shoulders, the water's driven constancy against himself.

Now I'm supposed to go home and have lunch, he thought. The idea is that I'll feed Eugene and play with him and give Susan a few hours off to sleep or work. That's what I'm supposed to do.

As he was approaching the dock, two fishermen—but fishing season hadn't started yet, had it?—were setting out in a small rowboat powered by an Evinrude outboard motor. Maybe they were going after sunfish. He could see, from the corner of his eye, that they had waved to him. He turned his face away from them but lifted his arm from one of the oars to wave back. He kept his head down.

What had he just done? He didn't know. He didn't know the word for it. There wasn't a word, he didn't think, for what had just happened. It was an *event*. That was all he could think to call it.

How soon would Cyril's body rise to the surface? A few minutes, a few hours, a few days? The water was so cold that it might not rise for weeks.

He tied up Hugh's boat and walked carefully and secretly with Cyril's cane to the parking area, stopping at Cyril's truck, at Li'l Devil. Cyril had left it unlocked, and Wyatt opened the passenger-side door and put the cane on the seat. Inside was the usual mess of Cyrilisms: old candy and gum wrappers, crushed filthy cigarette packs, a green cardboard Christmas tree that said *Pine Scent* on it, hanging from the rearview mirror. Cyril hadn't taken the keys out of the ignition. Had he thought that he was coming back right away? Or that he didn't want to cause anyone any trouble by taking his keys with him, down to the bottom of the river? Wyatt took the keys out of the ignition and dropped them on the floor, the way people did around here, not bothering to worry about theft.

When he glanced at where the keys had landed, he saw a note, addressed to himself, a folded piece of paper that said FOR WYATT on the outside. He grabbed it, shoved it into his trouser pocket, and jogged to his car. Once he had pulled out on the highway and had reached the speed limit, he pulled the note out of his pocket and opened it. Inside, there were two words: THANK YOU.

19

Behind him, the door slammed, and after he bent down to untie his shoes, he saw Christina playing with her building blocks in the sunlight on the east side of the living room. She had built a tower of the child variety and now was working on what looked like an airplane terminal next to the tower. Over in the dining room, Susan had finished paying bills. The stamped envelopes were in a neat stack next to her checkbook. She sat in a chair with her feet up on another chair, reading a book. Eugene was babbling as he crawled and cruised his way toward his father. Wyatt picked him up.

"Hi," Susan said, still reading. "Where'd you go?"

He had never been good at this business of little white lies. Maybe they weren't so little. Maybe they weren't white after all. "Oh," he said, pausing for a moment, lifting Eugene up, thinking of where he might have credibly gone, "to the appliance store. Thought I'd look at cassette decks." Eugene pulled at his hair.

"For here? We have one."

"For my car."

"But you don't drive anywhere. You drive four miles each day."

"Honey, it wasn't serious. It was something to do. Just to get out."

"I understand," she said. She dog-eared a page. "Listen, I have to get out of here myself." She scratched her eyebrow. She was beautiful. How easy it was for her. "I don't want to work on my rooms"—she meant the Joseph Cornell–sized rooms that she assembled in the basement—"or anything like that. I need to buy some clothes for Eugene. I have to go to the mall. And I want to buy something pretty. I need to look pretty again someday." Wyatt was about to tell her that, no, she didn't have to go to the mall for that, but she was already telling him what to feed Eugene, and suddenly Wyatt found it was an effort, a project, to listen and not to pass out. At the same moment that Christina's building-block structure fell over and she began to shout and scream, the telephone rang.

"I'll get it," Wyatt said, rushing into the kitchen, carrying Eugene close to his shoulder. After he answered, he heard telephone static and, in his other ear, Eugene's vocalizations. He said "Hello" three times before he heard a woman's voice replying, and it was a moment before he recognized the voice as Pooh's.

"That Christina there, yelling?" Pooh asked. Her voice was flat.

"Hi, Pooh," Wyatt said loudly, so Susan would know who it was. "Yeah, it's Christina. She's been practicing and perfecting her scream. What's up?" His mouth went cotton-dry. He wanted to wash his hands for a week.

"So why's she screaming?"

He tried to chuckle. It came out stagy, reeking of false humor. "She was building a tower. It just fell over."

"So. Did he do it?"

"Who?"

"Cyril."

"Do what?"

"Wyatt, just tell me if he did it. Don't make me ask these things."

"Well, he . . . he *told* you? He didn't say he was going to—"

"Of course he told me. So tell me. Did he go?"

"Yes. He went."

He heard her beginning to cry. "I'm so sorry," he said. He waited. "I should go."

"No, wait. Stay on the phone."

He stood in the kitchen, Eugene pulling at his hair, Christina still shouting in the living room, Susan bent over near her, and he listened to Pooh cry. "I'm sorry," he said again.

"Oh, ditto," she said. "He liked the water but he wasn't good at swimming." The words came out between sobs. "And he didn't like the pills."

"Pooh, whatever it was, it's over," he said quietly. He never knew how to offer comfort or solace. The wrong phrases leapt toward him. "Rest assured," he said, and as soon as he had said it, he wished he had never learned how to speak English or any other language.

" 'Rest assured'?" Her sobs mixed with an angry laugh. "My God, the phrases you use on me. Lucky you went to college. My God. 'Rest assured'! Oh, I'll rest assured, all right." He heard another low grieving sound start up in her throat before their line was disconnected.

Putting down the receiver, and then lowering Eugene to the floor, Wyatt understood that he had been an accessory to a crime, and he was astonished, not at the thought of the crime of aiding in a dying man's suicide, but at the recognition that he was slow-minded and hadn't thought of the legal term for his participation until now. The verdict on him, he now knew, was that he was obliging and careless, an accessory. He stood with his hands in front of his eyes, rubbing them. Outside, a truck rattled past, a pickup, the same year and model as Cyril's. Putting his hands back in his pockets, Wyatt could see through his front window his neighbor spraying his lawn with herbicide. He wore a yellow hat, with a visor. It made Wyatt want to scream. He stood in his own living room, repressing the impulse to scream.

"Well," Susan said, putting on her jacket, "I'm on my way." She touched Wyatt on the back. Down to his right arm went her hand. "Your sleeves are wet," she said, fastening her fingers around the cuff.

"Oh, that," he said. He couldn't think of an explanation, so he kept his silence. He had not screamed yet.

"What did Pooh want?"

"Just to know how Eugene was. She was asking about Eugene."

"She was? She never does that. What did you tell her?"

"I said fine."

"She was really calling about *Eugene?* That's odd. How's Cyril feeling?"

"I don't know," Wyatt told her.

"Well, I'm off." She stretched up to kiss him on the cheek. He thought: I don't deserve her. Probably I never did.

When Eugene became fretful, Wyatt changed his diaper. The process was slower than when Christina had been a baby, because now they used cloth diapers from Save-the-Earth Diaper Service, and Eugene's penis squirted half the time when exposed to the air. Wyatt kept another diaper free as a safety shield. In the kitchen, playing with Christina, Wyatt began to cry again but managed to wipe his eyes with his shirt sleeves so that his daughter wouldn't notice what he was doing. He walked over to the diaper bag and dried his tears with a diaper; then he gave himself a limit of thirty seconds to cry. He stood in the front hallway, his shoulders shaking, making sure his sobs were absolutely quiet. Christina walked up to him, saw his tears, pointed at them, and laughed. She ran away from him toward the living room.

Later, when Eugene was taking his nap, Wyatt hoisted Christina up on his shoulders and carried her around the backyard. The sun, as unyielding as ever, shining down on the wreckage of human history, seemed implacable now. The backyard had an appearance of normality, with its maple tree, its birdhouse, its little plastic play structure, its dirt beds for the garden they would soon plant, its wood fence. It was so normal, it felt strange, even to Wyatt. They had sent some birds over from bird-supply—the Fates had—and the birds made the backyard seem even more normal than it usually did. Wyatt pointed toward them. Sparrow. Goldfinch. Cardinal. Grackle. Christina shouted at them, and they flew away.

What was his mother's word for normality that was so normal it felt strange? Corilineal. All this was corilineal, with a vengeance.

He missed his mother, he missed his father, he missed Cyril, he missed Susan, he even missed Gretel—he would have to call her—and he missed the birds that had once been in the yard.

Back inside, with Christina watching *Sesame Street,* Wyatt sat down with the telephone directory in his lap. First he looked up Jerry Schwartzwalder's number. Then he began to flip through the Yellow Pages, until he stopped at an ad with a black curlicue border.

Tattoo You
Five Oaks Only Registered Tattoo Parlor
Walk-ins and Appointments
Clean and Fast!

Next to this information was a drawing of an eagle and a flower, followed by a telephone number and an address, an upstairs address—it was quite specific about this. You had to go up a flight of stairs to have this done to yourself. It wasn't a street-level activity.

Guy Smiley was excitedly shouting at the audience for *What Do I Do?* on TV. Sitting back in the big stuffed chair that he often claimed as his own, Wyatt imagined the steps to becoming not-Wyatt. Perhaps he had already started. Certainly a tattoo would help. Unusual pain went with tattoos. Everyone said so. He wanted some of that, and the sooner the better.

20

She had been rummaging through the south-west pile of newspapers in the hallway to the bathroom, looking for an article about the mating habits of Baltimore orioles—something about the manner in which the males fed the females, or displayed themselves, she couldn't remember—when Wyatt called her to say that Cyril had been found drowned in the river. After a long moment, during which her heart stopped abruptly, then started again, Ellen began to weep and laugh, before telling Wyatt that of course he was lying, and he might as well tell her what had actually happened. No, he said: Cyril had left his truck down by the boat dock, but he had forgotten his cane inside. Pooh had called in to the police to report him missing, and they'd dragged the river and found him. His balance was bad, Wyatt said, and always had been. Apparently he'd fallen off the dock. He'd been standing there, Wyatt said, probably gazing in one direction or another, and he'd just fallen.

She couldn't remember hearing Wyatt tell lies like this before, such elaborate fictions. It was quite new. She didn't want to make a point of it—he'd probably cooked up this death somehow with Cyril, and it was none of her business how the two boys had gone about it—but she was like God sometimes: she was curious. She couldn't help herself on that score.

"What were his last words?" she asked.

"Excuse me?"

"Oh *come on,*" she barked. "I'm not asking you for incriminating details, sweetie pie. This is *Ellen* you're talking to. I'm just asking about his last words to you. I'm not going to turn you in, after all."

"His last words?" Wyatt sounded distant and remote. " 'Thank you.' That's what they were."

" 'Thank you'? Ah, that sounds exactly right. 'Thank you.' Yes. He was always a mess, Cyril was, but he did try to be grateful, when he could be, for what he got. When's the memorial service?"

"Next Tuesday," Wyatt said, sounding like a talking ghost. "Czerny Funeral Home. You want to say anything?"

"I might. Sure." She was gazing down at her yellow socks. The color of the fabric was holding up pretty well. "Yeah, I'll say something."

•   •   •

She wore a string of pearls so that she'd look like the Queen of England, and pebble-sized opal earrings hidden under the mess of her hair. She liked the idea of wearing earrings to a memorial service for Cyril. Someone had to make an effort. Wyatt had worn a business suit, but Ellen couldn't remember a time when he had looked worse. He seemed to have forgotten to shave this morning, which gave him a certain Cyril-look. Even with Eugene on his arm, in the creepy false elegance of the funeral home with its headache-inducing spray of flowers, beige carpeting, and flocked gray wallpaper, Wyatt seemed both sick and angry. But all that was camouflaged under the official impassivity of his face. A too-short haircut and new pouchy bags under his eyes had aged him without maturing him. When she embraced him, he smelled of cologne.

Jeanne sat in the audience, vague and becalmed. And sitting next to her—Ellen could hardly believe it—straight-backed and observant, missing nothing, calmly at rest but not becalmed like her mother, was Gretel, who took in the whole event and seemed ready to diagnose it medically until Ellen saw what was clearly impossible: Gretel weeping, and blowing her nose into a handkerchief, and then, even more impossible, Gretel's mother, Jeanne, turning toward her daughter, and patting her three times, and nodding, giving consolation.

Near her were some of Cyril's high school friends, and Pooh and Otis, of course, and some others Ellen didn't recognize. A sparse crowd of mourners.

Various people came up to speak; Ellen didn't hear them very well. When it was Wyatt's turn, Ellen noticed that he was hunched over slightly to his right, as if he had a rock or a weight attached to him. He read a poem by Robert Frost, of all people, and then told a story about one of Cyril's teenage pranks: doughnuts in the municipal swimming pool. There were more stories. Wyatt was trying to make Cyril sound like fun, then respectable, having brought Pooh and Otis into the account.

Then he wavered. He became dissociative: he leaned forward, and his gaze flattened, as if he were about to take a nap with both eyes open. He swayed a bit before grabbing the podium to steady himself. Ellen leaned over to observe Gretel, who was watching her brother carefully.

"Well, I thought he was a good guy, and I loved him," he said. He sat down, two folding chairs away from Ellen, leaving in the air behind him a scent purchased at the Ralph Lauren counter at the local department store.

Ellen then rose and walked behind the podium. She knew that what she was about to say would get her into trouble. But she didn't know what she would say until she was actually standing there on the little raised platform and saw the faces staring up at her. She wouldn't say the words, they would say *her*.

She tilted her head and listened. The words fell on her in a flood.

"To start with," she said, "I don't think we know God's real name, and I don't think we're deserving to know it, either, any more than we know what's happened to Cyril over here." She took a breath. This would be a long-distance run. "Cyril wasn't much for responsibility. Wyatt was right about that, he kind of let things get out of hand, and maybe he was just like God that way, you know, the sort of person who starts on something and then just doesn't seem to care how it all works out. Sometimes I think God never grew up: all this death around us, all this suffering. I ask you: where's the plan? Not a sign of it, not a trace. I don't see any plan here. Don't get me wrong. I *liked* Cyril. I mean I loved Cyril, when he was being a bad boy, because he never hurt anyone, not really, not that I could see. He was just enjoying himself. He was one of those harmless hoodlums. God probably thought that that was the interesting part of Cyril. Let me tell you something. I think we all wake up at night out of those terrible dreams we have, and we know something dreadful is true about existence, but we can't say it, because the words vanish when we wake up. I've noticed that so many times, and I know you have, too. I'm trying to tell you about Cyril, now. After all, I half raised him, I tried to be a mother to him.'' She laughed quickly. "Oh, I know these remarks aren't coming out very well organized. Let me keep trying. I can't hurt anyone by talking. I see you're still sitting there. All right. I never had a steady job, myself, I mean one steady job, nine-to-five, and I never got myself committed to a long marriage, and I suppose the only thing I ever really committed myself to was helping to raise that man behind me who's about to be buried in the ground. I know you all think I was a single lady living out in a house full of newspapers. Cyril picked up all that oddness from me. I wasn't orderly, and neither was he. I was keeping those newspapers because I thought there was a story unfolding in them, and I found it, it's this: we once had a God who loved us, who took care of us, and treated us like children. No one knows what happened to that God, the one most people thought was a male, but He either died or disappeared. He left. Anyhow, now we've got another one, and I stand before you and swear to it: this God doesn't love us. The universe is too large for that. This God just does not care beyond being curious about how every event works out. I know about this God because this God is standing behind me right now. It does that, this spirit, it stands behind me watching everything that I do.'' She stopped and patted her right shoulder. "Right behind there, that's where it is. Just like a camera. This is the camera-God, except it's curious, this God-lens, this God-eye, and you know what we're doing for this God? We're putting on a huge *show*, that's what we're doing. We're entertainers. Oh I know this sounds like a horrible truth, I mean no one wants to know that the history of humanity is a history of a vaudeville for God's benefit, but it is, I mean it's at least *half* that." She saw some men stirring angrily in the audience and calculated that she had about another two minutes before someone came up and forcibly stopped her. "Everybody wants to have a good parent. But I can't see that God ever was or ever will be a good parent, so what we have to do is learn to be alone or to love humans. I don't want to hear from anybody that Cyril died because God wanted him to. God didn't care whether Cyril lived or died, it was all the same, a show either way. Maybe pain and suffering make for a better show, but I don't think God cares about the content, which is why if you're sitting out there in front of me, and you're looking up, and you're seeing a funny old woman who never went to a beauty parlor and who never learned how to be pretty or get married permanently, all the same you're seeing someone who's telling you something important about Cyril right now: God didn't do this to him. You want to blame somebody, you have to blame Cyril for doing gross harm to himself, or you have to blame that company out there that he worked for, but I don't want to hear anybody prattling on about the deity, prayers and so forth, because I have a personal experience of the deity, and I tell you that there is absolutely no love coming to us from that realm. None at all. You might as well pray to a telephone pole. I mean, if God loved us, we would know it, wouldn't we? You bet we would. We'd feel enveloped. We'd feel interfered with, wouldn't we? But no: this is hands-off, this God, and I think

Cyril knew that. How I loved him. How I loved that boy. He once carved a terrier dog out of a bar of soap and gave it to me. Whenever I was feeling low, he'd call me, find out how I was. He never had a penny. Spent all the money he ever had. Drank beer and smoked cigarettes and loved every woman who would love him back, and some who wouldn't. Well, I guess he's a pretty thin thread to spin on, Cyril was, I mean it's hard talking about the universe using Cyril as an example." One man was getting to his feet in the audience, and Ellen couldn't tell whether he was about to walk out, or advance toward the podium to muzzle her. "Let me finish," she said. "I'm almost done. Cyril loved to fish. As I remember, he loved to play softball. He loved to drink beer, and I seem to remember that he loved to amble around in the woods during the fall, kicking leaves. He just couldn't make sense of things, most of the time, and I don't blame him in the least, because I couldn't, either. Oh, all of you: go back to your houses and your homes and your families, and weep for Cyril if you feel like it. I have! But don't blame existence, because that doesn't make any sense, to do that. He just died. He was going to die. Maybe he brought it on himself or that company did. But I'll tell you, it wasn't God coming down on Cyril. That's just not how it works. There's not a bit more sense to this whole operation than to a robin eating a worm." All at once her gaze swept over Wyatt, who was staring back at her as if he had just been struck. "That's pretty much what I had to say, I guess. Oh: I just thought of something else. If there's anything better than love, I don't know what it is. Love gave Cyril a chance. And Pooh over there, she did, too. And their baby. Love is to me looking better than almost anything else. It's the only weapon we've got against this God. We've got to love each other, because God won't." She waited. Was there anything else to say? She had just made a spectacle of herself and wasn't

300

sorry. But it was complicated, when someone died, and the people who claimed that their thoughts were entirely in order weren't being honest. She had a last idea. "We have to save this world if we want to live in it, because God won't." That was enough. Ellen felt herself relaxing, the words that wanted to have their say having been said, and she was about to sit down when she saw Jeanne raising herself to her feet, holding up her hands, and applauding.

At the same time that Jeanne was applauding, a man—she could see from his balding head that it was Alan Stolmeyer, Cyril's classmate who worked now in the hardware store making duplicate keys—was getting up, his hand in the air as if this place had turned into a classroom, and he wanted to be called on.

"What you just said is an outrage," he said, his hardware-store voice trembling with fury. "And it's blasphemy. The purest blasphemy."

"She can say what she wants to," Jeanne said, from her chair, her voice sharp and as shiny as a silver carving knife, Ellen thought. She had developed some authority from her suffering after all these years. "You want to speak, Alan, you can."

Alan Stolmeyer continued to stand. He was wearing a moonlight-and-haystacks necktie. "An insult," he was saying, "in the face of God. If you read Scripture, the sixteenth verse of Matthew, you—"

"That's the wrong Bible," Ellen said, to the ceiling. "That one is about a God who left."

From the loudspeakers bolted into the wall, string music, "Abide with Me," had suddenly made itself audible.

"This isn't a town meeting," Wyatt said. He had returned to the podium. "We're trying to remember Cyril. Alan, you're out of line."

"I'm out of line? It's your aunt who's out of line! She should get down on her knees and beg forgiveness of Almighty God."

"Don't you tell me what I should do!" Ellen shouted. "Who are you to tell me what to think?"

"Who am I? Who am I? A God-fearing man who walks in the path of righteousness, that's who I am! And you should—"

Close to him, beside him, there had appeared, in a slightly worn gray suit, a gentle-seeming man with a receding hairline—perhaps balding men were sympathetic to other bald men—who was now quietly murmuring into Alan Stolmeyer's ear, just the way a parent might to a shouting child. The rituals of pacification: Ellen couldn't recognize this placid character, and then remembered that he had been Wyatt's friend and he sold Buicks out there at Bruckner Buick. His sister was a physicist. It was Hugh Welch, and he had gained some weight and he just hadn't looked like himself. He had his arm around Alan's shoulder, and now they were talking like a couple of old chums. If she ever bought a new car, Ellen decided then and there, she would buy a Buick. How she had wanted, at certain times of her life, for a man to speak into her ear that way, to calm her! That was one pleasure, one of the few, that had been denied her.

The funeral home director had reappeared and was now, to louder accompaniment of "Abide with Me," ushering everyone into a side room, for the reception, just prior to the actual burial. On a long folding table draped with hideous purple cloth were laid out various crudités and funereal snacks. She realized that she was standing alone. Others were speaking together or in small groups, but she had the north side of this table, near the window with the dusty venetian blinds, all to herself. She touched her pearls and reconsidered humanity and thought of how, at certain times of day, she didn't care for it at all.

"Well, now you've gone and done it." She felt herself being hugged and kissed by Wyatt, his cologne perceptible before he was. Next to him, Susan stood and smiled, carrying Eugene. And next to her was Jeanne, smiling crookedly, and Gretel, who leaned toward her and did what she had never done, in Ellen's memory: she kissed her.

"It just came out," Ellen said, before leaning down to kiss her sister-in-law on the cheek and then Gretel, whose skin was as smooth as a snowfield. At the moment that Ellen's lips touched Jeanne's cheek, Jeanne hummed.

"It's about time that someone spoke the truth in this town," Jeanne said, in that funny shortwave voice of hers. "The trees fall down, and nobody collects them, have you noticed?"

Ellen nodded.

"Poor Cyril," Jeanne said, all at once tilting her head to examine the ceiling. "At least it's only late April and not too early for planting. His timing was always off, but not quite."

Ellen nodded again. She turned to Wyatt. "Did you mind, what I said?"

"No," he said, "I liked it. It gave me permission."

"To do what?"

"Anything."

"You're not sounding like yourself."

"Good."

"So what are you going to do?"

He looked at her, and she saw behind or in his eyes the glint of desperation and violence, and she felt, at that moment, that she had never quite known her nephew or at least hadn't known him well enough, any more than his own mother had. Ellen felt that she had never understood anything about the undifferentiated anger of men, when they grew tired of decency and saw its inadequacy.

"I'll tell you one thing," Gretel said, putting her hand on her brother's arm. "Before I fly home, I'm going to take his blood pressure. He looks like somebody who's about to blow a few fuses."

Even though it was April, the hillside where they buried Cyril was cold: the maples had started to leaf out, but, in the shade they cast, the coolness of the earth seemed almost gravitational to her, pulling her toward it, and in between the statements and prayers—one high school friend of Cyril's who actually did believe in prayer was reciting a lugubrious verse from the Order for the Burial of the Dead—Ellen tried to hear the call of any bird, actively territorial or wild with its mating instinct, but she heard no sound from the trees except for the wind blowing through them. Behind her: God, watchful and indifferent; in front of her, Wyatt, exchanging a glance with her now, a glance saturated with anger and longing, but longing for what, she wouldn't have been able to say.

21

At the top of the stairs, his hand on the door-knob of TATTOO YOU, he waited for a moment, thinking, *This isn't me, I don't do this,* as he read the stickers fixed to the window pane to the side of the door. "We Reserve the Right to Refuse Service to Anyone." "Artistic Expression Isn't a Crime." "No One Under Eighteen Admitted." He went inside. Having left work early, he saw, in the reception area, an old-fashioned wood-encased pendulum clock that claimed the time of day as three-thirty. He had expected dinge and filth and spiderweb lighting, but in fact the outer room smelled of pine wood, and, lit by a large window facing south, it had a telltale aura of femininity: a Tiffany lamp, Art Nouveau illustrations on the wall, next to a bookshelf crammed with volumes about tattooing, folk art, birds, and painting.

Odd, he thought, after standing there for what seemed to be two minutes or so, before glancing over at the clock again. It was still 3:30, even though the pendulum was moving.

The office assistant, a large cigarette-smoking woman with a double chin and a complicated crucifix-and-chain earring apparatus, and who was dressed from shoulder to ankle in black, asked him if he had come for a tattoo. He said that he had. He sat down on the sofa, glad that no other customer was waiting here, and examined, without meaning to, the butterfly on her right forearm. On her other forearm was a lily.

She was sitting at a desk, writing on a notepad. "Do you know the size of the tattoo you want?"

He nodded and put the thumb and index finger of his right hand, curved to form a backwards C, into his left palm, and held that up for her. "About this big."

She nodded. "Method of payment? We charge forty-five dollars an hour. Minimum is thirty-five."

He had come prepared. "Cash."

She wrote this down. "And your name?"

"Cyril," he said.

"Cyril what?"

"Cyril Wilson."

"We require a thirty-dollar deposit on all work here before any work is actually done on you." She stubbed out her cigarette and lit another. He took out three ten-dollar bills from his wallet and gave them to her. "Where do you want this tattoo, Cyril?"

"I haven't decided."

"All right," she said, and he could tell at once that she was in a bad temper. "We don't do public skin: no face or forehead or neck, no hands and fingers, and absolutely no genitals or any tattoo that requires genital contact. Okay, right?"

"Right."

"We got some notebooks on the table there in front of you if in case you need some idea of what you want put on you." She puffed on her cigarette and daintily tapped the ash onto the back of a porpoise ashtray. "Well? What is it you want?"

"My name."

"Cyril? Is that it?"

"That's right."

"Just that? Cyril? Cursive or Gothic lettering or some other letterhead style?"

"Print. Plain print. Maybe something else too."

"Like what? What else you want?"

"I haven't made up my mind."

"Well, before you go into where the tattooist is, you better make up your mind. You should look in those notebooks on the table in front of you there. Like I said."

"All right."

The first one, the one on top, was labeled *Dead Stuff*. He opened it. Inside it, page after page, was a cornucopia of the underworld, a harvest of nightmare, a springtime full-flowering of celebratory lyrical menace and bloodflow: pictures of tombstones and wild skeleton cemetery orgies, windblown grim reapers with dead flowers in their buttonholes, then grinning and joyous skulls fixed at every angle, grinning vipers twisted around naked women with their heads thrown back in unconsciousness or submission, skeletons riding foaming horses or yellow Lamborghini convertibles, skeletons with clown faces ravishing nude standing or reclining voluptuaries, dripping-fanged cobras coiled around bloody daggers draining into lakes of blood, other huge orange-haired clowns (he hadn't expected clowns) with machetes and daggers raised high, poised for the ripping downward arc, raging lions one second away from their prey, then more skulls with roses for eyes, and that odd grim smirk most of these death-images presented, highstepping dancing cadavers, and a winged dragon enclosing the earth in its batlike wings.

"See anything you like?"

It wasn't exactly what he had in mind. It was all too happy for that, this joyful death-drunk party in the cemetery, the spicy hot-pepper delight in the image of metal flowers and gardens of ash. Oh joyful humpbacked Death, he thought, where was this smile the morning I rowed your boat?

"Not really."

"Men usually like dead stuff. Women get other things."

"I figured."

"We got a book of patriotic, too. Eagles and flags and Iwo Jima. Phrases, too, if you can't think of any. A.P.'ll be ready for you in a minute. She's just finishing up now. You can talk to her about what you want."

"Who's A.P.?"

"She's the tattoo artist. You want to look at the other portfolios? They're under there."

"Such as what?"

"Mister, I don't know what you want. We got flowers and birds. You can do mix-and-match, you know, some dead stuff and some birds. Women like birds. It's what they call a sexual difference. Then we got heroes. Elvis and Laurel and Hardy and Axl Rose. You want Madonna? A.P. did a Madonna last week. She's done Bruce and Prince and she did

Buddy Holly once. We also've got a sample book of vow tattoos, you want to see them."

"Vows?"

"Well, yeah, of course. Sure. Suppose you love somebody named Debbie. So you have a vow tattoo for her. 'Debbie until Death.' You know, like that. A vow. On a scroll. And, like, it's there *forever,* you understand that? These things do *not* wash off, believe me. It better be Debbie until death, 'cause that's how long it'll be on your arm. But I guess you don't want a vow, right?"

"Right."

"Just your name."

"Yes."

"Cyril."

"Yes."

She gave him an examining look. "You're Cyril?"

"Yes, I am."

"I'm asking," she said, "because we don't see many people coming in here, midafternoon, wearing a suit and a wedding ring, wanting his own name, but it's fine, we can do it, no problem. A.P., she'll be here in a sec."

The two women escorted him to a room with a chair exactly like a dentist's, and A.P., a short woman with long hair and glasses, said, "Yeah, it's a dentist's chair all right. Everybody asks. They're my worst clients, dentists. They don't like the pain. They can dish it out, but they can't take it."

He was beginning to feel that he was making a mistake, but a correct mistake, the sort of mistake he would feel grateful for later. The dyes were lined up in a multilayered box; the containers with the dye in them looked like squeegee bottles.

"So," A.P. asked, "what do you want?"

He explained about the name, and A.P. asked him what he wanted to go with it. "Nobody does just a name," she said. "That's not art. You need something to go with it, honey. Something to give it a feeling. I can do it, but you got to tell me, first."

"I want a shadow," he said.

"Excuse me? A shadow? A shadow how?"

He had thought of water, of a lake. He had considered a tiny pickup truck, or a scroll. But what he really wanted was a shadow, the very shape of a soul. "I can draw it," he said. "Give me a piece of paper and pencil. I'll show you exactly what I want."

The figure he drew, a human form from the midline up, was half shroud, half shadow, like a profile projected onto a wall.

"You want that?"

"That's it."

"What color?"

"Gray."

"You want a gray tattoo of a face with the name underneath."

"That's right."

"No color?"

"No."

"Not even for the name?"

"You could do the name in red, maybe. But the rest has to be gray."

"Okay. Now where do you want this?"

"Some place," he said, "where I'll know where it is, but no one else will see it."

"All right," she said, sitting back, "if that's what you want, I would put it here." She touched him underneath the upper arm. "You see, the arm is usually held toward the body, so people won't see it there unless you raise this arm over your head. Or I can put it on your buttock or your inner thigh."

"No. I don't want it there. The arm. Put it there, on my arm."

"Okay. You can hang up your coat and your shirt over by the sink. There're hangers. Just put 'em on the wall hooks. But I have to warn you about something. That area of the arm, where you want this tattoo, it hurts a little more than some other places in the body."

"That's all right. That's fine," he said, taking off his coat. "That's what I want."

While she was preparing her materials, and he was removing his undershirt, she said, "You can draw pretty good. You go to art school?"

"In college I majored in it."

"Me, too. I could always draw. Everybody else in art school, all the other kids, they were more into abstract expressionism, conceptualism, that stuff. But I was good at life studies. Nobody could do the body better than me. When I dream, it's in Art Nouveau. You put it in front of me, I could draw it," she said. "Okay, honey, let's take a look at you." She smiled. "You don't have much hair. That makes it easier. Raise your arm up." He did. "Smooth as a baby under there. Okay. First I'm going to disinfect it with Zephiran, and then I'll start the actual tattoo. You want me to explain what I'm doing while I'm doing it?"

"No." He examined her. She wore thick glasses that magnified her brown eyes. With both of her arms covered, no tattoos were visible on her anywhere. She wasn't at all pretty except for her eyes; they had a spark of sympathy, but the sympathy was cool and formal, like that of a social worker.

She didn't lose her way. He liked that. In her business, she didn't make judgments about people, only about shapes and colors.

"I don't need a stencil for this," she said. "I can do it freehand. I'm going to give it a little bit of color, a bit of blue. You want some music?" He nodded. She switched on a radio on the table behind her. Country-western came out.

"No," he said. "I've changed my mind."

"Okay, Cyril," she said, and she shut it off.

The pain, when it arrived, wasn't what he expected: not impact-pain, but more like a burning ripple, a small wave of pain splashing onto his arm, receding, and then coming back. He was disappointed. He had been hoping for more. He closed his eyes. The tattooist nattered on about her clients, the designs they sometimes wanted: the flag, Jesus, or the flag and Jesus together, *Death Before Dishonor,* a tree. He didn't want to hear that. He shut his ears against it.

It wasn't much pain, almost not enough to do the job, but it lifted him at last, until, inside his eyelids, a tree stood open at its trunk with a blue shimmering entryway into which he invited himself. Around him its roots and fibers closed so that he could play hide-and-seek inside it, and here with him was Gretel, his sister, the physician, examining him, but she must have been a bad physician because she listened for his heart by touching his shirt sleeve between her thumb and index finger, and then she pointed off toward the tunnel-darkness, and there, in the distance, at 3:30 in the afternoon, was his father. Cyril was standing nearby. They were talking. His father had raised a pair of scissors into the air and was cutting the air, cutting it in half. That was so like him.

He saw Alyse, then, in her office, and Jerry Schwartzwalder in his, and Schwartzwalder's house set on fire. He saw

everything himself, the avenging angel, a grim reaper hatch-
ing a cloak and a scythe, no, not grim, grinning, cobbled,
colloidal, at last on the winning side, humpbacked death, you
old Father.

"There," she said. "It's done."

She set down the needle bar, and he came back to himself.
She was explaining about preserving it: no bandage, she said,
but Monsell's solution, an anticoagulant. For the bleeding,
this was, and to prevent staining. She advised him not to put
anything else on it: no alcohol, for example, because it would
fade the design.

"Take a gander at it," she said, and he pretended to check
out the name and the shadow. In the mirror opposite him was
a man with his arm raised, but he kept his face turned away so
that he wouldn't see it, although he knew that, yes, it was
there.

"That was quick," he said. "Easy."

"You do something that size, it's easy."

"Thanks."

"No problem. You can pay on your way out."

Again the world made its way into his consciousness. He
heard the passage of cars, now, back and forth on the street
outside. A.P. was washing her materials in some sort of anti-
septic solution and then making out a bill. Without turning
toward him, she asked, "You aren't sick with anything, are
you?"

"Sick? No, I'm fine."

"You almost seemed to fall asleep. I've never seen anyone
fall asleep in that chair when I've been working on them. You
don't have any of those long-term illnesses?"

"No. What're you getting at?"

"Nothing. I didn't think so. I got to be careful. You

notice that I was wearing surgical gloves."

"Yes."

The name hurt, the shadow hurt, but not much, less than he had expected. Outside the window a breeze was loosening the crabapple blossoms and scattering them to the sidewalk.

"Look," she said, "it's none of my business, but can I suggest something to you?"

"What's that?"

"Take a vacation."

"Why do you say that?"

"Because I don't know the first thing about you, mister, but you sure look as if you could use one. You look okay and everything, but a little bit tired, no offense."

"I've been working hard lately."

"It's your eyes, Cyril."

"What about my eyes?"

"You look like you haven't been sleeping lately."

"Well, no," he said. "I haven't been."

"They got pills for that."

"Right."

"Okay, Cyril." She handed him the bill. "Well, listen. Take care of yourself. Don't go through the looking glass or anything."

"Why would I do that? What're you talking about?"

"You know damn well what I'm talking about," A.P. said.

22

With her face pressed against the pane of glass, and all the lights quenched in her room, Jeanne could detect the airless flow of the trade winds as they passed through the stumbled trees, and as these winds bore themselves soundlessly against the unprecise riveted disappearance of the ship, her stateroom tilted one way, and then another. Across the driven path of the night sky some calamity was staged for the sake of charity: planets, for example, held with their gravity their familial moons, their children. Those children did not fly away, nor were they contumed into the heavier gravity of the parent mass. Out here, where there was nothing but the occasional ecstatic breach of promise, the mother ship carried her further and further away into the vastness, unlike those astral bodies with their errant shadow plays. The winds of night tickled her window as she stood sentry for Planet Earth, in its vagabondage through the universe, past the wedding rings of the asteroids and the sorrowed orbits of the ruinous stars.

23

The sky had lately acquired a curious, stale calm. Maybe it wasn't the sky; maybe *he* had acquired it, but he wasn't interested in making such fine distinctions. He'd look out the window in the morning: there, in the upper atmosphere, would be the same cloud formations he had observed at twilight the night before, though they weren't cirrus clouds, these formations, "portents of rain," as the city manager liked to say in his offhandedly arcane manner. Probably these clouds were nameless. In any case, they were unmoving, the trade winds having been stilled. Despite the activity of his children through the house, he felt as if he were breathing the same air he had exhaled a week ago. Even the buds on the crabapple trees had the appearance of wear and age, a pawnshop feel to them. The tattoo on his arm didn't hurt, but it pulsated like a grim physical attachment, and he saw himself sitting down at his desk in the morning, *locating* himself there as if on a map, saw himself getting to work, a shadow nailed to his upper arm, and when he looked out of his office window he would see a cloud in the shape of a claw hammer, the same cloud he had seen three days before, casting a V-shadow on the street, V not for "victory" but for some other noun, which he would certainly think of eventually, "virtue," for example, or maybe one of those other unused nouns, like "vicissitude." He made love to Susan without paying more than generic attention to her, which was what, he thought, she gave to him.

The working day was like Halloween, except that all the masks showed businesslike and resolute expressions. The idea was to get on with things, crawl on one's belly like a reptile if that was what the situation demanded, but somehow remain a professional at all times. Was it possible to endure a dark night of the soul while wearing a cheerful face and a good necktie? At what time, on the day's schedule, would the nervous breakdown be penciled in?

At times he wondered if anyone really noticed who he was or what he was doing. Did people actually pay *sustained* attention to the activities of their fellow humans? The evidence, at least the evidence that he had gathered in the last month or so, based on the activities of his fellow citizens, was that they did not. It was just too much effort. Perhaps the explanation for the persistence of freedom in America was a vast and total communal indifference to the doings of anyone else. Everyone owned a spotlight, only to shine it upon themselves. Here he was, an assistant at a suicide, and no one had knocked at the door with questions, a pen and a spiral notebook in hand, gathering the evidence about Cyril. Except for Pooh and himself, no one seemed to miss him.

Somebody had told Pooh to wear black, so she was wearing a black T-shirt, black shorts, and black socks and black tennis shoes on the day that Wyatt had paid a call on her at the house on Maple Meadows Drive, and she had met him at the door with her eyes puffy and her hair teased up, layered and piled, as if she had been working at it all morning. Her hair was so huge, you could almost toss a coin in it and make a wish. "Come in," she said. "I've been doing housework." Baby Otis was strapped to her back, sleeping or overcome from hair-spray fumes.

They sat in the living room, still more or less bare of personal items, and with the picture of R. Stan Drabble gazing down at them, Pooh said, "I miss him. He was sweet to me. He was the first guy who was ever that sweet all the time." She began to cry, and her sobs awakened the baby, who saw Wyatt and began to cry himself. Seeing Pooh and Otis, Wyatt thought that the system of his nerves would collapse all at once. "I've been trying to help myself," Pooh said, "but I still cry all the time. My skin gets all rough and raw from the tears and the Kleenex."

He put his hand on her wrist. "I shouldn't have done it," he said. "I don't know . . . I don't know why or how. And I can't sleep anymore, and I miss him, too."

She began to shake her head back and forth with her eyes closed, as if dismissing him, or at least his regrets. "He wanted you to," she said. "Cyril never asked for very much, so when he did, you had to give it to him. I should know."

Taking the baby out of the carrier, she spread a blanket on the floor and put him on it. She had started to unclasp Otis's pajamas when Wyatt said, "Here. Let me do that. Please." Pooh raised her hands and moved back, and Wyatt took Otis's wet diaper off and handed it to Pooh, who carried it between thumb and index finger to a cloth sack with the words HAPPY BABY DIAPER SERVICE in the corner of the living room. She silently handed Wyatt the baby powder, and after drying off Otis's pink skin with another dry diaper, Wyatt powdered Cyril's son, who was looking up at him with baby-amusement.

"Sometimes they squirt you," Pooh said. "I've noticed this about boys."

"It's not personal when they do that," Wyatt told her. "Not usually." He brought Otis's legs up and slipped the clean diaper underneath him, crossed it, and pinned it.

"You're good at that," Pooh said, reaching for a cigarette, then putting it back. "Cyril only learned how to do paper diapers, he could never do these cloth ones, but he was sick by then. All those safety pins are pretty specialized."

"Yes, they are." He put on Otis's pajamas again and lifted him up to his shoulder, and the baby, who had stopped crying minutes ago, breathed quietly into Wyatt's ear. "Have you heard anything about the insurance, Pooh?"

She nodded. "They're paying it. They're paying all of it. They said the current near the dock where he parked his truck was enough to pull his body away to where they found it. They asked me if he'd ever mentioned suicide and I said of course not, it was against Cyril's religion."

"What religion is that?"

"They didn't ask, and I didn't tell them. Anyways, they're

going to pay all the life insurance, and Mr. Schwartzwalder, he's already paid me six months of Cyril's salary as, like, severance pay, and he bought me certificates for seven free dinners at Chez Steak. Maybe he didn't want me to sue him or something. I can cry and eat steak now, if I get in the mood. I wasn't going to sue him. I hate lawyers. That insurance is a lot of money. I've gotten an initial payment and the big one's coming. I only wish Cyril could see it. He would never have believed he was worth that much. And we had mortgage insurance, too. R. Stan Drabble says you should be insured for the times to come. Everybody's been real bricky. You, too."

Wyatt held on to Otis, patting him softly.

"You can give me the baby back now." Small tears were forming in the corners of Pooh's eyes.

"He's beautiful," Wyatt said. He lifted his fingertips to touch Otis's cheek.

"Well no he isn't," Pooh corrected him, holding Otis up and smiling at him, "but I never expected him to be. Between Cyril and me I thought we'd be lucky if he didn't attract, you know, extra attention."

"I've got to get back," Wyatt said. "Are you all taken care of, Pooh? Are you managing all right?"

"I'm okay. I'm not the first single parent there ever was. Only, I miss him, I miss Cyril, y'know? It's like the flu. I'm not getting over it. Maybe another man will help, but I can't do that yet. What about you? Are you all right?"

Wyatt shrugged. He was headed toward the door. "No," he said. "Goodbye, Pooh. Call me if you need anything I can help you with."

"No," she said. "You call *me*." She smiled. "You're not so lucky that you don't need help too, you know."

.   .   .

On the same May morning that Schwartzwalder had called to set up a golf game, Wyatt had been sitting in his office in city hall wondering when he would quit his job as assistant to the city manager of Five Oaks, or when, for that matter, he might be fired. People who got themselves fired were often imaginative, and he had mostly given that up. As soon as the Schwartzwalder call was finished, he walked down to Alyse's office. This was the day. His heart was pounding, and the tattoo throbbed.

He stood in her doorway and allowed himself to admire her, though he pretended to be doing something else. He was about to turn around and go back, but she shook her head and made a traffic-cop gesture of *wait*.

Her office had a pleasing disorder: a butter knife stood in her coffee cup, apparently to stir the cream; a poster of Mikhail Baryshnikov hung slightly askew; a diet Coke can had been pressed into service as a paperweight; and everywhere were papers, budget reports, torn message slips and telephone numbers. A pair of shoes, with high heels, were taking up the one chair, and a glass crystal hung from a thread in the center of the window, casting tiny spectra here and there in the office: yes, like the other foot soldiers in the growing army of the hapless and unlucky, she believed in crystals, and it broke his heart, but not so he couldn't stand it.

For a moment he blanked out, and when he came out of this reverie, Alyse was sitting there, staring at him.

"What?" he asked.

"What do you mean, what?"

"How come you're giving me that look?"

"Because you're standing in my doorway, and I was on the phone."

"To whom?" he asked.

"To a boring person with whom I do business day after day. He works in an agency. I think everybody works in an agency. Then you came in and leaned on my wall. What're you doing here?"

"I have an idea."

"Oh, that's good. You have an idea. What's your idea?"

He stood there. He let the seconds count away, while, outside, the clouds retained their exact shapes and placements in the sky.

"Oh," she said. "I see. You've come around."

"Yes."

She leaned back in her chair. "It certainly has been a long wait."

"Well, you know."

"Ah. I'm supposed to know. What happened? Did Susan disappoint you in some small but unforgivable way?"

Odd, to hear the typewriters and computer printers clacking from down the hall, the telephones ringing and the conversations, the dribble of the coffee machine. Maybe he wasn't actually hearing these sounds. They might be originating in his head. He closed the door.

"You closed my door. Well, it's not as if the invitation hasn't been open all this time," she said, taking off her reading glasses and dropping them with a gesture of dismissive contempt on her desk, next to the coffee cup with the butter knife in it. "Didn't you call me once or twice, at night, to talk, even though you had nothing to say? I seem to remember that you did."

"I think so."

"You think so. Wasn't it quite late?"

"Yes." He tried to smile and failed.

"But no follow-up. No follow-through. And now, here you are, darkening my doorway. Actually, my office. So what's your plan?"

"Do we have to talk about this? We could start with lunch."

"Ah. You mean today. You're talking about today."

"I guess I am."

"You guess you are. Well, I'm busy today. I may have been lovesick all this time, but I'm busy. I'm loaded down. I have lots to do. I just don't think it'll be possible. This isn't about your cousin, is it? Some weird consolation?"

She was smarter than he sometimes gave her credit for. "You mean," he asked, "not even lunch today or anything?"

"Maybe tomorrow. Maybe the following day. You didn't answer my question about your cousin."

He waited. Without wanting to, he broke her gaze by looking at her ceiling. Nothing up there but ceiling. "Why are you doing this?"

"This? Oh," she said, "you mean *this*. I'm making you suffer a little."

"Why?"

"Don't be obtuse. You know the cliché about what goes around?"

"Yes. I know that cliché."

"Well, so do I. I've had to wait. I've had to wait for you. I've had to sleep with someone else night after night, let's call him 'the wrong person,' while you were, well, on my mind, and I've waited and waited. A woman finds that hard, Wyatt. *I* find it humiliating. Well, it has been, making plays in your direction. You know what I love about you?"

"No."

"Your eyes. And you know where I've felt it?"

He was going to ask "What?" but thought that if he did,

he'd be missing the point so terribly that she might not speak to him again, ever.

"I felt it right here," she continued, tapping her chest just under her throat, near the collarbones. "Isn't that funny? My heart isn't up there. I don't even think that that's where your lungs are. It's medically kind of an empty space. Not much there except the esophagus, probably. Anyway, that's where I felt it. That's where I've felt not having you." She smiled at him, but the smile was not a kind one—in fact, quite the opposite.

"Funny to feel emotions up there," he said.

"Yes, isn't it?" she said, still smiling, and picking up a yellow pencil, which she baton-twirled between her fingers. "Funny to feel that feeling every time a guy, I mean you, walks by. Like a pressure. I guess most people learn to live with it. Or maybe they never feel it at all. Lucky them." She looked toward her crystal. "It thought it was going to rain today. I guess not. Why are you here? Because I don't think it was little old me that brought you down that hallway."

"Maybe it was."

"Well, then. Are you going to give me a compliment? At last?" she asked, staring at him. "Are you going to have something nice to say to me?"

"Yes."

"And what will it be?"

Looking at her, he said everything he could think of to say.

The motel carpeting, some sort of coarse orange-colored acrylic, hadn't been vacuumed with much thoroughness, and he could feel small particulate matter on the soles of his feet at the moment that he reached for Alyse and held her before they sat together on the bed. The trembling started in his shoulders and arms, and she whispered that she felt it, and it was sweet. She said it was in her knees. Her knees were weak. They'd been weak ever since she'd gotten out of bed that morning.

They were twenty-five miles out of town, near Harrisonville, in a room close enough to the freeway so that the Doppler-sound of trucks passing was clearly audible even with the windows closed and the air conditioning turned all the way up. He had brought some champagne and had offered it to her in a plastic cup, having poured himself one to settle his nerves. She had refused it. She said that if she was going to make love to him, she'd do it sober. But she had turned on the TV set, keeping the sound off: some midafternoon children's show, commercials for sugar-coated breakfast foods followed by Tom and Jerry cartoons, the worst.

He had also stopped to buy some apples and peaches. Without asking whether she wanted one, he quartered an apple and peeled it. She said that peeling it wasn't necessary, but he went on doing it because he had started. He was about to hand her the white fruit but then thought better of it and dropped it into the champagne in the plastic cup and then raised it to her mouth. She bit off a piece of the apple and chewed it, looking toward the curtains. One long-stemmed red rose, which he had bought for her, lay on the other bed. Their shoes were off, and she had removed his shirt and his undershirt but had stopped there. He fed her another quarter of the apple with his left hand, his right resting on her shoulder. The whole point was to slow down whatever was about to happen, to hold out their desire in the air in front of them, and to master it momentarily before it overcame them, as it would. With his help, she had taken off her blouse but nothing else except her shoes.

He felt as if future time had already arrived, as in a cubist drawing, and he had made love to her, had already kissed her on the side of her waist, that it was over, that he was leaving, all in one moment, and he said, "In less than an hour, we'll be here, and we'll be—"

She put her hand over his mouth, and he thought at that moment of Jeanne, his mother, though he couldn't imagine why. "Please talk," Alyse said. "I like that. I've always liked your voice. But make it irrelevant to what we say. The talk, I mean."

"Okay. Name a subject." He gave her another piece of apple, and she brought her hand up to his mouth and traced, with her index finger, his lower lip. Her fingers were longer than Susan's. He felt a slight soreness in his throat; Christina was getting a cold, and maybe he had been hit with the same virus. Alyse pushed her finger just inside his mouth, along the teeth, and he nipped at it.

"I love to travel," she said. "Give me a country."

"A country. You want me to *invent* a country? Is that it?" She nodded. He brought her to her feet and held her, and she lowered her head to kiss him on the chest. Then her hands were around his neck.

"I didn't know if you would ever let me do this," she said. "I didn't think you actually ever would." She kissed him and traced her fingers down his back, wedging her hands under the belt. "You have a nice body," she said, "And what is the name of this country?"

He thought of his mother, of her imaginary words. "Erezy," he said.

He closed his eyes, trying to imagine this nowhere place. He'd been raised and lived all his life in the Midwest, which, as far as he knew, possessed nothing exotic. "There are hills. Behind the hills, some fields. The growing season is short."

As he spoke, she unhooked his belt and lowered his trousers and underwear. She got down on her knees and helped him step out of his clothes. As she rose up, she touched the tip of her tongue to his thighs, then his hips.

"What do they grow?"

"They go out to the fields naked," he said. "I don't know what they grow." He reached toward her bra strap, but she brushed his hand away.

"Yes, you do. What do they grow?"

"Rice. No, not rice, it's a short growing season, and they don't have enough wet lowlands for that." She brought his hand back and let him undo her bra.

"You have a beautiful body," he said. "Alyse, you're gorgeous."

"No. Anyone can say that. Take me away. Take me away from here. Tell me what they grow. Tell me they grow fruits there, green ones, like kiwi, very sweet."

"Why can't I tell you how pretty you are?"

"Because then we'll be like every other damn couple in one of these rooms. Tell me about what they grow."

"Fruits, like kiwi, very sweet." She gazed at him, exactly the gaze of intimacy he had been missing with Susan, and Alyse, within a moment, was naked, and her hand was lightly around him.

"You're beautiful, too," she said. "What do *you* need?"

"I need a revelation," he said. "I could use one of those."

"It's hard to have a revelation when you're doing something as trashy as this," she said. She was caressing his back. "Here," she said, "put your arms around me." He followed her directions. He noticed suddenly that she had a birthmark beginning at her abdomen and circling around toward her buttocks, and on her right calf was a bruise. The usual imperfections. But her breasts were small and perfect, the nipples tiny, almost like a baby's, and they pointed up, and she had a small waist, the luxury of a childless woman. Looking at it, he felt the wind outside picking up, the clouds finally moving.

"You're beautiful," he said. "Where'd you get that bruise?"

"Staggering around at night in the garage, desperate," she said. "That country. That country you were describing to me. Erezy. I know something about it. After picking that fruit, the men get down on their knees." He did, and placed his lips on her belly. "They come in from the fields, smelling of leaves and grass and fruit, and they make love to the women. Oh, God," she said, and she suddenly sucked in her breath, a sound very close to a gasp. She had parted her legs for his tongue. "I can't stand any more," she said. "I have to lie down."

He bent down to kiss the bruise on her calf. From the next room, through the wall, came the sudden muffled radio blare of church music. Pious motel neighbors! Distantly, sirens screamed by on the freeway. When she let herself down on the bed, she reached over for the champagne and drank a gulp of it, then spilled the rest on herself, a few drops. He lifted her feet and kissed the insteps, first one and then the other, and then began to kiss his way up her legs. He rubbed the stubble of her leg hair against his cheek. It wasn't sex he loved. It was women. And he loved the desperation of this. On the TV set, the silent cartoons had stopped, and a rerun of *Car 54, Where Are You?* had commenced. What had happened to Fred Gwynne, a good actor, after that show?

"This isn't like you," she said, her hands in his hair. "Wait a minute. You're doing everything here. There's something I want to do." She moved him over, held him by the wrist with one hand while she teased him slowly, trailing her breasts and her hair and her mouth over his. "See how much of this you can take," she said. He saw that her moves were less physically sincere than Susan's. Apparently Alyse didn't take his desire for granted. Her physical expressionism, salted with petulance, gave her a style of sexual mannerism. Besides, she didn't really love him. He was sure of that. If she loved him, it would wreck everything.

He ran his hand down her spine. He rolled over so that he could put his tongue on the small of her back. It tasted of salt and pine wood.

Some essence about her smelled exotic: it might be her perfume or some other body oil, but now, when he breathed in, all he could breathe was her.

She was very busy now with her mouth. She had the busiest tongue he had ever known. Importunate and witty and fast.

"Oh, Wyatt," she said, "I can't wait another minute." Slowly he moved and felt her around him. She shivered, shook her shoulders back and forth as if she were trying to free herself from a scarf. After another moment, during which she closed her eyes twice, she said, "Well, how about that. I just came." She shuddered and inhaled twice again. "And there. That's two."

She stopped moving to get her breath back. She wiped the sweat off her forehead and put her fingers, with the sweat on them, into his mouth. She contracted the walls of her vagina around his penis. From the other room came the sound of a gospel singer.

"Can you wait?" she asked.

He nodded.

"I just want to feel this. You, down there. Still in me. Don't move. Just be there."

"Yes."

She wiggled a bit, a small suggestion of a shimmy, and

took another sudden breath. "Well," she said, "I hadn't expected that one." She put her hands down on his chest. "I have a short fuse. Maybe you've noticed."

"I've noticed."

"I invented orgasms," she said, in a voice just above a whisper. "Nobody had them before I discovered them."

"You're an inventor."

"Yes. I invented some of the basics."

"Such as?"

She turned him so that she could lean down and touch his cheekbones. Her breasts brushed against his chest. "I invented trees. We wouldn't have telephone poles without trees."

"Exactly right."

"I invented boiling water," she said. "And then, the next week, I invented ice."

"That must have been difficult." Her fingertips trailed down the side of his thighs.

"Yes, it was." She moved her hips sideways and came again. She kept her eyes closed. She was getting her breath back. "I invented the steering gear. I invented clouds. I invented basements."

"We're all very grateful to you."

"You should be. I invented cloudy days."

"It'd be monotonous with only sun."

"Well, that's what I thought. I didn't invent rain. Someone else did. But cloudy days, yes, I take the credit for that."

"Thank you."

"Here's something else I invented."

"What?"

"Take me by the shoulders and lower me." He did. "Now, put your arms around me and kiss me." He followed her directions. Her tongue was circling around his, and he had a sensation of dizziness. Breaking the kiss, she said,

331

"Don't wait any longer. Just start in on me." She began a rhythm with him, and when it increased in speed and intensity, and she was breathing in time to the movement of his thrusts, he looked down into Alyse's eyes, and it had all fallen away, all the protective stylishness, and there was nothing there now except her openness to him, which he thought he would probably misuse. It was the high passionate vulnerability, and if he hadn't known better, he would call it love, but he did know better, he thought, feeling his old skin slip away. Each person had a personal sexual style, and hers was desperate and excessive, and he wanted to thank her for a lesson in desperation and excess. Even with the blinds shut, the curtains drawn, he knew the clouds had started to move again, hurling themselves with a blind fury across the sky. If he stood at the window, he would be a sentry, watching the clouds as they advanced and retreated. It was a mad idea, the sort of idea his mother might have. He was here and not-here, Wyatt and not-Wyatt, and he felt the bonds attaching him to Alyse and felt himself breaking them even as they formed, knowing he might not come back to her or do this again. Groaning, and lathered with his own sweat, he felt himself beginning his career as a desperate man, a desperado; he would follow his mother's advice and burn down Schwartzwalder's house if he had to. He raised his arm so that, if Alyse wanted to see it—though she would not, with her eyes closed—she could see his shadow, she could see the name, and he cried out, and the day collapsed all around him.

24

The rabbit, Fred, had, over several months, developed a personality, a set of likes and dislikes, and chief among his dislikes was being pulled out of hats; he urinated with fear whenever he saw one. Susan respected him for this—she herself had never liked being awakened on Saturday morning when her mother, complaining about her lazy adolescent daughter, had snapped the window shades upward, pitching Susan into brutal Puritan morning sunlight—and so she stopped doing her magic act at children's birthday parties and sold her trick hats and the trick rings and the exploding handkerchiefs. The truth was, she had become as tired of birthdays as the rabbit, the spitball-throwing boys and the screaming girls.

She had continued her work at the recreational center because she liked the physical exuberance of children, once they were away from birthday parties, and were tumbling on mats, or climbing ropes. Allowed to be more like animals in the recreational center, they were actually more human. She had nagged at Wyatt to come down to watch her at work, some Saturday, but, after the first month, he had never returned.

She studied him, when she thought he wouldn't notice, and tried to figure out what he thought he was becoming, but she had no idea. It was as if he was beginning to carry on a secret life, and a few of her friends complained about their husbands in the same manner: not that they were having affairs, for example, but that affairs could become part of the secret life, the turning-in, the closed-mouthed reticence, and each time that she asked Wyatt how he felt about work, about this, or that, he shrugged and trained his eyes on the nearest window, as if the details of his job were the equivalent of the secret of the atom bomb.

He never drew anymore. He said there was nothing to draw. When she asked him to draw the children, he told her not to be a sentimentalist.

At night in bed, she wanted sometimes to pound him on the back, to make him breathe, or on the chest, to make his heart beat again.

So she went down to the basement, in her free moments, and worked on the little rooms, with Fred close by her, watching her from his cage, the peaceful sound of his carrot-eating keeping her company, and all the uneasiness she had started to feel about her marriage and about Wyatt went into the rooms. In the one that she had titled *Late Dinner,* the telephone on the counter was off the hook, and a saucepan on the kitchen stove appeared to have boiling water in it, and while all these signs of recent human activity were visible, no one sat at the dining-room table, where the place settings were neatly arranged, and the room itself gave off a somber feeling of human dishabitation, a word Susan had just thought of to characterize the mood of these thumbnail-sized objects, so small they had already become symbols.

On weekends, her two children occasionally in tow, Susan sometimes went to antique fairs, not for the human-scale furniture, but for the little pieces of dollhouse knick-knacks she happened upon, squirreled away in unswept corners. The air in these places was antique itself, so clotted with dust that if she had had asthma or any sort of bronchial condition, she thought, she might have collapsed on the spot. She felt the dust settling in her lungs, the smell of mold and age descending like grandmotherly ornamental lace on her skin.

She found the tiny saucepan in Old Things Corner, outside of Harrisonville. The stove and the dining-room table cost her $2.34 at Antiques Unlimited, in Five Oaks. The telephone turned up at Granddad's Attic underneath odds and ends of doll clothing and near, she was surprised to see, a Scottie-dog nightlight; and the rest of the materials she found at various flea markets she had attended. Wyatt helped her with the wiring from the batteries to the overhead light, which she purchased from a model-train catalogue. When the light was switched on, it cast a pleasantly gloomy illumination all over everything.

Because of their size, these small rooms were pleasing to

her, at first. They were models, all right, models *of* something or *for* something, and by mid-May, finally, she was beginning to think that these empty rooms—it amazed her that it took her so long to see it—constituted her life in this town with Wyatt. And then the rooms no longer seemed so pleasing.

Wyatt looked at the rooms and said, Well, they're very American. He complimented her, as he was always careful to do, looking and not-looking at the tableaux she had assembled, and then he went back upstairs to his children, his newspaper, and his headphones. Missing the point, as he sometimes did: ascribing to the culture what was actually located in himself. In a town without therapy, these rooms were her therapy, and one morning in late May she lined them up in the basement to study them and saw that if she didn't say something to Wyatt very soon—if she didn't *do* something to Wyatt soon—she would lose him, herself, the children, her life: that was what the rooms were telling her, in their clean orderly emptiness, their small eloquent vacancy.

She had never liked Wyatt's cousin Cyril without effort. With some effort and willpower she could bring herself to like him, slightly, the way she had slightly liked those goof-offs in high school who sat in the back row of civics class making belching and farting noises, but when she just thought about him, she could not. She was sorry that he had become sick and had fallen or pushed himself off a dock and drowned in that river, but she didn't think that he had added up to much as a human being, and Wyatt's attachment to him had puzzled her.

They weren't like each other at all. They had nothing in common. They were opposites.

There were parts of herself that she missed, after all, and she tried not to make a noise about any of that. She missed the girl in the ponytail who could, and would, walk on her hands on the balance beam in front of everybody, and she missed being the woman who lay in bed in the morning sunlight, the most beautiful, the most desirable thing imaginable, her hands raised to the light, part of the light itself. Maybe she could have used that beauty more somehow, but she had fallen in love with Wyatt, and married him, and come here. Whatever she had been, she didn't regret being herself, now; no one would call her "simple" as either a compliment or a critique anymore. She wasn't so simple as to be interested in Cyril, for example. She had seen through him, and around him, all at once, right away.

She had once desired Wyatt, and now she loved him. Getting from desire to love was one feature of adulthood that she thought she had mastered, and no one could convince her otherwise; the difference between desirability and lovability was the difference between not having a soul and having one, and *using* it—it wasn't enough to have a soul, you had to use it, once it was yours—to travel the distance between yourself and the person you loved. Love was soul-movement. There, she thought, I've figured it out.

She loved Wyatt in spite of himself, for his shadowy side, but the little rooms in the basement were clear enough about one thing: she wasn't sure whether he loved her. His soul was clean and sterile and secret. She was beginning to understand the rabbit better than she understood him.

One evening when Eugene was irritable and Christina bossy and demanding and just plain mean, Susan and Wyatt loaded them both into the car and drove the back roads outside of town until the children were quiet, and then asleep. It was a trick, driving them around, but it still worked. Susan rolled her window down and watched the lawns give way to fields and orchards.

When they stopped at an intersection, out beyond the places that Susan knew, Wyatt pointed to a field on her side of the car and said, "You remember seeing a softball game being played out there by some kids, some high school kids, a couple of years ago, when we were driving Christina around to settle her?"

Susan nodded. So he was getting nostalgic; nostalgia was her least favorite emotion. They drove past the intersection into a stretch of road bordered by forest growth, so close to the road itself that there were no shoulders on which to stop. "It's a shame," he said.

"What?"

She waited. Wind whistled past the open windows of the car. "Nothing," he said. That was hateful: making oblique teasing secret remarks.

"I hate it when you do that. Tell me at least what you mean," she said.

She looked over at him. With the headlights on, the road ahead of them was reflected on his glasses, though, miniaturized on the lenses, the road and the trees alongside it were mostly a blur. "I don't know what I mean. I wish I knew. When I say 'It's a shame,' it doesn't mean anything." He waited, then said, "I'm not exactly equipped. It must be I'm not equipped for American life."

"You're doing it again. What other life do we have?"

Up ahead she saw a possum, an ugly snouty thing with white eyes, scurry out of the path of the car, and Wyatt said, "There's a little stream off the road near here, a place that I found once. What I remember was, the water was clean. It was amazing. I think it's just up there. Right over there, next to that clump of trees."

With the car parked, Susan wondered if all this hadn't been planned: the twilight, the road, the possum, and now

this stream he claimed flowed somewhere out of these flat-
lands. With Christina and Eugene asleep in back, she stepped
out of the car and followed him through the grass, past rem-
nants of wildflowers, trillium in the shady sections, and Sol-
omon's seal and cornflower, and now she heard a stream after
all. He held her hand. Mosquitoes were clouding around her
face. The stream was only four feet or so across.

"Take off your shoes," he said. She had looked for no-
trespassing signs but hadn't seen any. He had bent down at her
feet and was slipping off her shoes and rolling up her jeans,
and she didn't want him to do that; she didn't want him to
touch her just now. She turned back to check the car. The
children were still sleeping. Wyatt, after taking his own shoes
off, raised his trousers, and, leading her by the hand, led her
into the water. His pastoralism was so hallucinatory, it was
hard to resist.

"Where are we?" she asked. "What's this place called?"

"Oh, I don't think it's anywhere," he said. "Thank goodness." He had leaned down and seemed to be washing her
calves with his hands, and when he stood up, he put his arms
around her, and she could feel his wet fingers on the back of
her neck, an unpleasant sensation. "You're beautiful," he
said. "You're so beautiful I take it for granted sometimes and
forget about it, but then I look, and I wish I could draw you,
and I remember."

"You always wanted to draw me, and you never could,
not really."

"No, I never could." He seemed to think for a moment.
"I've been experimenting on myself lately. I've been getting a
little strange."

"Wyatt, you *are* strange. You've always been strange.
That's one of the things I've loved about you. But you don't
like it. Other people fantasize about being weird or bizarre,

but you, your fantasy is that you're mainstream."

"You think so? Let's go back to the car. I want to tell you a story."

As he drove home through the dark, he kept both of his hands on the wheel, and his eyes were fixed on the road. She could tell that he could speak to her more easily if he didn't turn in her direction—if he spoke, instead, to the road and the darkness.

"I've been golfing with Schwartzwalder. He cheats. He comes out suited up in his sport shirt and cap, gripper gloves and cleated shoes, and those long-flight balls he orders through an eight-hundred number. All this regalia, and then he moves the ball when my back is turned and alters his scorecard to gain a few strokes' worth of advantage on me. At first I couldn't figure it out. Then I decided that this is a guy who's been permanently damaged by high school, and I'm supposed to be the audience for his new and continuing success. I'm the representative of the past, and I'm being shown.

"After all, I've been doing this thing: I pretend to be his friend. He confides in me. He tells me about the balance sheet at WaldChem. He looks out on the ninth fairway and talks about tidy profits. The business is privately held, so he doesn't have to say how large those profits are. Still, that's his phrase. 'Tidy profits.' He's not too fastidious about his adjectives. He doesn't mention my cousin, of course. Neither do I. That would spoil everything. That would be telling.

"But that's around the time when he informs me about the threatening letters. We're halfway through our game, and he has a six-stroke margin on me. It turns out that he's been getting anonymous letters in the mail, you know, the kind with words and letters cut out from newspapers and glued onto the paper. Just like the movies. They're meant to scare him. I can't quote these letters to you because he didn't quote them to me.''

Susan felt a queasiness in her stomach, as if she had eaten some spoiled crab, which had produced a discoloration of her emotions. The car's headlights pulled them forward into the dark.

"There are grammatical mistakes in these notes. The words are sometimes spelled letter by letter, and they're misspelled, which makes him think that somebody in the plant, one of the hourly workers, has got some grudge. I asked him if he'd shown the notes to the police, and he says, no, those guys are just Keystone Cops, he can handle this all by himself.

"Then we change the subject. We talk family, we talk high school. He loves to do that. He's *stuck* back there, somehow. He mentions to me one of our classmates who got arrested for breaking-and-entering in El Paso, Texas, last year. That's when he tells me about the prowler.

"Someone, he says, has been stalking around his house at night, throwing stones at and through the windows, lightly at first, scare tactics, and then harder, cracking the bathroom window, then breaking it. Others have been broken. This happened last week. Now there've been three broken windows. But my friend Jerry Schwartzwalder is not scared. He has a gun, he tells me, though he doesn't mention the caliber, and he says he can protect himself just fine. It's funny to hear him sounding like John Wayne, this little guy. It should be inspiring. I wasn't inspired, but I *was* impressed.''

He rubbed his hand across his forehead.

Susan thought of her boxes, those empty furnished rooms. She thought: Most things, when you look at them in a certain way, make sense. She shook off her fright as if it were nothing more than a brief chill.

"A couple of days ago, he thinks this prowler is out there in the dark, doing his vandal thing, and he gets his gun out, but then he has this better idea. His better idea is to grab a flashlight. One of those big flashlights, five or six batteries, a portable lighthouse. He beams it down and he gets a look, a look of the guy running away. He gets the rear view.

"He doesn't recognize him. He does notice something, though. A clue. We're on the putting green of the tenth hole, and he tells me this clue. He sinks his putt, and he looks up at me, and he says that the guy had long hair, was wearing a tank top, MTV attire, very young, and he's all built-up, as if he'd been taking steroids. This narrows the field, he says. Can't be too many guys like that in this city.

"Still and all, he's been getting more notes. Now the notes are threatening to burn his house down. Of course I'm appalled, and I say so. After all, he's no villain, he's just Jerry Schwartzwalder, my friend from high school, a product of this town, just like me. I tell him to call the police. I tell him he really ought to do that."

Susan waited on the passenger side. They were outside the city in a residential neighborhood that she knew fairly well. "What are you going to do?" she asked.

He smiled. "What am *I* going to do? That's a good question. I've asked Jerry that question, what *he's* going to do, and he says that he likes this town, it suits him just fine. He's stubborn. He's not going to move out of my father's house, and he's not going to be terrorized by punks. He's not going anywhere, he says. He's not going to be scared. It's that simple. He says it's a small thing. Some disgruntled employee probably. He can take care of it."

"So who's the kid in the tank top?"

He shrugged.

"That's all you're going to tell me, a shrug?"

"I don't really know who he is," he said. "I don't really know him."

"That's not what I asked you."

"I know. His name isn't all that important."

"Tell me."

"Here we are," he said, pulling into the driveway. "We're home. Looks like we left the light on in the living room. That's all right. It scares away the criminal element." He shut off the engine and the headlights.

"You aren't going to burn his house down, are you?" She tried to make it sound like an ordinary question. "Are you?"

He sat behind the wheel, staring toward the back of the garage.

"Where did you get this idea, sending him letters and throwing stones through the windows and burning down his house?"

He just sat there. Then, his voice seeming to come from another world altogether, he said, "Burning his house? That was my mother's idea."

"Wyatt," she said, "this is a terrible thing you're doing."

"You think so?"

"Yes. You're making it personal. What he did, what happened to Cyril, that wasn't personal."

"Of course it was. Everything is personal."

"You play golf with him during the day and then burn his house at night?"

"It has a nice symmetry," he said. "The devil has to be fooled."

"Why don't you let the agencies, the regulatory agencies, take care of him?"

"You're so naive."

"Don't you fucking condescend to me."

"I'm sorry. I'm not condescending."

"Tell me why I'm naive."

"Keep your voice down," he said. "You'll wake the kids."

"This won't work," she said.

"Why?"

"You can't do everything by yourself."

"All right, then, I'll do *this.*"

"What if it doesn't make him leave town?"

"I've punished him anyway."

"What if his family members are hurt? People get caught in fires, you know. They get killed."

"Funny you should mention that. His wife and child drove off for a visit to her mother the day before yesterday. Going to be there for a week."

"How do you know that?"

"We've become quite close, actually. He tells me every-thing. He trusts me. He wants to impress me. He's a very chatty guy."

"How can you stand to talk to him?"

"It's my job," he said. "Besides, I like him sometimes, when I don't hate and despise him. It's complicated."

"It's not complicated. It's nuts. It's not even pleasingly crazy, the way you sometimes are. It's all . . . it's all *erroneous,* what you're doing."

"No, it isn't," he said. "Think of me as a spy. An infiltra-tor leading a double life."

"I *have* thought of you that way. All the time, lately. Oh, Wyatt, don't do this. You're going to wreck everything. What makes you think that house will burn? You don't know anything about arson."

"I have faith and a lot of gasoline."

She reached for his hand. "No no no. Stop yourself. Please wait."

"Wait for what? I'm trying to make the world a better place. We're all on our own here. Everything is laissez-faire now. This is private resistance."

"It's revenge."

"It's that, too." He looked in the rearview mirror. "Let's take the kids in and put them to bed. Do we have any ice cream? I could use a snack."

After gathering up their children, they went inside.

Three nights later, at three-fourteen in the morning, he came into the bedroom, smelling of gasoline.

25

In the summer moon's muddy yellow light, he had crossed a narrow patch of night-dampened unmowed grass, the gasoline can sloshing with his every step, and he had reached Jellison Road feeling slightly out of breath but still strong enough to move a mountain three or four feet in any direction. His car was parked down the hill half a mile back in the Christiansen Landscaping and Nursery parking lot near some unsold baby maple trees. Things clung to him: mosquitoes on his neck and forehead, burrs on his trouser legs. The night birds, busy and unruly, chittered to him to think it over, but his heart beat with cardiac joy, and he felt criminal and wicked and justified.

Thanks to an atmospheric inversion, the night air smelled like an unclean clothes closet, mothballed-musty, and only the brightest stars, the ones with the names of heroes and animals, were visible. They did not twinkle. His impression was that they had not twinkled for years. He heard crickets weeping. Frogs croaked out their opinions. Nothing slept.

It was one of those nights for gasoline and disaster, one of those nights when things got done in this country: good-time violence, a show of hands, then flames and broken glass.

He stopped, took a breath, and mopped his brow with a monogrammed handkerchief given to him by his daughter, last Christmas. It had been at the bottom of his stocking and had been wrapped in ferociously festive red paper, which he had thrown into the fire while he bit into a chocolate-covered cherry. That was then. Now his left hand strayed downward into a patch of berries, and his fingers came back smelling of jam. Just under the handkerchief in that pocket were two books of matches that he had picked up from the floor of Cyril's truck.

He crept along the road just down from the shoulder, in case any cars approached, as they would not, he knew, this being a city where everyone went to bed promptly at eleven, even if they did not sleep or could not sleep or had no idea whatever of sleeping. It was the time of giving up and lying down and sinking into the citizenly duty of rest before the following working day. Only troublemakers, or the unfortunate nocturnal service class, stayed up and prowled about. Of course the citizenry remained conscious, marooned there between the sheets: for example, Pooh would be awake, alone in her bed, with Otis nearby. And Susan would be awake, waiting for her husband to return from his mysterious errand. Alyse would be awake—thinking about him, hating him, who knew? Ellen would certainly be awake, keeping her fixed gaze on her bedroom ceiling for some sign of that god of hers, or reading more of the evidence through her new glasses from Oak Opticians. And his mother, Jeanne, who never slept so far as he knew, would stay busy all night on patrol in the Universe.

But here *he* was, just off the shoulder of Jellison Road, a gasoline can in his right hand, his left hand swinging back and forth as he approached the unlit house, the house itself appearing to be dazed or asleep or just befogged, with Jerry Schwartzwalder, his new friend, his high school classmate, somewhere inside, perhaps awake, perhaps not.

Just to his left, now, ahead of him, was the solarium at whose windows his employee, that kid, Jeff Holsapple, had thrown his rocks before he had told him that enough was enough, and he had paid him off; and to the right were the unhappy displays of his father's architectural attempts to blend Colonial and Modern, windows both plain and ornate, a self-canceling style richly and recognizably his father's own.

He didn't know much about arson, but he was sure that if you poured enough gasoline over something and lit it, the substance underneath had a good chance of blazing up into visible heat and flame. He decided to do a tour of the house to settle on a site. Unusual for this style, the house had a separate two-car garage, the type with a rooster weather vane at its top, pointing, just now, at the madcap yellow moon. Of all moons, summer moons were the maddest. Next to the garage was a penned two-dog doghouse, undogged, the doghouse being a perfect miniature replica of the garage. On the north side of the house were planted rows of overwatered stinking peonies, droopy jungle growth, and, in front of the house, circles of red geraniums. Contemptible flower! Thriving on lovelessness and neglect.

He didn't like the flowers; he didn't like the two-car-garage doghouse; he didn't like garages with weather vanes, or front driveways like this one with black jockey hitching posts painted white to avoid the taint of racism. A bird with its head under its wing slept at the top of the flagpole. The downstairs bathroom window, translucent below, transparent above, suddenly flicked on with light, and he crouched down, stilling himself. From his distance, he heard the muffled torrent going on and on and on—Jerry Schwartzwalder had the bladder of an elephant—before the light and the window flicked off again, and the toilet gushed and gurgled.

The suddenly astonishing thought that he could go to jail appeared before him: he saw himself on one side of a plate-glass partition, speaking into a telephone to Susan, who sat on the other side. Eugene would be on her lap. Christina stood to the side, weeping.

It struck him then that what he was doing was absurd; that he did not know what to do; that the damage that others did was coherent but that his remedy was incoherent; and no one was more incoherent than himself. He had been a man of moral suffering and it had led him to this.

Nevertheless, he had the gasoline and the matches and the moon.

The same moon guided him toward the living-room windows, and he ducked down, thinking that he saw a patrol car cruising Jellison Road, protecting homeowners from people like himself. But if the car had been invisible before, it stayed invisible. He didn't know what intruding presence he had heard, or seen out of the corner of his eye. After stepping into a bed of pansies, he felt his shoe knock against a plastic ball. As soon as he had kicked it, the ball somehow started to play, almost inaudibly, "You Are My Sunshine." He tried to see it in the dark: it was one of those infernal plastic Fisher-Price toys that never broke or smashed, even when left outside. His own house and his back and front yards were seeded with toys like this one. He circled the house until he was at the back.

He stood straight to peer inside the window.

He saw bookshelves filled with trophies and dishes and little statuettes of dogs, rather than books; and a framed poster of a skier, with the word *Vail!* under the skier; and a photograph of the Schwartzwalder family sitting in a stiff photograph-studio pose. The man of the house had left a dim light burning in the den, and the photograph, cushioned in the shadowy soft illumination, revealed on Schwartzwalder's face an expression of implacable banality.

Crouching down, he tried to imagine Schwartzwalder inside the burning house, Schwartzwalder the captain of industry on fire, with little flamelets flicking up from his pajama cuffs and flames spurting out of his arms and eyes and mouth, *purifying flame,* it used to be called, and then the fire in the shape of a man walking through the house, burning the counters, the raincoats, the invitations to National Rifle Association fund-raising dinners, the trophies, and the VCR. He tried to regain a sense that he had the right and obligation to do what he was about to do. He gazed up to where he thought the moon was, for reassurance, but it had moved somewhere. It had gone off with his mother.

He imagined Schwartzwalder pointing a gun at him, and he didn't care in the least.

He saw a dog, scruffy and mongrel-like, panting and observing him, on the other side of the yard. He put his finger to his lips and shushed the dog.

His foot tapped against another plastic toy. He shook his head. He felt as if he had suddenly awakened. He was Wyatt again. He had traveled out of himself, but he had come back, and suddenly found herself underneath Jerry Schwartzwalder's window, a can of gasoline near his right hand and matches in his pocket. His father had designed this house. He couldn't burn it.

Half-crouching, he went back to the garage, almost tripping over a rake left out on the lawn: some sort of booby trap. With the garage doors closed, he couldn't tell if either of the Schwartzwalder vehicles was inside. If one happened to be in there, nesting, it'd probably explode. Too bad. Wyatt unscrewed the can and exchanged a glance with a blinking star, which looked insane with loneliness. Down splashed the gasoline, onto the grass and the exterior walls. Where and how—he was circling the garage, and now the dog, a strange mix of Labrador and poodle, apparently, was trailing along with him, wagging its tail and grinning—where and how had the myth arisen of the moon being made of green cheese? Because it was, as anyone with eyes to see could tell, actually made of lithium and insanity and God. The moon howled, and dogs heard it, and the dogs howled back. Not this dog, though, not just now, following Wyatt around the Schwartzwalder garage and sniffing dubiously at the gasoline he was splashing with generous applications against a rose trellis. An exploding car: he had seen a car explode once at the circus, its four cardboard sides dropping away to reveal a dog, very much like this one, behind the wheel, and two dogs with cockeyed circus hats and evening wear, like tuxedos, only tailored for dogs, riding in the backseat. It had been very impressive, that car. Now, with enough gasoline to leave a trail, he poured a path back and away from the garage, the weather vane, and the invisible moon, and when he was a safe distance, and already halfway home in his own mind, he capped the can and took out a matchbook.

Cyril had always liked a good fire.

He saw that CHICO'S SALSA DIP had been printed on the outside flap of the matchbook. Did they still print "Close cover before striking" in tiny print below? He closed the cover, lit the match, and dropped it into the puddle of refined fossil fuel at his feet. Then he turned. As he did, he expected to hear something like an explosion, but the sound was nothing like that: instead, he heard, as the gasoline apparently caught, a long breathing *whoosh,* like a giant's inhalation down into the lungs, a violent sigh, a god's sigh. He wanted to see the god but instead ran to his car. After putting the empty can into his trunk, he drove out of the nursery and headed home.

With his own car in its garage, he went inside, took a shower, checked on Christina and Eugene, and got into bed.

"Where have you been?"

"I went out."

"You smell of gasoline."

"I took a shower," he said.

"Why do you smell of gasoline, Wyatt?"

"I filled up the car at the Hop-in. Some of it spilled, you know, on my wrist and forearm. See?" He held out his arm toward her, and she drew back her head.

"Don't you do that," she said.

"All right."

At once she sat up. "Wyatt, we have to leave this town. We have to move. We have to do that right away. In a month or so. We can't stay here. We have to go." She was sitting cross-legged on the bed, wearing her nightgown. Her fingers were laced together in her lap. "We cannot stay here. Now tell me what you did."

"I set fire to his garage," Wyatt said, and, unexpectedly, and against all the rules of wakefulness, he fell asleep.

"Oh dear sweet Jesus God help us," she said.

26

"Nice sunny day," Schwartzwalder had said, wiping his forehead, just before Wyatt teed off.

The approach to the eighth hole was framed by two sand traps, and Wyatt would have felt humbled when his ball stalled in the air and then veered toward the kidney-shaped trap on the right, if Schwartzwalder's ball hadn't done the same, except in the opposite direction, so that the two men were separated halfway down the fairway, rather symmetrically. Schwartzwalder was getting a new look. He had a new blue hat with a visor, a knit yellow shirt, green cotton trousers with a white twill weave belt, and a shiny new sand wedge, with which, after a brief practice swing and a flurry of cloud-sand, he hit the ball to within four feet of the hole. He smiled and touched the brim of his visor with a modest acknowledgment of his own excellence. He looked like a one-man parade.

Wyatt was having a bit more trouble. His stroke sent the ball up too far into the air, with not enough lateral force, so that it came down like a little damaged rocket right on the edge of the green. He himself wasn't feeling so dapper, and he had forgotten to wear a hat, so that the sun, which he had hated ever since it had bothered to shine down on Cyril's last day, heated up his hair and made his scalp prickle. Stroke: up to the middle of the green. Stroke: close to the cup, but not in it. Stroke: in it went.

Schwartzwalder had his characteristically comfortable lead.

Wyatt had heard nothing on the radio, nor had he seen anything in the paper about it, about the fire. Today, with the sun drooping toward the west, and barn swallows following them overhead as they progressed through the course, Schwartzwalder had brought up the subject of skiing trips. Just past the second hole, he had said that far too many areas like Vail and Park City were being spoiled. Too many people, the wrong kind.

Yes, Wyatt said, what a shame. He shook his head. Unbelievable. Had he spoken that word, or had he only considered it? He repeated it. "Unbelievable." Certain of his words stayed inside his mind despite his conviction that he had actually said them. This was one.

As they approached the tee for the ninth hole, Wyatt saw

a tree, an elm that had somehow survived all the recent diseases, standing there, behind the tee, offering its shade, and he imagined for a moment that the sight of this tree, old and weathered, undiseased, would make him burst into tears. He had become a hero of disguise, and he was beginning to experience his emotions with an intolerable intensity.

Schwartzwalder was smiling into the sun, his confederate, as he walked. As he pulled his club dolly, one of its wheels squeaking, *er er er,* he turned to Wyatt. "Did you hear about me? My little adventure?"

"No," Wyatt said. He himself was carrying his clubs.

"They tried to burn down my garage."

"What? No. Jesus, Jerry. What happened?"

"Not much, actually. Two nights ago. They splashed gasoline on it and tried to set it on fire. A real amateur job."

"You saw this?"

"Sure I saw it. I was awake. There was all this gasoline in a line heading toward the garage, and there was a pool of fire near the garage's south wall, but the gasoline on the wall hadn't caught."

"The garage didn't burn?"

"Nope. Just a line of gasoline on the lawn. The gasoline pools didn't connect. I got out my hose and put it out until the fire department came. I got lucky, those little bastard creeps. I've put out movement detectors now. Don't know why I didn't do it before. I got a security system and patrols, the whole shot. They come around again, we'll get them. I'm drawing the line."

"How'd you know there were two of them?"

"What?"

"You said 'they.' "

"Oh. Just a guess. Teenaged punks work in pairs for their fun. That's what I've noticed."

"Ah, Jesus. I'm sorry. That's terrible."

"Hell, it could've been worse. It could have caught. It could have jumped over to my house. Thank God it didn't."

"Thank God," Wyatt said. "Nobody hurt, though."

"Unless you count the dog," Schwartzwalder said.

"The dog."

"Yeah. It's weird. I was awake anyway, I don't sleep too well in the summer, the heat, especially when I'm alone in the house. Usually I just watch TV or read, you know. Magazines, the sports page, box scores, that sort of thing. And I was upstairs, when I look out and I see this line of flames heading toward the garage. Hadn't heard it, of course, until then."

"Right."

"But that wasn't the most amazing thing."

"What was that?"

"Well, I looked out, and there was this dog, our neighborhood stray named Burton that everybody feeds, a real sociable mutt, and I guess some way or other it had gotten some gasoline on itself, maybe rolled in it, who knows? I'll spare you the details. You don't want to hear the details."

"No," Wyatt said.

"But there was Burton," Schwartzwalder continued, "running in circles, barking like mad, then rolling around my yard, his coat on fire. Terrible. You should never see a dog on fire. I didn't know until the day before yesterday," he said thoughtfully, "that dogs could scream."

The elm was beginning to swim a bit in front of Wyatt's eyes, and he noticed that cold sweat was breaking out on his forehead.

"That's awful," he said.

"Can't get it out of my mind," Schwartzwalder said. "Could it be that a person would pour gasoline over a dog? Set a dog on fire? It's disgusting. It made me sick to see it. I

357

tried to douse him with water. He ran away from me. They had to put Burton down. He was burned all over. Too bad."

"I'll say."

Schwartzwalder was bending down with an orange wooden tee in his hand, and now he was sticking the tee into the ground, the grass, the soil, and now, in apparent slow motion, he was placing the ball, the Big-Flite Special, on top of the tee, and then standing—he, Schwartzwalder, was standing—no, addressing the ball, with his driver, before hitting it and watching it sail off into the distance; and Wyatt, who had never felt sick in his adult life, that he could remember, watched Schwartzwalder hit the ball and saw it direct itself toward the hole and then hang in the air, as Schwartzwalder watched it, and then Schwartzwalder turned to see Wyatt and to smile and to exchange some kind of glance at him, a look of expectancy, it seemed, prompting Wyatt, in the very center of his nausea, to say, "Good one," before he himself drove his ball off into the air. He walked the length of the fairway, and sank the ball after a total of five strokes, one over par, before saying to Schwartzwalder, after looking at his shimmering watch, that he had to stop, get home, he was late, and, on top of everything—how strange it was!—he wasn't feeling at all well, he felt lousy in fact. Also: Christina had had a bout of flu, sorry: he would have to go home. He picked up his clubs, following Schwartzwalder's nod. Schwartzwalder had always been a companionable guy. Wyatt carried his clubs up to the clubhouse, stripped, and went into the shower. In the shower he fell to the floor in his stall and lay in the stream of water until he came back to consciousness seconds or minutes later. No one else was there with him, and no one had seen him, as usual. He stood up. As he stood, he saw in his mind's eye a boy with cash in his hand reaching with strong strokes toward the center of the river.

He had had enough. It was time to leave, to move on. He would pack the boxes, his clothes and his lamps, he would pack it all, if he had to, by himself, and go to a place that they couldn't spoil anymore, because it had already been spoiled a century ago. He didn't hate the Midwest, he didn't hate it exactly, that wasn't the reason: he loved it too much to hate it more than he already did or to collaborate in its further ruination by grabbing the money and swimming into the river.

He dried himself off, put on his street clothes, and drove home. He would tell Susan to help him pack; they would take Jeanne with them.

27

Without knocking or caring to knock, or even, for that matter, noticing where the door was, he found Alyse at her desk at the end of the day, her feet propped up near the windowsill, twirling her hair around her index finger, and when she turned, he saw her expression of annoyance and uneasiness; he couldn't tell if she was angry or embarrassed or both, and the distinction didn't matter anyway.

"Come with me," he said.

"No."

He reached for her, but she batted his arm away. Nevertheless, she put on her shoes. As she did, she said, "Don't tell me we need to talk."

"I wouldn't say that. We don't have anything to say."

"That's the spirit," she said. "I love it how sex ruins everything." He stood waiting for her, surveying the chaos of her office, a recently expanded and enlarged chaos, a more fully ripe disorder. In the west corner a violet was dying in slow stages. A butter knife stood in her coffee cup as a stirrer, and across her desk was spread an abstract expressionist tableau of unread memos and letters.

"We're going for a walk. But I don't think we need to say anything," he told her. "I just think we need—"

"A walk? Oh. All right. I know where. You want to walk, I'll show you something. You might actually like it." She explained that where they were going, what they were about to see, was known *only to her*.

On the passenger side of his car, she was rigid and cool, though not actively hostile or rude, and he thought of how in college his friends, after they got past the bragging in the early stages of drunkenness and were deep into intoxication, would say, *love spoils sex*, but it didn't, really; sex was just heat, it just cooked what was already there. She pushed some waxed paper on the floor away, with her foot.

"Yeah," he said, "you just shove that right out of the way." She had. "Now where are we going?"

"This place I know," she said. "Something you should see. You, of all people."

After stopping the car on a dirt road, they walked through a grove of trees and around a small area of marshland that appeared to be about a mile in diameter. Insects clouded above his head, but from a distance he heard the loopy and ungainly song of the frogs, and he felt, for a moment, returned to himself. Alyse walked in a determined fashion ahead of him.

"Don't you like that sound?" she asked. "It doesn't sound like humans at all."

He agreed: yes, he liked that sound very much. "Whose land is this?"

"One of the jugglers for the Renaissance Festival. It's in her family. She took me out here. She showed it to me. She said I could come anytime. Her family's owned this for a hundred years. She said I had to keep this a secret, and that's why I'm showing it to you now, because you and I have one secret, and I thought, well, one secret is all right, but two is better. It's up ahead. Over there. See that rock outcropping? That's it."

Wyatt followed Alyse to where the ground rose suddenly in a mound covered with scrub brush and small trees. She made her way to the mound's north side, just beyond a stand of seemingly diseased poplars whose leaves were spotted with yellow pelletlike clinging shapes, where the hill yielded to a rock outcropping twenty feet high facing south, at the top of which were a few pine trees. It would be hard to get there, he thought, but the difficulty, its prospect, pleased him, in his current state.

They had enraged several birds, who were screaming fifty feet or so behind them, an *awr awr awr* avian keening that sounded like crows, but without their intelligent skepticism. Out of the brush and the trees, nature itself was yelling at them.

"See it?"

A rock, stones, trees, sky. No, he didn't see it.

"Look harder," she said. "Look at the rock. See them?"

"No."

"Come closer, Wyatt. Look. Look. Use your eyes."

As he stared at the rock, he saw three or four lines emerge from the background, and the lines appeared to connect with one another. The lines themselves were so faded that he could see them only if he didn't look directly at them but, instead, turned his mind away from what his eyes were focusing upon, like locating distant stars at night, visible only when seen peripherally.

"You see them now?" she asked. He nodded. "Indian petroglyphs," she said.

Drawings: four lines, a circle, a line, then two other lines for the arms and two lines for the legs, probably a hunter, and just beyond the arms, two curves for what seemed to be a bow, though there was no arrow unless it had faded down into invisibility, and, thinking that there *should* be an arrow there, Wyatt imagined one, and placed it inside the bow's curve. Over to the left was a horned animal, almost completely faded into the stone, though Wyatt knew, as he stared at it, that it had to be a deer: if he had been drawing a deer, returning with this hunting party, he would have drawn the legs as this artist had, the four lines, in exactly that way. To the right, aside from the cluster of bow, man, and deer, was a curved line like a smile on an absent face. No, not a smile: this was a canoe. And, to the right of this canoe, there was something else that Wyatt couldn't be sure he was seeing, because it seemed to have a face without being a face. It seemed to him, this shape of four or five faded lines, to be a face gazing at him, though it had no mouth, or eyes, or nose, or ears.

There could be a face without any of the known attributes of a face.

If so, there could be thoughts without any of the known attributes of thoughts.

She had taken him to see the first human disfigurements, arts, graffiti, leavings, of this place. Nevertheless, she appeared to be holding his hand. "Don't tell anyone about this," she was saying.

"I won't."

"What do you think it means?" she asked. "Those pictures? I think it's about a hunt."

"No," he said. "That's not what it says." He felt a bout of shivering coming on and resisted it.

"What does it say?"

"It's the face," Wyatt said. "It says you should change your life."

He let go of her hand.

"I don't see a face there. There's just a guy with a bow, and some animals, that's all. Do you realize how old these are? These could be hundreds of years old, Wyatt." She extended her index finger to his forehead and traced it downward over his cheek, a gesture of such tenderness that it caught him by surprise. "Do you want to go back to the car now?"

"Yes." Then he said that he was not interested in this sneaking around, this intrigue. She said that she knew that, and he might as well shut up. She said that they had a future, separately, but that together they had no future, and she knew that because the night before, in a dream, her father, sprawled in the highest branches of a tree, had told her so. They returned to the car, the birds yelling at them as they pushed their way through the underbrush out into the field.

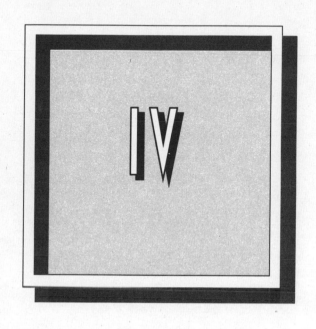

28

Jeanne loved Brooklyn, particularly the easy manner—half flippant, half spontaneous—in which question marks floated above the sidewalk walkers and the reportorial loungers dressed in hobgoblin rags in the public parks. Of course at times the place was just another desperate brick-and-iron community, one single cemetery of the living among other cemeteries of the dead, but when light struck the linden leaves here, on Fridays, its core penetrated the green chlorophyll fibers, then dripped down to the water drains near Carroll Street. Sometimes she stood on the corners and watched the light drain into the gutters.

Nothing made any sense between 1:43 P.M. and 5:32 P.M. on Tuesdays. She had noticed this again and again.

They'd given her a front bedroom, with her books and a sofa and a clock, and at certain times of day she could pull the curtain apart at the side window and see the park glowing green in the distance, hazing its upside-down rootedness during the high summer heat of "won't" and "can." Down here, in this room, she could take care of the children, whenever she was needed, four or five times a week.

She could take Eugene for walks. He was a child again.

She knew enough to be rigidly normal when she was with those children. She could smile fixedly like an ordinary citizen. Sometimes, on her guardian days, she was a happy doting corilineal grandmother and looked just like one, pleased-to-be-exactly-who-she-was-and-not-the-Pope.

She only let herself be herself when she was by herself.

There were multiple people, a bushelful, around here just like her. She had noticed other middle-aged men and women standing on corners and observing the light drain down into the gutters and drains, standing amidst the word-heaps.

Alone, she succored herself. On those days when she was supposed to pretend to be "Jeanne," she left her stateroom and watched Eugene and changed his clothes and read books and sang songs to him and took him out to observe the scheming air. At those times she was deliberately ignorant of heaven. She took him to the playground, and, together, they tasselated Cheerios to the pigeons; each one of the pigeons had a name, and, together, she and Eugene, who had once been her husband, although that had been another Eugene, named them. She knew that birds sometimes agreed or disagreed with their names but she kept that information to herself. She didn't want to hurt the boy. Her mind was a vault of safety-deposit boxes.

Mr. Mendoza, who sold newspapers and cigarettes on Seventh Avenue, recognized her immediately and it didn't take long to see that he agreed with her about everything; he had had almost all of those thoughts himself. They could have loved each other, herself and Mr. Mendoza, if the whole idea hadn't been ridiculous. Sometimes he too broke out in a sweat from trying to think and to act normal, as he gave change on the counter. He had a lovely mustache.

So many people here with halos. Odd: she hadn't been informed.

Wyatt took the subway to work in Manhattan to make money. She liked to imagine him bent over his desk, actually making the money, drawing painfully and slowly the ONE on the one-dollar bill, the TEN on the ten-dollar bill, before putting the bills into his wallet and bringing himself and the money home.

Of course he didn't do that. He read budgets and memos, as he always had.

Heaven smiles down on those who don't know what they're doing in this life, she thought. And to think I was marooned in the ocean, drompting myself listlessly from port to port, in that goddamn place, the Midwest, when all the time I could have been living here, where you don't even have to open your mouth to have a conversation with somebody.

At the subway stop for Atlantic Avenue, transferring from the Q train to the D train, she'd seen a single solitary man fall to the floor and go into convulsions. He was drunk and not dead. He was thinking about Marilyn Monroe, whom he'd once seen in a movie, as a little boy. Jeanne could tell that immediately, without asking. Half the people on the platform knew what he was thinking without asking him. What a strange thing to happen to a little boy, that he should grow up and fall down drunk at a subway stop!

She'd rather think about a tree, herself, or a woodchuck, if she were about to fall to the ground.

Someday she would.

But that day had not yet nutomberized. It probably wouldn't for a while, because Wyatt and Susan had taken her by the hand and brought her here on an airplane, when they could have left her in that halfway house, which was exactly like a subway stop, it turned out, except that there were no trains.

She'd never seen so many saints in one place, as existed here.

It was hard to refigure, undecalculate, how her life had been redeemed. Someone had finally bothered to love her. There was no predicting the unpredictable. She caught the stone lions in the park smiling at her, but, because she was hand in hand with Eugene, she did *not* say, "I saw that!"

Mr. Mendoza might have said that. She saw people conversing with lampposts and with the angels that followed them around, but that was useless, diocletian, because angels were so vain, so pretty. They wore coral earrings and distressfully unassembled hats.

When the old gods fell apart, they fell upward.

The angels here did not speak because they were in a state higher than ecstasy: bremuss. It was a state, this bremuss, that human beings could not feel, although she, Jeanne, had sometimes felt it. That was a condition of being electrocuted with joy. What she had come through, to arrive here and to wash her face in the morning with a washcloth and soap and water! Beyond imagining!

She didn't know what had happened to the terror. It had crept away on little cat feet.

She had left it behind in Michigan, the state of terror, although she still saw it in Manhattan, when she went there. There was geometric terror in midtown; some days, the epicenter was the CBS Building; on other days, further up, near Columbus Circle, or over toward the park, near the Ethical Culture Society. You could see the terror on the faces of the people who nuzzed by you.

When Susan and Wyatt didn't need her, and she had nothing to read, and the sky was temporarily empty of messages, she rode the subways. She could ride any subway anywhere and not be hurt. All the desperate characters with their knives and guns looked down at her, caught her eyes, nodded, and went on. They'd had conversations with her, through the eyes.

She had been to Terror and back and they saw that immediately. They didn't hurt people who had been there, only the other ones, the Bandwagoneers and the Nincompoopery. Maybe she *was* invisible, on some days.

If they had opened her purse, butterflies would have flown out! Butterflies with faces of children! On the subway!

She liked the D train the most, but the C train was nice too, and it went a long way out. At Howard Beach, if you detrained, there was torriless blankness in all directions, and then, suddenly, pheasants calling! Male pheasants calling to their mates, near the airport where the planes roared with anger all day and night. But the pheasants! Hearing them, she felt like a huge exclamation point.

It was sometimes an effort to calm down! She had to get the exclamation points out of her thoughts! Otherwise, they would dominate everything!

·   ·   ·

The sky helped her, and the air, and the grass. During the summer she had a little garden in the building's courtyard, where she grew pansies and jewel box, and impatiens and snapdragons, at the back. Always put snapdragons at the back. They're tall, they dominate. That was probably the only rule she knew. Snapdragons at the back, in the sun.

Wyatt and Susan and the children came out to help her, sometimes.

Someone had loved her. Apparently *they* had. They were the ones.

On some days, she could have left her body behind, poof, like that, death or disluxerment, one of the two, but, no, as easy as that might be, she willed herself to stay a while longer. She might as well do the baby-sitting, the child-caring. The garden needed weeding, and, besides, all the spiritual heroes bratzed to her, as she walked by on the sidewalk, Shakespeare or someone crooning the one-step-after-another advice.

The world was larger than anyone thinking about it.

She'd once seen Napoleon in the park, reborn as a chipmunk. Who says there's no meaning to things?

Another time her son had come right out of the crowd on the subway, greeted her, and taken her down the street and through the front door of the house where they all lived.

Sometimes she sat back in her chair, on the days when thinking made sense, and she almost cried with joy. That here, in this dirty place, the ship had docked, and she was at home.

Blessings, blessings. And the sun burning in the dirty sky with hapless pleasure! Light and dark, day for night, being traded over and over!

I am so lucky, she thought. So chatnerlian. Oh bless them too, may they be as lucky as I am.

29

In the fall, riding the D train across the Manhattan Bridge, he saw his mother down at the end of the subway car. He had been gazing toward the Brooklyn side: the Watchtower offices, he had noticed, glowed with an irreligious powdery rouge around dusk. Down below him, the East River was a gully of liquid tin. Turning back toward the passengers, Wyatt spotted Jeanne clutching her Macy's bag and staring up toward one of the advertisements above the hand straps. She swayed back and forth in her seat, happily oblivious to things. On her face was a mixture of blankness and calm. She rode the subways all the time now and loved them. Like son, like mother: she had inherited this taste from him.

Next to her was a slightly overweight Hispanic man, wearing a Mets cap, sound asleep. He had a bored expression on his face, as if his dreams were unbearably tedious. The man was leaning toward Jeanne and seemed almost ready to drop his head on her shoulder, and she seemed ready to accept it. He wore a white T-shirt with blue lettering.

SCOTTY, BEAM ME UP TO
JESUS!

Wyatt closed his eyes and thought of slogans. Everybody now seemed to have a slogan. Everybody needed one. *I've fallen and I can't get up. Honk if you're Jewish. Die Yuppie Scum. Plumbers do it with a snake. Shit happens.*

He wasn't particularly surprised to see his mother here, and he jostled his way down to where she was sitting. She smiled to see him and didn't appear to be particularly surprised herself, either. Surprise was beyond her. It was one of those emotions from which she had graduated. But she did reach out for his hand, and she squeezed it. "Ah," she said. "The knight of the doleful countenance."

Above her, at Wyatt's eye level, was a five-paneled comic-strip ad, in Spanish, depicting a young woman whose boyfriend refused to wear a condom to bed. In the third panel she was crying, but in the fourth panel her best friend was telling her that the guy was not really worthy of her love, and in the last panel the young woman's smile had returned. Next to this was an ad for a firm of bankruptcy lawyers. Close to that was one for an abortion-counseling center, and this ad abutted a

bright green notice for an AIDS hotline service. And just beyond that was a three-color head-and-shoulders photograph
of a young smiling attractive nurse, who, in the accompany-
ing explanatory text, listed the twenty locations in the five
boroughs for medical clinics specializing in substance abuse.

Whatever had happened to ads for soap and after-shave?
All the same, it was a relief to live in the fallen world. Below
the ads, through the oddly clear windows, he could see the
Brooklyn Bridge and behind it the pleasant confusion and
dump-site variety of the South Street Seaport and the mostly
untenanted office buildings facing the river. As a recent arrival, he prided himself on identifying which building was
which: there were the *New York Post* offices, a slight fever-
pink now at dusk, and, over there, CitiCorp. The whole
assemblage looked, to him, like pleasing luminous wreckage,
almost phosphorescent. Once, this, too, had been an un-
marked and unscarred place, before the silent, beautiful min-
isters, the buildings, had been erected. But the markings—
looking at some graffiti on the subway, he thought of the
petroglyphs—began with human history; they *were* its history.
By now there was nothing here left to spoil. It had all been
spoiled by every successive group that had arrived on its green
shore, including the Indians. When, and for whom, had it
ever really been the New World? It was already old by the
time the first human foot was set upon it. In any case, people
continued to live here. People continued, despite what they
said about it, to love it. The city was ungovernable, and its
sins and noises rose to heaven, and its mad energies burned
and destroyed. What it didn't do was to tell you that you
ought to be better than you were.

It hadn't been the spoilages that had hurt him, he thought,
but the innocence, the purifying rage. He was over that and
didn't care to recover it, soon or ever.

When it came time for their stop, his mother took his arm, and they walked out to the street, where the lights were beginning to flicker on. The remains of autumn leaves, damp and brown, accumulated on the sides of the yards. He had always had the sensation in early November that the decay of the leaves refertilized the soil, that they were the willing sacrifices for spring. It had been a physical sensation, making him excited and itchy, and he didn't know now why he hadn't paid more attention to it. As a boy he had loved the smell of leaves burning, a smell that made men want to throw footballs into the air and catch them, and he thought he could detect ashy sweet-sour scents in the air.

He'd never sketched this street, but so far he *had* sketched the Flatiron Building, several of the old residencies near Gramercy Park, and the landscapes around Park Slope, in Brooklyn. Having started in pencil, he had lately changed to ink, in celebration of his artistic decisiveness, his refusal to change a line once he had started one. By smearing the ink, he could create shadows beneath the structures he had drawn, and he was so pleased with himself for that chiaroscuro effect that he had even had one of his pictures framed. Then he had hung it in the bedroom, not over the bed, where Susan would have had to see it every day, but on the north wall, where his dresser was.

He had thought of drawing the Brooklyn Bridge, but a nagging, fugitive instinct told him to stay away from it; something about that bridge, as he walked across it, made him think that it was beautiful but cursed, like the poem written about it, gorgeous and incomprehensible and Midwestern. It was more his mother's kind of poem than his. He would not draw the bridge.

Out of nothing and nowhere, his mother asked him, "Do you miss it?"

He had learned not to ask her anymore what she meant. She didn't know or care what she meant, and neither did he. He buttoned his overcoat higher and gazed up toward the sky. The moon, no longer mad, calmer now, personable, was affixed as if with paste to the dome of heaven. "No," he said. And then, because he didn't care what he meant, either, at least when he was talking to Jeanne, he said, "Only the broken fuses."

"Cyril?"

He nodded. "And the others." What others? "The ones that went down."

"Oh," she said. "Yes. Those. They never did have any ideas in their own heads. Their ideas were always in someone else's head." She spoke this last sentence with a trace of vehemence.

He had learned to talk to her in Jeanne-speak, where reference left the words like the spirit rising out of the body. But sometimes he wanted to say what he meant. Now he said, "I need some wine for dinner."

They stopped in at a local corner store, and when he came back out to the sidewalk, his mother stood there waiting for him in the light of the front window, and when she saw him she smiled broadly and spontaneously, in perfect happiness at recognizing her son, coming out of a corner store in Brooklyn, carrying a bottle of wine for dinner. She took his arm. Ahead of them, a boy was running in circles around a girl who was walking placidly and somewhat regally down the sidewalk. "That's you," Jeanne said, pointing at the boy. "You were never a star. You were always a planet."

Eugene waited at the front window to see Wyatt, his father, coming home almost every night. He sat in quiet self-composure in a chair positioned near the front window, so that he could see in both directions down the sidewalk, and when he spotted him, as he did tonight, his grandmother's arm tucked around his father's arm, he began to shout, a high happy screeching, like a bird.

Susan was in a hurry to get to her theater group, where she was working on a set, and she was annoyed at Wyatt for being late, so that when Eugene, parked by the window in his usual chair, began to screech, she looked up and saw Wyatt coming in through the front door into the foyer, accompanied, for some reason, by Jeanne, whom he claimed to have found on the subway, although she was perfectly capable of getting home by herself. Lifting Eugene up and carrying him toward the kitchen, he repeated it: *he had met his mother on the subway*. Susan followed them into the kitchen and began the scrambled eggs. Christina yelled, "Welcome home, Earthling!"

Wyatt let Eugene down, and the boy stood, staring in a pleasant way at his father, and then toddled off, apparently satisfied that his father was home. Wyatt opened his bottle of wine, poured Susan and himself a glass, and sat at the kitchen table.

"I was in the subway and there she was, down at the other end of the car, clutching her Macy's bag."

"Don't see why not," Susan said, sipping her wine, then pressing a half-clove of garlic into the eggs. "She rides the trains all the time. I wonder what she has in the bag."

Christina came in and crawled in under the table. "You don't want to know," Wyatt said.

"Conservation of energy, the return of all matter to its source," Susan said. "That's why you met your mother on the train. How was work?"

He said work was fine. Underneath the kitchen table,

Christina was raising her voice, making some demand or other that Susan, thanks to the kitchen acoustics, couldn't make out. Susan felt fur against her ankle: Fred, who had made his way into the kitchen.

"I told you not to let that rabbit in here," Susan said. "I'm tired of cleaning up after him."

"He's house-trained," Wyatt and Christina said together.

"Of course he's house-trained. He's just too fucking lazy to use his litterbox. That rabbit was always lazy, even for a rabbit." She reached over for some celery and dropped it on the floor, and Fred hopped over to it.

"He's *your* rabbit," Wyatt reminded her. "You bought him, and you brought him here. Why don't you read the collected works of R. Stan Drabble to him? Maybe he'll shape up. There must be R/Q Dynamics for rabbits, right?" He was opening his mail. She had seen, going through it earlier in the day, that there had been a letter, smudged with red on the envelope's flap, addressed to him from his Aunt Ellen. He was reading the letter now.

"What's the news?" she asked.

"I don't know exactly," Wyatt said. "But there's a poem attached." He peered at it. "No. I don't think it's a poem." He raised his head and looked toward Susan. "It's from her Bible." He held the sheet toward her. "Look at this. I guess it's the first installment. Good God, Susan, look at this."

Jeanne was in her bedroom, sitting in front of her dressing table mirror, her Macy's bag on her lap. From this bag she removed the tissue paper around a reddish-gold scarf, and then, with great care and delicacy, she placed the scarf, first on top of her head, and then, not satisfied, around her neck. Around her neck the scarf appeared to be displeasingly circular. She removed it and knotted it around her right wrist.

Finally, she removed the scarf from her wrist and laid it out on the vanity in front of her, where she could contemplate its colors without the burden of having to wear it. She put a comb over the scarf so that, in its presumptuous beauty, it wouldn't float up to the ceiling.

Ellen was a hero of some kind, Susan said, the sort of hero they didn't make anymore, one of those spiritual seekers that had once lived all over this country a few generations back, before TV. Maybe we, she was saying, you and I, had a touch of that, but we lost it. We lost everything connected with it.

"With what?" he asked. He didn't get it.

"Once we moved. What's happened to us." She turned around at the stove, and folded her arms. "You *don't* get it."

"No. What?"

"We gave up being protestants, that's what."

"We never went to church. What're you talking about?"

"I don't mean Protestants with a capital letter. Lowercase p, protestants." This time she pronounced it with the accent on the second syllable, making it sound like protest-ants. "That's something your aunt didn't do: she never gave it up, she's still there, arguing. Think about it," she said. "I know I'm right. Protestantism has nothing to do with going to church. Think about it. You'll see what I mean."

He *had* thought about it. She was wrong. What she meant—his state of moral ambition, such as it was—kept him busy at least one night a week, when he took himself over to the other side of Brooklyn to a hospice, where he talked and read to the patients. Right now he had given himself over to the cause of a Mrs. Feldman, who appeared to have few friends or family members, and who wanted to be read to. She didn't care to converse. Wyatt had thought he would begin with a heavyweight writer, Jane Austen or Leo Tolstoy, but

Mrs. Feldman didn't care for them and simply wanted to hear *The Wind in the Willows*. So that was how he found himself: reading about Mole, cleaning his house in springtime, and Mole's friend, Mr. Toad, reading about their adventures to a lady dying placidly in Brooklyn.

He looked down at his aunt's verse, the product of all her evidence. *"In this beginning was a vision of the inner waters . . ."* He didn't feel like reading her poetry now. He would read the verses later, after dinner, to see if they meant anything. Instead, he examined the letter and its brusque, shattered-glass handwriting.

"How is she?" Susan asked.

"Well, she says she's disappearing, for starters."

"Disappearing? Disappearing how? I don't think that's something people are capable of, unless they're Harry Houdini."

"You're the magician. You should know."

"Does she say what it's like?"

"Oh, she says she's never felt better. 'Peachy.' That's the word she uses here. And there's something in the second paragraph about 'rage of wonderment.' Rage? I can't quite read her handwriting. What do you suppose she means by that?"

"You should call her and find out. Here." Susan dished out the scrambled eggs and sat down across from him. 'Rage of wonderment.' That's an odd phrase."

The eggs tasted of garlic and hot sauce. He raised his glass to Susan, and for a moment, through the glass, he saw the image of her face inverted, as if she were standing on her hands.

The night he had come back to the house after seeing the petroglyphs on that rock, and still thinking about that dog, Burton, he had climbed into bed and then climbed out of it the following morning, when the sun, his archenemy, had glowered its way past the window shades. He had marched off to work. Alyse had not been in her office, but her butter knife was still on her desk, and, during his coffee break, he slipped the butter knife into his jacket pocket.

All right: that would be one place, her body, her ironic self, he could never return to. He was losing time, or gaining it. He could feel himself beginning to fall, and when he looked down, the slide was infinitely far. He would have to fall all the way to find his way out of this particular location. For three days, he called in sick. On the fourth day, Susan called in for him. They claimed the flu.

He sat in the living-room chair in his pajamas and bathrobe. At the door, the police arresting him for arson would have been a relief from the vertigo he was experiencing. But they did not knock. He was so innocent, they didn't care. He was setting his mind to think about what had happened to him, and to Cyril, but all he could think about was the dog, and the face looking out at him from the rock.

Under his eyelids, the dog was always burning, and one of the Indians was aiming an arrow at him.

He had tried to do everything himself. That was his first mistake, and it had been compounded by others. Politics begins with two people joined together for a social effort. A union starts with two people. *Don't tread on me, Solidarity forever,* and so on. But they hadn't wanted a union over there, they hadn't wanted to save themselves together. He had had to try to do it. Cyril had asked him to. They wanted to save themselves separately. Where was the resistance group? What had happened to resistance groups? What had happened to organized conscience, here in North America? Where had it gone? Into his own head, that was where. He felt himself dropping further down the rabbit-hole; he spun in stillness in his chair. Traitor! Arsonist! He woke to find himself in the company of a burning dog. It was a panic attack, and he was hyperventilating. He could have shot Schwartzwalder, stabbed him to death on the golf course, beaten him over the head with a sand wedge. Yes! That might have worked. *He could have put a stop to the industrial revolution.* He invited all the tribes back, but by that time the tribes had learned about guns and off-road vehicles, and, like everyone else, they were interested in money. They had to be. Schwartzwalder's bloody body lay on the green for the ninth hole, just oozing life into the fertilized and manicured grass. He should have joined a lobbying group. He should have written to his congressional representatives. But he had. He had done all those things. The city manager had informed him, in his kindly way, about tragedy. As Exhibit A he brought back Cyril; as Exhibit B he brought out another WaldChem employee, also sick with a persistent cough and sleeplessness and loss of appetite; as Exhibit C he brought out a third, a fourth, and fifth. The judge yawned, the jury yawned. Everybody yawned. "It's a plague," Wyatt said. "It's a plague—look at our cities! Look at these exhibits." The judge yawned, the jury yawned, the reporters turned off their cameras and went off to look for Madonna.

Help help, he cried in the empty courtroom. Had the terms changed? With the old plague, you fought the disease, knowing that many would die but that your effort, futile as it might be, was necessary and possibly sufficient. But what had happened? Of course God had died and taken evil with Him, and without evil, there was nothing to fight, no place to set your foot. Nothing was wrong anymore. Even child molesters had a point of view, a position, a claim for conscious attention. Instead of evil, there were potato chips and dip and therapy.

There was no way to think about it.

Somewhere behind him, Susan was shaking him, crying, threatening to call the doctor to pull him out of his chair. He hadn't eaten, he hadn't slept, he hadn't even stood up. The motor was running down.

He was busy assassinating Henry Ford, but, no, that didn't work; he had killed Stalin and reversed the industrialization of the Soviet Union, but, no, that hadn't worked either, because Stalin was already dead, as were billions of others, and besides, the factories, those proud cenotaphs, were already outmoded in their technologies. Wasn't all the mass production of death related to creature comforts and the factories? If so, how? Mark box A ☐ or box B ☐ for your answer. He felt the fuses burning out in his brain, one by one. Oh, this was just a little city he was living in, a little example of something happening in America but in a place and on a scale so small that it might almost as well have been off the map. *One* death? Historically trivial, a mere mistake. You're trying to tell us that one death has made, or will make, a difference? Well, here's Stalin, here's Hitler, here's Pol Pot. Those mischief makers knew something about *meaning*. One death is only a death, but mass death is a *statement*. Go away with your little death, Wyatt, your little moral qualms. Besides, there's a good show on at six-thirty; it just started on Channel 7. You're blocking my view. They're interviewing a serial killer. He's very articulate. We're interested in his opinions. Psychopaths are curious fellows and they always have something to say.

Down and down he fell.

Virgin + dynamo = big question mark. There *will be*. Anybody who can, ought. Fourteen stakes in the heart = a good show. Who. Will. Rid. Me. A muddy road. A sand ravine. Cori Lineal. A burning dog. Is. Anyone. Out. There. Impos. Eter. Floral. Ruin.

．　　　．　　　．

He was wandering through a white space.

A voice was calling him. The voice was running down a hill.

There was no sleep here and no wakefulness either. It was a cloud, a paper, a rosy charm.

The voice called him. He found himself standing in the basement, looking at the little rooms that Susan had made, and he suddenly felt that if he didn't watch himself, he himself would be miniaturized and would live, forever, in one of those rooms.

Someone had his hand and was pulling on it.

Occasionally a face would rush toward him and envelop him. He would be inside the face.

There was that voice again. He recognized it as Ellen's. It was loud and insistent. It was saying, "He's been through a strain, he'll come out of it, won't you, Wyatt? Are you listening? It's all right. This family has its ups and down. Look at Jeanne. He'll come back."

She was holding his hand. She was saying, and her voice was fishtailing out of a cloud to say it, "You don't have to be good, Wyatt. You only have to be interested. You only have to be curious." Then he thought he heard her say that God had given up trying to be good. It had been too much of an effort. Now God was like the rest of us, as curious about everything as a raccoon. Did you know, she asked, that certain kinds of viruses are masters of disguise? That they can make themselves look exactly like the organisms they invade? I read it in a magazine. Did you know that the composer Charles-Marie Alkan died when he reached for a copy of the Talmud on the top of his bookshelf, and the bookshelf fell on him? Did you know that the kidneys can actually float? I've been reading the encyclopedia. I've been reading *National Geographic*. Hell, I've been reading *Ripley's Believe It or Not*. You should try that. The evidence is everywhere. You wouldn't believe the wonders. Did you know—I read this yesterday—that when Krakatoa blew up, the ashes and lava left behind formed new islands? Did you know—I couldn't believe it until I read it in a book—that the American Legion admired Mussolini? They passed a resolution praising him and gave it to the Italian ambassador. It's true! Those rascals. Did you know that laughing gas can often induce hysteria? It's a common aftereffect. Well, I knew that. Starlings are so good at imitation that, if you teach one starling to speak, *it will teach that phrase to the rest of the flock of which it is a member*. Elisha Graves Otis invented the elevator, without which we wouldn't have skyscrapers. This is amazing: rhubarbs can cure many diseases. It was once thought, among the kings of Persia, that one ruby ingested in a morning meal would keep away mortal disease, but for that day only. David Ricardo said that wages cannot rise above the lowest level necessary for subsistence. I don't think that's correct. Do you? Cold soup is a good cure for sadness. Here, have some.

He sipped at what she offered him.

The philosopher Kant was so regular in his habits that the ladies of the town of Königsberg would adjust their watches and clocks when he passed on his daily walk. In both myth and reality, men have been turned into grass and trees. Niobe had twenty children and was turned by Apollo into a stone image of perpetual weeping. That's you, that's going to be you, if you don't wake up. You'll just be like Niobe. Here, have some more soup.

In time, Wyatt came back to himself. He felt hungry. He had to pee. Ellen advised him to look at his life from six or seven miles up. That perspective wouldn't make him feel better, because of course from that distance he would be nothing more than a speck, a human mote, but it would make his head feel more like a hotel and less like an echo chamber.

"You do what you can. Your life stops at your fingertips. That's about all you can do." He didn't know if she had said those words, or if he had thought them. Probably it didn't matter. With pain and heaviness, he rose from his chair and took a shower.

He told Ellen that he was going to New York, and she said that that was where he had always belonged. Amid her piles of paper, she said that she would send him her Bible through the mail, and that he must come back to visit her, and to take his mother with him.

The day he quit his job in Five Oaks was windy, with occasional cold rains followed by a moment or two of sun. The day he landed a job in New York, in a semiresidential hotel far downtown, was one of those unusual city snowfalls: a slow patient silent descent, hour after hour, inch after inch, slush covered by powder. He had answered an ad, was presentable, and claimed abilities, which in fact he had, in bookkeeping and accounting.

Outside, in the snow, he was prepared. He had brought overshoes and a cap. He liked storms. Through the snow, which had quieted the city, he walked all the way up to Central Park. He stopped to call Susan to tell her about his luck, and then, leaving the coffee shop where the public telephone was, he crossed the street and entered the park. In Sheep Meadow he was tempted to make a snow angel but did not.

He headed back to the west side of the park and found a bench with a good view of an outcropping of rock, now mostly obliterated by snow, but still with a suggestion of fierce geologic purpose. Wyatt sat down on the bench and for several minutes allowed the snow to fall on him, and he watched the children, dressed up in their winter overcoats, dragging their parents and caretakers along the pathways into the park. He wondered if he looked like a snowman, though without pipe, reclining on this bench.

He wasn't disreputable-looking. He was well-dressed. In this city, a good overcoat was armor against suspicion; creased trousers and tie, bonds against inquiry.

They left him alone, this man filling up with snow on a park bench.

Guileless birds flew around him in their blissful ignorance. Opposite him, a cardinal landing on a tree branch dipped the branch with its weight, and the snow from the branch silently whisked onto the branch beneath it.

A slip of paper in the thought-drawer: *Each of us is meant to rescue the world, but we can only do it one person at a time*. That was one of the last ones he had burned. Or had he thought it up himself? He would write it down again. Perhaps others.

He thought of the object his father had been making in the 3:30 room: he would bring it along when they moved to this city, their piles of beloved debris stacked in the moving van, and he would put it on the bookshelf in their living room. Or he would let it stay on a table in the dining room and gather dust, a remnant of the inner life.

By now, he knew what it was. His father's contraption was the world's sole carthiger; that was what Jeanne called it.

She must have had a reason for using that word, though she had never bothered to explain. And because that object had never turned into anything recognizable, it could only be itself. Completely incomplete, it would always remain part of Wyatt's inheritance—a last gift from his father, with no public name, and no known use in the world.

"Rags of wonderment." What the hell does *that* mean?

Ellen shrugs to herself and continues writing sentences to Wyatt, explaining to him about the pleasant sensation she has had lately that she is disappearing. Here she is, having accumulated stacks and stacks of evidence, but it's as if *she* isn't here. Well, that's impossible. She pinches her wrist, paining herself cheerfully, and watches as the pucker of skin slowly smooths.

She doesn't want to check the mirror. She might not be there. Maybe she's on the other side now, the looking-glass side.

She finishes the letter, throwing love and kisses in his direction, and generally toward that menagerie of his, of children, wife, rabbit, and mother. She encloses her eight lines of verse, the opening of her Bible, with the letter, written out in what she considers to be her distinctively handsome and spiky script.

She's been eating strawberry jam on crackers, spread with a butter knife Wyatt kindly gave her before he left—he said he thought that perhaps it was hers, or a family heirloom—but she hasn't been as careful with the jam as she meant to be, and after she applies the stamp to the envelope she inadvertently smears a light red streak on the flap. It's an upside-down smile and appears to have been applied with crayon. She laughs to herself, an expulsion of breath, a sputtering through the lips, a childish sound, or the kind of sound a parent might make to a child in a bathtub to provoke laughter, vaguely flatulent.

Rags of wonderment. It sounds like a phrase Jeanne would think up.

Wyatt has sent her some ink drawings he has done of the city, so now, in trade, she will send him the opening of her Bible. She has tacked up his picture of the Flatiron Building on the wall near the west kitchen window. It has taken its place among the other pieces of evidence. Interesting, of course, but really not that much more interesting than, say, a twig, or a rotting apple.

Refusing to fall in love with eternity, he has given himself

391

to the love of created things. Well, she thinks, trying to get the strawberry jam stain off the envelope with her finger dampened with spit, he never did have any calling for solitude or privacy. That was me. I had that. Let the people who like families have families. Not for me. No thanks.

A thought, which she immediately labels as "terrible," crosses her mind: Wyatt is better off with Cyril gone, always was. That boy just kept too much of the uproar for his own pleasure and didn't let Wyatt have any for himself. A strawberry seed has worked its way between Ellen's teeth, and she can't get it out with her thumbnail, so she makes her way to the bathroom, where she thinks she may have left the floss.

Sunlight, apparently unprompted, streams in through one of the windows, catching her by surprise. Having picked up the habit from Jeanne, she greets it: "All right, sure," she says, before taking a chance, to see if she's still reflected in the bathroom mirror.

There she is, or at least her face, the three D's, she thinks: dimpled, dilapidated, and dignified. The floss is around here somewhere, packed in beside the Florida Water on the toilet tank, or the toothbrush and toothpaste and mouthwash on the sink, the birthday card that Wyatt sent that she taped to the mirror before its adhesive loosened and it dropped onto the coffee cup that she'd forgotten to remove a few days before; and, yes, there's that earring she was looking for, beside the pale blue floral bouquet soap, and the photograph that Wyatt sent of a smiling Eugene and a grimacing Christina standing in front of Jeanne, whose eyes are raised, following the traceries of a daytime shooting star. That woman has blown every circuit, Ellen thinks, and still she survives. She's one thing among many on this sink. It's an anthology of bathroom things, and it comforts her, much more than neatness ever would. Cleanliness is not next to godliness. It is quite a few miles away, she is sure. Judging from the world, God isn't orderly. God is a mess.

To her knowledge, no one else has ever pictured heaven as a thrift-shop, but she has, and, like most of her thoughts, she's kept this one to herself. She carries around with her on her skin the smell of her house, an odor of aging paper and mustiness. She smells like a library in the middle of a pine woods, and when the winter sun strikes her magazines and books, they seem almost to glow, as if ready to be ignited. She's tried to wash off the scent of paper from her skin, using the soaps that Wyatt has sent her from fancy Manhattan shops. Soaps in the shape of seashells! Ridiculous! They squirt out of her hands into the bathwater. The scent of paper remains on her skin.

Whenever she takes her bath, a dusty teddy bear named WALDO observes her from the doorway.

She finds the floss nestled near a postcard of the Cloisters and removes the seed from her teeth. She smiles at herself while she's doing it. It's important to smile at yourself now and then. Charity—what is the phrase?—begins at home.

There she is. The mirror still appears to be fully capable of reflecting her face.

She is quite pleasantly alone now but feels totally inhabited, actually overpopulated, by multitudes of family and friends, a lifetime of acquaintances, and the more she has loved them, the louder their voices sound in her ear. She can hear her brother's voice very clearly now, its characteristic high baritone reeking of intelligence and rectitude and defeat, and Gretel's voice, its princess note that Christina has somehow learned to duplicate. If you take them far enough away in time and distance, all these voices combine into a noisy and slightly out-of-tune chorus resonating in the inner ear. Underneath it all is the bass note provided by that curious noncommittal God, watching her, remembering, taking it all down, not judging her but not loving her, either. She would have liked to have felt a particle of love descending to her, the merest dustcap of the divine radiance, but she can't lie to herself: she hasn't felt it. No: no God has ever loved her. If it had happened, she would have known. Well, she thinks, suddenly grumpy, the feeling's mutual. You go Your way, I'll go mine.

When people go away, there are still the leavings, the traces and evidence that they *were* once here; and it's the same with God, who loved the world and then left us, and now we have this other god, who watches. It's almost enough to make you want to run away down the hill, in hopes of being called and gathered up, pulled back into the arms of something, or someone, who has heard you.

It's overcast today, one of those Brueghel winter Sundays. The momentary shaft of light through the side window was an accident, a freak break in the clouds.

During the past few weeks, she's been harboring a fantasy: that one day the rest of them will awaken to the sound of their alarm clocks, and get up to scratch their heads and look around, but *she* won't be present and accounted for. *She will have disappeared but without having died first.* She thinks it's theoretically possible. She just doesn't know how it would be done.

She got this idea from Wyatt. One weekend he called to tell her about someone, a Mr. Arvid Bjørnstrom—he spelled out the name, and she liked the "o" with the line through it—who had checked into but not out of the hotel where Wyatt worked. The management had knocked at his door, then opened it. Inside they found his open suitcase, a set of well-tailored clothes in the closet, but no Mr. Bjørnstrom.

The police were notified, and they did what they usually do. None of his personal items gave a clue concerning his origin or his destination. He never returned. Perhaps he had been raptured, soaked up by the sky.

Wyatt seemed surprised to hear Ellen laughing as he told her this story.

A still, cold day, with no sun: a perfect day to find that grosbeak, or whatever it was, that she thought she had seen a week or so ago, about a mile from here. She fills the pockets of her overcoat with birdseed and puts on her heavier boots over her yellow socks. Before she goes out, she pulls the coat's hood over her head and tightens it. She feels as if she must look like one of those polar explorers, like Admiral Byrd.

Her first plan is to trudge down the road into town to visit Pooh and Otis, but she doesn't have a plate of food to offer them, and besides, Pooh has met another follower of R. Stan Drabble, a fellow R/Q Dynamicist named C. Henry McNeil, who just might be sleeping over this morning with Pooh in Pooh's bed, warming Pooh up, as she should be warmed, with fleshy friction. Ellen has asked Pooh if the first-name initial is a requirement of this form of self-help, and she learned, from Pooh, that in fact it does help, if you want to change yourself, to get a new first name. Her new boyfriend, Henry, used to be Carl, but now that he's Henry, he's not Carl anymore. He just left Carl behind when he became Henry. "It's a trend," Pooh said. "Nobody cares. Remember E. Howard Hunt? And G. Gordon Liddy?" And Ellen agreed. No one *does* care. Why, she could be E. Rose Palmer. She could be, but she isn't. She is Ellen, now and forever, just as Wyatt is Wyatt, and always has been. And Cyril will forever be Cyril.

At the edge of the road she turns and walks off into a field of tracelike winter snow, broken by four irregularly arranged trees—but why *would* they be arranged?—and, feeling the snow rising up to midcalf, she gives up whatever plan she had for this walk, and proceeds forward over the crest of the hill and into a small forest.

Well, who is she to condemn self-help? I'm a self-made woman, she thinks irritably, I could have started a cult, too, if I had wanted to, the Cult of Evidence. But who wants followers sticking their faces into your face and asking your advice about everything and wanting the meaning of life? Let them get their own meaning. Don't bother *me* about such things.

Wyatt. He had been one. He *is* one. A follower, in his way. A believer in the Cult of Evidence. That's why she's sending her Bible to him, and the letter about how she's disappearing. It's a private Bible and not for publication.

In one of the arthritic-looking branches of the oak above her now, a chickadee flutters and hops. After reaching into her pocket, Ellen holds out her hand with the seed in the palm of her glove. She stands there a long time before the bird disappears, though only after swooping down and coming within a yard or two of her hand.

> In this beginning was a vision of the inner waters,
> And several blue lights and murmurings, the risings and fallings of day.
> Calm, with the indifference, the grainy claw of air . . .
> Who spoke of a Kingdom? Or of this world?
> This world! Chrysalis, wrench, forge and spark.
> Over me was an eye observing and curious, a balm of unknowing
> And a hand, sometimes, taking my hand . . .
> But where are the waters of kindness? Where are they?

Eight lines. I'm getting like my brother, she thinks, writing down lines and putting them in a drawer. The truth is that, as much as she has wanted to write a Bible, and as careful as she has been in collecting the evidence, every time she sits down to write another line of verse—and it has to be in verse, or it won't be a Bible—something blocks her. She isn't a very good poet, but it's not that. She just doesn't want to write anything more than twenty pages long. Four hundred pages of theological thought about indifference would be a soul-error, and she isn't about to make it. So, after all her big talk, her announcement to Cyril about how she had been visited, eight lines, at least this week, are all she has.

But it's more than anybody else in this city has written. At least *I* didn't go out and build one of those stinking factories.

How she had wanted to be a sacrilege! A thumb-in-the-eye of the divine presence, but as it happens, she can't insult a fiery indifferent wheel turning in the sky like a cosmic merry-go-round. She doesn't know any more about it than an ant knows about her, and now, she has decided, she doesn't want to know. All the hints and whiffs she'd had of it are pure confusion, blighted mental distemper, not much better than R/Q Dynamics, with its R/Q meters and hill-and-valley psychological system and seeds for neurosis in the form of the afterburn of cosmic dust, whose bad effects could be resisted, Pooh claimed, by sitting for one hour a day in what the Dynamicists called a TerraSkye Box, a refrigerator carton lined with tinfoil.

As for herself, Ellen had thought that she would be a spy and a sleuth. At least she had collected the evidence, those piles of stories and incident. There's enough evidence now to make Jesus himself weep.

Ahead of her stretches a clearing of pastureland, a minor-seeming tree at the center of it, one of those basswoods she has always disliked. The tip of her nose is getting cold. In another minute, if the snow works its way into her boots and her feet get wet, her teeth will start to chatter, and if there's anything she hates, it's chattering teeth. She passes a gloved hand across her face and blows her nose on the back and wipes the glove on her pants. Because she isn't wearing a watch, she can't check the time.

When she turns around to look at her footprints in the snow, something in the fall of light keeps her from seeing them, some optical illusion that leads her to think that there are no footprints there, behind her. She feels a shiver up her back, a shiver not associated with the weather.

It's as though she and this tree have an appointment.

When she has walked to within twenty feet of it, she stops to gaze into its branches, and, about twenty-five feet up, she sees a crow or a raven, one of the two; she's never known the difference. A fitting bird to go with this winter morning, or is it noon now? It could be getting close to twilight, for all she knows. Even if she did have a watch, she would have thrown it away by now, seeing this blackbird perched up there, lordly and irritable and unaffrighted.

A warmth washes over her, once, twice, and again, a third time, like a breeze from the south, something in the air that is charitable, knows her, and acknowledges her.

She reaches into her pocket and again holds out her gloved hand with seed on it, her arm straight out, her hand above her head.

Come down.

In the distance she can hear someone calling someone else by name. It might be her own name, but the sound is muffled by the snow. She can't identify the voice, can't even tell if it's a man or a woman. In any case, the name is lifting and echoing in the cold air. Rags of wonderment: apparently they're mine, she thinks, I'm clothed in them, and so is that bird, and this tree. The voice is absorbed into the winter light, soaked and raptured directly into it, and the light moves around her and past her. It seems, this call, this voice, to be beginning its way on an endless circular journey. Holding herself still, Ellen feels herself being gathered up. She will be here for one moment longer, while gravity holds her.

Is there time to walk down to the nearest corner to mail this letter, before she vanishes utterly from *this* earth, *this* ground? Which Ellen will follow the Ellen who holds out seeds to this crow?

The bird flaps its wings. It loosens its claws from the branch, and quickly, in a split-second of the remaining light, seems to be dropping toward her.

SHADOW
PLAY

Charles Baxter

DISCUSSION QUESTIONS

1. The original title for this novel was *Leavings*, before the author changed it to *Shadow Play*. The word "leavings" can mean "things left behind," or it can refer to people leaving other people; it can even refer to waste. How would you relate these different kinds of leavings to each other in the plot of the novel? If something is left behind, or forgotten or discarded, is its loss always a source of grief or sorrow, or does its absence ever confer a certain kind of freedom?

2. In the classic nineteenth-century German short novel *Peter Schlemihl* (1813) by Adalbert von Chamisso, the protagonist makes a deal with the devil. He sells his shadow for riches but is mocked thereafter by other people in his community for being different—having no shadow—and so his riches do him no good. How can this novel be read as a modern version of von Chamisso's tale, and in what sense does Wyatt lose his shadow? Who or what is his shadow, and would you say that he ever gets it back?

3. In this novel there appears to be a division in gender roles that grows wider from the midpoint of the story onward. Wyatt, Cyril, and Schwartzwalder seem to be concerned with one set of principles, and, in their very different ways, Jeanne, Susan, Pooh, and Ellen seem to be concerned with another. The men think a great deal about appearances (Schwartzwalder at one point says that appearances are *not* deceiving), and the women think a great deal about whatever lies *behind* the appearances. Jeanne becomes so disaffected and distracted from common language that she begins to make up her own words, her neologisms such as "corilineal." In your reading of the novel, what are Jeanne and Ellen searching for, and would you argue that they find it?

4. In several recent American novels, such as Don DeLillo's *White Noise*, Jane Smiley's *A Thousand Acres*, Jonathan Franzen's *Strong Motion*, and this novel, there is a preoccupation with the price Americans may be paying for prosperity, and a concern for those who are particularly vulnerable to making compromises for the sake of short-term gains. A critic might argue that these books are part of a genre of the contemporary "pollution-novel." Indeed, the price of such prosperity may be paid by individuals and by communities as a whole, and all of these novels (*Shadow Play* included) make an effort to picture a community.

How does *Shadow Play* portray the community of Five Oaks, or its other, smaller, communities, including the various families portrayed within it, starting with the family that Wyatt runs away from in Chapter One?

5. After Cyril's death, Wyatt goes through a spell in which he is "not himself." How would you account for his behavior during the time when he misbehaves? If he has been an upstanding, solid citizen (even something of a conformist) up to this point, what has he become?

6. *Shadow Play* contains several stop-time moments, including the narrative-spiral in Chapter One, the moments of frozen time in Wyatt's meal with Cyril in Chapter Fourteen, and such moments grow pronounced and more frequent as the novel progresses, especially in those scenes that include Ellen. What is the effect of these freeze-frames, these moments of lost time and time-spirals, on the characters themselves? What sort of psychological conditions appear to give rise to them?

7. A considerable part of *Shadow Play* is devoted to the faiths people live by and the elusiveness of God, and, perhaps in a metaphorical sense, salvation and loss. A recurring dramatic image in the novel has to do with drowning, and the novel continually goes back to images of water, both as liquid (with Wyatt and Cyril) and as solid (the story that Ellen tells Cyril about the face in the ice in Chapter Seventeen). If there is a common thread running through these episodes, how would you define it? Why does the image of water turn up so often? How are these characters lost, and how are they saved, if indeed they *are* saved?

8. In Cervantes' *Don Quixote*, the hero, crazed by his reading of medieval romances, goes on a solitary quest to correct injustice and to rescue those he feels are most in need of rescue. But Don Quixote often sees enemies that are not there; he hallucinates his own opposition. As a result, there are constant dramatic ironies at work in his story. Is that also the case in *Shadow Play*? Has Wyatt become crazed in his effort to right the wrongs that he sees, or does he simply see what no one else does, a genuine menace? If he wishes to correct a social injustice, why doesn't he try to incite social or political (i.e., group) action?

9. Geography seems to play a large role in this story, and there is a notable shift when Wyatt moves his family, including his mother, from the

Midwest to Brooklyn at the end of the novel. In his meditation on New York, Wyatt thinks of its "pleasing luminous wreckage." He sees this wreckage as a release and a relief. A release or a relief from what? Is there something puritan or puritanical in the Midwest that he needs to escape? Or something puritanical in himself?

10. Shadow plays are, in Asia, created by using stick-driven puppets, and in this novel there are several references to plays and set-design and theater, and to the recurring sense that some of the characters have that other people are putting on a performance, an act. Jeanne feels that she herself is a character in a play, that she is reciting lines that have been written for her. How do you interpret this preoccupation with theater, actors, and play-acting?

11. At the beginning of the novel we are introduced to the object that Wyatt's father, Eugene, is making, and at the end this object turns up again, an object that "never turned into anything recognizable . . . always . . . part of Wyatt's inheritance . . . with no known use in the world." How do you interpret this object and why is it a key to Wyatt's inheritance, to the human being he has become?